The Stolen Ones

The Stolen Ones

SHY KEENAN

HODDER

First published in Great Britain in 2011 by Hodder & Stoughton
An Hachette UK company

1

A CIP catalogue record for this title is available from the British Library.

ISBN 978 0 340 97866 5

Typeset in Plantin Light by Hewer Text UK Ltd, Edinburgh
Printed and bound in the UK by CPI Mackays, Chatham ME5 8TD

Hodder & Stoughton policy is to use papers that are natural, renewable
and recyclable products and made from wood grown in sustainable
forests. The logging and manufacturing processes are expected to
conform to the environmental regulations of the country of origin.

Hodder & Stoughton Ltd
338 Euston Road
London NW1 3BH

www.hodder.co.uk

ACKNOWLEDGEMENTS

With special thanks always to my own family and dear friends, I love you. To all those I have worked with and who have supported me over the years, thank you more than you will ever know. I could never have done this without David Riding, Tara Gladden, Isobel Akenhead and all of the team at Hodder – thank you all for helping me realise what I thought was an impossible dream.

I dedicate this book with very special and sincere thanks to my dear friend Del, forever thank you for everything always.

Chapter 1

I closed my eyes and wished myself away and it worked cos they didn't choose me. Not this time.

But whether I'm on my bunk or there with them I'm still the hero. Sometimes bad things happen to heroes like they go to a nasty school or they get bullied or they have to fight monsters or their mummy and daddy die. Sometimes much worse than that. But whatever He says, I know my mummy and daddy aren't dead. They're trying to rescue me and it's up to me to help them. To be super-smart, like Daddy always says. Be like Harriet the Spy. Like the little princess who has to sleep in the attic. Heroes always escape the bad stuff in the end. That's the rule.

They think I'm stupid because I clamp my teeth down and refuse to say The Things but I'm not stupid and I'm not dirty and I will escape. They're hurting one of the others, but they can't make me see and they can't make me hear if I don't wanna. At the dentist's, Mummy told me stories so I didn't think about the dentist sounds, and now I tell the stories. Except bad things happen all the time now so it's safer not to stop the stories, let them go like cartoons one after the other, with no bits in between. But with me, it's not really a story cos it's real. I'm *going* to escape, and my mummy and daddy are going to help me.

Down here there are no storybooks. Down here there is TV, but we have to behave for them to get them to turn it on. It's too high for us to reach, and it's hard to behave. So I do my messages.

I write my messages. I write them so they're not in my head. In the dust on the floor I write 'Save Me' and 'Save Me' and 'Save

Me' so my mummy will see it. And she'll find me and take me away.

But now He's looking at me. The Old One. I stop my messages. I know That Look. That Look means I have to pretend. That Look means it's going to hurt. That Look means he's not going to stop when I cry.

Savemesavemesaveme.

It's happening now.

Chapter 2

This third kick in the sequence was hardest of all, hitting home dead centre with a seriously satisfying smack.

'Now that's more like it.'

A swig of water and Cordelia Hunter was back in fighting stance, T-shirt wet against her back, core muscles engaged. Her eyes locked back onto the leather punch bag. In her mind, there was only ever one opponent, and he never left the fight in one piece.

Across the room the phone was ringing, but as usual she let it go to answer machine. The only people she picked up for were her sister Jess or her boss Allyson, and they knew to call her mobile. Same rules for the loft apartment's video intercom. Unless she'd ordered a delivery there was no way she was opening the door to a stranger. Not even a crack. She remembered reading about how vampires couldn't cross your threshold without a specific invitation, and she figured the same should hold true for double-glazing salesmen, tabloid journalists and old flames. Even for their voices.

But this wasn't one of those calls.

Cordy broke off from a series of roundhouse kicks so that she could listen better, letting the punch bag sway in front of her.

The voice was briskly feminine, clear and to the point.

'Dr Hunter. My name is Detective Chief Superintendent Fiona Andrews. I'm calling from the Elite Child Protection Unit. Obviously I can't go into details over the phone, but Head

Office read your article for the *National Psychiatric Journal* – the one about the police's handling of the recent case of the prostituted children – and we would like you to come in and consult on a current case. If your schedule permits you to come in for an appointment early next week, I can lay it out for you . . .'

Cordy waited to hear the contact details and then unleashed a powerful sequence of jabs and upper-cuts to the bag, bringing her hands back to shield her face after every punch. Soon her breathing was ragged and her fringe was stuck to her scalp. Keeping light on her feet, as her trainer had taught her, she danced round the bag, letting loose a vicious volley of kicks and punches while her mind analysed the call from every possible angle.

It had been a couple of weeks since the article had come out, and since then she'd been ducking calls from news programmes and daytime TV asking her to appear on their shows. She always emailed back press releases, giving Justice4Children's official response to current news stories, but she got the distinct impression that the programmes were less interested in her victim advocacy work and more interested in speculations about her personal history. Which she never discussed.

Usually no one would take much interest in a small article in a specialist medical journal, but a reporter from the *Daily Mail*, keen for a new angle on a controversial topic, had spotted it, and reprinted it alongside a blown-up version of the tiny headshot that had accompanied it. Now everyone seemed to want a piece from her. And this, she admitted to herself, was not just thanks to her qualifications, her work as a child protector or even rumours of her troubled past – a past that was easy enough for a researcher to uncover, if they bothered to look through the newspaper archives and court records. No. Journalists were mostly interested in her because of the way she looked.

'I mean, all that lovely hair. And those legs. You could be a newsreader or something,' one freelancer had gushed, thinking it would persuade Cordy to do a Q&A for a weekly women's magazine. 'Our readers will definitely be able to identify with you. You certainly don't look like any sort of victim. Not at all.'

'Well, appearances can be deceptive,' she had shot back. 'You, for example, sound like an idiot. But I'm sure you're just trying to do your job.'

Cordy found herself smiling at the memory. The journalist had barely been able to mumble out an apology before she hung up.

Guess she won't be saying that to anyone else anytime soon. But, she thought ruefully, *in the end it's really my own fault.*

She knew she should never have agreed to being photographed, but the section editor had explained that they wouldn't be able to run the piece without the headshot, and Cordy hadn't wanted to let her colleagues down. Her boss, Allyson, had helped coax her into it.

'I know you hate flash photography, love, but remember, it's not a tabloid. It's not like they're going to dress you up or anything. And I'll be right there with you. No one will touch you. Bet you can even do your own hair and make-up, if that's what's bothering you. Though, to be honest, I'd love someone to do all that for me. Give me a bit of a makeover.'

'I know that it's good publicity for the foundation. And it's an important piece. It's just that . . .' Cordy had trailed off, embarrassed.

'It's not just the camera, is it?' her boss had asked. 'Bet I know what's got you all twitchy. You don't want the world to discover how – what do they call it? – *media-friendly* you are?' Allyson had laughed at the expression on her face. 'Jesus Christ, woman. I should fire you. Then I'd get to be the glamorous face of J4C. If that's not a contradiction in terms.'

They had both looked round the dingy office, which they shared with a couple of bright-eyed interns and a broken photocopier, and laughed.

'Yeah,' Cordy had quipped. 'It's right up there with *X Factor* for pure glitz and glamour.'

'Whatever. It's your turn to put the kettle on, twinkle-toes. The photo'll be fine.'

But as it turned out, Allyson had hit the nail on the head with the 'media-friendly' thing. In fact, Cordy had vowed last night (after yet another call from a sparky young researcher from *Daybreak*) that the next person to tell her she 'would look lovely on the sofa' would get an earful about the demeaning portrayal of women in popular culture. As much as Cordy loved working in the victim support and children's advocacy field, there were limits and, for someone who guarded their privacy as fiercely as she did, having a video camera shoved in her face was deeply unpleasant. Some of her most terrible memories had been played out in front of a camera flash. She'd had enough of that sort of attention to last her several lifetimes.

But this call was about something completely different. This wasn't about providing a smile and a two-minute soundbite (sandwiched in between celeb gossip and the footy results) but about actually being part of a case. But working with the police . . . with a load of strangers . . .

At this point in her workout, Cordy usually hit the mat for her daily series of stomach crunches, but instead she walked over to the answer machine and pressed replay. Swigging down a glass of iced water, she gazed out of the window at the heath as the message played out again. The woman didn't give her very much to go on. Like everyone in her field, Cordy knew about the history of the Elite Child Protection Unit – the ECPU. In fact, as part of her Child Psychology studies she had taken a module on the history of the Unit, and its pioneering work in combating Internet paedophilia. However, after a year at J4C, the Unit had grown larger than life in her mind, a strange realm of amazing technology and crushing bureaucracy, which held itself aloof from charities and foundations like hers.

Outside a young couple were lounging on a tartan picnic mat while their dog licked their plates clean. A little blonde girl fell over mid-cartwheel, but her father ran over and brushed off her knees before she'd even had a chance to start crying properly.

Cordy turned away from the window and back to the phone. What were they doing calling her all of a sudden? Surely they must have their own experts on the payroll. What were they trying to prove by bringing her in?

After scribbling down the contact number on the pristine white notepad she kept by the phone, Cordy went into the kitchen to fix herself a snack. As usual her flat was spotless. Women's magazines might be full of Cath Kidston cushions and vintage chic, but for Cordy clean minimalism trumped chintzy clutter any day. Admittedly, it wasn't simply an aesthetic choice. Looking around, Cordy once again admired the soothing white of the sofa, the shining hardwood floors, the square footstool that rested firmly on the floor, with no sinister black shadows underneath it. That was another of her rules. She'd even had a raised platform purpose-built for her bed to rest on, so she would never have to check underneath it.

In the kitchen she opened her fridge and took out a Tupperware box of blueberries and a fresh tub of Greek yoghurt. This was her regular post-workout snack, and the routine of spooning the fruit into the yoghurt pot soothed her. She always got a kick out of the way the colour leached off the berries, dyeing the creamy yoghurt blue. Smiling, she remembered the way her father would shake his head and say,

'Simple things please simple minds', when he caught her and Jess swirling their ice cream and chocolate sauce into a delicious brown slush.

Of course, since the accident, even the thought of ice cream made her feel nauseous. It had joined the long list of things that belonged to a former life, one that she knew she'd never get back.

But she worked around it, like she did everything else. Hence the yoghurt.

Cordy forced her mind back to the present. She'd call the Unit back in the morning. At the very least she should go to the meeting and find out what it was all about. Maybe they were right. Maybe she could help. Maybe this was just the chance she'd been waiting for: to effect a real change from the inside, rather than making noise from the margins.

Or maybe it was just a PR stunt.

She meticulously washed out the pot and put it in her colour-coded recycling bin and then checked her watch. Four thirty. Time for half an hour on the treadmill before she went to visit her sister Jess. Smiling to herself, she pumped up the volume on her stereo and let herself get lost in the pounding bass and the smooth rhythm of her stride.

Chapter 3

The rain-slicked streets of South London were flashing by her, but for Cordelia the only real thing was the voice in her head muttering that this was a bad idea. That she should stick to working with the people she knew. That she should turn right around and go back. What the hell did she think she was doing anyway? The police worked by completely different rules. She'd publicly criticised them in the past. Hell, they'd probably only brought her in to shut her up, to stop her saying negative things about their operations again. They'd just be waiting for her to slip up. And meanwhile there'd be . . .

'Shit!'

The bike juddered under Cordy's body as she braked to avoid a cyclist who'd cut in front of her.

'Watch it!' she yelled, but already the courier had his head down, and was sprinting over the crossing ahead. 'Bloody idiot.'

By the time she pulled up in front of police headquarters her heartbeat was back to normal – in fact she felt calmer than she'd done all day. Unlike her boss Allyson, she wasn't into stuff like yoga or meditation. Cordy found that no amount of New Age chanting could clear her head like a good old-fashioned surge of adrenaline – hence the bike, the kickboxing tournaments and the handsome, aloof men that she'd sometimes sleep with but never let sleep over.

Cordelia Hunter, she reminded herself firmly, *you set your own agenda, and if the police want to work with you they'd better remember that.*

Her confidence started to sag as she locked up her Suzuki Hayabusa and took a closer look at the building. All the ground-floor windows were blocked off by grey concrete barriers, giving the place a tough, unwelcoming look, like a bunker. *Or a prison*, Cordy thought grimly. The only way in was through a covered walkway, manned by armed guards. The nearest one (a gangly young blond man) gave her a quick once-over, but went back to staring into the middle distance when she shot him a scornful look.

Taking a deep breath and slinging her helmet under her arm, Cordy marched up to the front door. To her relief she saw that once inside it looked just like an ordinary waiting area, complete with bored-looking receptionist and scuffed leather chairs.

After looking around in vain for a bathroom, she approached the desk. 'Sorry, I'm heading for the ECPU. I have a meeting with Fiona Andrews. But I really need to get changed out of these leathers first.'

The girl hurriedly stowed her copy of *Heat* magazine under some files and gave Cordy a curious look. 'I can see that. The Ladies loos are round to the left. I'll give *Detective Chief Superintendent* Andrews a call to let her know you're here.'

'Fine,' Cordy said, ignoring the dig. 'I'll be right back.'

A couple of minutes later she emerged wearing a sharply tailored trouser suit and black court shoes, her long brown hair pulled up into a severe ponytail. The only signs of individuality were the bulging bag of bike gear she carried over one shoulder and the half-heart gold locket she never took off.

This time the receptionist managed a vague smile. 'Right. Here's your security pass. They said to go straight up. Fifth floor.'

She had turned back to the horoscopes before Cordelia had a chance to thank her.

In the lift Cordy fiddled with a rebellious stray hair, trying to tuck it neatly back in the elastic. She'd only just given up on it when the doors opened onto the fifth floor and a handsome man in his early forties stepped forward to greet her. He was tall – six three at least, Cordy figured, factoring in the extra inches her court shoes gave her – with dark hair trimmed short at the back and sides and an expensive-looking suit, cut to make the most of his athletic build. The man exuded confidence. *University education*, Cordelia guessed. *Travelled quickly up through the ranks. Type A, but highly developed people-management skills . . .*

'You must be Dr Hunter,' he said, cutting short her impromptu assessment. 'Welcome to the Unit.'

'Thank you, umm . . . ?'

He gave her a warm smile. 'Anthony. Anthony DeLuca. It was me that emailed over the directions last week.'

'Oh, of course.'

'So you found your way here OK, then?' he asked, guiding her along the corridor with a hand in the small of her back.

'Mmm,' she replied, moving discreetly away. Thanks to her history, she wasn't mad keen on physical contact with strangers – even very handsome ones.

Luckily Anthony didn't seem to notice anything odd, and Cordy was able to take a good look round while he pointed out the various departments.

She'd never been a fan of cop dramas, but Cordy had still expected the ECPU headquarters to be more . . . dramatic. There were no cells, no uniformed officers, no perps sitting around in handcuffs. Instead it was like walking through a technology showroom. Everywhere she looked there were semicircular banks of computers, with screens piled up to the ceilings. Interactive whiteboards turned the walls into yet more screens, making it hard to see where one office ended and another began. Amongst all this hi-tech gear, the staff looked a little out of place, hunched over their computer screens or standing around in corridors shooting the shit. It was almost a relief to spot a break area, its cheap plastic tables littered with dirty coffee cups, its low-tech noticeboard dominated by a flyer about an inter-departmental football league.

'The chief is just in here.'

Anthony held the door open for her. Inside the bare, functional room was a short black woman with a distinctive streak of white in her bobbed hair. She offered Cordy a firm handshake.

'Dr Hunter. Thanks so much for coming in today.'

'Well, I only hope I can be of help,' she replied. 'So far no one's really told me very much . . .'

'Oh, it's a sensitive case, as I'm sure you can imagine,' Detective Chief Superintendent Fiona Andrews said briskly. 'But, before we get into all that, I thought I'd tell you a bit about the work we do here. If you'd like to take a seat. Tea, coffee?'

'Water is fine,' Cordy said, sitting down.

The handsome male detective – Anthony DeLuca, Cordy reminded herself – nodded and left the room. Fiona shut the door firmly behind him and took up position in a big leather chair on the other side of the desk.

'So.' She glanced down at a sheet of paper, as if reminding herself of the pertinent facts. 'Although there's been an increase in dedicated funding for child protection in recent years, there has long been concern in the service that not enough was being done to protect the more vulnerable members of our society – specifically the under-eighteens. In this country we've had special procedures for dealing with young *offenders* for over a hundred and fifty years – since the Juvenile Offenders Act of 1847, but it's only much more recently that we've been able to focus on what we can do to help child *victims*. Which is where the ECPU comes in. Since the legislation change of—'

Cordy, who'd been nodding and smiling politely up until this point, cut her off. 'It's OK. You don't really need to do the whole spiel. I know about the ECPU's background. I'm really more interested in why you want to talk to *me*.'

'Well, I'll get to that, of course.'

'Why not get to it right now?'

The chief superintendent looked at her hard for a beat and then nodded. 'Fine. If that's what you prefer, we can jump straight in. Save us both some time. Well, firstly, you're here because of your specific area of expertise. After someone sent me the article, I took a look at your research work into victim speak. Impressive. As is, of course, your work at—'

There was a knock, and the door opened again. Anthony appeared with a tray of glasses and a large bottle of mineral water.

'Tap would have been fine,' Cordy protested.

'I'll remember for next time,' he said, smiling and setting the tray down carefully on the desk.

The chief leaned across and with a sharp snap of the wrist opened the bottle and started to pour herself a glass. 'Thanks, DeLuca. Now look, can you get the team together? I want to show her the clip while she's here.'

'You're going straight into that?' he asked, raising his eyebrows. 'I thought you wanted to fill her in on the background first?'

'Seems like Dr Hunter doesn't want to beat around the bush.'

He reached over, filled a glass and passed it to Cordy. 'Whatever you think best, Chief. I'll call down to the Ops Room now. The others should be ready to go in ten. Are you sure she's ready to see it?'

'See what?' Cordy asked, looking back and forth between them.

Fiona gave her an appraising look. 'I take it you're used to hearing about these video nasties in your line of work. Well, we're not allowed to show you the whole clip, but there's something I think you should see. It's from an Internet site we've just found that offers a—' She glanced up as the door opened, and a big, grey-haired man walked in. 'What did you call it, Bob?'

'Pay-as-you-go kiddie porn.' The man put the laptop down on the desk and grinned at Cordy, who recoiled slightly.

'Although obviously that's not the term we use in official reports, DCI Sampson,' Fiona said primly to the grey-haired man.

'Let me get this right, the victims are abused . . . to order?' Cordy stammered.

'Yes, horrific, isn't it?' Anthony said, coming in with a slim blonde girl in a short denim skirt. 'This is Detective Constable Tammy Reynolds, also on our team. She helps us a lot with our undercover work.'

'Yup, I'm the resident jail-bait,' Tammy said wearily. 'Not exactly what my parents had in mind when they paid for all those acting lessons, I bet, but there you go. All in a good cause. And who knows – maybe they'll have me on *The Bill* one day. Or *Law and Order SVU*.'

Cordy didn't crack a smile. She must be in her early twenties, she thought, sizing Tammy up, but she could definitely pass for someone much younger. Especially with that lilting, little-girl voice. Catnip to a sexual predator.

As if she could read her mind, Tammy retreated to the corner with a muttered, 'Nice to meet you.'

'Wait – so you've found this site,' Cordy backtracked, 'and it's live? I mean, it's still operating? You haven't shut it down yet?'

'Well, of course we could make the web host remove it. That's what we do with sites that distribute images and videos from outside sources. We aim to break the link in the supply chain. But this is something very different,' Fiona said. 'Maybe I wasn't clear. They're making these clips themselves.'

'It's like the difference between a supermarket and a farm – if you're a pervert, that is,' the grey-haired man – Bob Sampson, was it? – explained.

Cordy couldn't help but wince at his analogy.

'In this instance, our major objectives are to get the children into a secure environment and press criminal charges against the offenders,' Fiona explained. 'In that order. And those objectives will be easier to achieve if we don't force the perps to go to ground.'

'That makes sense.'

'Unfortunately we don't have a lot to go on so far,' the chief continued. 'The men's features are hidden, and even their voices are digitally distorted. The children don't seem to match any of the missing children reports we've dug out so far . . .'

'But you must have the basics, right?' Cordy insisted. 'You must have an idea of what country they're operating out of. Who registered the site name? What ages, races and genders are we talking about here?'

'Perps are adult white males. We're interested in the three regulars in particular: a tall dark-haired twenty-something, a sandy-haired guy who seems to be in charge, and an older male who looks to be the most violent of the three. And in terms of the victims there's quite a diversity in age and gender,' Fiona replied.

'Sort of a pick'n'mix,' Sampson added. 'You've got yer regulars, you've got yer one-offs; you've got yer boys, you've got yer girls; you've got yer older kids, you've got yer—'

'All right!' Cordy interrupted. 'Jesus . . .'

'Rein it in, Sampson,' Fiona ordered testily. 'She's only been here five minutes.'

'The indications are that it's hosted in Britain, which is why it's us and not the Feds who are dealing with it,' Anthony said, his calm voice soothing Cordy's rising nausea. 'We do have one lead. This clip. Which is where you come in.'

'Thanks, DeLuca. I think I can take it from here, guys,' the chief said smoothly. The other officers nodded and stood up to go. Bob winked at Cordy, but headed out through the door before he could see her answering look of disgust. 'Now, Dr Hunter, like I said, your qualifications are impressive and the department has heard great things about your activism work.'

'Well, thank you . . .' Cordy stammered.

'And I note that the organisation you work for, Justice4Children, had quite a few criticisms of the way the police handled the recent Norwich Children's Homes case.'

Although her cheeks were flaming, Cordy stood her ground. 'We weren't the only ones to suggest that more could have been done to protect those children.'

Fiona sighed. 'You can say that again. Seems like everybody thinks they're an expert on paedophiles these days, thanks to our friends in the press.'

Cordy raised her eyebrows, but the chief had already moved on.

'Now look, let me be frank. We could really do with your help on the case. But that's not the only reason you've been called in. Basically, we can't afford another PR disaster with this one. When this breaks to the press, the police need to be seen to be doing everything in their power to smash this paedophile ring. And I mean *everything*.'

'I think we're wasting time here,' Cordy said bluntly. 'I thought you were going to show me the clip?'

'Right. The idea the powers that be have had is that, with your experience in this field . . .' Fiona paused. 'Anyway, here it is. It's only a few minutes long but, well, you'll see . . .'

When she clicked 'Play' the screen filled with the image of a pale-skinned girl, probably about seven or eight years old, Cordy guessed, but so skinny that her dark eyes seemed too big for her delicate face. The girl was staring intently at the camera, her lips moving softly.

'Can you turn up the sound any higher?'

'The sound's not good,' Fiona admitted, 'and anyway, it seems like she's speaking under her breath. But we've got an expert who lip-reads, and she says it's just a nursery rhyme.'

'Nursery rhyme?' Cordy's voice came out telltale husky. It was heartbreaking to think of the girl clinging on desperately to a scrap of her childhood . . .

'You're watching, right?' Fiona asked, a hint of scorn in her voice.

On screen the girl's lips were still moving, but something was different.

'Wait, can you rewind the clip?' Cordy asked. 'Just those last few seconds.'

Detective Chief Superintendent Andrews glanced at her watch, but did as she was asked.

This time Cordy was ready. Ignoring the painful lump in her throat, she stared at the screen.

And that's when she saw it – something unmistakeable and painfully familiar. Something that catapulted her back fifteen years to a time that she couldn't bear to remember, but could never afford to forget.

She had to force herself to slow her breathing, to take it all in. To check that she wasn't seeing something that wasn't there.

But no. There it was. Like a ghost captured on screen.

After glancing around warily, the girl looked straight into the camera and blinked three times in rapid succession.

'She's . . .' Cordy swallowed. When she tried again her voice was firmer, more professional. 'She's signalling, isn't she?'

Fiona crossed her arms in front of her ample chest. 'Just wait.'

The girl blinked three more times slowly, then three times more quickly again. Abruptly the screen went blank.

'You don't even want to hear what happened next,' the chief said firmly, but Cordy was barely listening.

'S-O-S,' she murmured. 'The girl's a messenger.'

'Right. She's using Morse code.' From the look on Fiona's face she was surprised that Cordy had even got that far.

'And has she signalled again?'

'Poor Bob – Detective Chief Inspector Sampson, I mean – has been tracking the site, but so far no more blinking. Looks like that might be the only bit of code she knows. Makes sense I guess. They teach it in primary schools, Brownies, Girl Scouts, that sort of thing.'

Cordy looked down and noticed that while they'd been talking she'd twisted long strands of her ponytail round her fingers. Releasing the hair, she locked eyes with the detective. 'Well, if she's trying to get a message out that won't be her only attempt. I've . . . seen this before. Can someone pull out footage of her and look for words, hand gestures, scars?'

'Scars?'

'When you're in a desperate situation, you work with what you've got.'

'Tell me about it,' the older woman quipped.

Cordelia didn't smile.

'So you'll work with us then?' Fiona asked.

Cordy nodded slowly. She knew she'd have to think over the practicalities at some point, but as soon as she saw that hunted look in the girl's eyes she knew she couldn't just walk away. 'And Detective Chief Superintendent, I'd be grateful if you'd set me up with a computer. Sounds like this is on a mainstream, surface-web server, but we should be trawling the deep web too, in case they're marketing the site in unpatrolled domains or using the darknet to distribute old clips.'

'Wow. I didn't know you were a techie. You'll fit in well here.' Fiona smiled. 'Sometimes I walk into the Ops Room and feel like I'm working on the set of *Star Trek*.'

'I'm not a techie. It's just that you can't work in the child protection field these days and be a complete Neanderthal.' As soon as she'd said the words she saw the chief's face harden.

Great job, Cordelia. She thinks you're making a dig at her. Way to lose friends and alienate people.

But when Fiona responded her voice was level. 'Well, in any case, we have a dedicated department for that sort of thing. We're not recruiting you for your computer skills. What we need is someone who can give us a psychological insight into the situation – particularly from the victims' point of view. As you can see for yourself, we have a child who seems to be attempting to communicate with the outside world. We need to know how best to make use of this opportunity.

'You would, of course, help the team to profile and identify the suspects, but what we most need is to get inside that girl's head. Which means that we need someone with specialist knowledge of the effects of this kind of sustained, systematic abuse. Someone who can read the situation from the inside out. Who can put themselves in this girl's place.' Here the chief tried to catch Cordy's eyes. The younger woman felt her cheeks flame, but willed herself to return the policewoman's gaze without flinching. In the end it was Fiona who looked away first. 'I don't mind telling you that this comes straight from HQ – part of a skill-sharing initiative with the not-for-profit sector. Your brief is to be a consultant psychologist, profiling the victims and suspects and helping the team formulate the tactical aspects of the investigation. You'd report to DI DeLuca, who reports to me, as does DCI Sampson separately. Detective Constable Reynolds would occasionally be available as a resource for you, but generally you'd be expected to operate as an independent team member. Does that make sense?'

'It does.' Cordy pushed back her chair. 'If it's all right with you, I'll get started right away.'

'Hold your horses,' the chief said. 'It'll take me a few days to get the paperwork in order. After that, I'll call you in and have DeLuca give you an orientation.' Fiona stood up to walk her guest out. 'He'll explain to you more about the way we work here, and get you set up with payroll. But make sure you give yourself some time to get settled in.'

Cordy shrugged. 'I'm sure I'll be OK.'

'It's not a suggestion,' Fiona said firmly. 'I'm sure you're very capable, but you're new to our systems here. All the evidence suggests we're up against organised criminals and we can't afford to make any mistakes. Plan on spending a week shadowing DeLuca before you get your hands dirty.'

'Fine,' said Cordy. 'Just one more thing.'

'Hmm?'

'What's the girl's name?'

The detective chief superintendent had already started picking up files from her bulging in-tray. 'They call her Alice on the site. You know, like *Alice in Wonderland*? Very unlikely to be her real name, but better than calling her Girl 1, or whatever, like she's just some anonymous corpse.'

Cordy bit her lip. 'Right.' She was about to leave the chief to her paperwork, when she realised that there was something she'd forgotten to ask. 'So how long should I plan on being here for?'

'You'll be on a short-term contract – initially for a month, but probably for however long it takes us to wrap up the case. I hope that it'll be no more than two – three tops.'

'Three months?'

'At the absolute limit,' Fiona assured her.

Cordy swallowed. 'Oh . . . My understanding was that this was only a temporary assignment. I'm not sure I can take a sabbatical from my job at Justice4Children for that long. We're quite a small operation . . .'

'We've actually already cleared it with your boss. So, if it's OK with you, then we'd like you to join us. If you can't do it, we'll find someone else.' The chief didn't look too upset at the prospect. 'Like I said, this directive comes from Head Office, but I doubt they'll worry themselves about the details.'

This was Cordy's chance to walk away without losing face. To go back to her exhausting, rewarding job at the foundation, where she knew the rules of the game. Where she wouldn't have to stare into those blank, dark eyes and be reminded of exactly what was going on behind them.

But, then again, she wasn't a quitter and she certainly wouldn't have made it this far without a hell of a stubborn streak.

'I'll make it work,' she said, trying to convince herself as much as Fiona. 'Sign me up.'

Chapter 4

Two days later, Cordy was called back to the ECPU. After being issued with a pass, she took the lift up to the fifth floor and got her first good look at the Ops Room. Fiona's *Star Trek* comparison wasn't so far off. As soon as she walked in through the door she felt the thrum of high-speed processors, like something alive. Inside, she saw that the desks were arranged in a semicircle, each with multiple screens showing digital map images, old newspaper articles, the results of online database searches and criminal mug shots. For someone like Cordy, who prided herself on always knowing her immediate environment inside out, the effect was disorientating. There was too much to process all at once, and it took her a few beats to notice that a couple of the desks were unoccupied, and that these seemed to function as dumping grounds for broken computer components, perilously stacked reports and what looked and smelled like a pile of unwashed jockstraps. Against the flickering, hi-tech backdrop, this human detritus looked even more shabby and out of place.

Anthony was leaning against a filing cabinet, chatting to Tammy, the 'jail-bait' detective, who was perched on the table in the centre, slim legs crossed coquettishly at the ankle.

They stopped laughing when they heard her come in. Cordelia tried not to feel like the new kid in school – the one no one wants to play with.

'So,' Cordy said, wracking her brains for something funny

to say. Something that'd make her look less like an interloper, 'apparently I'm supposed to sit on my arse for a week so I can see how the *experts* do things around here.'

'Well that makes sense,' Tammy said brightly. 'You wouldn't want to go messing the investigation up, would you?'

'Well no, I didn't mean . . .' She petered off lamely.

There was an awkward silence.

Anthony took pity on her and waved her over towards the least cluttered of the spare desks. Cordy calculated that the hardware half hidden beneath the mess was worth more than Justice4Children's annual turnover. She told herself firmly not to feel intimidated.

'Here, this used to be Saunders's. Officially he's still on sick leave, but I can't see him coming back any time soon, to be honest. Or if he does he'll get a transfer.'

'Who's Saunders?' Cordy asked, gingerly gathering the dirty coffee cups that had accumulated around the computer. 'And no offence, but don't you guys have a cleaner?'

Anthony shrugged. 'We can't really expect them to tackle that mess on their wages. Think it's a couple of poor sods who do the whole building at some ungodly hour of the morning. Usually the admin staff help clear up a bit, but they're a little overstretched at the moment.'

'Yeah, don't get the chief started on budget cuts or you'll never get round to doing any police work,' Tammy put in. 'Or, erm, consultant work. Is that your title, by the way?'

'Apparently.'

'Reporting to?'

'Me,' Anthony supplied. 'Which I hope you're OK with.'

'Mind you don't let DeLuca run you ragged,' Tammy said, with a mischievous smile. 'He can get like that.'

Cordy changed the subject. 'You were saying about Saunders . . .'

'Nothing to tell, really,' Anthony said. 'Nice bloke. Really good child protector. But the cases started getting to him, especially after his youngest was born.'

From across the room Bob, who'd been hunched over his computer, let out a derisory snort. 'Bri Saunders was all right. But he lost it, basically. He won't be back.'

'This afternoon I can show you where the cleaning closet is, if you like,' Anthony offered. 'I don't blame you if you don't want to sit amidst all that crap. Some of it's left over from when we used to have a Unit rugby team. Before some of us got all fat and lazy.'

'What was that, pretty boy?' Bob called. 'You're saying I'm fat? Well, I reckon any man that spends as long in the gym as you do must be compensating for some serious inadequacies.'

'If you say so, Sampson,' Anthony said lightly.

'And by that I mean a small penis.'

Tammy groaned theatrically. 'You know, Sampson, you seem to spend an awful lot of time thinking about DeLuca's package.'

'Look who's talking!' he retorted. 'I don't flatter myself that you're wearing that belt of a skirt for my benefit, missy.'

Cordy accidentally caught Anthony's eye. He gave her a wry grin. Flustered, she glanced back down at the pile of dirty sports kit. 'So go on then: where are you hiding the rest of the squad?'

'Oh, it's not just us,' Tammy assured her.

'Though it feels like that sometimes,' Bob muttered.

'There're teams on the other floors. And then there're the tech guys, the trauma therapists, the foster parents from the safe houses . . .' Tammy ticked them off on her fingers. 'And that's not even counting the resources we share with other departments.'

'Sounds like a big operation,' Cordy said quietly. She wondered how Allyson was getting on without her back at J4C. The thought of all the strangers she'd be working with made her head spin.

As if he'd read her mind, Anthony shooed the others away – 'Don't you lot have work to do?' – switched on her computer and showed her how to set up a password to access the shared files.

'And if you have any questions, you're usually better off asking Bob Sampson to take a look. The tech boys tend to take a while to get back to you. Either they're really busy or just really disorganised.'

'Sampson?'

'Yeah.' Anthony lowered his voice. 'I know he seems like a bit of a dinosaur – been in the force longer than anyone cares to remember – but he's actually surprisingly computer-savvy. Think one of his grandkids got him interested in it, or something like that. Anyway, it's good to have him around, because these babies can be a little temperamental.' He patted the nearest monitor affectionately. 'Not that I'm complaining. You should talk to Sampson about what they had to work with when he first started at the Unit. Mental really. It's hard enough with all this.'

Cordy smiled. 'You should see what we've got at our office. My PC broke and now, unless I lug my laptop in, I'm on something that's pretty much one step up from an abacus.'

'Well, I'm sure you'll get the hang of it.' He gave her an appraising look. 'Fancy a cup of tea or anything before we get cracking?'

'I think I'm all right,' Cory said briskly. 'Let's just get started.'

'Right.' He waited for her to stand up and then pushed her chair over to his desk. Cordy couldn't help noticing the framed picture – of him and a pretty redhead posing on a beach – that sat on the shelf beside them. 'We'll get you a proper briefing with Mick in the tech department if you want, but I can give you the basics. I'm sure you know all about the OSC, or Online Sex Offenders' Community?'

'You could say that.'

'Well, then, you know the sort of message boards where they congregate. Ones like BoiLovers, Wondaland . . .'

'Littlefriends?' Cordy offered.

'Yeah, those type of sites. Ones that are not explicit enough to be shut down immediately. Or ones run by scum who'll just start a new site as soon as you take the old one down. And usually you need to be in deep with the codes or it all seems like nonsense. Anyway, links get posted to these sites directing users to live clips of child abuse. As far as we can work out, a lot of these clips are coming out of the same place. Same kids too, far as we can tell. Soon as we worked that out, we knew we were in for the long haul – no point just targeting the webcast and leaving the kids there. Especially since all the signs point to it being a cellar kids situation.' He sighed. 'We're seeing more of these – in this country as well as overseas. Fritzl wasn't a one-off, you know. And of course, there's the copycat effect to factor in. That's why we're always careful about what info we release to the press.'

'An actual cellar, you think?' She tried to keep her tone as matter-of-fact as Anthony's, but it was difficult with the image of the girl – of Alice – still burning behind her eyes.

'Cellar. Attic. Garage. Somewhere with little natural light, as far as we can see,' he said. 'Anyway, it's not a bedroom or a living room, which is what you'd expect if it were a family set-up.'

Cordy didn't answer. She just nodded and turned back towards the computer.

Anthony gestured to the screen, where he'd brought up some text which he'd copied and pasted from the Wondaland website. 'As you can see, basically they post a variant on "get a load of this" and then a link. But the links are never up for very long, so even being optimistic we're probably missing seventy per cent of the output. We've got an online software bloodhound trying to track down other activity from that ISP address, but so far not a lot of joy. That's one of the problems – the guys we're dealing with aren't stupid. Not by a long shot. They mostly keep their faces out of the frame, or else wear masks. Apart from the obvious areas . . . we only get the odd ear, or glimpse of hair colour, but not a lot to go on. And so we're left sifting through profiles of known offenders and missing children to see if there are any likely matches. Which is what you'll be helping with, for starters.'

She looked up. 'The chief was saying that there's an . . . an interactive element.'

'Yeah. Viewers can pay to request certain things being done to or by the children,' Anthony said. 'I know, it's really sick—'

She cut him off. 'So if they're using PayPal or something, surely you can find out where the money's going to? Find the people, do a raid, close it down. Isn't that what the Unit's for? Surely there's no time to waste . . .'

Anthony swivelled to face her. 'Look, I told you these guys were clever bastards. Or at least one of them is. Not only do we have the problem of half the banks refusing to give up the "customer details", but even with what we can find out, these guys are using an online checkout, and when you trace it back the money is going through a whole series of foreign bank accounts, all in different names.'

'So where does that leave us?'

'Well, the fraud squad are supposedly helping us with the money trail but, like Fiona says, unless one of these guys is implicated in terrorism or drug smuggling, we're just not going to be top priority. Besides, the money trail is the most complicated way of getting to them. Believe me.'

As this point Bob butted in. 'Yeah, but say they were using the kids as drugs mules.' He'd drifted over from the corner and was now leaning over their shoulders. Cordy instinctively put her hand on her throat to check her shirt buttons were safely done up. 'Or some terrorist shit. Whatever. You can bet your arse we'd have that money trail tied up like *that*.' He clicked his fingers, and carried on strolling towards the door. 'Cos that's a *priority*. But sadly it seems like the perps haven't got round to that bollocks yet.'

'Yes, that is a shame,' Cordy said, before she could stop herself. 'Because, you're right: it is pretty amusing to think of ways those kids' lives could get worse.'

'Looks like you'll have to watch yourself around her, Sampson,' Tammy called, but the older officer just shrugged.

'I'm sure she can take a joke.'

'Yeah, but I'm just not sure how much of *you* I can take,' Cordy shot back. She tried to match his light tone, but knew her blazing eyes gave her away.

'Keep your hair on, love,' he said mildly. 'No point starting off on the wrong foot. We've all got to work together here. Lighten up a bit or you'll go mad, dealing with this shit day in, day out.'

'I can deal with *this shit*,' she assured him. 'Don't you worry about that. What worries me is the way you're talking . . .'

He turned and stared at her, stopping her midstream.

'*The way I'm talking?* You've got to be kidding me. *Sweetheart*, it might all be political correctness and hearts and flowers where you come from, but over here we actually do something to stop these perverts, rather than whining to the press about them.'

'I don't know what—'

'Save your breath, love, we all saw the article in the *Mail*. Chief emailed it round, in fact. Particularly liked the parts where you bitched about the way the police handled the follow-up. Shame you've got no clue what you're talking about.'

Cordy leapt to her feet. 'You know nothing about the work I do. You know nothing about me. But if we're going to work together you're going to have to stop talking about the victims like they're lumps of meat. Because that's exactly how their abusers treat them.'

He laughed dismissively. 'Now, no need to get your knickers in a twist. If you're going to survive here for two minutes you're going to have to grow a sense of humour. And some balls. Because I'll tell you something for nothing: a lot tougher folks than you have had problems hacking it. If that's what you decide, fair dues. Go back to reading books and writing press releases or whatever it is you do. But, in the meantime, it wouldn't kill you to have a bit of respect. We're on the bloody front line here.' Without waiting for an answer he walked out. Cordy stared at the back of his head, eyes burning.

'Ouch,' Tammy said, wincing dramatically. 'Sampson One, Hunter Nil.'

'Ignore her,' said Anthony. 'In fact, ignore them both. Sampson's bark is much worse than his bite. He's actually a pretty solid copper. He was a good mate of Brian Saunders . . .'

Just then Bob Sampson poked his head back round the door.

'Sorry, love, just yanking your chain. No hard feelings, eh? Can I get you a cuppa?'

Cordelia shrugged.

He seemed to take that as a yes and came back a few minutes later with his peace offering.

'Thought you probably didn't take sugar . . .'

'Because I'm sweet enough?' Cordy finished the sentence icily.

He gave her a wink. 'Got it in one.'

Chapter 5

clewis: Did you like the things I sent you?
           The one with the girl with the red hair?
spurs101: spot on
clewis: Told you she was begging for it
           Watch her
           She loves it
spurs101: hey mate
           thanx 4 all ur help
clewis: Any time.
           Sometimes you just need to talk about it.
           Let it out.
spurs101: I didn't really know what I was lookin for
clewis: Yeah, it's easy to spot someone new in the
           chatroom
spurs101: what cos they dont know their arse from there
           elbow???
clewis: Pretty much.
           Thought you were a copper at first.
           Getting paranoid in my old age.
           You still there?
spurs101: evry time u open a paper seems like the worlds
           gone crazy
clewis: True.
spurs101: why cant people just mind their own business
           and leave other people alone
           ????

clewis:	surely they have more important things to worry about?
spurs101:	as long as there not hurting anyone i mean
clewis:	Like global warming.
	Or their own messed up lives
spurs101:	right
clewis:	Anyway, got something else you might be into.
	From the states. Nice quality.
spurs101:	sounds good
clewis:	I'll just send it to your hotmail again?
	You didn't give me a work one
spurs101:	no that ones good
clewis:	You know I could probably help you more if I knew a bit about your situation?
	You know you can ask me anything?
spurs101:	thanx
clewis:	Like I said, it can help to talk.
spurs101:	sorry gotta go

Chapter 6

Cordelia surveyed her desk with a grin of pride. It was only her third day at the Unit and already she had managed to create an oasis of calm and order in the high-tech chaos of the Ops Room. The desk gleamed and she could now work on the fancy computer without her fingers sticking to the keys. She still wasn't quite used to the banks of screens, and the interactive whiteboards the team used to share data and to chart their progress, but she was a fast learner, and she was already plotting ways that Justice4Children could upgrade their technology and improve their overall functionality. She was currently working her way through a dozen or so inter-linked digital files, documenting the team's work over the last few weeks. She also had open a four-page memo – 'Elite Child Protection Unit: Updated Standards and Procedures' – which Fiona had suggested she read through twice.

'You wouldn't want to miss anything,' the detective chief superintendent had insisted, when she'd called Cordy into her office for a brief orientation on the Unit's systems and protocols. 'These days it's not good enough just to catch criminals. Unless you've got every single piece of official documentation in place, their lawyers will weasel them out of it. Even bring a charge against you for defamation of character.'

Cordy nodded obediently, but Fiona wasn't finished.

'It's easy to bitch about bureaucracy. But when you've seen the smug look on a rapist's face when their case is chucked out of court, then you'll know what I'm talking about. It's the paperwork that gets them behind bars. And it's the stats that keep the funding coming in.'

'Fair enough.' Cordy's eye caught on a picture taped to the wall – a butterfly finger-painted on a grubby white piece of card. She gestured her head towards it. 'Cute. Our office at J4C is papered over with those.'

'Oh yeah?'

'From the kids who come on the family camps we organise,' Cordy explained. 'It's getting to the point where we're going to have to take some down, or there'll be no room for the new ones. But I dread to think what the walls look like underneath. We've got a bit of a damp problem ...' She stopped when she realised she was rambling. She admired the chief superintendent, but something about her reminded her uncomfortably of a headmistress she'd had at primary school – Miss Davis – who had had a thousand-yard stare and a reputation for being tough on troublemakers.

'My daughter made it. Sophia, my youngest.'

The look on Fiona's face didn't invite further inquiries, so Cordy just thanked her and left, memo in hand.

Back in the Ops Room she'd asked Anthony what Fiona was like to work with.

'The chief's great. Good at her job.' He paused, and looked around, as if to check she wasn't standing in the doorway. 'If she's a bit short with you it's only because she's under a lot of pressure from the bigwigs. You know her predecessor was sacked, right?'

'I think I read something about it . . .' Cordy said vaguely, not wanting to reveal that she'd spent the last couple of evenings staying up late and reading everything she could find on the Unit's history. She'd always hated feeling unprepared.

'Well, I arrived from the drugs squad halfway through it, but basically a case we'd been working on for months – hundreds of man-hours – folded because of witness intimidation. The bastards got away scot-free.' He shrugged. 'Not exactly the last chief's fault, but it was obvious that someone's head was for the chop.'

'She's got kids, right? Detective Chief Superintendent Andrews, I mean.'

'Yep, three,' he said. 'And I get the impression their father isn't really in the picture any more. But she doesn't really talk about her personal life much. Not like Reynolds here . . .'

'Oy, I heard that,' Tammy called, shooting a look at him from beneath her long lashes.

'Although you'd need a PhD to keep up with her love-life,' Bob chipped in. 'Those panties of hers must have hit the floor more times than Paris Hilton's.'

Cordy bristled and swivelled to face his desk. 'And why has Detective Constable Reynolds' private life got anything to do with you?'

'Oh, he's just jealous,' Tammy said. 'I wouldn't waste your breath.'

'*Detective Constable Reynolds*,' Bob mimicked in a high, squeaky voice. 'Should have expected you birds to stick together. There's so much bloody oestrogen in this room that I'm starting to grow a decent pair of tits myself.'

'I don't think man-boobs count,' Cordy shot back. 'And since I don't reckon the rest of us fancy picturing you and your missus in the act of sexual congress, I suggest you lay off Reynolds. Her knickers are really none of your business.'

Tammy laughed at that, and put her hand up for a high-five.

Bob mimed being shot through the heart, but when Cordy didn't respond he turned grumpily back to his computer.

A few minutes later the regular percussion of keyboards started up again.

Cordy was just getting back into her research when Anthony nudged her.

'It's great to see someone giving back as good as they get. We're all so used to Sampson we just let him shoot his mouth off. But it's a whole lot more fun when someone fights back.'

She tried to stifle a smile. 'Thanks. But I'd better get on with this. Come Monday, I'll be okayed to help move the investigation forward and this is all' – she gestured at the files – 'pretty new. A lot to get my head round.'

'Course,' he said. 'Just shout if you have any questions. And if you happen to be free over lunch I'd love to pick your brains a bit. You promised you'd tell me more about Justice4Children. Did I tell you that my mother raises funds for you guys?'

She shot him a look to check he wasn't teasing her. 'Really? What's her name?'

'Kathy DeLuca. Nothing major. Just does bring-and-buy sales at her school, that sort of thing. But she thinks you guys are amazing.'

Cordy was about to ask him about how his mother had got involved when Tammy sashayed over.

'Thanks for that, Hunter,' she said, flashing her perfect white teeth.

'No problem. Hope I wasn't too harsh. Sexists bring out my inner terrier.'

'Ah, Sampson knows that you shouldn't give it out if you can't take it.' Tammy turned to Anthony. 'So, boss, when are you going to bring your gorgeous wife out on a double-date with me and Klaus?'

'The famous Klaus. He's still on the scene, is he? Yeah, we should get something fixed up.' Anthony moved away from Cordy's desk to check through his diary. 'The missus is on nights until next week. But maybe Tuesday after next? We could do that pub quiz again. Cordelia, you should join us. What's your specialist subject?'

'I guess I'm OK on music. But, to be honest, I'm not really much of a drinker.'

Tammy leaned over and said in a stage whisper, 'You should come along anyway and meet Angie. They're so adorable together. Just got married last summer. We were all invited. And she's *beauuutiful*. She's a nurse. Bit younger than you. They're such a lovely couple.'

At a normal volume Cordy replied, 'Thanks for the invite. I'll let you know.'

Message delivered, Tammy sashayed off. Amused, Cordy looked over at Anthony, but he was at his computer, back hunched over, nose inches from the screen. *I wonder if he's had his eyes tested recently*, she caught herself thinking. Smiling, she turned back to her screen. *I'm getting as bad as Tammy. If his wife's a nurse, I'm sure she's got it covered.*

As her eyes skimmed over the case documents, her smile faded. She couldn't afford to let herself get distracted by office politics. She had a job to do.

Maximising a series of documents, she looked again at the single word she'd typed on the first page.

Alice.

The letters floated eerily in the white space. Cordy frowned down at the screen, fingers hovering over the cordless mouse.

Who is she? And how the hell do I get her out of there?

Chapter 7

Cordy cleared her throat awkwardly. A couple of heads turned curiously, but most people didn't bother looking up from their screens.

'Sorry to disturb you, but is Leela Simons in this office?'

'Next door,' a middle-aged woman said, without looking round, or taking off her hands-free headset. 'Desk near the window.'

'Thanks. I should let you get back to your . . .' Cordy's voice trailed off. All round the open-plan office, phones rang out and fingers clacked on keyboards. It was obvious no one was listening.

The second office looked like a carbon-copy of the first, apart from the fact that above the whiteboard someone had pinned up a poster of a cat clinging on to a branch, with the words 'Hang In There' picked out in bold red letters. *Original*, Cordy thought, scanning the room for a likely Leela.

A woman with long dark hair happened to look up from her bank of screens and catch her eye as Cordy hovered in the doorway.

'Dr Hunter is it? Detective Chief Superintendent Andrews said you might want a word.'

Cordy smiled gratefully. 'Sorry, I know I said two o'clock but it's a bit of a maze down here.'

'Is it easier if I come upstairs?' Leela asked. She was already taking off her headset and saving her files.

'If you don't mind. It's about that clip . . .'

Upstairs Leela took out a pad and pen from her neat leather bag and sat down in front of the screen. Cordy had reserved one of the single offices to ensure there would be no distractions. It was one of two small rooms that had been carved out of a much larger one, and, as if to make up for the lack of natural light, a fluorescent strip gleamed harshly down from the ceiling, causing shadows to pool beneath the single computer desk.

Cordy pulled over another chair from the corner, and resisted the urge to bend down and check there was no one lurking in the darkness. Angie wouldn't bat an eyelid if she did that at Justice4Children, but Cordy didn't want Leela telling her colleagues what a weirdo she was.

Although maybe I could pretend I had to sort out the wires underneath . . .

No. Cordy forced herself to sit down and log on to the spare drive.

'Sorry, it'll just be a minute . . .'

'No worries,' Leela assured her. 'Any excuse to get away from my desk for a bit. It's been a long day.'

Cordy shifted uncomfortably in her seat. She knew she should ask about the other woman's job, but she'd never really had much of a talent for small talk. Instead she blurted out the first thing that came to mind.

'So you're not deaf then? I mean, hearing impaired.'

Leela raised her eyebrows. 'No.'

'So why . . . ?'

'My little brother lost his hearing after a viral infection when he was little. We all learned it. In my family I mean.' Leela toyed with the pen in her hand, twirling it like a baton. 'He lives in Canada now so I don't use it that much day-to-day, but sometimes I watch TV with the sound off to keep my eye in.'

'Must be useful.'

'Good for spying on people's private conversations,' Leela agreed. 'Although sometimes you end up hearing things you shouldn't.'

'As long as you only use your powers for good,' Cordy quipped.

Leela looked a little confused, and they lapsed into silence.

'Great,' Cordy said briskly when the computer had finally logged her in. She opened the shared case file and clicked on the video clip that Fiona had shown her at their first meeting. 'Now, if you can just take another look at this.'

'Sure. Although I remember it's pretty creepy. Like something from a horror movie, don't you reckon? What was that film with Jack Nicholson and those scary children? Redrum, and all that?'

When Cordy didn't reply, Leela uncapped the pen and obediently focused her attention on the screen. Halfway through the clip she turned back to Cordelia.

'Like I said before, it's a nursery rhyme. "This is the way the lady rides." I'm not sure if that's the official name, but—'

'Could I get it word for word?' Cordy interrupted.

'Sure, if you think that'll help.'

Cordy reset the clip and this time the other woman made notes. She asked for it to be played again, and then again.

After the fourth time Leela put down her pen. 'Think I've got it now. Sorry, it's a bit difficult because she's not using her mouth that much. When people speak aloud the movements are usually more distinct. Or maybe I'm just a bit rusty.'

But Cordy was already looking at the page over her shoulder.

'Can you read it? Sorry, I've got terrible handwriting.'

'How confident are you that you've got this right?' Cordy asked. 'Give me a percentage.'

Leela shrugged. 'I mean, I wouldn't bet my life on it, but . . .'

'Seventy-five per cent?' Cordy persisted. 'Eighty?'

'Eighty,' Leela said defensively. 'Maybe eighty-five.'

Cordy read aloud. '"This is the way the captain rides. Hobbledee. Hobbledee. Hobbledee. And down, into the dark." That right?'

'Well, it should be the way the old man rides . . . and ditch, I think. Down into the ditch. That's the bit where you tip the kid upside down. My dad used to do it with us.'

'No, I mean, that's what she's saying?' Cordy asked. 'I read it right?'

Leela nodded. 'Yeah, I haven't heard that variation. And there's a couple of verses missing in the middle. Maybe she just learned it wrong. My daughter always sings The Beatles' song like it's "Yellow Summer Dream". Cracks up my husband.'

Cordy didn't smile. She was thinking that Alice was a little old to be getting mixed up like that. In fact, she was a little old to be singing nursery rhymes, full stop. At first Cordy had assumed it was just the usual type of regression you'd expect to see in traumatised children. *But given the blinking* . . .

Noticing that the other woman was looking up at her curiously, Cordy pushed back her chair and stood up. 'Thanks. That was very useful. I won't keep you any longer.'

Leela took the hint, stood up, and made to take the notebook.

'Do you mind leaving that page?' Cordy said quickly.

'Sure. But you'll see that the first verse is just normal. "Trit trot, trit trot" and all that stuff.'

'Still, if you don't mind . . .'

As soon as she'd safely packed Leela off downstairs, Cordy sank back down in her chair. Smoothing out the torn-out page she carefully typed it up and saved it on the communal drive. Somehow in blunt Arial type the words looked less mysterious, less pregnant with meaning.

Frowning, Cordy turned off the computer and went back to the Ops Room to look for Anthony. Already, she'd worked out that he was a good sounding board, and right now she could do with some reassurance that she wasn't barking up the wrong tree.

Anthony and Tammy's desks were empty, but Bob was in his usual position in the corner, slumped over his keyboard. Cordy's first instinct was to quietly go over to her own desk, but then she paused. Just because Bob rubbed her up the wrong way didn't mean she should underestimate his ability as a policeman. After all, she knew from bitter experience how keen people were to put labels on each other. Maybe she'd been a bit quick to judge.

Clocking the empty mug on his desk, she walked over and asked if he fancied a cup of tea.

'Ooh, that'd be lovely,' he said, passing it over to her. 'Just the one sugar. I'm trying to cut down.'

When Cordy came back he'd moved to the middle table. Reassured by this friendly gesture, she placed the steaming mug down in front of him and pulled up a pew.

'Watching your weight, are you?' he asked, nodding at her herbal tea.

'No. I just like peppermint,' she said, trying to ignore the snap of irritation in her belly. 'Not all women are on permanent diets, you know.'

'Fair dues.'

With the preliminaries out of the way, Cordy pulled out the neatly folded page of notepaper.

'What do we have here then?' Bob asked, fishing his glasses out of his shirt pocket.

'It's what Alice is saying in the clip. I was trying to figure out what she's trying to tell us. You see how she's changed the song?' Cordy ran a highlighter over the odd words in the last verse. 'I mean, I could be completely wrong, but it seems like it's worth thinking about. If she's smart enough for Morse code, then she's probably smart enough to try other kinds of messages.' As Cordy warmed to her subject she picked up pace and started to gesture with her free hand. 'What I've been thinking is: Who's the captain? And is the mention of horses significant? Maybe she's in the countryside, and can hear them outside her window? Or—'

Bob held up a hand to cut her off. 'No offence, love, but not only does she probably not have a window. But it all seems a bit' – he looked around as if searching for a word – '. . . far-fetched.'

Cordy swallowed. 'I know it sounds like a long-shot, but I thought it was worth kicking round some ideas.'

'Right,' said Bob, not bothering to hide his scepticism.

'So what do you think?' Cordy persisted. 'If we can narrow our investigations to the suburbs and the countryside, that'd be something at least. Or do you think it's the word "captain" that's important? Should we be thinking about ports? After all, if the children are smuggled into the country—'

'Slow down there, missy!' he said with a chuckle. 'It could also mean bugger all. I know you're new to this sort of investigation, but I'm telling you, we don't have the resources to go off on wild-goose chases. Any line of inquiry has to start from solid, verifiable facts. I mean, that's pretty basic, isn't it?'

Cordy bristled at his patronising tone. 'But it seems to me you guys aren't making much progress. The girl's risking a lot to get messages out. Don't we owe it to her to take them seriously?'

Bob put down his cup of tea. 'You're looking at this all wrong. It's the perps' heads we need to get into, not the kids'. Look, I don't even want to talk about the shit I've seen from that place, but I can tell you something for nothing: with the best will in the world, that little girl will be fucked up beyond belief. Who knows if she even realises what she's doing or saying any more. Wouldn't blame her if she was a total nut-job. Our job is to get her out of there, and that means we can't afford to arse around. We've got to do everything we can to track these guys down.'

Nut-job? Cordy bit her lip. Now wasn't the time to get into an argument about prejudice against victims. Instead she forced her voice to come out calm and reasonable. 'That's exactly why we shouldn't be closing off lines of inquiry, surely? I'm going to start off by compiling a list of towns near major ports – I mean, Dover's the obvious starting point – and look at which ones have riding stables in the vicinity. Then maybe tomorrow morning Reynolds can help me to—'

'Look, I didn't want to be blunt,' Bob said, 'what with you being new and all, but that sounds like you're, um, flogging a dead horse.'

Cordy ignored the pun. 'That's just your opinion.'

'No,' his voice had a hint of steel in it now. 'That's a fact. What you do in your own time is your concern, but, if I'm not mistaken, they've put you on the payroll for this, right?' He didn't wait for her to reply. 'So when you've finished with your blue-sky, out-of-the-box thinking, I could do with a hand going through the Sex Offender Register. The chief thought it'd be useful to make a list of all the dirty buggers who've ever fancied themselves as the Martin Scorsese of the kiddie-porn world, and I have to say it sounds a lot better idea than mincing around with horseys and sailors or whatever it was.'

Cordy barely registered the dig. 'I really hate that phrase.'

'Hmm?'

'Kiddie porn. Or child porn, for that matter.'

Bob shrugged. 'Ugly phrase for an ugly pastime, surely. No use sugar-coating. I hate all that PC-gone-mad stuff.'

He sounded irritated, and Cordy knew she should probably just drop it, but instead she tried to explain what she meant.

'It's not that. It's just that it makes it sound like a legitimate industry, you know? Like something erotic? You have your straight porn. You have your gay porn. You have your child porn.'

Bob looked back at her blankly.

She tried again. 'It's just playing into their hands. I mean, do you think those children self-define as porn stars?'

'You've lost me there, love.'

Cordy crossed her arms in front of her chest. 'OK. Fine. Of course I'll help with the register, if that's the priority. And maybe you're right about the nursery rhyme thing being a red herring. But, in general, can we just agree to use the phrase "obscene images of children"? I mean, that's what we're really talking about, right? It's like the difference between "child prostitute" and "prostituted child".'

'Oh, thanks for setting me straight.' Bob's voice dripped with sarcasm. 'Because for a minute there, I thought *I* was the one with over a decade's experience banging up paedos.'

'That's got nothing to do with it. I just think—'

'Right. So apparently none of that counts if I don't use the current *terminology*.' He said the word like it left a bad taste in his mouth. 'Good job you're here to set me straight.'

Cordy threw up her hands in frustration. 'Calling it kiddie porn is offensive to victims. That's *all* I'm trying to say.'

Bob drained his mug and stood up. 'Now if it won't offend your delicate sensibilities too much, I've got actual police work to be getting on with. Give me a shout when you're bored of playing Nancy Drew and maybe you can give me a hand.'

Without a word, Cordy put down her tea, picked up her bag and walked out through the door. She felt a surge of hot anger behind her eyes and when she pushed the button for the lift she realised her hands were shaking.

Temper, temper, Cordelia.

The voice in her head was her uncle's, and she had to force herself to count down from a hundred to keep the memory of his mocking smile from floating to the front of her mind.

By the time she'd reached the ground floor, the wave of rage had left her body, but the doubts that replaced it weren't much better. She should really swallow her pride and go back up there. It'd only be worse tomorrow.

'Cordy!' Anthony swiped through the barrier, Sainsbury's bag tucked under one arm. 'Thought we'd stock up on biscuits. Want one before we let Sampson loose on them?'

She flinched away from his outstretched hand. Behind him, Tammy must have caught the movement because just then she looked up from her iPhone.

'Hey Reynolds, I'll see you upstairs,' Anthony said firmly.

'Sure thing, guv.' Tammy shot Cordy a curious look before getting into the lift.

'Hunter, are you OK?' he asked, after the young detective had gone. 'You look as white as a sheet.'

'Yeah. Sorry. Just need a bit of fresh air.' Cordy tried to sidestep past him but he followed her outside into the watery sunshine.

'What's up? Sampson been giving you a hard time?' Anthony asked.

Cordy shrugged. 'It's not really that ... it's ... nothing really.'

'Here, you forgot your coat.' He took off his own suit jacket and laid it over her shoulders. Until then she hadn't realised how cold she'd been. 'That's better.'

'You're right. Thanks.' Usually Cordy liked to keep her distance from people – especially new people – but there was something strangely comforting about the warm smell of the fabric, the weight of the jacket on her shoulders. About Anthony himself, come to that: something solid and appealing.

'Wanna talk about it?' he asked. When he saw her face he added: 'You don't have to if you don't want to . . .'

Cordy hesitated. It was on the tip of her tongue to just blurt out everything. About her parents' accident. About the shock and the ache that never went away. About the visits from her uncle, which seemed at first like a holiday from their grandmother's sadness and rules and frailty. Which became confusing, shaming weekends that she and her eight-year-old sister didn't have the words to explain to anyone; weekends where her uncle and his friends would lock up Cordy and Jess and take pictures of the brutal, sadistic things they did to them. Pictures that still probably existed in the darker corners of the web.

She could tell him about their grandmother's death. About the years of therapy and endless determination that she'd needed to come out fighting. How she'd learned to use her terrible first-hand knowledge against other sexual predators, rather than let it destroy her. She could even tell him what it had done to Jess – what it was still doing to her baby sister.

Telling people made it more real, but it also took a small part of the horror out of it. And something about Anthony made her feel that he'd understand. That he would be able to listen – really listen – without flinching. And not just because of his job.

When she looked up, he smiled. 'Remember, you're part of the team now. We look out for each other.' He leaned over and put a warm hand on her shoulder.

The physical contact broke the spell.

He was a colleague. She was being unprofessional – letting her history get in the way of the investigation. And Cordy Hunter never let that happen.

'Thanks, DeLuca,' she said, edging away, 'but I'm just not feeling great. I'll be back in tomorrow. And don't say anything to Sampson, will you?'

'Wouldn't give him the satisfaction.' Anthony was still looking at her intently. 'Go home and get some rest. I'll see you in the morning.'

After he'd gone back inside she aimed a kick at a pebble, and tried not to imagine that it was Bob Sampson's self-satisfied face.

Chapter 8

The night had started to draw in as Cordy followed the discreet black and white signs to the final turn-off to the clinic. It was a journey she could make in her sleep – seventeen minutes door-to-door from her Blackheath flat, unless the rush-hour traffic got in her way. This evening the roads were clear and there was a bracing chill in the air. She shivered as she pulled up at the gatehouse, grateful that she'd remembered to grab her spare biker jacket before she left home. Putting her foot down for balance she took her left hand off the handlebars to reach across for the buzzer.

She didn't recognise the voice that asked for her name. Usually Cordy tried to get here earlier, so maybe it was just a guard from the later shift. At least, that's all she hoped it was. One of the things that had most appealed to her about the clinic was their low turnover of staff – even their security guards. To outsiders, it might have seemed like a minor detail, but given how terrified Jess was of strangers, continuity was important.

'Evening. It's Cordelia Hunter. I'm here to see Jessica Hunter.' Cordy hesitated. Even after all these years she still hated having to say this next bit. 'She's in Ward Seven. The high-security wing.'

There was a short pause before the barrier lifted to let her through.

She released the throttle and was soon powering along the winding drive that led to the clinic. Although the house's elegant proportions and landscaped grounds made it look like a country manor (Cordy had once joked to her sister that she felt as though she should be arriving in a carriage rather than on a motorbike), its isolation, high wire fence and the preponderance of CCTV cameras made it impossible to forget the building's true function. Although some of the short-stay patients on the ground floor were there for drug rehabilitation programmes, this was nothing like The Priory – a fact underlined by a gut-wrenching scream that tore through the night air as Cordy pulled up.

One of the permanent patients, she thought miserably. *That'll set off the others.*

Please let this be one of Jess's good days.

The young girl at the reception desk smiled when Cordy stepped inside, helmet tucked under her arm.

'Good. You made it. I was worried that you might not be able to come in today.' She passed the book for Cordy to sign in. 'Jess'll be pleased to see you.'

'Have you ever known me to miss visiting hours on my visiting days?' Cordy asked, signing her name with a flourish.

The girl smiled and looked back to her computer. She didn't even look up when an alarm went off, and a young doctor and a burly hospital porter came running in from the break room, carrying restraining equipment.

Cordy moved silently out of the way.

The Forest Clinic was a calm, safe environment for Jess to live in. Compared to other high-security mental health institutions, it was progressive – the best doctors, the newest facilities, the latest treatments – but still it broke Cordy's heart every time she stepped inside. While other twenty-somethings were busy planning their futures, Jess was struggling to deal with the horrors of her past, and the ugly raised welts on her arms, legs and belly were constant reminders of the deeper scars she lived with. *And it was all* his *fault*, thought Cordelia bitterly. *So much easier to smash apart a life than to try to put one back together, piece by piece.*

As Cordy climbed the set of stairs at the side of the building, she tried to push those thoughts away. She'd long ago made it a rule not to bring negative energy with her when she went to visit her sister. Jess was far too fragile to deal with Cordy's professional or personal problems, and both sisters were careful about alluding to the past. That meant that, much as she'd like to vent, Cordy knew that she'd keep quiet about her run-in with Bob Sampson. Jess only ever got to hear a very carefully edited version of her big sister's life (*match highlights*, Cordy sometimes thought), and the closer that her work got to the nightmare of the girls' shared past, the less she was able to share. She'd never forgive herself if she set Jess off on one of her terrifying downward spirals.

Approaching door 704, her sister's room for the past four years, Cordy fixed a smile to her face. She knocked, but there was no answer.

'Jess, it's me. Can I come in?'

Silence.

She tried again. 'It's Cordy. I'm going to come in now, if that's OK.'

She waited a few beats just in case, then cautiously opened the door. Patients like Jess were not allowed locks on their doors, and most of the furniture was bolted down, but it was always best to be careful. During one of Jess's episodes, Cordy had opened the door and stepped straight into a pile of her sister's faeces. It was one of a number of 'booby-traps' her sister had rigged up against their uncle and his cronies. The fact that a decade ago the men had skipped the country, just as Cordy was helping the police build a rock-solid case against them, did nothing to help Jess's bouts of paranoia.

This time there weren't any booby traps. Jess was sitting

quietly in a corner, staring out through the shatter-proof window at the clinic's dark lawn.

'You all right, love?'

Slowly Jess turned, and Cordy's heart caught at how thin and vulnerable her baby sister looked.

Looking at Jess was like looking in a fairground mirror. Cordy was slim and tall for a woman; Jess had a good few inches on her, but was so frail and hunched that she seemed much smaller. It was only when you looked closer that you saw the genetic echoes. Same bone structure. Same deep, dark eyes. Same rare smile that lit up when the two were together.

When she's taking her meds properly, Cordy added silently, remembering the worrying email she'd got from Jess's case manager late that afternoon.

'How are you feeling?' she asked, filling plastic tumblers with water for them both and sitting down. The clinic was careful about which 'clients' got to use glass receptacles.

'Good,' Jess said, after a long pause. 'You look nice.'

Cordy looked down at the grey polo neck she was wearing. 'Not too boring and conservative for you?'

Her sister shrugged and looked away.

Jesus, Cordy thought, *if she can't even work up the energy to tease me about my fashion sense, she must be in a pretty dark place.*

'Dr Hunter?'

Outside in the corridor, a short, round-faced nurse stopped her. Visiting time was over, and Cordy had just said goodbye to her sister. Neither of them really went in for hugging, but they touched fingers as usual, and Cordy had been alarmed at how cold and shaky her sister's hands were.

'Nurse Jacobs, how are you doing?'

The nurse smiled quickly, and then gently pushed Cordy a little further along the corridor, away from her sister's door.

'Sorry to keep you, but we're a little worried . . .'

Cordy's heart sank. 'What happened? I got the email about the meds. Is there anything we can do?'

The nurse sighed. 'That's not our only problem. Jess is getting quite secretive. Refusing to be examined.'

'Really? Recently?'

'Yes. This afternoon. So naturally we're worried that . . .'

Cordy rubbed her eyes. Suddenly she felt exhausted. 'You think she's cutting again?'

The nurse shrugged apologetically. 'Given her history, it's a worry. Although we didn't find any sharp implements last time her room was searched.'

'Shall I talk to her?' Cordy said, turning back, but the nurse gently put a hand on her shoulder.

'She'll be eating in a minute. Probably not a good idea to disrupt her routine.'

Cordy nodded. 'I'll be back on Saturday, as usual. Maybe I could have a word with her doctor?'

'Of course,' Nurse Jacobs said, walking with her down the stairs. 'You know, I don't mean to worry you. It might be nothing. It could even be a healthy sign – you know, that she wants a bit more privacy and independence.'

'Thanks for bringing it to my attention.'

The two women said polite goodbyes, and Cordy walked slowly out to her bike.

After unlocking the heavy chain she gave herself a minute to gather her energies before riding off. It'd been a long day.

Looking up at the beautiful lines of the clinic, Cordelia remembered with a shudder the ward that she had found Jessica on when she'd tracked her down after she'd turned eighteen and finally been given access to their records. After their grandmother's death, there had been no one else in the family able to look after them, and the two sisters had ended up being sent to foster homes at different ends of the country. In the days before email, it had been all too easy to lose touch

– letters were returned to sender, phone calls to local child services offices went unanswered. But the reunion, when it happened, was not what Cordy had been dreaming of for all those lonely years. She still remembered the sickening reek of bleach and vomit and excrement. The obscenities shouted by a man with tattoos over his face. The exhausted staff trying to hold down a woman who was bucking and spitting and clawing. Jess was on a mixed ward and beds were pushed out into the corridors due to the high demand. The room was so chaotic that no one stopped Cordy as she wandered between the patients. She could have been anybody.

Cordy hadn't even recognised Jess the first time she walked past her. In fact, she had had to check the chart to confirm that this emaciated teenager with the bandages and the dead eyes was really her beautiful little sister. She'd had her bedding and clothes taken away from her ('Too high-risk,' the young healthcare assistant told Cordy. 'It's hospital policy with level three patients'), so was lying shivering on the bed in a thin hospital gown, open at the back, looking impossibly vulnerable.

At the time Cordy had just wanted to pick her up and run out of there – take her somewhere calm and quiet and safe. Somewhere where she wouldn't be shocked and drugged up to the eyeballs and left to lie half naked in a room of strangers. *And that's what I managed to do*, she reminded herself, *eventually*.

Even with the money they had inherited from their parents and from the sale of their grandmother's house, it had been a struggle finding the right place for Jess. The Forest Clinic was world renowned. Jess had access to one-on-one, round-the-clock nursing care, as well as the best psychiatrists and occupational therapists money could buy. She was luckier than most in her position.

But was it enough? Would anything ever be enough?

Chapter 9

Stories say that grown-ups never understand anything by themselves, and we kids have always got to be explaining things to them.

The corners of Mummy's eyes crinkle up when she smiles or it's sunny and Daddy says she should wear sunglasses or she'll get old and wrinkly. When the ground broke, I didn't see Mummy but I saw the sunglasses – the pretty new sunglasses from the market – and they were smashed into little pieces. They looked like an elephant had stepped on them but there wasn't an elephant, which would be funny. Just the ground shaking like a ride that you couldn't get off of and everyone screaming and me losing Daddy's hand as things started falling and then silence so bad I couldn't even cry. And then waking up in the hospital and everyone speaking funny and then *his* hand. The Captain.

That day is like a film that won't stop playing in my head. If I rock the film can't play properly, like a stuck DVD, but then the men laugh at me and look and it's safer to tell my stories instead. In my stories everything is all right in the end and this is just an adventure. They think I'm a kid but *really* I'm a secret agent and I leave messages for Daddy and Mummy. A message before I can sleep. A message after they do The Things to me.

I'm not the only one with messages. The men have their own messages. Secret words they think that I can't hear, but I can. Lolly says *play dumb* and so that's what I do. But when they say the pills will help me sleep and I nod, I put them in the side of my mouth and spit them out when I go on the bucket. They make my head fuzzy so it's too heavy to hold up. It hurts worse without them but a top-secret spy needs to stay awake if they want to escape.

The eye is watching, just like they said it would. But maybe Mummy and Daddy are watching too. Not the bad stuff. They'd never ever ever watch that. But the messages. Maybe they're watching the messages. Maybe if they know the men's secret words they can stop them. *Knowledge is power*, Daddy says when I don't want to go to school. I miss school now.

Chapter 10

clewis:	I remember what it's like at first.
	You're scared but you're excited.
spurs101:	no way
clewis:	There's a whole new world of possibilities. Not just clips and stuff.
	The real deal. Live action.
	Because after a while you want to get involved.
	Want to touch them for yourself.
	Dont you?
spurs101:	im not into that
	couldn't do that
clewis:	Whatever you say
	If I were you I wouldn't be so touchy.
spurs101:	meaning????
clewis:	I know more about you than you think
spurs101:	thats bollocks and you know it
clewis:	You reckon?
	I'm not the only person you've talked to about this, am I?
spurs101:	whats that to u?
clewis:	We're a small community. We've got to watch each other's backs
	Last bloke got scared when he found out you were with the pigs, right?
	But he didn't even know which pigs, did he?
spurs101:	what u on about???

clewis:	Whereas I
	I did my research
	Shouldn't have given Gaz your real name
	And you definitely should have changed your screen name once you came out to him as a copper.
spurs101:	you threatening me????
	fucking pervert
clewis:	Takes one to know one.
	Don't worry, I'm not going to go shooting my mouth off
spurs101:	I dont need shit from you on top of everything else
clewis:	There's no need to get all het up
spurs101:	what do you want
	why dont you just leave me alone
clewis:	It's a bit late for that
	You should have told me what you are
	Did you think I'm stupid?
	That I wouldn't find out?
spurs101:	dya blame me
	fuck
	ur gonna tell everyone aren't you
clewis:	No.
	But some things are going to have to change around here
	So if I were you I'd have a bit of a think about what matters to you
	And how we can help each other
	You still there?

Chapter 11

'Good lunch, Princess?' Bob called, spraying half-chewed bits of sausage roll all over his copy of the *Sun*.

'Fine, thanks. Just went to Prêt.'

'Classy lunch for a classy lady.'

Cordy forced a smile as she sat down at her desk and turned on the computer. It'd been a week since their run-in, and – on the surface at least – their working relationship was surprisingly cordial. She got the distinct impression that Bob actually enjoyed riling her, so her new policy was to try not to take the bait. So far the truce was holding. They'd been working closely together on the Sex Offender Register, and Cordy had been grudgingly impressed by Bob's no-nonsense efficiency. Less so, it had to be said, by his personal hygiene.

'Hunter, can I talk to you a sec?' Anthony asked, appearing in the doorway of the Ops Room with a Costa cup in hand. His dark eyes looked unusually serious.

'Shoot.'

He pulled over a chair and sat down beside her, close enough for her to smell the freshly ground coffee and the clean citrus tang of his aftershave.

'The good news is that we've managed to capture another link to the site. From the discussion boards, it looks like the clip will be live in about ten minutes. I know you're not going to like this, but I think it might be better if you sit this one out.' He looked at her steadily. 'It's not that anyone thinks you can't handle it. But trust me, what they're putting out there is pretty brutal – particularly the ones featuring the old guy – and there's really no need for you to watch it live.'

When Cordy didn't reply straight away, he leaned closer and tried to catch her eye. 'I mean, we'll obviously be recording it, and capturing a series of screen-grabs too. You'll be able to look at the relevant sections first thing tomorrow; as soon as it's passed through the edit suite.' He glanced down at his watch. 'Sorry, but I should go help Reynolds set up. Incidentally, she's not watching it. And that's not us being sexist, it's just—'

'No,' Cordy said firmly, getting her notebook out of her leather shoulder bag. 'I appreciate your concern, but I should know exactly what we're dealing with. I need to watch it from beginning to end so I can see the set-up for myself. It might help me profile the abusers and get more of a handle on the victims. Isn't that what I'm here for?'

Anthony looked as if he might be about to argue, but Cordy was already halfway to the door.

'Shouldn't we get going?' she called.

'Yeah. Don't know what the chief's going to say but . . .' He shrugged. 'OK, fine. If you're all right with watching it, I'm sure your insight would be really useful. You coming, Sampson?'

The older man let out a noisy puff of air and wiped his hands on his trousers, leaving behind a few crumbs of pastry. 'If I must. Can think of better ways to start the afternoon than with a load of kid—' He glanced at Cordy. 'With a load of *obscene images of children.*'

Cordy rolled her eyes and moved aside to let the two detectives out of the Ops Room. She followed them down the hall to a small technical suite made even more cramped by a bulky camera, tripod and microphone system that Tammy had set up to record the clip. As Cordy peered inside she tried not to think about what she was about to see and hear, but still a tight knot of dread formed in her stomach. Child abuse didn't scare her – for her there was no terrible mystery to it, just a sad mundanity – but watching grown men brutalising children was never fun.

Anthony held the door open, and as she passed he rested a warm hand lightly on her shoulder. The contact made her jump, but she forced out a quick, brittle smile before moving away. The knot in her stomach loosened a little. They were all in this together.

'Right,' said Fiona, as they knocked and entered. 'Good afternoon, you lot. Take a seat. I'd appreciate silence while we're watching the clip. We'll debrief afterwards. Reynolds, you can leave now. Dr Hunter?'

Anthony jumped in. 'It's OK. She's watching it too.'

Fiona gave her a hard look, and Cordy hoped that she looked tougher than she felt inside.

'Fine,' she said at last. 'Sampson, pull another chair over, will you? I think there's one under that desk in the corner.'

When they were all seated and Tammy had stuck a 'Do Not Disturb' notice up outside the door as she left, there were a few painfully long minutes of silence. Cordy was sure the others must be able to hear her heart thudding in her chest, as her fight-or-flight instinct kicked in. It took all her determination to stay sitting there in front of the computer, her fingers gripping her pen so tightly that her knuckles turned ghostly pale.

The page they'd been directed to was fairly basic. It could almost have been a rudimentary version of YouTube, except the box that dominated the page was still dark, and there was no way to replay old clips. Down the sides were the names of the 'performers': Alice. Lolita. Kurt. At the bottom of the screen was a button that allowed you to email requests to the site. There was a flat fee of £100.

'So cheap?' Cordy blurted out.

Bob snorted. 'Yeah, looks like they want to offer value for money. It's a wonder they don't make it £99.99. They offer extras, for extra cash too.'

Fiona shot them both a stern look, but Anthony leaned over and whispered: 'And there could be hundreds of customers all requesting similar . . . well, you know. And it's not like anyone's going to ask for a refund.'

Cordy's throat filled with bile. She tried to choke it down, but the thought of all those predators, from all over the world, glued to the screen at just that second, waiting for it to begin, made her insides revolt. Waiting, just like she was. What did that make her? And meanwhile, on the other side of the camera, that little girl was waiting too. Maybe even waiting to find out if today was her turn to be abused.

Just as Cordy was convinced that she'd have to make an excuse and dash to the toilet, the dark box whirred into life.

Out of the corner of her eye she saw Fiona's face stiffen, and recognised the effort it was taking her not to turn away from the screen. It was Alice again. After the dart of recognition came a toxic anger that blurred her eyes and made her whole body tremble. Knowing she had a job to do, Cordy battled to channel her hot rage at what was being done to the girl into cool analysis. Ignoring the tears that were running down her cheeks she treated the webcam image like a grid system, and examined every coordinate in turn (left to right, top to bottom) with ruthless efficiency. She barely flinched when she found herself staring into Alice's eyes. They stared back, as bleak and empty as black holes. No blinking. Cordy moved onto the next coordinate. It wasn't until she'd reached the bottom left of the screen that she saw something.

Biting her lip, she scribbled a single word in her notebook and then shifted her eyes right and carried on.

The 'show' lasted nearly forty minutes. When the webcam was switched off it took them all a few beats to recover themselves. Bob was slouched in his chair, looking suddenly years older, and Anthony, usually so practical and upbeat, looked as though he was about to break down. When he caught Cordy looking at him he managed a watery smile.

Fiona was the first to recover. She stood up, snapped the screen off, and turned to face them.

'All right. Thoughts, people.'

Anthony cleared his throat. 'I think they're getting worse – more extreme I mean.'

'You mean rougher?' Fiona asked.

'Yes.' His voice was a little unsteady. 'It's like they don't even realise they're hurting her.'

'Agreed,' Fiona said briskly. 'And that fits with the trend we've been noting in Internet images – not just from this site. I think we can all agree that distributors are increasingly tending towards the very littlest victims, more violence, more extreme practices. Although, in this particular case, the perps could have been responding to one of the requests. Anything else?'

'Looked like the older guy this time,' Bob said. 'Face obscured as usual, but I think we got a clear shot of his arm and hairline. I'll run it through the database and see if there're any matches.'

'Good,' said Fiona. 'At least that'd be something. And hopefully we'll be able to take a closer look at the video. Dr Hunter, any thoughts?'

'Dormouse.'

'I'm sorry?'

'There was a word written on the mirror,' Cordy explained. 'Bottom right. You could see it more clearly as the room heated up.'

'Go on.'

'Well, I'd guess the other men you've identified were watching from the sidelines, and from the low ceilings it looks like quite a small space. Since they're obviously interested in monetising the abuse, it's likely that they were also filming for the DVD market. So certainly one monitoring the webcam, making sure it was all in shot. Maybe another one watching the other kids. Plenty of body heat to steam up the mirror.'

'Anyone else see this?' Fiona asked.

The two men shook their heads.

'You can check it,' said Cordy bluntly. 'But it was there.'

'Dormouse?' Fiona checked. 'Can't say it makes a whole lot of sense to me. But the perps must have put it there for a reason.'

'Maybe it's some sick sort of joke?' Bob suggested. 'We already know this lot fancy themselves as clever fuckers.'

'What's the significance, then?' Fiona asked.

'It's another *Alice in Wonderland* character,' Cordy said. 'Which fits. You know how Lewis Carroll has become a cult figure for paedophiles? All those pictures he took of Alice Liddell and those other children. Maybe he was just a sentimental Victorian, but that hasn't stopped him being turned into a weird sort of figurehead.'

Anthony consulted his iPhone. 'Yeah, there's a dormouse at the Mad Hatter's tea party. Well, that makes a sort of sense.'

Fiona nodded. 'Great, well let's get on line and throw it around. See if we get any bites.'

Bob turned the screen back on and brought up the favourites panel. 'Where did the link go up again?'

'Littlefriends,' Anthony said. 'You can use the Wonka screen name – I don't think they've busted that one yet.'

Bob started typing furiously, and in a few seconds he turned, looking triumphant.

'Bingo. We've been invited into a private chatroom. That took, what, less than a minute?'

'Nice one, guys. We're really getting the hang of their systems. We'll shut these bastards down soon, I can feel it.' Fiona stood up and motioned to Cordy to take her chair at the front. 'Look, I'm afraid I've got to leave you lot to it. They're coming in to do yet another audit next week.'

'Shout if you need a hand,' Anthony said, turning from the screen.

'Thanks, DeLuca,' Fiona said, giving him one of her rare smiles, 'but I think I got it covered. And by the way, good work, Dr Hunter.'

Anthony elbowed Cordy playfully in the ribs, but her eyes were glued to the screen. The conversation was horribly mesmerising. The people in the chatroom obviously fancied themselves as connoisseurs. They were commenting on the clip as if it were a sports event, or an Oscar-nominated film: rating its best moments, debating whether Alice or another child, Lolita, got 'more into it', arguing over who had made what requests. For Cordy, so used to working to support victims of abuse, it was like falling down a rabbit hole, into a world where all perspectives were dangerously skewed and all the characters were terrifyingly deluded. And once again, she realised with a flash of horror, *it's like we're one of* them.

'Get this,' Bob said, jabbing at the screen.

One member was boasting about being a regular visitor at the cellar.

Big_Mark: an if you wanna visit, don forget that i can
           sort u out
           4 the rite price . . .
dragonwarrior: whats the deal???
Big_Mark: well theres a discount if you bring a little
           friend

'Seen this guy before,' Bob put in. 'He's a regular on the message boards.'

'Reckon he's local?' Anthony asked.

'Wait!' Cordy said. 'There was something about Kilburn, just after we signed in.'

Obediently Bob scrolled up, and they both spotted it at the same time:

king2000:	I reckon I know where this place is it's that house that's always shuttered round the corner from Kilburn Tube, isn't it?
Big_Mark:	nah mate totally at the wrong end of the line ;)

'So we reckon Docklands or East London?' Bob asked. 'Other end of the Jubilee line?'

Cordy nodded. 'Guess that makes sense.'

'Or he's bluffing, and he doesn't know shit,' Anthony warned.

'Can't we just ask where the house is?' Cordy said. 'I mean, we're in the chatroom, aren't we?'

Bob made a face. 'Doesn't work like that, love.'

'But if this Big Mark guy actually knows where this place is—'

'Then there's no way he'd tell the others,' Anthony said. 'Look, I know it's frustrating but Sampson's right. You can see how careful they all are. No names. No details. No explicit language. It's all hints and codes and that kind of thing. If we start asking questions we'll be thrown out straight away and we'll just have all that work to do again building up a screen name they trust.'

'And,' Bob said, gesturing to the screen, 'if they suspect there's police involvement they'll up security. Our best bet is for them to relax and get sloppy. Maybe it's already happening – we've never got a codeword before.'

'So we just stay silent and hope no one takes any notice of us?' Cordy asked.

'Safest that way,' Anthony said, with an apologetic shrug.

When they scrolled back down, they saw that the chat had got progressively more graphic. What made it so sinister was the way the screen-names twisted ordinary words and made them do appalling things.

king2000:	So i found myself a sweet little girlfriend.
	putting her through her paces
	training her up
glkdogg:	gotta get me one of those
Big_Mark:	I'll send you a link to this boyband fansite
	girls are fuckin gagging for it on there
	they look all innocent and shit but you
	know their typing one-handed
glkdogg:	send it over
Big_Mark:	keep watchin. Bet I can get some fresh
	meat for the next broadcast
	some honey whos really beggin for it
	but she wont have to beg for long

'Jesus Christ,' Anthony muttered. 'Cordelia, you really don't have to read this.'

'I'm fine,' she snapped, fishing out a stick of gum from her bag. The spearmint helped calm her stomach and she steeled herself to read on.

'It's like a bloody nest of cockroaches,' Bob said.

'Yeah,' Cordy agreed. 'Shame we can't just stamp it out.'

Bob let out a mirthless laugh. 'With you on that one, Princess.'

'This Big Mark guy sounds like a bullshitter to me,' Anthony put in, 'but if he's not . . .'

'Then this is a decent lead. About time too,' Bob said, leaning back on his seat.

Cordy lost track of how long they sat there in the darkened room, staring at the screen.

Eventually Bob turned to face the others and broke the silence. 'Look, kids, it's getting late. No point us all sitting around here. Why don't you guys go home and get some kip and you can take over bright and early tomorrow?'

'We can't leave you to do it all yourself,' Anthony protested. 'That's not fair.'

But Bob was insistent. 'It's fine. Look, the wife's supposedly having this "book club" thing tonight.' He said the words disdainfully. 'So I'd be banished to the pub anyway. And to be honest, it's easier if I just get on with it.'

'If you're sure . . .' It was clear from Anthony's voice that he was wavering.

'Look, scram, both of you,' said Bob. 'See you in the morning.'

'Do you want me to get you some food or something?' Cordy offered, suddenly desperate to leave the stuffy little room and the afternoon of horrors behind her. 'I could nip down to the canteen.'

'No worries, love. I've still got some of the leftover curry in the fridge.'

'Well, call me if there are any problems,' Anthony said.

'Right you are.'

With Anthony close behind her, Cordy stepped out of the dark little room into the welcome neon glare of the corridor.

'Tough day,' Anthony said, shifting his notebook from one arm to the other.

'Yeah, I feel like going home and pulling out my toenails would be light relief after that,' said Cordy grimly. 'Come on, let's have a cup of tea before we leave. Your missus won't thank you for taking this shit home with you.'

'OK.' Anthony rolled his neck around and let out a sigh. 'You know, Hunter, we're lucky to have you here.'

For the first time in many hours she smiled. 'You'd better believe it.'

Chapter 12

Just as the lift door closed, she heard a familiar voice yell: 'Oy, wait a sec!'

Cordy jabbed at the 'Open Door' button but the lift was already moving up.

'Sorry, Anthony,' she said under her breath, and when she reached the fifth floor, where the Unit's offices were located, she waited in the corridor for him to emerge.

Last night he had insisted on buying her a cup of tea from the posh Italian place round the corner, rather than chancing their luck at the police canteen.

'Although you realise it's sacrilege to go to Mariana's and not drink espresso?' He lowered his voice. 'If anyone found out, they'd take my Italian passport for sure.'

Cordy laughed. 'I didn't know you had dual nationality.'

Anthony pulled himself up to his full height, making him a good six inches taller than her. 'There's a lot you don't know about me, Dr Hunter.'

As usual, it was hard to tell if he was joking or flirting in earnest. Cordy decided that it was safest to assume that he was just mucking around.

They'd lingered in the café longer than Cordy had intended, and she'd ended up having to head straight to the clinic, rather than going home and getting changed out of her formal work clothes, which was her usual routine. Still, it'd been worth it. Anthony got her laughing with his scarily spot-on impressions of Fiona and Bob, even down to Bob's hunched shoulders and

Fiona's habit of lifting her right eyebrow when she thought you were talking bullshit.

'Ha! I've definitely seen that look before,' Cordelia said, narrowly avoiding snorting tea all over the table. 'Now I'm scared you've got one of me too.'

Anthony dipped his biscotti in his tea and gestured across with it. 'Didn't you realise that I had an ulterior motive for getting you here?'

'You wanted to observe me at close quarters?'

'Uh huh. And now I can add you to my repertoire.'

'Great. Now I feel self-conscious,' Cordy said, shielding her face with her hands. 'Should have guessed. Don't they say there's no such thing as a free cup of tea?'

'So that'll be two pounds sixty, please.'

'Daylight robbery.'

'Don't worry, I know some guys in that division too,' Anthony said, giving her a grin that got the pretty young waitress rushing over to see if there was anything else she could do for them.

After they'd settled up, Anthony asked her how she was doing. 'I hope you don't mind me bringing it up, but you really seemed upset the other day. Is there anything I can help with? Short of setting a hitman on Sampson, I mean?'

Cordy laughed. She thought about fobbing him off again, but something about the way he held her gaze so steadily opened a door that Cordy usually kept firmly locked and bolted. 'Well, you probably don't want to hear about this . . .'

'Try me.'

She lowered her voice. 'It's a little complicated and not . . . pleasant.'

'I'm a smart guy and I deal with pretty terrible things every day,' Anthony assured her. 'I can handle it.'

'Well, there's a reason I got into child protection. A pretty personal reason . . .' Haltingly, she explained about the years of abuse that she'd suffered at the hands of her Uncle Herbert, after her parents passed away in a car accident. 'I mean, now I know it was actually a pretty standard story – there's a family crisis and a predator moves in. We never knew why we'd never met our father's younger brother before. We'd always just been told he lived far away. But suddenly, there he was – buying us ice creams and offering to have us to stay to give our grandmother a break.'

'Us?' Anthony asked, but Cordy carried straight on. It was one thing to share her story, quite another to offer up Jess's to a man her sister had never even met.

'Well, you can guess the rest. Once he'd won our trust the abuse started – gradually at first. Just some rocking on his lap to start with. We'd make jokes about his face getting red. But it got worse. A lot worse.'

On the table next to them a baby started to cry. Cordy took a deep breath. When she continued her voice was calmer, her tone matter-of-fact.

'The first time he raped me, I was eleven years old. He told me that if I ever told anyone my grandmother would die too. That we'd live with him all the time, and he'd do it every single day. He said he'd killed my parents and got away with it. That no one would believe me. That he could kill me too, like that.' She snapped her fingers.

'Jesus, Hunter.' Anthony leaned over as if to take her hand, but paused midway. 'Sorry. No wonder you like your personal space.'

She laughed bleakly. 'You noticed that?'

He nodded. 'But I didn't mean to interrupt you.'

'Well, not much more to tell. My grandmother fell ill, and went into a nursing home. We ... I went into a children's home. Got labelled as a difficult kid. Couldn't trust anyone. Screamed if one of my foster fathers got too close. Things started to get better when I was sent to an all-girls school ...'

She stopped, and looked at her watch. 'Shit. Didn't realise how long I'd been rambling on. I really have to go. So sorry.'

He held the door for her as she rushed out of the café. Outside on the street she paused for a minute.

'You'll keep this to yourself, right?' Cordy said, suddenly uncertain. 'I mean, it's not like it's a big secret, it's just that . . .'

'It's no one's business but yours.'

'Exactly.'

For a second they just stood there on the street, letting people stream past them, until they had to move out of the way for a woman with a pushchair and a load of shopping bags.

'So I'd better . . .' Cordy said, moving to go.

'Yeah, course,' Anthony said, but he didn't move.

'See you tomorrow.'

'For the record,' he said, his voice stopping her in her tracks, 'I think you're very brave. One of the bravest people I've ever met.'

At that she flashed him a genuine smile. 'Thanks for letting me chew your ear off.'

'Any time.' He returned the smile. 'Seriously. Any time.'

Despite what Cordy had seen and spoken of that afternoon, she was able to behave in front of her sister as if nothing was wrong, and had even managed a decent night's sleep – give or take a few nightmares.

And now today . . . today she felt hopeful. The investigation was moving forward. By now Bob would have a pretty rounded profile on this Big_Mark guy, and who knew how many other familiar characters had shown up in the chatroom after she and Anthony had left?

When he finally emerged from the lift, Anthony, too, looked much more chipper than he had yesterday afternoon.

'Thanks for holding the lift, Dr Hunter,' he said with mock sternness.

'Any time,' Cordy shot back. She felt her stomach unclench. It wasn't going to be awkward. Anthony wasn't going to treat her like she was made of glass. 'Now, if you're done griping, maybe we could go and track down some criminals?'

'Great idea. Why didn't I think of that?'

'Because you don't have a PhD,' she said, grinning.

'Yeah, well maybe you can tell me which site you bought yours on and then there could be two doctors in the department.'

She narrowed her eyes 'Shut it, you.'

As soon as they walked into the Ops Room, the banter died on their lips.

Bob was slumped over the middle table, looking grey and exhausted.

'Bad night?' Anthony asked, taking a seat next to him. 'I take it the chatroom's quiet now? Not even perverts are chatty at this time in the morning.'

'I wouldn't know, mate,' Bob said, leaning his elbow on the table and propping up his head with his fist. 'Bastards shut down the site not long after you guys buggered off.'

'But they seemed to be in full swing when we left,' said Cordy, her heart sinking.

Bob shrugged. 'Who knows? Maybe they changed the password.'

'You should have gone home,' Anthony said. 'You don't look good.'

'Well, I didn't want to give up that easily,' Bob said, 'so I tried the "dormouse" thing on a load of other sites. Waste of fucking time. Up all night and all I got was a heap of aggro.' He looked down at the table. 'Sorry, but I think we're going to have to put Wonka out to pasture. Don't think I'll be long behind him.'

Anthony gripped his shoulder. 'What are you talking about? I'd have done exactly the same thing. Just bad luck, that's all.'

'Get off me, you poofter,' Bob said, but he sounded too tired to care. 'Guess there's still that music website he was on about. Might be worth a trawl.'

'Yeah, I'll mention it to Reynolds.'

Cordelia was still hovering awkwardly behind them. She'd never seen Bob looking this wretched.

'Can I get you guys a cup of tea? Sampson? One sugar is it?'

'Better make it two,' Bob said. 'Ta, love.'

On the way to the kitchen, Cordy passed Fiona in the corridor.

'I don't know if you've debriefed him yet,' she said, 'but you should send Sampson home. He's exhausted.'

'Thank you, Dr Hunter, but when I need staff management tips, I'll ask for them.'

Before Cordy could answer, the chief was striding towards the Ops Room, her high heels clicking on the lino floor.

When Cordy returned with a tray of mugs, Anthony was already collecting Bob's things together and Tammy was phoning for a taxi.

'You can't go on the Tube like this,' she insisted, when he'd protested that it was a waste of money. 'You'd sleep past your stop and end up in the back of beyond.'

After he'd left, the others all took a seat round the middle table.

'Right,' said Fiona. 'So it looks like the password changed –' she looked down at her notes – 'about two and a half hours after it was set up.'

They all nodded.

'Maybe I'm being stupid,' Tammy said, a little hesitantly, 'but I don't get it.'

'What don't you get?' Fiona asked.

'Well, you sent round that screen-grab of the mirror. Good spot by the way,' she said, turning to Cordy.

'Thanks.'

'But why would they circulate the password like that? I mean, if they wanted to make it obvious, they could have posted it on the site or even had it written on a bit of cardboard. Why would they arse about with writing on a mirror, when people might not even notice it?'

'You've got a point there,' said Anthony.

Tammy flashed him a mega-watt smile. 'And if they wanted to be subtle about it, or, you know, restrict who got in the chatroom . . .'

'They'd have emailed around their associates,' Fiona put in. 'Yes, that has been worrying me as well.'

'Well, I think the solution is obvious,' Cordy said.

'Really? Don't keep us on tenterhooks then,' the older woman drawled.

'The men didn't write it. Alice did.'

'I'm sure that that would have been the last thing on her mind,' Fiona said. 'Come on, she's just a little kid. She might not even know that word. Any other thoughts?'

But Cordy refused to be bulldozed. 'I don't think you should dismiss the possibility out of hand. To be honest, it's the first thing that occurred to me when I spotted the writing.'

'The writing on the wall,' Tammy murmured.

Cordy ignored her. 'We know Alice leaves messages. Maybe she overheard the men talking, or something.'

Fiona drained her mug before replying. 'Look, I know you feel a connection to this girl. But it's really important that we get inside the perps' heads and work out what they're trying to do with this password thing. If we can work out the system, it'll be so much easier to tap into it, and get the next password and the next one.'

'But if Alice is the one leaving the messages, they might not even have realised that their current password was jeopardised. Unless they spotted the writing. I mean, that would explain why Wonka got locked out of the chatroom.' Cordy looked round for support.

'It's an interesting idea, but I think the chief's right,' said Anthony, throwing her an apologetic smile.

Tammy nodded. 'I mean, obviously I wasn't there yesterday, but it seems like we should really be concentrating on figuring out how these guys operate.'

Cordelia was about to protest, but then Fiona cleared her throat.

'All right, thank you all for your input. So this is where we go from here . . .'

Cordy slunk down on her chair, only half listening to the discussion about who was going to do what next. All her instincts were telling her that they were working from the wrong assumptions, looking in the wrong place. But until she had something more solid to work on than gut instinct and wild theories, there wasn't much she could do about it.

Chapter 13

More than once that morning, Cordy had found her gaze drifting to the window of the Ops Room. Outside the sky was a cobalt blue, with small clouds scudding lazily across it. It was the first bright day after a week of rain, and although the temperature had dropped there was something enticing about the crunch of the leaves and faint tang of woodsmoke in the air. What Cordy really wanted to do was to take a long walk around the heath, to clear her head. Or perhaps she could even get permission from Jess's doctors to take her sister for a stroll in Greenwich, climb Maze Hill and look out over the city. It would be good to see a little colour in her sister's pale cheeks.

Turning back to her computer screen, Cordy's heart sank. There was no way she was leaving her desk while it was still light outside. Every day there seemed to be more and more to do – names to cross-check, descriptions to verify, data application forms to fill out – and a creeping sense that none of it seemed to be getting them anywhere.

In the last week or so the investigation seemed to have stalled. After the session in the chatroom, they'd focused on tracking down this Big_Mark character. However, what had seemed like a good lead was looking more and more like a rambling dead end. The strict rules about letting civilians access the police databases didn't help. It felt ridiculous to be surrounded by banks of computers and having to work off a bulky print-out. There were plenty of 'Marks' on the Sex Offender Register, but the ECPU hardly had the resources to investigate all of them, and anyway (as Anthony had pointed out, at the end of yet another interminable 'catch-up meeting'), they didn't even know if that was his real name, or if he had previous form.

Meanwhile, Fiona had pulled some strings to get them more man-hours from the tech boys. Thanks to round-the-clock surveillance, they were catching more links to the pay-per-view clips. In fact, she realised, glancing at the digital clock on the bottom right of her screen, she'd better get going if she were going to watch the recording of the one that they'd filmed last night. The chief was a stickler for punctuality, and since Cordy had insisted on watching all the clips in full she'd better be in the media suite by twelve on the dot or Fiona would start without her, just to make a point. Looking round, she noticed that the others had already left.

Great.

With the weariness of a much older woman she stood, gathered up her notebook, and made for the door.

The email that had gone round that morning had mentioned that the latest clip featured a small boy and an older girl – maybe eleven or twelve years old.

'Kurt and Lolita, by the looks of things,' Fiona was saying as Cordy knocked and entered. 'Although clearly those are not their real names.'

'So I guess they chose Kurt because it's that Scandinavian kink they all seem to have, right?' Anthony suggested. 'And obviously Lolita is the girl from that Russian guy's novel.'

'Nabokov,' Cordy supplied.

Bob looked as if he was going to make a crack, but the sombre faces around him must have put him off because he sank back down in his seat and crossed his arms over the shelf of his belly.

Yet again, they sat in sickened silence as the clip played out. This one was shorter than some of the others. After a long time of waiting around – probably waiting for the money to come in – the abuse lasted no more than five minutes before the camera was switched off. It had gone live almost exactly twelve hours ago.

'Witching hour,' muttered Bob, but no one responded.

There was something deadening about the horrible banality of the clip, the guiltless violence, the twisted abuse. To her dismay, Cordy was finding that each time it was a little easier to distance herself from what was going on, to put up a protective barrier between herself and the victims' ordeal. Her growing numbness felt like a betrayal.

'Whaddya reckon?' Bob asked, when they were back to staring at a blank screen. When no one answered he looked over at Cordy. 'What are those *leetle grey cells* telling you, Poirot?'

'Well, I can't see any messages.'

Cordy thought she spotted Fiona rolling her eyes. It was clear that the others hadn't forgotten the argument about Alice.

Swallowing down her annoyance, she continued, 'But did you see the way Lolita's eyes kept on flicking to one of the men, as if for approval? It happens a few times. Once, right at the start.'

'What, to the old guy?' Anthony asked.

'No, the big one with the dark hair.'

Fiona stepped over to the video camera. 'I hate these things. But we should be able to replay . . .'

'It's saved on the hard drive, so you can just use the media player,' Bob offered.

'Right. OK, give me a sec.'

After a bit of faffing she managed to reset the clip. The team watched the first seconds before Fiona clicked the mouse (a little harder than necessary) to shut it off again.

'She's right, you know,' Bob said.

Cordelia nodded. 'I know it's not a recognisably domestic location, but I'd say there was a family connection here. Older brother, father, stepfather, something like that.' She didn't say *uncle*, although that was her first thought.

'That makes sense,' Fiona said. 'Something to think about, anyway. Family Services might even be able to help us. They must have a list of at-risk children in this age range in the local boroughs, if we do think it's London.'

Bob snorted mirthlessly. 'It'll be like getting blood from a stone.'

'Well, they know they're supposed to cooperate with our investigations,' Fiona said sharply. 'By the way, have we had any luck with the Missing Children's reports?'

Anthony, who'd been sitting quietly in the corner, stirred himself at this. 'Still no likely matches, I'm afraid. Most runaways are older, but I'm still trawling through cold abduction cases. Will let you know if I find anything.'

Fiona thanked him, and got up to leave. The team looked as though they had just run a marathon, only to discover they still had another one to go.

Just as the chief opened the door, Cordy heard herself blurt out: 'How long since you first found the site?'

Fiona turned and looked at her dead on. 'Almost a month now.'

'And we're still nowhere near shutting it down? Nowhere near getting those kids out?'

'There's no point shutting the site down and cutting off our only source of information.' Fiona didn't bother to hide her irritation at Cordelia's outburst.

'But still, I mean—'

Fiona cut her off. 'And unless you have some fantastic new piece of evidence that you've been keeping from us all, then no, we're not in a position to get them out. Which is why we should all get back to work. *OK?*'

'Ouch,' said Cordy, after Fiona had left them to take down the equipment. 'Should have kept my mouth shut.'

'Maybe.' Anthony shrugged. 'You can't blame the chief for being stressed out.'

'It's just the thought of those children, and how they must wake up each morning and realise that it wasn't a nightmare, that this really is their life. And meanwhile we're pissing around—'

'Speak for yourself, love.' Bob was unscrewing the tripod, folding it up so that it'd fit back into its battered black case. 'I haven't got home in time for dinner once this week.'

'It's not that, it's just . . .' Cordelia trailed off hopelessly.

Bob gave her a wink. 'Ah, cheer up. It'll be all right. There's always a bit where you feel like the investigation's ground to a halt – the Italian Stallion can tell you that much.'

'Something will happen,' Anthony agreed. 'They've poured a lot of resources into this investigation. It's not like they're just going to drop it.'

When Cordy didn't respond, Bob sighed. 'I know, I feel bad for the poor little fuckers too, but we'll—'

Cordy dropped the chairs she was stacking and swung around. 'Don't call them *fuckers*.'

'Relax, I was only—'

'No.' She walked over until they were only inches apart. 'If you think it's OK to talk about raped children like that then you're as sick as those bastards.'

'Now hang on a minute . . .' said Bob, his face turning puce. 'I've had about as much as I can take of your holier-than-thou crap.'

'No, you hang on.' Cordy's voice was ragged with fury. 'Do you think they enjoy it? They make them act as if they like that, you know. They hurt them more if they don't.'

'Is this an effing joke? It's just an expression, for God's sake. Don't get hysterical.'

'You're the joke,' Cordy spat out. 'You're a fat old has-been who hates women, so why don't you do us all a favour and retire?'

'I don't have to listen to this,' Bob said, walking out and slamming the door behind him.

'Fuck!' Cordy said, and collapsed onto the nearest chair.

Anthony approached warily. She had almost forgotten that he was there.

'At the risk of getting my head bitten off too . . .'

She covered her face in her hands. 'Go on,' she said, eventually, not looking at him.

'There's a gym on the second floor. No one really uses it. It's a bit grotty, but maybe you could um . . .'

'Go there until I calm down?'

Anthony ventured a little closer. 'I find it clears my head. Look, you can even borrow my spare set of gym stuff. It's clean – I think.'

'You think?' Cordy said, looking up with the ghost of a smile.

'Cleanish. You up for it?'

Cordy shrugged, but pulled herself to her feet.

'That's a girl. I'll come too, and then we can set the world to rights between reps. And you can finish telling me about all that stuff you started talking about the other day.' He must have seen her face shut down because he quickly changed tack. 'Or we don't have to talk at all. Just sweat it out. But I warn you, I'm pretty strong. Don't feel bad if you have to keep putting the weights down a few levels.'

'You reckon?'

He flexed an arm. 'Look at that.'

She rolled up her sleeve. 'Two can play that game.'

'Hmm,' he said, giving her bicep a squeeze, 'not too shabby. For a woman.'

'I've just picked up the phone and the 1970s want their opinions back,' Cordy deadpanned.

'Ouch.'

Cordy laughed. 'Seriously, you're as bad as Sampson.'

'Who, the fat old has-been?' Anthony asked.

Cordy winced. 'Shit. Shouldn't have said that. Or that stuff about retiring. I just get so . . .' She trailed off. 'Jesus. I'd better go and apologise.'

Anthony shook his head. 'Give him a while to calm down first. In the meantime, prepare to be humbled by my physical prowess.'

'Bet you say that to all the girls.'

'Only the ones who look like they can kick my arse.'

Cordy decided not to tell him about her kickboxing. Not just yet.

Chapter 14

'What's wrong, sweetheart?'

Jess stopped pacing long enough to touch hands with her sister, but even when Cordy pulled her down on the sofa with her, Jess's fingers were still fidgeting out an incessant percussion beat. Cordy had to force herself not to put her hand over the top and physically stop the drumming. Instead, she lowered her voice and tried to make eye contact.

'Jess, love. What's up? Has something happened?'

Her sister shrugged her thin shoulders and continued to look at the floor. Her long dark hair fell limply over her face. It was tangled at the back, as if she hadn't bothered to brush it that day.

Cordy let out a deep breath. 'Well, if you're not going to talk to me, I'll have to leave. There's a ridiculously handsome Arabian prince waiting outside, poised to whisk me away on his private jet. Apparently he wants to shower me in diamonds and build me a castle made of white chocolate.' She stopped when she saw the flicker of a smile on Jess's face. 'But I said I'd rather hang out with my little sister.'

'Then you're an idiot.'

'Ah, it talks!' Cordy said, giving Jess's hand a squeeze. 'What's wrong? You having problems with the new meds? They screwing up your sleep again?'

'It's nothing,' Jess muttered.

'Tell me anyway.'

'Fine.' Jess looked down at the floor. 'But don't have a go at me, OK?'

'Would I?' Seeing her sister's face, Cordy relented. 'I won't. I promise.'

'OK. So.' Jess started rocking back and forwards very slowly. She reminded Cordelia uncomfortably of an animal in captivity, exhibiting signs of trauma. 'I told you about the new nurse, right?'

'Yeah. Polish girl? You said she was nice.'

'She's all right.'

There was a pause. Cordy was about to prompt her but Jess let out a sigh and the story came out. How she'd woken up to find the young nurse checking her arms for cuts and had freaked out.

Jess's eyes were empty. 'I know she's just doing her job, but . . .'

Cordy shook her head emphatically. 'No, she's not. The agreement is that they don't touch you without your permission. We even got that in writing. Did you talk to Dr Rubin about it?'

'Yeah. The nurse said sorry. She brought those.' Jess gestured to a rather tired-looking bunch of flowers that were still propped up in the sink.

'I'll put them in water, shall I?' Cordy offered.

While Cordy was undoing the elastic band that held the stems together, Jess mumbled something.

She turned around. 'Sorry, I didn't catch that.'

In a barely louder voice, Jess asked: 'Why am I such a freak? I mean, we all know *why*. But I screamed at her, Cordy. Really screamed. Now she looks nervous every time she comes to give me my meds. They must all think I'm a psycho.'

'Course they don't,' Cordy said, putting down the flowers and reaching for her hand. 'It was her mistake.' Jess didn't look convinced. 'Anyway, who cares what they think?'

'That's easy for you to say. You're not the fucking loon. You're not stuck in here.'

'You're not a loon. And it won't be forever, Jess,' Cordy said, with more conviction than she felt that afternoon. 'You know it won't.'

Jess didn't answer.

Cordy laced her fingers in her sister's. They felt cold and delicate, her bones like a bird's. 'Well, at least the nurse knows the score now, so it won't happen again. That's good, isn't it?'

'I guess.'

Jess let go of her hand, and Cordy's heart sank. The Forest Clinic was the best that money could buy. She'd never tell Jess this, but year after year it was slowly but surely eating up the money the girls had inherited from the sale of their grand-mother's home. For an instant Cordy felt a pang of regret at the well-paid interviews she'd turned down a few months ago. If Jess was unhappy there, she'd have to move her again, and, truth be told, they were running out of options. *If they ended up having to relocate to the States to find newer, better treatments* . . . Firmly, Cordy shook the thought away.

'Just give me a sec,' she said, arranging the flowers in a colourful melamine vase she'd found for her sister in a local vintage shop. 'There. That's better. They'll perk up now they're in water.'

Jess barely glanced at the carnations. 'Thanks.'

'So . . .' Cordy sat down. 'Did you want to watch a film or something? I brought *Calendar Girls* with me. We haven't watched that for ages.' There was silence. Her sister had glazed over. 'Jess?' she said, more loudly.

'Whatever you want.'

'We don't have to. We could play cards or something.'

Again there was that hopeless shrug.

'Cup of tea? Biscuit?'

'Stop fussing,' Jess snapped. 'You don't have to stay, you know.'

'Well, I don't mind keeping my prince waiting. It'll give him more time to decide where to take me for a shopping spree: Paris or Milan.' When Jess didn't even crack a smile, Cordy changed tack. 'Anyway, have I told you much about my new colleagues at work?'

'You never tell me anything about work,' Jess said, accusingly.

Cordy had to admit that this was true. Given her day-to-day contact with child molesters and perverts, it seemed safer that way.

'Well, I told you I was working in a new, erm, office, right? Well there's this guy Bob . . .'

'Tall, dark and handsome?'

Cordy smiled. At last her sister seemed to be perking up a bit. 'No. Short, balding and stout. And sixty, at least. Maybe even older.'

Jess sank back down, clearly disappointed.

The silence grew between them. Eventually Jess looked round, as if remembering that Cordy was there.

'Sorry . . .'

'I was talking about work,' Cordy said gently, making a mental note to talk to her doctor about Jess's meds. Her concentration seemed even more shot than usual.

'What are the rest of the people like?' Jess asked. 'Or are they all old and boring?'

'No, there's actually a girl about your age,' Cordy said. 'Tammy. She's pretty, but she knows it. Think she might have a bit of a crush on her boss.'

There was another pause. Often trying to talk to Jess was like wading through black treacle, but at least she seemed vaguely interested for once. 'And he is?'

'Oh, just another guy in the office.'

'*Really?*' Jess drew the word out. For a second she sounded like the bubbly little girl that Cordy remembered from twenty years ago. 'Tall, dark and handsome?'

'His name's Anthony. And he's married,' Cordy said firmly.

'Shame. But that doesn't stop him being tall, dark and handsome.'

'I haven't noticed . . .'

'Oh yeah?' Jess dug at her, a smile playing on her lips.

'Oh stop it,' Cordy said. 'Anyway, thought you wanted to watch a film?' But as the trailers rolled she smiled to herself. Jess's hand was finally still on the armrest, and her dark eyes had lost some of the hunted look of earlier. She would be mortified if Anthony ever realised that he was such a hot topic of conversation. But, to be honest, it would be worth any amount of teasing to see her sister looking less broken.

Chapter 15

In books you need a magic cloak or a magic spell to be invisible, but here you don't need anything because they talk like you aren't there. Like right now. They talk and talk but it doesn't always mean anything. They twist stuff until it makes no sense. The Captain is saying he wants Lolly to have a baby but that doesn't make any sense cos she's not married and she's not even in big school yet. Or at least she doesn't go. She says she hated school anyway, but mostly she doesn't say anything. We share a bunk but it's not like girls in boarding school stories. It is not like that at all.

Her stepdaddy is saying it's too much hassle. He says this about emptying the bucket too when it's his turn. Even when the flies get really bad. He says that baby stuff is sick and twisted and that they should concentrate on mainstream stuff. Mum says I shouldn't say 'stuff' when she asked what I learned at school. She says it doesn't mean anything. But nothing means anything down here.

I'd like to dig a hole and get us to safety but Kurt might tell because he wants to be the favourite. But maybe he would come too. I turn to ask Lolly what she thinks but her face is blank and she's watching the men like they're a TV and even when I pinch her she won't look away.

What they don't say in books is that being invisible is a lot like being dead.

Chapter 16

'And another one,' Tammy called from her desk in the corner. 'Blimey. All the pervs are out today. It's like shooting paedo-fish in a barrel.'

'Yeah, except we keep putting them back in the water,' Cordy sighed, pushing away her stack of files. The young detective's running commentary made it impossible to concentrate on anything else.

'What, you mean rather than gutting them?' Tammy asked, with a wink. 'Admittedly, that would be more satisfying. Did you read what the last one wrote? Sick fucker.'

Cordelia came over and leaned over Tammy's chair. Just as she had said, up on the screen was yet another explicit message that Honeybun1998, Tammy's teen alias, had received from a grown man. Although Cordy had heard plenty of horror stories from her clients at Justice4Children, this was her first live experience of paedo-phishing, and she was finding it pretty depressing. For all the articles about paedophiles 'grooming' children on line, the reality was even more stark. As soon as Honeybun appeared on the fan site, she started to receive instant messages, many asking in the same breath what subjects she liked at school and whether she had any naked photos.

'Is it always this bad?' Cordy asked.

'Today's pretty active,' Tammy told her, checking back through her log. 'But you always get at least a few bites. This is the fan site that that Big Mark fella was on about, but whether we'll catch anything useful . . .'

'And this doesn't count as entrapment because . . . ?'

'Because the definition of entrapment is coercing someone into doing something illegal that they wouldn't ordinarily do.' The young detective grinned. 'So I don't pose as some nympho fifteen-year-old, coming on to all and sundry. That'd get thrown out of court. But if it's clear that they're the one soliciting sex from an obviously underage person, well, then we can bang 'em to rights. Even if I'm a few years older than I claim to be.'

'A few?'

Tammy shot her a withering look.

Just then Anthony came in with a sandwich from the deli across the street.

'Mind if I join you girls?'

'Might put you off your lunch,' Cordy warned him.

'What, no home-made shepherd's pie today?' Tammy asked, eyeing his BLT. 'Standards are clearly slipping in the DeLuca household.'

'Maybe we went out for dinner last night.'

'Ooh, fancy.' Tammy swivelled away from the screen. Today her blonde hair was loose around her shoulders, falling in soft layers around her face. Cordy, whose dark hair was caught up in a neat ponytail, suddenly felt old and frumpy by comparison. 'Where did you take her? Pizza Hut? Maccy Ds?'

Anthony turned to Cordy. 'Reynolds thinks I'm not romantic because I gave my wife an exercise bike for Christmas. But that's what she *wanted*.'

'So where'd you take her then?' Tammy persisted.

'We just got a curry.'

'I rest my case,' she said with a smirk, turning back to the screen.

Anthony caught Cordy's eye and shook his head ruefully. 'I just can't win with that one. Hope she doesn't give Angie any ideas. Anyway, how are you lot getting on?'

Cordy didn't sugarcoat it. 'No local guys so far as we can tell, and nothing that seems to connect back to the main case.'

'It'll come.' Anthony pulled out a chair and sat down at the middle table. 'You want a bite?'

Cordy shook her head. 'Thanks though.'

Anthony glanced over at Tammy, who was now typing away furiously. 'Ah, she's got another one, by the sounds of it.' He turned back to Cordy. 'Did Reynolds ever tell you about Brian?'

'Not much. Extended sick-leave guy?'

'Yeah, that's the one,' Anthony said. 'Haven't seen him in a long while. But back in the day he was quite a character. Before we got Tammy, he did lots of the paedo-phishing. Had a knack for sounding like he was a kid on email. I remember one day when I was still training Reynolds up, we sat in on one of his sessions. He was pretending to be a young girl, and this guy was pressuring him to strip off and turn his webcam on. Brian eventually agreed – but only if they did it at the same time.'

'Let me guess: when the pervert looked at the screen he got the shock of his life,' Cordy said with a grin.

'Exactly. His trousers were around his ankles and he found himself staring into Brian's ugly mug.' He lowered his voice. 'Never thought an erection could wilt so fast. Like someone had let the air out of a balloon.'

'Thanks, mate! Lovely image,' Cordy said, putting her hand over her mouth.

'What are you two giggling about?' Tammy called, sounding put out.

'Nothing,' Cordy assured her, regaining her composure. 'Do you need a hand?'

'Well, you both might want to come and have a look at this.'

'Who is it?' Anthony asked, tossing his wrapper in the bin.

'Wait for it. He calls himself . . . "Marky14Mark".'

Cordy shrugged. 'Surely no one would be stupid enough to use their actual name on these things?'

Tammy looked put out. 'You'd be surprised. And they'd definitely be stupid enough to use the same alias twice.'

'Could just be a fourteen-year-old?' Anthony suggested. 'Unless that's supposed to be a Marky Mark reference?'

'What you on about, DeLuca?' Tammy asked.

He shook his head. 'Before your time, Reynolds.'

'Postcode,' Cordy said. 'Marky14 – Mark, E14. That'd fit.'

They all crowded round the screen. Anthony offered to get Cordy another chair but she insisted she was fine standing. She and Anthony stood shoulder to shoulder behind Tammy, who was using the mouse to highlight sections of Honeybun's latest exchange.

Unlike some of the other guys, Mark's messages started fairly innocuously.

Marky14Mark: Hi honEbun. I saw this guys in
                    concert last week and he ROCKS . . .

'Maybe he's just some teenage boy, like he says he is,' Anthony suggested. 'I mean, I know we're all programmed to assume the worst, but it sounds like he's just trying to set up a date.'

'Get a load of this photo though,' Tammy said, clicking open an attachment. 'Maybe he was seventeen . . . in the early nineties. Look at those trousers. He's like a white MC Hammer. And who scans in photos these days?'

Cordy nodded. 'And see what he says about her "sounding mature" and how he can bring "booze and ciggies"? Definite warning signals.'

'Nice,' Anthony said, rubbing his hands together. 'It's a pretty common name, but if it turns out to be the Big_Mark guy from the chatroom, then this could be a really strong lead.'

Just then another message flashed up on the screen.

Marky14Mark: So you up for meeting then?

'Fantastic,' Cordy said, turning to Anthony. 'Now how do we play this?'

'We put him off,' Tammy cut in. 'Give ourselves time to do some groundwork and see if it's worth getting a warrant to investigate him. That's right, isn't it, guv?'

'But won't he just move on to the next girl?' Cordy asked. 'We'll have lost him . . .'

'It's always a risk,' Anthony admitted, 'but think about it. We haven't got much to go on so far. The name thing is probably just a coincidence. And there's no way that we can arrange a meeting without proper back-up. You must know yourself how danger-ous these guys can get when they realise they're cornered.'

'I mean, I'd happily do it,' Tammy assured her, 'but like he said, there's no point until we get the right paperwork. Until then our hands are tied.'

'Well, how soon will that be?' Cordy asked, more sharply than she intended. 'And in the meantime, shouldn't we reply? Mark's probably getting bored of hanging around already. We don't want him to smell a rat.'

Tammy shrugged. 'If he thinks he's got some prepubescent girl on the hook, he'll wait as long as it takes.' Anthony shot her a look. 'But yeah, guess we might as well.'

She looked down at the keyboard for a beat, and then typed out:

Honeybun1998:   errr sorry mark mums here chat u
                 l8rs xxxxxxxx
Marky14Mark: youd better believe it HB M xxx

'Happy now?' Tammy asked.

Anthony glanced down at his watch. 'Sorry, guys, but I said I'd update the chief on what's been happening with the case. At least I have some good news for her now. Good work, Reynolds.'

'Cheers, boss.'

'But what's the timeframe on getting an investigative warrant?' Cordy asked again. 'We don't want to let this guy get away.'

Anthony was already halfway to the door. 'Like I said, I'll run it past the chief and see if she thinks it's worth pursuing. Reynolds, see if you can get another good bite now you're on a roll.'

'Will do.'

Cordy slumped down in her seat in frustration.

'Goodbye, Honeybun, hello, Twi-lite,' Tammy said, cheerfully. 'How old shall I be today?'

'Eight,' Cordy replied, dully.

'Like Alice?' Tammy asked. When Cordy didn't reply she turned back to the computer. 'I'll say ten. Kids like to round up, and paedos will factor that in.'

Less than ten minutes later she let out a long breath.

'What do you make of that? Half twelve? And there it is. First catch of the afternoon.'

Chapter 17

The day seemed to drag on forever. Cordy's eyes kept straying down to the time display at the bottom of her screen, but the digits seemed to change with painful slowness. The Ops Room had never felt so cramped and oppressive. Every time Bob made one of his wheezy little chuckles or Tammy's cutesy ring-tone went off she felt like screaming.

The fact was that the mingling of excitement and dread in her stomach made it difficult to apply herself to her work and her mind was going back and forth as if she was watching a tennis match. *Should she, shouldn't she, should she, shouldn't she?* It was the waiting that was wearing her down. If she'd just been able to do it straight away, as soon as the idea occurred to her . . .

Her frustration mounted as six o'clock came and went and they were all still sitting at their desks.

Don't you people have homes to go to?

At the start of the week there'd been a memo from Fiona saying, in no uncertain terms, that there'd be no overtime available on this case, but with the exception of Bob (who'd finally sloped off at half five, muttering something about his grandson's birthday), the team was still hard at it.

Across the street, the clock on the local Catholic church chimed seven, and Anthony finally looked up from his screen.

'God, didn't realise it was that late. Come on, let's finish up here and nip across to the Fox and Hound for a quick pint. It's been a long week.'

'Now that,' said Tammy, shutting off her computer with a flourish, 'is a great idea. Just give me two minutes to go to the loo and sort my face out.'

'Your face looks fine to me,' Anthony called, but she was already busy rifling through her handbag. 'Hunter, you'll come along for a bit, won't you? I might not drink tonight either. I'm supposed to be training for that ten-k run next weekend.'

'I don't think I've sponsored you for that yet,' she said, playing for time.

'Thanks. You're a sweetheart.' He gave her a smile that did nothing to calm her jittery stomach. 'Actually, I should probably send another email round. So far I've got a tenner from Fiona and a couple of quid from one of the secretaries on the floor below and that's about it.'

'Yeah, people just forget, that's all.'

'So . . .' he said, easing into his leather jacket, 'quick drink?'

'Actually,' Cordy said, turning away, 'I might just look over the case files one more time before I go. I feel like I've been missing something.'

'Oh come on,' Tammy said, who had just come back in. She'd retouched her make-up and taken off her jacket to reveal a chic scarlet vest top, cut in a generous scoop neck. Cordy couldn't help but notice Anthony's eyes flicking over her slim figure. 'You know what they say about all work and no play . . .'

'Well, fine. Maybe I *am* a dull girl,' Cordy snapped. She bit her lip. 'Sorry, it's just I'm tired, and I've got a lot to get through. Why don't you guys just go ahead and I'll see you on Monday?'

As she turned back to her screen, Cordy was almost sure she saw Tammy roll her eyes to heaven.

Anthony touched her gently on the shoulder. 'You all right? I could always stay and give you a hand if you like.'

Her face softened. 'That's OK. You should go for a drink. I, erm, might join you guys there later.'

'Well, here's my mobile number,' Anthony said, scribbling it down on a piece of scrap paper. 'Call if you want to check we're still there. Or if you have any questions about the case files.'

'Thanks. I will.'

'K. See you on Monday!' Tammy said, grabbing Anthony by the elbow and steering him out. 'Don't worry, boss, first round's on me.'

Cordy waited a couple of minutes and then sneaked out into the hall to check they'd left. She even knocked on Fiona's office door, and was relieved to get no answer.

Back in the Ops Room, she closed the door behind her, leaned against it for a beat, and then, decision made, booted up Tammy's computer. Cordy had already noted that the young detective kept her passwords on a pink Post-it note on the wall behind her desk.

Top-level security, she thought wryly as, less than a minute late, TReynolds logged on to the intranet.

Crossing her fingers, she typed in the web address of the fansite that Tammy had been phishing on earlier in the day.

'Come on, come on . . .' she muttered, but a quick scan of the message boards showed no sign of Mark. 'Arse.'

At a noise in the corridor she froze, ears straining. With her mind whirring through a list of possible excuses for being at the wrong desk (her computer was broken, she couldn't find a file, she thought it'd be funny to change Tammy's backdrop), she shut down Internet Explorer and wiped the history clean, expecting one of the team to appear any second.

But when she poked her head round the door she saw it was only a cleaner going round emptying the bins.

'Err, don't worry about doing us today,' she said, trying to sound casual.

The woman shrugged. 'If that's what you want, only—'

'Thanks,' Cordy interrupted, 'and have a good night.'

As soon as the door was safely closed, she was back on the computer. Clicking the site open again she saw there were a few random messages for Honeybun but nothing from Mark.

Minimising the fansite, she opened a new window and, in a flash of inspiration, went to a teen networking site that Tammy had mentioned that morning as a 'paedos' paradise'.

Tammy must not have logged off after her last session, because the site took her straight to Honeybun's home page. Better still, the toolbar showed a flashing mail icon.

'Is this our guy?' she murmured.

But before she even had a chance to open it, an instant message popped up.

Marky14Mark: Hey, its me. Mark
                 We were talking earlier
                 This is the same Honeybun, right????
                 Got a feelin ur 1 of a kind ;)

He sounded so smug and confident. Cordy itched to wipe the smile off his face, to tell him what she thought of perverts who trawled the net for girls barely into their teens. Instead she tried to remember what Honeybun had sounded like that afternoon. With shaking hands she started typing.

Honeybun1998:   Yeah I remember u mark
                 Howz things????

To her relief he wrote straight back:

Marky14Mark: Good – now I'm chattin 2u again!!!

Although Mark didn't seem to notice the switch, the chat moved a lot slower than it had when Tammy had been at the keyboard. Cordy found it tough to stay in character, and had to double-check every message before she sent it out. She knew the longer she was on line, the more likely she'd be to trip up, so after a bit of back and forth she cut to the chase. Before she had time to think too hard about whether she was doing the right thing.

Honeybun1998:	So u wanted to meet up . . .
Marky14Mark:	Yeah, when???

Cordy hesistated. *Oh well, no point in backing down now.*

Honeybun1998:	Tomorrow???
Marky14Mark:	Cool
Honeybun1998:	Shall I come round to urs then?

This time Mark didn't reply straight away. Cordy bit her lip. *Shit, I've given the game away by being too pushy. It's just that if we had an address . . .*

The screen flashed.

Marky14Mark:	Nah, lets meet round somewhere like Victoria Park. Down near the canal?

Cordy's heart leapt. *East London.* This guy was sounding more and more like Big_Mark. But a meeting in such a secluded space would be a logistical nightmare. *And potentially dangerous*, a little voice inside her said.

Honeybun1998:	Mcdonalds near whitchapel tube??? eleven????????
Marky14Mark:	Perfect
	You look great in them profile pictures, by the way

Honeybun1998:   Thanx ☺
Marky14Mark: Specially the beach ones
                 Bring a friend if you like n we can
                 double-date

Repressing a shudder, Cordy typed back:

Honeybun1998:   May b next time cant wait 2 cu
                 2mozzza!!!!

And shut down Tammy's computer, wiping the history once more and being careful to make sure that nothing looked out of place.

Going back to her own desk, she sat for a long time in silence, listening to the hum of the Hoover on a downstairs floor and the laughter drifting up from the Friday night revellers on the street below. Trying not to think about tomorrow.

Chapter 18

clewis: Thanks for keeping in touch.
          In 10 years time there won't be persecution like
          this. But for now, better safe than sorry, eh?
spurs101: you didn't give me much choice
          do you have any fucking idea what would
          happen if this got out?
          my life wud be over
clewis: Well, it's appreciated anyway
          Just glad we could work something out
spurs101: if you can keep your mouth shut we can
          so what was it you wanted to know
          you know we always have a load of investiga-
          tions going on at once right
clewis: I'm learning a lot of stuff I didn't know about
          the boys – and girls – in blue
spurs101: look Ill go if ur gonna be like that
clewis: sorry
          Just want to make sure none of my friends are
          going to get in trouble
spurs101: Nice friends u got
clewis: Glass houses, my friend.
          So . . . anything going on down our neck of the
          woods?
spurs101: what do u mean
clewis: Come on, you know exactly what I mean
spurs101: well there's always stuff, you know

clewis:	But anything specific?
	Close to home?
spurs101:	and that'd be???
clewis:	London
spurs101:	youd have to be more specific than that
clewis:	east London.
	that good enough?
spurs101:	There is something
	I don't know if you know anyone involved in a pay-per-view site
clewis:	Go on
spurs101:	because there on our radar.
clewis:	Right
	As in, someone should tell them to get the hell out of dodge?
spurs101:	nah, not yet
	not by a long shot
clewis:	well, keep me to up to date, would you?
	like I said, it'd be appreciated
	by the way, there's another site you might want to have a look at
	Just your kind of thing
spurs101:	I probably shouldn't
clewis:	Well, I'll send you the link and then it's up to you, isn't it?

Chapter 19

A ragged scream came from the blackness of the heath. Cordelia bolted upright, knocking over the full glass of water she kept on her bedside cabinet.

Shit.

She ignored the water puddling on her floor as she strained to listen.

Nothing. Not even the low rumble of the night bus.

Just a fox, you idiot, she told herself, sinking back down. *Now go to sleep.*

Cordy pulled the spare pillow over her head and screwed her eyes tight shut. Usually she enjoyed the feel of freshly washed Egyptian cotton against her cheek, but tonight she couldn't seem to find a comfortable position to lie in. Even though she'd followed her usual evening routine, her body jittered as if she'd been hardlining caffeine all day. *Or doing shots of Jagermeister like she was just one away from a good time,* she thought wryly.

These days the younger, wilder version of herself felt like a stranger who happened to share the same name. There weren't many pictures of those reckless student years she'd spent in Manchester, but whenever Cordy happened across a blurry Polaroid she barely recognised the thin, manic girl looking back at her through dark, kohled eyes.

Those were the days before she realised that the buzz alcohol gave her wasn't worth the loss of control. All it took was one dodgy situation at a house party, with a guy who wasn't inclined to take no for an answer, and she was ready to swear off booze forever. That was back before she'd started the kick-boxing training, but she'd still managed to give the creep a broken nose to remember her (and his manners) by.

Cordy reached for the water glass a beat before she remembered knocking it over. Frowning, she drew her arm back beneath the warm covers. The afternoon's events were whirring round in her head, and even thinking about her plans for the next day made her feel dizzy and nauseous. This would be the first time in her adult life that she'd voluntarily come face to face with a paedophile. Her work with Justice4Children was solely focused on supporting the victims and their families. Seeking out a predator was not something she'd ever thought she'd do.

Part of the sick feeling came from knowing she was going behind the team's backs. Of course, if Mark turned out to have a connection with the case, it'd be a massive step forward. But if he didn't, or if something went wrong . . .

Cordy propped herself up on her elbows. *It'll be fine*, she told herself firmly. *He's a cowardly pervert who preys on little girls and you're a grown woman. What can he do to you?*

She shook her head. That wasn't a helpful train of thought. The problem was that she could all too vividly picture the ways he could hurt her. No one who had survived a childhood like hers could ever imagine their body as invulnerable.

She tried again.

Look, you heard what Anthony said about his hands being tied. And every day we waste getting paperwork together is another one that Alice and the others are going through absolute hell. If this Mark character has nothing to do with the case then we haven't lost anything. And if he is, then we'll be one step closer to getting those kids out of there.

The fox cried out again, and Cordy gave an involuntary shudder. She knew it was just a mating call, but there was something so uncannily human about the sound that it set her teeth on edge.

A glance at the clock told her that it was past two. She'd been tossing and turning for hours. Time to accept that she wasn't going to get to sleep any time soon.

Turning on her bedside lamp, she eased herself out of bed and wrapped herself in her thick cotton dressing gown. Methodically she went around the whole loft apartment, checking that all her windows and doors were closed and locked, that her fire and burglar alarms were set and that all the plug-sockets were flicked off. She knew it was a strange little routine – you didn't need a degree in psychology to recognise that it was more than a little OCD – but it calmed her. *And besides*, she thought defensively, *it's not like there's anyone here to judge me.*

Usually Cordy loved the fact that she lived alone. When she'd first moved back to London, she'd shared a small terraced house with another graduate student and had hated every minute of it – the unexpected interruptions, the lack of privacy, the constant pressure to be sociable. These days she even avoided having lovers back to sleep over, prefer-ring the clean, controlled anonymity of a hotel room. That way her home stayed exactly as she wanted it: a refuge from the complications of the outside world. And the man of the moment could be under no illusion that just because she felt like sharing a bed with him it meant that she wanted to share the rest of her life with him too.

But tonight was different. Tonight she'd have welcomed someone to talk things through with. Someone to reassure her that she was doing the right thing. The only logical thing.

Cordy sank down on her white corner sofa. Her phone was on the coffee table still, and absently she scrolled through her contacts. Jess . . . no way. Her boss, Allyson, had a huge heart but she could be a bit of a mother hen. She'd be horrified at the idea of Cordy breaking the rules and putting herself in harm's way. Allyson would demand that she returned to Justice4Children straight away, and there was no way that Cordy could abandon Alice and the others now.

She scrolled back up to Jess's details, and let herself imagine for a second what it would have been like if their Uncle Herbert had never got the chance to destroy their childhoods. She pictured a rounder, healthier Jess. A Jess with a career. A Jess with a boyfriend, eating dinner at a romantic little restaurant rather than using plastic cutlery in the canteen of a mental institution. A sister she could lean on, confide in. But, as far as Jess knew, Cordy did a boring administrative job at a charity. And there was no way that she'd worry her about something like this.

Cordy snapped her phone shut.

Enough sitting around.

Not bothering to change out of her pyjamas, she grabbed her helmet and leathers from the hall closet and kitted up.

Minutes later she was tearing down deserted lanes, letting her doubts and worries stream out of her into the cold night air. Her visor was down and the night seemed to blur around her as she picked up speed along the straights and arched her body into the curves.

When she stopped at a set of traffic lights, a taxi pulled up alongside and the driver wound down the window and mouthed something.

Cordy lifted off her helmet, worried that he'd spotted something wrong with her suspension.

'Nice bike, sweetheart,' he repeated. He leaned forward and gave her leather-clad body a leery once-over. 'Sure you wouldn't rather be wrapping those legs round me?'

'This beauty rides harder and faster than you ever could, mate,' Cordy retorted, and roared off before the taxi driver had a chance to pick his chin off the floor.

When she'd bought the Suzuki Hayabusa a couple of years back, the dealer had tried to steer her towards something less powerful, something more 'sleek and chic', but she'd insisted that it was the bike for her. Now she was grateful for its brute power. There was something so private about speeding along, ears muffled by the helmet, feeling powerful, sexy and completely anonymous. Maybe statistically it was dangerous, but she *felt* safe because she was in control. And that's what really mattered.

It'll be the same following Mark, she realised. She'd be the one calling the shots. She'd be in the driving seat.

Keeping her eyes on the road she started meticulously planning what she would do tomorrow. Given that the whole case could be at stake, she couldn't afford the slightest margin of error. With so much to concentrate on, she hardly even registered that the fox was still calling desperately for a mate.

Chapter 20

Bodies are not private here but my arm is still *my* arm and I scrape messages on my skin with my finger on the inside part where there are veins and bruises and seven freckles (two on the right, five on the left). In school there was a boy who was ambi-something which meant he wasn't a lefty or a righty but an ambi-something, and maybe I am now too because I make ambi-messages. Ten on one, ten on the other, again and again and again. Because their fingers are hard and rough I make my finger gentle, baby-soft, and it hardly touches but if you had a magic spell you could still see the messages, and the writing would be little like in a book from the Gold Reader shelf in the school library.

When no one's looking, which is lots of the time, I can make better messages with my nails. You don't need magic to see these because after a while they bleed. I used to be scared of blood but that's silly because it's just blood and the men say there's no need to make a fuss. And I can use the blood to make more messages too.

These special messages are actually just one message and it is the thing I see when the Captain hurts me. I look and look at it because I don't want to see his face all red and the poppy veins on his eyelids or his dirty stuff and so the thing I look at is burned behind my eyes and I see it before I go to sleep. I want to show it to my mummy and daddy because they've seen it before, and now they can see it again through the camera's eye, because the Captain doesn't know everything and they're not dead and they *are* getting my messages. My secret messages. And then they'll come and take me home.

Chapter 21

The young mother gave Cordy a funny look as she moved aside to let her and her double-pushchair past.

'Aren't you getting on then?'

Cordelia blushed. 'Go ahead. I'm waiting for the number, erm, ninety-three.'

Glancing up at the new electronic display board, she saw that if there was such a thing as a 93 bus, it definitely didn't stop here.

So much for playing the undercover detective.

Luckily the woman was already manoeuvring the bulky buggy through the doors and onto the crowded vehicle, which, minutes later, joined the Saturday afternoon traffic crawling down the Whitechapel Road. Looking down, Cordy noticed that one of the babies had dropped its teething ring on the floor. Not wanting to leave it lying in the dirt, she picked it up gingerly, placed it on the bench and went back to watching the McDonald's across the street.

Was that him? In the white shirt?

Her body stiffened, but the middle-aged man strolled over to a guy who was already in the queue and slapped him on the back.

Guess not.

Cordy went back to methodically scanning the place, table by table. It was one of the smaller branches – only one level – and despite the heavy traffic she had a pretty good view. She'd picked a spot where there was a break in the market stalls, and

while there was nothing she could do about the buses that
trundled by now and then, blocking off the other side of the
street, a bump in the pavement added to her natural height
advantage.

She'd aimed to be there a quarter of an hour early, but she'd
been so worried about being late that she'd already been standing here for forty minutes and it was only just past eleven –
the time she, pretending to be Honeybun, had suggested for
the 'date'.

As yet another guy turned to enter, she fiddled with her
hoodie. As a rule she hated wearing anything that cut off her
peripheral vision, but during last night's ride she'd decided
that it'd help her feel less conspicuous. She also had her
favourite battered old running shoes on – just in case.

There'd been plenty of false alarms already that morning,
but there was something about this man that made her take
a closer look. Maybe it was his boxy leather jacket, or the
way he smoothed down his hair before he went inside. He
certainly had a – what? – a *swagger* about him. With shaking fingers, Cordy reached into her backpack for her digital
camera.

'Sorry, you don't happen to know how I get to Spitalfields?
Spitalfields market?'

When Cordy looked up a girl clutching an *A–Z* was standing in front of her. A young, lanky guy hung a little way back,
looking embarrassed.

'I'm a little . . .' Cordy said, then shook her head wearily.
It'd be quicker just to tell them. When she'd hurriedly pointed
out the right direction, the girl thanked her, shot a triumphant
look at her boyfriend and finally moved out of the way.

Cordy's eyes leapt across the street.

Where the hell is he?

At first she thought that she must have been wrong – that
the man had just bought a burger and left. After all, there was

hardly a queue now at the counter. One of the servers had even left her till in order to wipe over the spare tables.

Then she saw him. He was leaning right against the window, next to a gaggle of four teenage girls. From this angle she could see that he wasn't as old as he'd been in her head – maybe late twenties, early thirties, and clearly no stranger to the gym. He had a certain cheap glamour, Cordy saw at once. Muscles. Tan. 'Or maybe not so cheap,' she muttered, as a heavy gold chain around his neck caught the light. The girls threw the man a couple of glances, causing Cordy to inhale sharply, but a minute later they were gathering their shopping bags and strolling out onto the street, arm in arm, laughing loudly enough to get disapproving looks from passers-by.

It could be him.

It could be Mark.

As soon as the group were gone, the man slipped onto a high stool by the doorway and got out a paper, jerking his head up a few times as girls walked past him. Cordy cursed her camera, which only had a x12 lens. Even with the zoom on maximum, the couple of pictures she sneaked of him looked grainy and indistinct. More useful was the mental image she was compiling of him.

Hair: Straight brown, cut medium short (number 3? number 4?) receding at temples, product
Skin: White, tan (fake?)
Clothes: Black leather jacket (expensive-looking), beaten-up Adidas trainers, Levi jeans, tight T-shirt, gold chain
Height . . .

She paused. It was hard to work that out when he was still sitting down. She checked her watch. Almost twenty past. How much longer was he going to wait?

As if in answer to her question, the man folded his paper and got down from the stool. After a last look around he walked out through the door. He didn't even have any wrappers to throw away.

Barely stopping to look for traffic, Cordy nipped across the road and followed him down the street. He walked quickly despite the market stalls that spilled out onto the pavement, and she struggled not to lose him in the weekend crowd. In fact, she almost missed it when he turned right, and then right again, away from the touts and bustle of Brick Lane and into one of the dingier streets that ran at right angles to it. She'd assumed he'd just head for the Tube, but maybe this would be even better. As usual at the weekend there were track works, and the trains and platforms would be busier than ever. There was no guarantee she'd be able to squeeze into the same carriage and, even if she did, she might end up being closer than she'd like. Too close for comfort.

Cordy shuddered, but then forced herself to concentrate on the task in hand.

Every now and then the man she was trailing would scan the girls passing by, as if he still hadn't quite given up hope of spotting Honeybun, but Cordy made sure there were always at least a few people between her and her quarry. Up close, she could see that his skin was pitted in acne scars, that his hairline was starting to recede. This new information was like power she held over him. Cordy felt a familiar shot of adrenaline coursing through her veins. Almost without realising it, she engaged her core muscles, as if readying her body for a fight.

I've got you, you bastard.

By the time he turned for the third time, the crowd had thinned out, so Cordy paused at the corner, pretending to tie her shoelaces. Glad of the hood falling over her face, she looked up and saw Mark walk over to a pimped-up blue Audi.

She waited until she heard the growl of the ignition before standing up, plugging in some headphones and jogging past the parked car.

Her stomach lurched as she passed within touching distance of the Audi's gleaming bonnet. The driver had one arm round the back of the seat as he reversed out past the rubbish cans and the chained-up bicycles. He turned back to the front, and for a horrible second she thought that he might have caught her eye in the rearview mirror. His eyes were unexpected – a cool grey, the pupil ringed with black. They seemed to fix her, strip away her weak disguise, know her for what she was.

Stop being paranoid, she told herself sharply as she jogged round the corner and collapsed against a grimy brick wall. *In ten minutes, he won't even remember he saw a jogger today. Why would he? If I'm right about him, I'm too old to be of any interest.*

She memorised the registration number: L59 RGH.

It echoed in her head like a good-luck charm as, slowly, she jogged back to her bike.

The whole encounter with the man who might be Mark had lasted less than twenty-five minutes, but she felt as if she'd run a marathon and could sleep for the rest of the weekend. On the way home, Cordy tried not to entertain the possibility that she'd followed the wrong man. That the real Mark (if there even was such a person) was still sitting out there: eating in McDonald's, browsing on Brick Lane, drawing up alongside her in that blacked-out SUV.

Spotting a gap in the bus line, she weaved to the left, and watched the SUV get smaller and smaller in the bike's rearview mirror until it disappeared altogether.

Chapter 22

'So I ask my mate's missus why she didn't join the women's league at the Anchor over in Hammersmith, if she's set on playing darts, that is. Which is a fair enough question, right?' Bob looked round, but when no one answered he just ploughed straight on. 'Exactly. So she was all on about her high scores and how it wasn't like she was worried about chipping her nails or anything and that's when I stopped her and I said, 'Look, love, no offence, but if you were a bloke you wouldn't even have brought that up.' He chuckled to himself, shot a sly glance at Cordy and took another gulp of tea. 'Anyway, then she got on her high horse and was talking about equal opportunities and going straight to the club secretary, but I said that if she wanted to play that badly, I wasn't going to stop her. So now this bird is in a regular league match down our local and I'll tell you something for nothing – after all that fuss, turns out she's not a bad player. Not that I'd tell her that, like.'

He turned to wink at Cordy but she carried on staring at her computer screen. Clearly disappointed not to have got a rise out of her, he folded up his paper and pushed his mug into the centre of the table. 'Right. Guess I should be getting back to work.'

Once again the only sound was the whir of the ancient air conditioners and the clicking of mouses.

'You all right?'

Cordy jumped. She hadn't heard Anthony coming over, and yet here he was, leaning over her desk, so close she could smell something clean and citrusy on him. *Soap? Shampoo?*

'Fine. Yeah,' she stammered. 'Good weekend? Sorry I didn't make it to the pub in the end.'

He set down his mug on her desk and put a cool hand across her forehead.

'What are you—?'

He laughed at her startled expression. 'Just checking to see if you had a temperature. Couldn't think why else you'd let Sampson get away with that kind of macho bullshit.'

'I didn't hear *you* say anything,' Cordy said irritably, pulling away. She felt much closer to Anthony since she'd confided in him about her past, but that didn't mean she wanted to be poked and pawed. He should have figured that out by now.

Anthony grinned. 'I like an easy life. But that doesn't mean I don't enjoy watching you two slug it out.'

Cordy glanced uneasily around. 'Look, I'd better get on.'

'Of course.' He paused, fixing her with his deep brown eyes. 'You just seemed quiet, that's all, so I was wondering if there was anything I could help with?'

When she didn't reply he shrugged.

'Sorry. Probably none of my business. I didn't mean to disturb you.'

'Wait!' she called impulsively as he turned to walk away. 'Do you have time for a quick coffee in the canteen? Now, I mean?'

'That muck? Well . . . I've got a report to write for the detective chief superintendent.'

'It'll just be quick.'

'You're on.' He gave her a stomach-flipping smile. 'After you.'

Compared to the hi-tech ECPU offices, the canteen looked as though it was stuck in a time-warp. Not only were the curling lino and brown plastic seats pure 1970s, even the food looked past its prime. The smell was of boiled chicken bones and dirty cleaning rags and, in the harsh fluorescent light, even Anthony looked a bit peaky.

'God, I never come down here,' he said as he pushed open the double doors on the third floor. 'And now I remember why.'

Now that she'd decided to get Anthony's help, Cordy couldn't bear to wait another second. The words were straining to get out, like water kept under high pressure. While they were still waiting to add water to their herbal tea bags ('Trust me,' Anthony had warned, 'you don't even want to think about drinking the shit they call coffee'), she asked if there'd been any progress on Tammy's paedophile from last week.

'It's only Monday,' Anthony reminded her. 'I don't think Reynolds is even scheduled for another paedo-phishing session till the end of the week. In the meantime, I can do a search for that screen-name, but to be honest we don't have much more to go on.'

'What if you had a car registration plate?' Cordy said hurriedly. 'Would that help?'

Anthony turned round to face her, ignoring the queue building behind them.

'Where would you get that kind of information?' His voice was serious now. 'Hunter, what the hell's going on?'

Aware of dirty looks being sent their way, Cordy hurriedly paid for the tea, pulled Anthony over to a table and filled him in on her Saturday morning adventures.

'Jesus.'

He leaned back in his chair and looked at her carefully. It was difficult to tell if he was impressed or appalled. *Maybe a bit of both.*

'So what do you think?' Cordy said, chewing on the inside of her lip. 'Helpful or not?'

'Not if the car's stolen, of course,' he warned, 'but otherwise . . .'

'Otherwise it'll help?' she asked hopefully. 'You can use it?'

'Not officially. But I suppose, unofficially . . .' He shrugged. 'Worth a try, isn't it?'

'You think?'

'Why not? I don't mind running it through the system.'

'Oh, I knew I could count on you!' Cordy reached across the table and covered his hand with hers. Immediately, she felt her friend's fingers stiffen. Mortified, she drew back. 'I'm sorry, I just—'

He cut her off. 'It's OK. You surprised me, is all. You're not usually . . . well, you know.'

Cordy slunk down into her own seat, certain her face was aflame. She thought she heard a few sniggers from a nearby table, but she told herself she was just being paranoid.

'Sorry,' she said again. 'I've just had lots on my mind with one thing and another and, you know . . .'

Anthony was concentrating doggedly on his tea, refusing to meet her eye.

She trailed off. After her fraught weekend it felt like such a massive relief to have someone else's help. To have someone to confide in. But of course Anthony must be used to women throwing themselves at him all the time. No wonder he got the wrong idea. She flushed at the thought of herself in the role of the clumsy seductress. *Surely he wouldn't think that?*

For a minute there was silence, and then both of them spoke at once.

'Maybe we should . . . ?'

'Do you think that . . . ?'

They laughed awkwardly, and Anthony put out his palm. 'Sorry. After you.'

Cordy took a deep breath and tried to sound businesslike. 'Do you think that there's a way of looking into this . . .'

'Without the chief being involved?'

She nodded. 'Well, initially. Until we have solid facts.'

Anthony drained his cup with a grimace. 'Even the tea tastes bad here. Look, why don't we go and see if one of the rooms on our corridor is free? If so, we can run the registration through our databases and see what we find.' He stood up before she even had a chance to answer.

Cordy trailed after him, glad to leave the glare of the canteen behind her. She wanted to kick herself for making things weird between them. *Was it worth explaining that she just wanted to be friends? Or would that make her look even more pathetic?*

She tried to persuade herself that she was making a mountain out of a molehill, but the sour taste of rejection continued to rankle at the back of her mouth.

Five minutes later, Cordy was punching the air in triumph.

'Ha! That idiot even used his real name.'

Back in their familiar stomping ground, the coolness between them had started to thaw, although Anthony's arms were still folded in front of his chest, as if to ward off further PDAs.

But Cordy was too elated to stay embarrassed.

'Now that's a result,' she crowed, jabbing at the display.

On the screen was not only the man's name – Mark Jones – but an address in Hackney.

'Wait a sec . . .'

With a few clicks, Anthony copied and pasted the details into another database. After a quick search he looked up at her. 'This is promising. He has history. We've been called out to domestics and he's done time for theft when he was a juvenile.'

He clicked to open the mug shot.

'Yep, that's our charmer,' Cordy said, rubbing her hands together. 'I can't believe this. So, what do we do now?'

Anthony didn't return her grin. 'Hunter. You know these are dangerous people, right?'

Cordy nodded, still looking at the mug shot. *Six foot two.* That sounded right.

'Under no circumstances should you go near this Mark character again.'

This caught her attention. 'I understand your concerns, but—'

Anthony interrupted her. 'I'm serious, Hunter. This isn't a game. In any case, you're getting ahead of yourself. This guy might not have anything to do with the case. All we know so far is that he's a nasty little shit with a thing for teenage girls. I mean, Mark is, what, one of the top ten most popular names in the country?'

'Top thirty,' Cordy admitted, 'for this age range. I looked it up. These days it's all Jaspers and Barneys.'

'See!'

'Fine,' she said, 'there are a lot of Marks. But how many paedophiles are called Mark and live in East London? You've got to admit that that's a smaller group. I could probably do a statistical analysis, in fact . . .'

'You're jumping to conclusions.' Anthony ran a hand through his thick, dark hair. Cordy noticed a sprinkling of grey at the temples. 'It's not a crime to flirt with an underage girl over the Internet. And anyway, statistics show that "teenophiles" rarely go for younger children. Just because this Mark's a sleazy bastard doesn't mean he's got a load of kids locked in his cellar. If it did, it'd be a pretty scary world we're living in.'

'It *is* a pretty scary world,' she retorted, remembering Alice's empty stare.

Anthony's voice softened. 'Look, I'm worried about you. Seems like you're too close to this case. You're letting it get personal.'

For the first time, Cordy regretted opening up to him. 'DeLuca, all that stuff I told you about is ancient history. It has nothing to do with Big Mark and Alice and . . .'

He looked sceptical, but changed tack. 'If you say so. But you think he might have seen you, right?'

'I don't know; it's just—'

'Well, then you might be compromised,' he pointed out. 'We can't take any chances on a case like this. And then there's your safety to think of.'

She shrugged.

'I'll tell you what we'll do. We'll get Reynolds to apologise for standing Mark up and see if we can get anything more out of the messages he sends her. Don't worry, I'll tell her it was all my idea. She'll be cool with it. She's a good girl.'

Cordy felt an irrational flash of irritation. 'I thought you said we should keep this to ourselves?'

'Well, I just don't want you getting chucked off the case, which is what'll happen the minute the chief finds out,' Anthony explained. 'But Reynolds can keep her mouth shut. In fact, I've got a few mates in uniform who might be able to help us with a bit of background. See who talked to this Mark character last time they were called out.'

'See if they noticed a cellar full of children?'

Anthony laughed grimly. 'That sort of thing.'

He glanced at his watch.

'Shit, I'm supposed to be in a meeting. Are you OK to shut down this computer?'

'No problem.' She opened her mouth to say something more, but then shut it again. She'd already taken up too much of his time.

'Oh, and in case I forget to say it, nice amateur sleuthing,' he said as he strode out through the door, with a smile that made her feel a little less like an idiot. 'But try not to get yourself into any more adventures this afternoon.'

'I'll do my best,' she said, but he was already gone.

★   ★   ★

A couple of hours later, Cordy was getting ready to leave for the night when Bob stopped her.

He cleared his throat. 'Sorry, love, I was wondering if you had plans for dinner tonight?'

From the corner Tammy laughed. 'I think you're a bit old for her, Casanova.'

Bob gave her look. 'Don't be getting jealous now, little Missy. There's plenty of me to go round.'

'You can say that again,' Tammy deadpanned.

This time he ignored her. 'What I meant was, if you don't have plans you should come have tea with me and the wife. You can tell just by looking at me that she's a good cook.' He gave his beer-belly a rub and lowered his voice. 'Seems to me like maybe we haven't had the best sort of start, but I'm sure we can fix that.'

'Did someone put you up to this, by any chance?'

Bob looked awkward. 'I suppose the chief might have mentioned something . . .'

Cordy laughed. 'Well, that's really very kind of you.'

'But you've probably got plans already?'

She hesitated. She didn't want to reject Bob's peace offering, but there was so much going on in her head that the idea of making small talk over meat and two veg sounded hellish.

'Something like that. But another time would be lovely.'

Bob nodded. 'Fair enough.' He raised his voice. 'Maybe next time I might invite young Reynolds too. Double the eye-candy.'

'What about your wife?' Tammy called.

'Have you met Jean?' he asked. 'Because "eye-candy" is not the phrase that immediately springs to mind. "Battle-axe", maybe . . .'

Cordy left them to their banter and slipped out of the door. As she passed Fiona's office she heard Anthony's deep, measured voice and was gripped with a brief, childish fear that he was telling on her.

Get a grip, Hunter, she told herself as she waited for the lift. *Get a fucking grip.*

Chapter 23

clewis: You all right?

It's been a while.

spurs101:   yeah guess so

hope ur not caught up in that site I was on about

clewis: Why's that?

spurs101:   cos looks like shit is hitting the fan

their putting a lot of resources into it

clewis: Are you fucking kidding me?????

spurs101:   calm down

clewis: Look, we had a deal.

If I go down, you go down. I'm not kidding.

You know what they do to people like us in jail?

Because if you don't I can explain in graphic detail.

spurs101:   what are you on about jail for?

clewis: Because this shit is serious

And we're in it up to our necks

spurs101:   well sorry but I cant help you anymore

clewis: Both of us

spurs101:   ive got enough to do to watch my own back

what do you expect if people cant take reasonable precautions???

don't you think it'd be safer to drop contact for a bit

just for a while

clewis: Safer for who?

spurs101:   for everyone

clewis: LOL LOL LOL

spurs101:   what???

clewis: You'd like that wouldn't you? Just sweep it all
              under the carpet?

spurs101:   thats not what Im saying

clewis: Well, whatever you're saying, I want you to
              picture everyone's faces when they find out
              what you're really like.
              Can you do that for me?

Chapter 24

There had been a three-car pile-up on her road into work this morning, and even when the traffic was moving again, the rubberneckers had made the going slow. By the time Cordelia got into the office it was quarter past nine, and the team meeting had already started. Fiona glanced up as she walked in.

'We were wondering where you were. Grab a seat.'

Cordy murmured an apology and took the chair next to Tammy. Looking around, she sensed a buzz of excitement in the room. Everyone's movements were sharper and cleaner than normal, from the way Bob cleared his throat to the way Fiona ticked off the bullet points on her sheet.

Anthony looked up and gave her the briefest of smiles as she put her jacket on the back of the chair and hurried to get out her notebook.

'And now that Dr Hunter's here, we can take a proper look at this. Tammy, can you pass these round?'

'Right you are.'

The young officer laid out the pages blank side up as if she were handing out a test.

'So can we take a gander then?' Bob asked. 'Or is this some sort of psychic challenge?'

'Turn them over,' Fiona said curtly, 'and take a good look. This is our first confirmed image of the guy we reckon is the ringleader.'

There was a whir of paper as they all flipped the sheet over. Cordy was so desperate to know what was on the other side that it took her a few minutes to process what she was look-ing at. The distorting effect of the blown-up picture didn't help, making the familiar strange and uncanny. Gradually the pixels unjumbled themselves. An ear. A patch of grey-ing stubble. Straight brown hair, long enough to touch the collar.

It was only when she felt a surge of disappointment that she realised how much she'd been counting on seeing a picture of Mark in her hands. But the hair was too long, the skin too smooth. This fragment of a stranger told her nothing. A white male, anywhere from thirty to sixty. He could be anyone.

She looked up, but Anthony was still staring at the image, his brow furrowed. No one else seemed to share Cordy's dejection.

'About bloody time,' Bob said. 'Now we're finally getting somewhere.'

'They're getting sloppy,' Tammy chimed in. 'They've always covered their heads before.'

'Well, this is taken from the middle of the clip.' She looked down on her notes. 'Most of the screen time is taken up with an oral sex act.'

'So he's probably a bit distracted,' Bob put in.

Cordy shot him a warning look.

'But yes, it's a good sign,' Fiona continued. 'I was worried that they might have caught on to the fact that we used their password, but so far there's no evidence of that. They're care-ful, sure, but they'll slip up again. They always do.'

'You've run the image through the Image Recognition Database, right?' Anthony asked.

'Tech boys are doing the IRD check now,' Fiona confirmed. 'They should have results for us any minute. I know it's just a partial, but remember what happened with the Highgate case? If someone's spotted this guy before, we could be in a position to get a positive ID by the end of the day.'

Tammy put her hand up for a high-five, but Fiona either didn't see or chose to ignore it.

'Let's not count our chickens,' Bob muttered.

'What are the other images?' Cordy asked, pointing to another pile under Fiona's photo.

'Ah,' the detective chief superintendent said, 'I'm not sure how useful this will be. But in our initial meeting you said to look out for scars, and this one's a beauty. Here, take a look.'

Cordy reached for hers, and then stared wordlessly at the picture in her hands. Like the last one it was heavily pixellated, but the content was clear. Alice, her lank hair covering her face, was stroking her own arm. Beneath her pale fingers was an angry red scar, the only bright spot of colour in the photo.

'What you're looking at is another screen-grab from the broadcast that went out at ten o'clock last night. From the end this time,' Fiona said. 'The night shift have the whole clip for us to watch, but this is another of their edited highlights.'

'You have this in a better resolution?' Cordy asked, still staring at the photo.

'Obviously the perp is our priority at the minute but, yes, we'll try and get a better version of this too. It looks almost like a brand to me,' Fiona said, tracing the distinctive lines of the scars. 'But anyway, I thought it'd be useful for your psychological profiling. What does this kind of physical abuse tell us about the type of men we're dealing with? That sort of thing.'

'Do we really need more evidence that they're sick bastards?' Bob put in.

Cordy stopped him with a frown. 'From what we've seen, these guys are quite comfortable with causing the children pain, but it's always functional or specifically sexual. So hair-pulling, physical restraint, slapping, violent penetration – that all fits – as well as the full range of passive and active neglect. But we've seen no evidence of textbook sadism or violent fetishes.'

Anthony nodded. 'Cordelia's right. And we haven't seen any knives used. Though of course, that could have been a special request.'

Cordy stood up abruptly. 'If it's all right, I'm going to go to the tech room and see if they can get a better version of this image. I think it could be important.'

Fiona shrugged. 'Well, this is what you're hired for. Try Mick – he can talk almost like a normal person. He's the one with the white-boy afro. Let me know if you run into any problems.'

Upstairs in the tech suite, it was easy enough to spot which one was Mick. His sandy-coloured hair curled out in a mad frizz that bobbed about in time to some unheard music. As Cordy got closer, she felt the rumble of bass escaping from his over-sized Bose headphones.

He jumped when she tapped him on the shoulder.

'I'm busy,' he muttered.

'Mick, is it? Cordelia Hunter.' She put out a hand. 'I'm working with the ECPU.'

He sighed heavily and swivelled round to face her. But once he'd had a chance to give Cordy a quick once-over, his whole demeanour changed.

'Erm, sorry 'bout that,' he said, whipping off the headphones, leaping up to his feet and wiping his hands on his jeans before taking hers. He was tall and skinny, with a prominent nose and a couple of days' stubble on his jawline. 'Jeremy Micklethwaite. But, umm, Mick is fine. You must be new?'

'I'm temporary,' Cordy said. 'But I'm assigned to Detective Chief Superintendent Andrews' team and she said you'd be able to help. Can you do anything to make this clearer?' She handed him the picture of Alice. 'It's saved on the system. The file address is written on the back.'

'Sure. But I'll need your department's password to access that drive.' He gestured brusquely. 'Take my chair; it'll only take a few minutes.'

'I can go get another one.'

'No, it's fine. I don't mind doing it standing up,' Mick said, then blushed to the roots of his hair and turned away.

Cordy suppressed a grin. He was even more socially awkward than she was.

Mick made a big show of turning away while she was typing in the password for him.

'It's probably one of their dog's names or something,' he grumbled. 'I keep on sending round emails about how to create secure passwords, but it's not like anyone seems to take any notice.'

Cordy kept quiet. The password was in fact ECPU1 ('nice and easy to remember,' Tammy had told her).

'There. I'm in.'

'Just scooch over a sec.'

Because of his height, Mick had to bend almost in half to work on the computer.

'Are you sure you don't want the seat?'

'I'm fine,' he muttered. 'Just give me a second.'

Cordy watched as he opened the file in a multimedia programme and set about separating out the layers and refining the image.

'It's the arm I really want to see. Can you focus in on that?'

'On the scar you mean? The one that looks like—'

Cordy spun round to look at him. 'Go on! I'm not being crazy. It looks like a symbol or something, doesn't it?'

'I was going to say that it looked like it was infected. Nasty. I managed to hammer a nail into my hand a couple of years back and it went like that.' He zoomed in and showed the discolouring around the scar's edges. 'Hope she's getting some antibiotics.'

'Unlikely,' Cordy said, sinking back into her chair. 'I don't think her wellbeing is their top priority.'

Mick frowned. 'No offence, but the stuff you lot are working on – the stuff with kids – is really fucked up. And I seem to get assigned more than my fair share.'

'It's definitely fucked up, but someone's got to work on it.' Cordy turned back to the screen. 'So you've saved the hi-res version in the folder? Could you also print me out a copy? Our high-definition printer downstairs is on the blink.'

'Whatever you want.'

After a few clicks of the mouse he straightened up. A printer whirred into life behind them.

'Great. Well, I'll let you get on with your other work,' she said, standing up. She didn't miss the surreptitious glance he gave her legs as she smoothed down her skirt.

Mick gave the print-out a once-over before handing it to her.

'You might be right, you know,' he said. 'The symbol thing. The shape does look familiar, but' – he thrust it at her – 'I couldn't say where from.'

'Yeah, I can't quite place it. It's annoying.' She shrugged. 'But someone will recognise it.'

Downstairs the atmosphere was decidedly more casual than when she'd left. Fiona was back in her office and the other three were cross-referencing a long list of dates and names.

'Any luck?' Tammy asked. 'How's Mick doing?'

Anthony cracked a smile. 'She's always going up there and terrorising the poor boy.'

'Oh, he loves it really.'

'Only because of that time you dressed as Princess Leia and turned up at his Halloween party.'

Bob winked. 'Was that a light saber in his pocket, or was he just pleased to see you?'

Tammy groaned. 'I walked right into that one.'

Ignoring the banter, Cordy stuck the picture of Alice's arm up on the whiteboard. 'Sorry I haven't made copies yet. But would you all mind taking a look at this?'

'It'll be useful when we come to court,' Tammy commented. 'Juries are tougher when they get to see physical evidence of brutality.'

'If it even gets that far,' Bob muttered.

'No luck with the database search?' Cordy asked.

'Well, we scanned in the partial image we had, and we got quite a few likely matches. Problem is, they're all unsolved cases – or, at least, dead-end leads,' Anthony explained. 'Most of the matches come from DVDs we seized from an American guy coming back from Bangkok. But he just claimed to have bought them in a market there.'

'So at least we know the suspect's been in Thailand.'

'Yeah, him and every other perv who can get his hands on a couple of hundred quid,' Bob said. 'It's cheaper than the Costa del Sol these days. And a lot easier access to, err, prostituted children.'

And they say you can't teach an old dog new tricks, Cordy thought, as she saw him casting about for the correct term.

Anthony shrugged. 'He's right. We can put a request in for the DVD, but there's no guarantee that it'll show any more of his face than we've already got.'

'Well, we know now that he's a prolific paedophile,' Cordy said. 'With a certain amount of disposable income.'

'And that's about all we know,' Bob said glumly.

'But back to this scar . . .'

Bob gave it a cursory glance.

'What about it?'

'Well, I have a theory.' She cleared her throat. 'It looks familiar, doesn't it?'

There were shrugs all round.

'If you look at it long enough,' Anthony said gently, 'it sort of does. But isn't that the same with lots of things?'

'My cousin found an image of Jesus at the bottom of his coffee cup,' Tammy pointed out. 'He tried to get a picture of it in the papers, but apparently they get quite a lot of that sort of thing.'

Bob laughed. 'Sounds like brains run in the family.'

Cordy struggled to keep her temper. 'So my theory is this: if Alice is trying to get out another message it must be significant somehow. And if we can just work out what it means . . .'

'So you think she scarred herself? Like self-harm?' Anthony asked. 'Well, we've seen plenty of that before.'

'Yes and no. I mean that the scar itself might be a clue.'

Bob pushed the paper away without another glance. 'Look, love, I don't think anyone's in the mood for playing Miss Marple right now. Go Google Image it or something. And then maybe you can get us all a cup of tea. I think it's your turn.'

Anthony stood up. 'I'll get them.'

As he passed by her, Cordelia asked quietly, 'Any progress with Mark?'

He stopped, and pretended to look at the print-out. 'Reynolds is chatting to him, but nothing concrete so far. Let's have a catch-up tomorrow.'

'And the scar . . .'

But he was gone.

Chapter 25

We are supposed to be sleeping now and the other kids are and they look different when they sleep. When their eyes are closed it's easier to think that we are on a sleepover or a school trip except if we were boys would be in different rooms because that's the rule. If I met Lolly in the playground I'd give her a friendship bracelet because she doesn't have any because the other girls are jealous that the boys like her. My friendship bracelets are still at home. I have six. Two from Jemma Swanton, and one each from Amber, Heather and Poppy, as well as that one from Kayla who I'm not friends with any more but the bracelet's still pretty so I keep it. They've all got them from me too. You are never supposed to take them off as it's bad luck but Mummy said that was just superstition and I didn't want to lose them, did I? If they're still at home I didn't lose them, although I don't have them now.

If I met Kurt he'd be with his mummy and they'd be eating number 99 ice creams because he said that was his favourite thing. My daddy says that it's a waste of money and that it'd be cheaper just to buy a whole flake and stick it in, and then you'd have more chocolate and more money but we never did that in the end.

When I am rescued I will sneak back in and help them escape. Lolly has long legs so she'll be OK, but maybe I'll put Kurt on my back because he's only little and he'll have to cling on like a little monkey while I climb the walls to the roof where there'll be a helicopter. They will be really happy with me and buy me things and probably make me friendship bracelets too, or at least Lolly will. Maybe Kurt's mummy will make one for him to give to me. She will be really happy. Lolly says her mum is a fucking bitch, so she can live with me. Her daddy won't be allowed to come and find her. He's not her real daddy anyway. If he does my daddy will beat him up or maybe shoot him.

Kurt can come and visit us. His hair is soft, like a cat's. Very carefully I let it fall through my fingers like sand at a beach. The top of the sand is hot and you can fry eggs in it but underneath it's cool and wet. But I'm not careful enough with Kurt's hair because he wakes up and is scared like I'm going to hit him and then he hits me and calls me a stupid slag. I try to say sorry but he turns over and curls up again like a woodlouse. I didn't mean to wake him up. He didn't hit me hard.

I go back to my messages.

Chapter 26

Cordelia Hunter had had enough of waiting around for leads that didn't lead anywhere.

If they fire me, they fire me, she thought grimly, looking around for a good hiding place. *But at least I'll know I actually did something. Anything rather than sitting around on my arse and waiting for the case to miraculously solve itself or for the perps to have a sudden crisis of conscience and turn themselves in. Because, at the minute, that's looking like our only way of getting those kids out of there anytime soon.*

A middle-aged woman with a terrier who was passing in the opposite direction did a double take, and Cordy realised that she'd been muttering to herself. With an effort, she pasted on a bland smile and tried to figure out how best to blend into the background.

Her object was to see without being seen.

Over the last few days, Cordy had spent hours trawling the Internet for anything that looked like Alice's scar. The problem was that she didn't really know what she was looking for, and by the time she caught herself checking out hieroglyphics and Chinese kanji, Cordy knew she was really scraping the barrel. The others weren't much use either. Anthony was as charming as ever, but since the incident in the café it had been impossible to get him on his own. They never did have that catch-up about Mark, and she didn't like to push in case he thought she was using it as an excuse to spend time with him. The thought made her stomach clench in embarrassment.

What was she, twelve? Why couldn't she be friends with an attractive man – an attractive married man – without making everything awkward?

It's not like she'd ever mess around with someone else's bloke. That just wasn't her style. Surely he could see that?

To make matters worse, Tammy was always there, hanging on his every word and, although Anthony insisted she was trustworthy, Cordy got the distinct impression that the younger woman was more than a little sceptical of her methods.

'I've got a freckle you might want to take a look at,' she announced to the team one day. 'It just looks, very, you know, *significant.* Like it might have a *secret meaning.*'

Cordy ignored the first few digs, but when Tammy started humming nursery rhymes under her breath she snapped. 'Look, I'm sorry for whatever I did that put your nose out of joint. But seriously, grow up. We're all just trying to solve the case here.'

Tammy spun around in her chair. 'Is that supposed to be an apology? You logged onto my computer without permission. You used my aliases. Do you know how hard I've worked building those up?'

'DeLuca told you then?'

'Of course he told me.'

'Yeah. OK. I am sorry, actually,' Cordy mumbled. 'You're right. I shouldn't have gone behind your back like that.'

Tammy muttered that it was fine, but Cordy noticed that she'd taken down the Post-it note with her passwords on.

Generally, team morale was low. It didn't help that Bob's gloomy predictions about the Thai DVD had all come true. Their US counterparts, who'd impounded the film, were slow to get back to them. When they finally did, they explained the DVD had somehow been filed in the wrong place. When the file finally arrived, Fiona had despatched a team to pick it up. But when they opened it they found that it was a montage of dozens of different clips, some grainy and amateurish, some given a lurid sort of professionalism by bright lighting, a script of sorts and steadier camerawork. Although a couple of the girls and boys were clearly underage, with most it was hard to tell. Were they adolescents made old before their time or young adults who'd worked out that they could get more money passing for minors?

'That's why images of Asian kids are generally less valuable to European paedophiles,' Fiona had said grimly. 'Less guarantee of authenticity.'

It had been hard at first to pick their suspect out of the procession of faceless white men. When they did, it was only to discover that he had only a few minutes of screen-time performing sex acts on a skinny young boy, and this time even less of his face was on show.

'Let's run the others through the database too,' the chief had said. 'See what comes up.'

'But there's no evidence that they were filmed in the same place or time. There could be no connection whatsoever between the men,' Cordy had pointed out.

'If you've got any better ideas,' Fiona had said coldly, 'I'd be very pleased to hear them.'

No you wouldn't, Cordelia thought now, bracing her back against the stone wall next to the entrance of the park. *I can guarantee that you'd rather be in the dark about this one.*

It was early morning and the grass was still dewy from the night before. Apart from a couple of dog-walkers and a few Lycra-clad joggers, she had the park to herself. Late last night, when most of the lights were off in the houses, Cordy had scouted out the neighbourhood. The best view of Mark's semi would be from the little corner shop at the end of his street but, given her uneasy encounter with him last time, Cordy was determined to put safety first. The park was a much better bet. The road in front was busy with city commuters heading for the Tube and groups of kids making their way to the school round the corner. Cordy tried not to think too hard about the implications of Mark having a couple of hundred schoolgirls on his doorstep.

For the want of a better idea, Cordy was back in her tracksuit and T-shirt, having hidden her bike round the corner. If anyone had been watching too closely, they might have wondered why she had spent the last hour or so standing in the same spot doing stretches, but now she'd stopped speaking under her breath, no one gave her a second glance.

The idea of staking out Mark's house had been bubbling away ever since she and Anthony had got his address off the database. At first Cordy had dismissed it as too danger-ous – after all, her amateurish sleuthing might already have been noticed. But as the days went by without fresh leads, she became more and more determined to find out as much as she could – either to put Mark in the frame, or at least elimi-nate him from their inquiries.

Now she wished she'd told someone – Anthony, maybe – what she was planning. He might have been able to give her some ideas of what to look for. *Or he might have just talked you out of it.*

It was just after eight in the morning and the neighbour-hood was waking up. Cars that had been parked for the night on the stretch of road outside the park were being driven away, one by one. Cordy would have preferred them to stay there – a protective barrier between her and him.

She looked across the road at Mark's house. Nothing. Litter had blown into the front yard and the door could do with a lick of paint, but apart from that it looked pretty much like every house in the street. Respectable. Private.

Nine o'clock. Still nothing.

Always good to be limber, Cordy thought wryly, reaching down for the umpteenth hamstring stretch. *If he doesn't get up soon, maybe I'll start on the yoga.* Given the quantity of litter and dog shit around her feet, though, the idea wasn't very appealing.

Half an hour later, there were signs of life. A light went on in the left-hand upstairs window. A curtain pulled open, revealing a glimpse of a man in boxer shorts. A side window opened to let out a rush of steam.

Cordy felt a stab of excitement mingled with fear. It was strange to feel that the tables had turned, and that – for that morning at least – the predator had turned prey. *And vice versa.*

The thought shocked her a little. Certainly there was some-thing voyeuristic about lurking in a park and spying on a stranger, but it was in a good cause, wasn't it? Cordy shook herself. This wasn't the right time to be having an ethical crisis. Not when Mark was opening the door and stepping outside.

Adrenaline pumping, Cordy slunk along the wall out of sight. She pushed herself into the ivy, flattening her body as much as she could. Once safely tucked away, she forced herself to count to twenty before letting herself have another look. It took forever – like a nightmare version of hide and seek – but when she looked up Mark was gone.

Without giving herself time to think about what she was doing, Cordy sprinted out of the park and across the street. After quickly checking that all the lights were off – *why hadn't she double-checked whether he lived alone?*, she looked around desperately for anything that might link Mark to the pay-per-view site, or tell her where the children might be hidden. For a mad second she considered scaling the drainpipe and climb-ing in the bathroom window, but then she checked herself. For all she knew, Alice and the others could be inside the house – in the cellar, the attic, anywhere. If they were being left unguarded, there could well be booby-traps. There was just no way she could jeopardise their safety like that.

Looking around, Cordy did a split-second risk assessment. She was standing in the front garden, partially obscured by a scraggy tree that leaned in at an angle from the house next door. So far the people passing on the street hadn't given her a second glance, but the longer she stayed there, the more likely it was that a curtain-twitching neighbour would get suspicious.

A quick glance both ways down the road told her that Mark was still nowhere in sight.

I guess that's something.

Taking out her camera she took a few snaps through the window into the front room. This wasn't one of the more gentrified Hackney neighbourhoods, but it was clear that Mark was doing all right for himself. A single leather recliner was set up next to one of the biggest flat-screen TVs she had ever seen. A games console sprawled over the floor. She shaded her eyes and leaned closer to the glass. No. As far as she could see, there were no family portraits on the mantelpiece.

Looks like a bachelor pad, Cordy thought. But that didn't stop her straining her ears for the sound of a footstep or the flush of a toilet from inside.

At first it looked as if she'd have to go the long way round to get to the back yard, but then she noticed an alley almost hidden behind a pile of rubbish bags.

A lover's lane, Cordy thought, trying not to inhale as she clambered over the bags, which were seeping a foul-smelling liquid out onto the concrete below. She winced as she slipped, smashing something inside the nearest rubbish sack.

Cordy froze. *Damn Mark. Hadn't he heard of recycling?*

Thankfully, no one seemed to notice, but Cordy glanced down at her watch, determined to be out of there in the next ten minutes, just in case a local busybody had thought to call the police. *Because it'd be a hell of a lot of fun explaining what I was doing sneaking around a suspect's house, without an official search warrant.* Frowning, she pushed the thought away. *Concentrate, Hunter. You're here now.*

The alley was littered with fag butts and a load of takeaway menus that some kid must have got fed up of posting through letterboxes. On the right side was a grimy brick wall, about six feet high, carved out with initials and obscenities. On the left side was Mark's house, but Cordy was disappointed to find that there weren't any windows at ground level. Looking up, she spotted a window on the first floor. But it was the curtains that really caught her eye: cartoonish flowers in purple and yellow, completely at odds with the sleek bachelor pad décor downstairs.

Shit, that's a kid's room. A little girl's room. I've got to see inside.

Suddenly grateful for her punishing push-up drills, Cordy hoisted herself up onto the brick wall opposite Mark's house, and crouched there a second to get her breath back. The alley was only a few feet wide, so, when she eased herself into a standing position, forcing herself not to look down, she had a direct view right into the window. She was also completely visible from the street, but she tried not to think about that too much.

Those flowery curtains were only half drawn, so inside the room was shrouded in gloom. A quick glance told her the bed was empty. Peering in, Cordy felt a growing sense of dread. She was right: it was a little girl's room, complete with posters of dolphins and a lipstick-pink duvet set. But it was so tidy. Unnaturally tidy. *What has he done with her?* was her first panicked thought, and she methodically scanned each section of the room, as if expecting to see a child-sized corpse poking out from under the bed.

Keep it together, Hunter.

Mind on the case.

And then she spotted it. On the dresser next to the window-sill was a photo – a family shot of a woman, a man and a smiling girl in a heart-shaped plastic frame. Keeping one arm out for balance she angled her body closer for a better look. Although she was expecting it, it still made her flesh creep to see that the man was Mark. He was even wearing the same leather jacket. The woman had mousy-blonde hair, tired eyes and heavy curves. For a split second, Cordy's eyes refused to look any further. Then her gaze slid down the photo.

For a breathless moment, Cordy thought the girl might be Alice. The two faces swam together in her mind. But a second glance told her they looked nothing alike. This girl was older. Blonde. The realisation was both a relief and a bitter disappointment.

Then she remembered the other girl – the older girl from the clips. *Lolita.*

It's him. She didn't know whether to punch the air or throw up. *That's her. It's him. I'm looking into their house.*

The realisation made her dizzy, and she had to squeeze her eyes shut and crouch down on the wall to regain her balance. When she opened them up again her nausea had been replaced with an icy resolve.

That bastard's going down.

She eased herself up to standing again. There was a digital alarm clock by the bed, and when Cordy looked at it she realised that it had been about ten minutes since she left the park. It felt like seconds and also years. The world always slowed down for her in dangerous situations.

Time to get out of here.

Getting out her camera, she forced her hand steady and took a series of images of the family photo, on the highest res setting.

She was just checking there was nothing she'd missed when a sound from the road stopped her in her tracks.

Probably nothing.

This time it was unmistakeable.

Shit, it's the gate! I've got to get out of here.

Flattening herself along the top of the wall, she saw Mark in the front garden with a paper under his arm.

Fuck. It's too late. He's going to find me and he's going to kill me.

Panicked, she looked around the alley for somewhere to hide. But the thought of crouching behind the dustbins while he paced around out front . . .

Maybe I should just confront him? After all, I know I can handle myself.

But the thought of jeopardising the case made her ease out of fighting stance.

No. Just get out of here. Now.

She was waiting for the sound of the key in the lock, but instead she heard him pause.

Shit. I didn't move the rubbish bags back into place. And if he happens to look up . . .

Cursing her own foolhardiness, Cordy slipped down off the wall and assessed her options. She could wait until he went inside and then just dash out the front, hoping he didn't happen to be looking outside. Or else try to get out the back way, and loop back round to the park. Yes, that would be safer – obviously 'safer' being a relative term here.

Finally she heard Mark go inside and shut the door. That was her signal to move. Already her T-shirt was dark with sweat. Downstairs the TV was turned on high, and Cordy told herself that it'd cover the sound of her escape. Despite the solid walls in between her and Mark, it still felt like the thudding of her heart would give her away any second.

Cordy crept along the alley, looking for some way out: a gate into a garden, anything. She swore under her breath as she realised that the end of the alley was blocked off by a chain-link fence. It looked like the house that backed onto Mark's was being renovated, and they must have secured the area around it. Backing up, she realised she had two options: make a dash out through the front, or heave herself over the wall and take her chances with whatever was on the other side. Berating herself for not having assessed her surroundings more thoroughly, she pulled herself back onto the wall and looked out in the other direction.

Thank God. There was a car park on the other side – she wouldn't raise the alarm by jumping down into some old biddy's rose bushes. But this time the dismount didn't go so smoothly. Her hands were slick with sweat and she didn't have time to get her body in position before she began slipping down. Her hands and feet clawed for purchase as the bricks scraped the skin off her arms and legs. She landed with a yelp of pain on a pile of sharp rubble.

When Cordy struggled to her feet she was covered in grime. Gingerly she flexed her wrists and ankles. Nothing broken. She had a sudden impulse to laugh out loud – she must look ridiculous. *Bob was right, Nancy-bloody-Drew.* But the sound died in her throat when she looked up and saw Mark staring at her from the kitchen window.

'What the fuck? Wait there, you crazy bitch, and I'll . . .'

Cordy didn't wait to hear the end of the sentence. Ignoring the cuts and bruises she limped off towards the park. She had to get to her bike before he got to her.

Seconds later she heard the sound of a door slamming shut. Without looking back she speeded up, cursing herself for having locked the bike up. Her breath was coming out in ragged gasps as she pushed her aching body to its limits. She could hear footsteps now. He wasn't far behind her.

'Where are you, you stupid interfering bitch? Did Tina send you to spy on me?' he shouted. 'You can tell that fat slag that she's not getting a penny from me.'

It seemed to take forever to get the bike upright and wrench the lock off. By the time Cordy was sitting on top of it she could hear Mark round the corner and heard the footsteps stop as he spotted her. With fumbling fingers she jammed the helmet on her head.

She couldn't look. It was years since she'd felt this kind of terror. It took every ounce of willpower not to freeze where she was. Instead she flicked the ignition and the engine growled to life.

'It's you.'

Now she had to look, because she would have to ride past him to get out of the park. She pushed the visor down and fought the urge to cry.

'You're not Tina's mate. So who the hell are you? Hey, I'm talking to you.'

He stood, barefoot, blocking her path. His face was blotchy with anger.

'You police?' He narrowed his eyes, and then laughed derisively. 'You're never police.'

Not knowing what else to do, Cordy drove straight for him. He stared her down, only stepped out of her path at the last minute.

'Oy!' he shouted after her. 'I'll find out who you are. Don't think I won't find out who you are. And when I do . . .'

As she rounded the corner his voice was lost on the wind.

Cordy was still shaking when she arrived back home. She put her camera down carefully on her coffee table then got in the shower with all her clothes on and washed off the acrid sweat and the smell of the dirty alley. Even when she had stripped off her sodden clothes, dried off and wrapped herself in a thick dressing gown, she couldn't stop shivering.

Chapter 27

clewis: You heard what happened?

spurs101:   what?

clewis: Don't play the effing innocent with me

One of your lot's been sniffing around one of my mates

Too close for comfort

Much too close

spurs101:   nothing to do with me mate

who was it

clewis: Tall skinny bitch. Long hair.

spurs101:   oh shit

clewis: You know her then?

spurs101:   maybe

clewis: Right

Enough fucking about

We need details

Name

Home phone

Mobile

Email address. All of them.

spurs101:   what if I don't have all that

clewis: Don't worry, we'll find the rest.

We need to make that bitch understand that she can't afford to mess with us.

Chapter 28

When Cordy woke up the next morning it took her a couple of beats to remember why her body still felt flooded with adrenaline.

Tentatively, she wiggled her fingers on her left hand and then her right, and then both sets of toes. Then she traced her fingers over her ribcage, feeling for any tenderness. It was a routine she hadn't had to do in over a decade, but her hands knew the score.

There were a few bruises and lacerations from her fall off the wall – including a small gash down the side of her face – but nothing too desperate.

Just as well. Even now, she hated submitting to medical treatment, and having to come up with a cover story would have brought back too many bad memories. It was the mingled pity and discomfort on the nurses' faces that always used to get to her. She remembered desperately wanting them to challenge her version of events – the neighbourhood kid who got a bit rough sometimes, the fight at school, the accident in gym class – and at the same time needing to believe that everything was right as rain and they'd get her fixed up in no time.

Her thoughts were interrupted by the peal of her alarm: six thirty. After the quick once-over she eased herself into a sitting position and looked around. Her wet clothes were still dropped on the floor where she left them, and if it hadn't been for her aching limbs, Cordy would have jumped up and put them in the laundry basket. Disruption made her twitchy.

Easy does it, old girl. You can get them on the way back.

Standing under a pounding hot shower, Cordy felt her limbs start to loosen and a bubble of something like excitement form.

We've got him now. I can't wait to see the looks on their faces . . .

She winced as the water made contact with the abrasion on her cheek.

Next time you try to play the action hero, she told herself, *don't be so clumsy.*

Not that there'll be a next time.

A couple of hours later, Cordy was tapping her toes, cursing the lift for taking so long to get to the fifth floor at ECPU. Since she'd been feeling too fragile for her morning exercise routine, she'd had plenty of time to formulate a plan of action. The first step would, of course, be round-the-clock surveillance. From the video evidence they were amassing, it wouldn't take too long for Mark to lead them to the house. Unless the children were actually hidden in Mark's house somewhere. The attic. The basement.

They could have been there all the time. Listening to me scrabbling outside. Willing me to rescue them . . .

Cordy was so disturbed by the thought that the doors had already started closing before she realised that they were on her floor.

'Oh, sorry. That's me.'

Ignoring the grumbles, she stuck out her hand to stop the doors closing, and squeezed out into the corridor. She was a little early, but hoped the others would be around already. The camera felt weirdly heavy in her bag, and on the ride to work she'd been paranoid about dropping it or leaving it behind somewhere – sabotaging their best lead so far.

When she walked into the Ops Room Tammy's chair was empty, but both Bob and Anthony were already sitting around the table, scanning through the morning memo.

Anthony sprang up when he saw her. 'Jesus, did you cut yourself shaving or what?'

Cordy touched her face self-consciously. 'Oh, that. It's just a scratch.'

She resisted the urge to squirm as he gently held her chin and turned it to get a better look.

'You might want to have someone take a ganders at that,' Bob said, coming over to join them. 'What happened, love? Been scrapping in the playground?'

'Did someone do this to you?' Anthony asked sharply. 'You have to tell us.'

Cordy broke free from them both. 'Look, it's nothing, OK? Accidents happen. Just drop it.'

'You didn't crash your bike, did you?' Bob persisted. 'Seriously, love, that thing's a deathtrap.'

'Jesus, no. You're like a pair of mother hens, the two of you, fussing over me.'

She saw the two men exchange a look, and then slink back to the table.

'Thank you. Now I can breathe again.'

'By the way, where did you get to yesterday?' Bob asked. 'You weren't answering your phone.'

'We were worried about you,' Anthony added. When she didn't reply he patted the chair next to him. 'Fine. We don't have to get into it now. Sit down, and we'll catch you up.'

Bob tutted. 'Give her a minute. The poor girl's looking a bit peaky. Are you sure you don't want to go home?'

'I'm not going home,' Cordy growled.

'You do look a bit flushed,' Anthony said. 'Do you want a drink of water or something?'

'Really, I'm all right.' She reached into her bag. She couldn't wait any longer.

'You don't want a scar,' Bob said, 'not with a pretty face like yours.'

Cordy shook her head impatiently. 'Take a look at that,' she said, scrolling through her pictures and then plonking the camera down on the table in front of them. 'What do you reckon? Can we do anything with it?'

Anthony leaned in to take a closer look. 'What the . . . ?' He turned to Cordy, eyes steely. 'Where the hell did you get that from? Or don't I want to know?'

'Jesus. That's one of the kids from the site, isn't it?' Bob asked. 'What is this? You found a family photo?'

Cordy nodded. 'And this is one of our suspects. I've got the name, address, everything. Now I realise it'll take the chief a while to get extra detectives assigned to the case, so in the meantime I thought we could take shifts tailing him. DeLuca and I could—'

'What?'

Bob was looking at her as if she were mad.

'DeLuca and I could take the first one,' Cordy said, avoiding his eye. 'And meanwhile you and Reynolds can do a background check. Get a positive ID on the girl, for starters.'

Bob let out a mirthless laugh.

'Problem?' she snapped.

'The problem is,' he said slowly, 'that you've just fucked up our case. Congratulations. Paedos One, ECPU Nil.'

'What case?' Cordy said icily. 'Because from where I'm looking, we're just going around in circles. This is our guy,' she said, jabbing at the camera screen. 'Now we're actually getting somewhere.'

This time Bob didn't hold back. 'Sorry if it's not exciting like it is on the telly, *Dr Hunter*. But in the real world you need to build a proper case. You can't just make it up as you go along. What did you do? Sneak around and snap this through a window?'

Cordy crossed her arms over her chest but didn't say anything.

'Bloody hell. You did, didn't you?' He put his hands over his face. 'Are you insane? This isn't like being in the Famous Five! They'll laugh us out of court.'

She turned to Anthony for support, not sure how much to say, but he was shaking his head. 'I hate to say it, but he's got a point.'

'Too right I have. How the fuck did you . . . ?' Bob caught himself, and stared down at the table for a few beats. When he looked up, his face was less puce and his voice was calmer. 'Look, love, it's not just the investigation I'm thinking of. Those guys are dangerous.' He put a hand on her arm. 'I didn't mean to shout at you, but really, love, what were you thinking?'

She shook his hand off irritably. 'Of course they're dangerous. I thought that was why we were trying to arrest them.'

'We?' His expression hardened. 'Look, I thought the boss lady had explained this. You're a consultant on this case, not a trained detective. Any leads, you go to us. Any feelings in your water, you go to us.'

She was about to speak when Anthony cut her off.

'To be fair, she did come to me with this name after Reynolds hooked him a week or so ago. It didn't seem that strong a lead at the time . . .'

'Great,' Bob said. 'Everyone's in on it except me. In which case I won't feel bad about leaving you lot to explain it all to the chief.' He sighed, closing his eyes and rubbed his temples. 'So how exactly did you come into possession of that image, again, or don't I want to know?'

'And more importantly,' Anthony cut in, 'what are we going to say when the scumbag accuses us of casing out his property without a surveillance warrant?'

Cordy wanted to stamp her feet in frustration. 'Here,' she said, pushing the camera towards them, 'Mark Jones, Suspect number one; Lolita, Victim number one. Don't you two get it?'

This time it was Anthony who snapped. 'There's no need to be so patronising, Hunter. I told you not to interfere, and you ignored me.'

'Well, you didn't—'

But he wasn't listening. 'What you seem to forget is that Sampson and I do this for a living. Have you even thought about what'll happen to the kids if they realise we're onto them?'

'What about what they're doing to them now?' Cordelia took a deep breath and pointed to the photo. 'Look at her. We need to get her out. While there's still a child to rescue.'

'Have you listened to anything we've said?' Anthony asked, turning away from her. 'Have you listened to a single word?'

Cordy opened her mouth to protest, then shut it again. She was in the right, wasn't she? The ends justified the means. *Didn't they?*

No one spoke for a few long minutes.

Eventually Bob broke the silence. '*While there's still a child to rescue?*' he muttered.

Cordy shot him a sharp look.

'Jesus,' he muttered. 'Any minute now she'll want to play Good Cop, Bad Cop.'

Despite herself, Cordy's lips quivered into a smile, and she heard Anthony let out a hoarse laugh. Suddenly the tension seemed to seep out of the room.

As if sensing the change in mood, Bob turned to Anthony. 'Watch where you leave your handcuffs, mate. She's clearly into the old role-play.'

'Careful,' Anthony warned.

But Cordy wasn't taking the bait. She caught Anthony's eye, her face serious. 'Have I really jeopardised the investigation?'

Bob was the one who answered her. 'Ah, maybe we'll be able to fudge it somehow. It helps that you're a consultant, not one of us, so we can say it was you acting independently, if needs be. But like I said, there's no way I'm in the room when the chief hears about whatever shenanigans you've been up to.'

Anthony let out a puff of breath. 'We'd better go now, I guess. Let's hope she woke up in a good mood.'

Cordy rose to her feet and straightened her suit. 'If this had just been the warm-up act, then . . .'

'Who did you say this was again?' Bob said, pushing the picture towards her. 'Mark Jones?'

'That's him. February the fourth, 1978.'

He gave her a wink. 'Next birthday behind bars, eh?'

Cordy held up a pair of crossed fingers, and readied herself to meet Fiona's wrath.

Chapter 29

I don't have any granddads any more, but he looks like one from off the TV. His hair is grey and he's got a big belly like he's going to have a baby except it jiggles a bit like when Mummy's belly was full with my brother. You could see it moving when he kicked, and Dad said we've got the next Beckham in there and Mum said maybe his daughter was the next Beckham and he shouldn't be so sexist.

But he's the one I have to watch. The other two are nasty and stupid, like big bullies. When they pretend, their smiles don't reach their eyes and no one's fooled. With the old one you can forget and think he means it but then it's worse when you were his darling and sweetheart and sugarlips and now you're a stinking whore and he's hitting you so hard you can't see. Yesterday he gave Kurt a nosebleed when he said he didn't want to and then he made him anyway.

He watches me. I can't make messages when he's in the room. But now he's gone home and I can.

I used to use my fingernail but now I have found a proper nail, which is better for putting messages in the wood of the bunk. I thought there were two lots of sleeping sounds but I'm wrong because Lolly's head comes down from above and what am I doing she asks and I say nothing and please don't tell. But she says not to be so fucking stupid and give me that for a sec and I give her the nail and she leans over and writes something. She smiles when she's done as if it was something nice or clever but it's just his name with a heart around it. Mark. The heart is wobbly. I ask her why she did that when he hurts her and she says he does it because he loves her and I'm too young to understand. I ask if he loves me too and that girl last week but then she says I'm a jealous bitch and won't speak to me again, even when I say I'm sorry.

When she is asleep properly this time I scratch out the name so the heart is empty again.

Chapter 30

Once safely home, Cordy dropped her keys into the bowl on the hallway cabinet and went to check her face in the mirror. Carefully unpeeling one edge of the plaster she saw that the thin gash was already beginning to heal.

Lot of fuss about nothing.

As soon as she'd arrived at Jess's clinic for her regular midweek visit, the nurses had insisted on cleaning and dressing the scratch before letting her in to see her sister. Despite Cordy's protests, one called for a doctor to check her over. They didn't let her go until every last scratch on her body had been assessed and treated.

'Nothing serious,' the doctor said, eyeing her sternly. 'But you really should be at home resting. How do you expect your body to heal if you're gallivanting about the place?'

Conscious that Jess was upstairs waiting for her, Cordy found herself hurriedly promising that she'd take the next day off work just so they'd all leave her alone.

I don't shell out thirty-five grand a year to be treated like a child by the staff here, she thought, as she creaked up the stairs to her sister's floor, having grown tired of waiting for the lift. *Who the fuck do they think I am, Humpty Dumpty? Maybe if they spent more time worrying about the patients and less time sucking up to the relatives, Jess would be getting better by now.*

When Jess opened the door and saw Cordy, her eyes widened in alarm and she put both hands to her own face.

'What . . . did he . . . ?'

'Wait! No!' Cordy said firmly, grabbing her arm. 'Nothing like that!'

'But—'

'It's fine. We're fine,' she insisted, holding Jess's eyes, willing her to believe it. 'It's just a tiny scratch under there. *He* had nothing to do with it. Jess, I told you not to worry about that.'

Her sister was still rigid in the doorway, but some of the colour had returned to her cheeks. She pulled away roughly and crossed her arms across her chest. She started up that horrible slow rocking motion that always made her sister feel slightly sick.

'I'm sorry, I didn't . . .' Cordy shrugged helplessly, knowing there was nothing she could do when her sister was in this state. 'Sorry, I shouldn't have come.'

Jess didn't look at her. Instead she worried her half of the heart-shaped locket, turning it over and over in her thin fingers. 'You scared me.'

'I said I'm sorry.' Suddenly Cordy felt exhausted. Usually she was good at anticipating her sister's reactions, but today she'd been blindsided. With so much going on in the world outside, it was easy to forget that for Jess there was still just one enemy, one overriding threat to their safety. 'I was at kick-boxing practice and the bag swung back and caught me in the face. Silly really.' She forced a laugh. 'Good job I wasn't fighting a real opponent.'

Jess didn't say anything, but her rocking seemed to lessen in intensity.

Cordy grabbed at the chance to change the subject. 'Want to watch a film?' she said brightly. 'Something funny? I could do with a laugh today.'

Back home, she collapsed on the chair, worn out but fairly hopeful that she had calmed the worst of her sister's fears. She felt guilty about feeding her a line, but it was all for her own good.

I shouldn't have gone in till the cut had healed, she thought. *I should have made an excuse.* But then again, it had been good to see a friendly face. All in, it'd been a pretty tough day.

Fiona had not reacted well to news of Cordy 'going rogue', as Anthony put it. And the worst of it was that the official dressing-down had been postponed. Cordy didn't even know if she was still on the case. It felt as though she was waiting for the blade to fall.

Despite her protests, Anthony had insisted on going in first on his own. 'To soften her up a bit,' he said, with no discernible irony. To Cordy's surprise there had been no raised voices, only a grim murmur of voices. It would have been painful to overhear what was being said – but it was torture to stand outside, not knowing what was going on. The minutes ticked by, and she debated whether she should just knock on the door and be done with it. *But then ignoring Anthony's advice was what got me into the mess in the first place . . .*

Cordy jumped when the lift doors at the end of the corridor pinged open, and Tammy stepped out, still chatting on her mobile. She mouthed a 'hello' as she trotted past.

After what seemed like forever, Anthony had opened the door a crack.

'Hunter, the chief is in meetings for much of the day, so if you could pop by tomorrow morning, that'd be great.' Before she got a chance to reply, he carried on. 'And we all think you should go home and get some rest.'

'But I'm fine, and—'

'It's not a suggestion, Dr Hunter,' Fiona said, from inside the office.

Her tone left no room for argument.

Of course, with a head full of the case, rest had been the last thing on her mind, and she'd spent most of the day Googling Mark Jones. The common name made for slow progress.

When she typed 'Mark Jones, London' into Facebook's search engine, she came up with 400 entries, and even when she'd whittled it down to a handful of likely profiles, obscure pictures and tight security settings made it difficult to say for certain whether any of them were definitely his. However, with a bit of cross-referencing across different social networking sites, she managed to come up with some basic information about their suspect. She typed out a list of organisations the team could contact to find out more: his secondary school, a garage he used to work at, the local football team he used to be goalie for.

Even if they don't want to work with me any more, she thought grimly, *they might be able to do something with my leads*.

Cordy had got so caught up in putting together a profile on Mark that she hadn't had time to eat before she went to visit Jess. Now it was getting late and she couldn't be bothered to cook for herself. Grabbing a banana from the bowl on the kitchen cabinet, she rebooted her computer.

Might as well do another hour or so.

Part of her was still hoping to stumble across something so vital to the investigation that they'd overlook her rogue moment.

As usual, she did a quick scan of her J4C webmail. Her inbox was teeming with little red flags and the 'To Be Actioned' folder was bursting at the seams. There were three urgent emails from her boss alone.

Maybe it's just as well ECPU are probably kicking me out, Cordy thought, vowing to spend Saturday getting on top of her other commitments. *Otherwise Allyson might do the same.*

She quickly checked her Yahoo account. Since only a couple of old university friends and a few work contacts had her address, all she usually got was spam, but today amid the usual money scams and offers for herbal Viagra was an email from an address that looked kosher. A female name.

Vaguely familiar. Maybe a friend from Manchester who'd got married?

After a moment's hesitation she clicked it open.

I'm jerking off to a picture of you. Right now. Your hair is darker these days, but anyone could tell it was you. Do you think your colleagues might like to see it? Or the papers? See how seriously people take you then, you stupid bitch.

Jesus.

Cordy's throat filled with bile, which she struggled to choke down.

She scrolled down. That was it. No signature.

When Cordy typed up a hasty reply ('Who are you?') the email bounced back. The provider no longer had an account registered under that address.

How the hell did they find me?

She generally only gave out her J4C address or a Gmail one that she used for Internet shopping. It was one of the ways that she created a safe space for herself. And now that space had been violated.

The thought made her leap up and double-check the locks on the door. Her hand shaking, she put the chain on and did a round of the windows, switching every light on in every room to banish the shadows.

Only then did she return to the computer. The toxic email still filled the screen. There was a file attached to it, but Cordy couldn't make herself open it. She'd worked in this area long enough to assume that scanned-in images of her as a child were still making the rounds, but this was the first time she'd had the chance to find out for sure. The logical part of her brain tried to persuade her that it would be better to just open it and see, but then there'd be another image burned in her memory. She'd lived it: she didn't need to see it again. And there could be a virus or spyware . . .

No.

Hastily she deleted it, then clicked to empty the Trash folder.

Are you sure? the computer asked.

'Positive,' she said grimly.

Giving up on the idea of working, she changed out of her work clothes (she'd wanted everything to be normal for Jess) and pulled on a pair of shorts, an oversized T-shirt and trainers.

In the rest periods between her high-intensity intervals, she tried to think dispassionately about the email, imagining what conclusions she'd reach if she'd heard of it being sent to one of her J4C clients.

Was it from Mark? Of course the timing made it seem like that, but that could just be a coincidence. Apart from anything else, the word 'colleagues' didn't seem like something Mark would use to describe the police. *If he'd called them pigs, then maybe . . . Unless,* she thought with a shudder, *he's got his cronies involved.*

After the first few miles her body stopped complaining and found its natural rhythm. The endorphin hit helped her panic subside, and let her consider the other options.

In all likelihood, it was from some other pervert she'd clashed horns with in the past. The guy whose file-sharing site she'd been campaigning to close? Maybe. Or the church group leader who got put away because she encouraged his victim to speak out? Allyson had sent her a worrying report about prisoners' access to mobiles and Internet, even in high-security jails. She'd call her in the morning.

Despite her best efforts to keep her mind and body busy, Cordelia still found that in the vulnerable moments between wake and sleep the unwelcome memories took over and she was, once more, the girl in front of the camera. Naked. Split open. Humiliated. Lying in her own filth while he sweated on top of her and his friend leaned in for a close-up.

Chapter 31

Cordy reached out and switched off her alarm clock before it got a chance to ring out. For a few minutes she lay still, staring at the ceiling, gathering her energy for the day ahead. Despite her troubled night, her head was clear. She wasn't going to tell Anthony and the others about the email. They'd only use it as further proof that she shouldn't have gone after Mark herself and, besides, it didn't really pay to put it around that you were a victim of child abuse. Cordy had seen enough promising romances, friendships and career opportunities go sour to figure out that most people were only comfortable around her when she kept her mouth shut about her past.

And as an educated, middle-class white woman, Cordy knew, she got off lightly.

'It's infuriating,' she'd admitted to Allyson, not long after she'd started working at Justice4Children. 'Every time some psycho goes mad with a meat cleaver, the first thing that the newspapers report is that they were molested as a child. As if one thing necessarily leads to the other. And it's worse if there's a sexual aspect to the crime. I mean, you don't just assume that a rape victim is more likely to be a rapist, do you? So why is there this easy assumption that a victim of child abuse will become an abuser themselves?'

'You're preaching to the choir, love,' her boss had told her. 'Our clients run up against this all the time. What I really want to do is get bumper stickers made up that say, "Paedophilia is not a sexually transmitted disease".'

'Catchy. I can see that on a T-shirt.'

'Yeah, but that's the whole point,' Allyson had said, suddenly serious. 'Who the hell would want to be seen wearing it?'

Cordy smiled ruefully at the memory. Part of the reason that she'd moved into the not-for-profit sector rather than continuing her psychology research was that she had kept running up against advisers who made it clear that in their opinion Cordy's personal history clouded her judgement or, worse yet, made her somehow suspect herself. They didn't see that – terrible as the experience was – it could be turned into a strength, rather than a liability. Allyson got it. But Allyson was one in a million.

Later that morning, faced with Fiona's grim countenance, Cordy was glad she'd kept the anonymous email to herself. The older woman didn't need any more ammunition.

'I thought that I made your brief perfectly clear, Dr Hunter,' she said, pushing a copy of Cordy's temporary contract towards her. 'You report to Detective Inspector DeLuca. Your role is advisory. You've agreed to be a resource for the team, for the duration of the case. And, as an *untrained, uninsured* civilian, there is no question of you being involved in hands-on undercover work. With your impressive academic background, and your groundbreaking work with child victims, I really thought you'd be an asset to the team. But if you're going to go off on your own initiative, without consulting the rest of the team . . .'

'It won't happen again,' Cordy promised.

'No? Well, I hope I have your word on that,' Fiona said, sitting back and looking down at her notes. 'I guess that just leaves the small matter of about a dozen basic operating procedures that you've trampled all over. If you've talked to Sampson and DeLuca already, you'll know that I'm not the only one whose nose is out of joint.'

'I'm sorry. I just saw an opportunity to move the case forward—'

'And you grabbed it.' She didn't wait for Cordy to protest. 'Look, part of the point of you being here is to circumvent another media disaster, not cause a fresh one. Sneaking around a suspect's house, without any intelligence, without back-up. Without a warrant. Really, what were you thinking?'

There was a long uncomfortable silence, during which the ticking of the clock seemed to get louder and louder.

Eventually Fiona broke the silence. 'Well, I hate to say it, but it seems you were right about Mark. I'm sure we'd have made the connection sooner or later but . . .' She rubbed her forehead. 'Well, anyway. Yesterday I wasn't sure you were right for ECPU work, but today I'm more focused on following up that lead. Must be going soft in my old age.'

Cordy didn't smile. It was only just occurring to her that secretly she might actually have been relieved to be taken off the case. For the decision to be taken out of her hands.

But Fiona had already moved on. 'So for now, at least, we'll continue as before.'

'Thank you—'

The chief cut across her. 'As long as it's absolutely clear that you're on a short leash from now on.'

Cordy frowned. *What was it the email had called her? A stupid bitch?* Before she could stop herself she muttered, 'Fine. But I'm not a dog.'

'What?'

'I said I'm not a dog.'

Fiona fixed her with a cool stare. 'No. You've got the potential to be one of the most highly respected child protectors in the business. But at the minute' – she gestured to her desk – 'you're also a pile of paperwork that I don't need. So from now on everything is by the book. If you're in any doubt, ask. If you have a hunch, report it up the chain of command.' Seeing

Cordy's face, her voice softened slightly. 'Look, we really need your psychological profiling skills right now. We need someone who can get us in that room with those victims and those predators, who can help us find them, help us formulate an arrest and rescue strategy that won't end in those kids disappearing off the grid completely and the perps skipping town. But try to think in terms of accountability. I know it might seem tedious to you, Dr Hunter, but the protocol is there for a reason.'

She nodded dismissively, but Cordy stood her ground.

'So I can carry on investigating Mark?'

'You can present your information to the rest of the team and wait to be instructed on how best to proceed with helping them secure a warrant of investigation,' Fiona corrected her. 'I've got a feeling that things are going to start moving ahead now.'

I'm jerking off to a picture of you ...

'And in the meantime Mark's free to do as he pleases?'

Fiona put down her pen. 'In the meantime we'll be working on it night and day. But, as I said, it takes time to build an airtight case.'

I'm jerking off to a picture of you. Right now ...

'As long as all the protocol is followed and all the forms are filled out correctly, who cares about his victims, right?' Cordy was aware that she was speaking louder than necessary, but somehow wasn't able to stop herself.

The chief rose to her feet. Even in heels she only came up to Cordy's shoulder, but her eyes blazed. Her voice, however, was cool and measured. 'Like I told you, we could use your expertise right now, but if you're not happy with the way the investigation is being run, then we can always release you from your contract. It's completely up to you.' She sat back down and reached for a file. 'Now, if that's all, I have work to do . . .'

Cordy left without another word, blood pounding in her ears as she stormed down the corridor.

She breathed a sigh of relief at finding the Ops Room empty – the last thing she needed was to have to explain to Bob and Anthony what Fiona had said. *Or how I got her riled up again after everything was sorted out*, she thought bitterly. *Nice one, Cordy.*

As she waited for her computer to start up, she straightened up the keyboard and wireless mouse so that the angles neatly aligned. Fumbling in her bag for a piece of gum, she noticed a flickering sign on her mobile. She had a voicemail. Unknown number. Worried that it might be one of the doctors calling up about Jess, she dialled 901 to retrieve the message. At first she couldn't quite make out what was being said. *A bad connection? The caller had a cold?* Then the message became all too clear.

'. . . so fuck off because I know where she lives and I've got some friends who'd be more than happy to pay her a visit . . .'

She dropped the phone as if it was infected. It *was* infected. There was no way she was ever using that number again.

A male voice, deliberately muffled. *Could be Mark. Could be anyone.*

Mechanically, she logged in and clicked on Internet Explorer. After accessing her account details she called Carphone Warehouse and arranged to have a new SIM card with a different number couriered to the Unit. Without a moment's hesitation she agreed to their offer to upgrade her handset at the same time, for a nominal fee. Next she left messages at Justice4Children, ECPU's admin department and at the clinic, letting them know her new contact details, in case of emergencies.

When that was done she wrote down the few telephone numbers she needed and didn't know by heart, turned off the phone, took out and destroyed the SIM card, before dropping it and the phone itself in the bin.

She could handle this. After all, she'd got through much worse.

By the time Anthony and Tammy came back up from the canteen, she was able to act pretty much like normal.

'Bit of a roasting,' she said. 'Nothing I didn't deserve.'

'Rather you than me,' Tammy said. 'I had to go over my report on the paedo-phishing yesterday afternoon and she bit my head off about my grammar. Seriously, I got a half-hour lecture on the proper use of apostrophes.'

Cordy shrugged. 'Sorry.'

'Forget it,' Tammy said. 'My mum's always on at me about that too. I'm like, I won't send you postcards and stuff if you're going to get all angsty.'

'Well, I'm just glad it's all sorted out,' Anthony said, coming over and sitting on Cordy's desk. 'Because there're a few things I wanted to run by you . . .'

As Anthony laid out a plan to identify Mark's associates – the man they'd seen in the Thai DVD, and the grey-haired guy – Cordy caught herself thinking back to the phone call. She knew she should feel reassured that whoever it was didn't know much about her and her family. Maybe she should even be grateful that she didn't have a niece or nephew for them to target. But still she hated the thought of someone dialling her number, hearing her voice on the recorded message. Maybe trying again, right this second. Maybe finding some other way to get to her.

'You all right?' Anthony asked, putting a hand on her arm.

'Peachy keen,' Cordy replied, automatically moving away. 'Just repeat that last bit, will you?'

Chapter 32

When she turned up unannounced at the Justice4Children office, it sounded as if all the phones were going off at the same time.

'Can you grab that?' Allyson shouted to a serious-looking girl with long brown hair. Cordy's boss was flicking through a heavy folder, her mobile clamped between her ear and shoulder. 'Yes,' she said, turning back to the desk, 'the court date's been set for April the second.' There was a pause. 'Right. Right. I know.' She swivelled again, caught sight of Cordy and waved. 'Yes, it's understandable that she's nervous. But she should be able to give evidence by video link-up. And we can always arrange a dummy run, so she'll know what to expect . . . Wait one second.'

'Sorry. Should I come back later?' Cordy asked. 'I just thought I'd drop by . . .'

'Nonsense. Great to see you. Just give me a few minutes,' Allyson said firmly. 'Go and make us all a cup of tea or something.' She transferred the mobile to her other shoulder. 'Sorry about that. Now where were we . . . ?'

Across the room, the brown-haired girl was taking messages while typing at a furious rate. Cordy wondered if this was Natasha, the girl that had emailed the charity and offered to overhaul their website for them. Allyson said she was a treasure, and she certainly had an air of quiet confidence about her, despite her young age. Cordy tried to get her attention to offer her a cup of tea, but the girl was too engrossed in her multi-tasking to notice.

Oh well. She doesn't have to drink it if she doesn't want to.

As Cordy made her way to the cramped kitchen, she noticed, with a pang, that her desk was now being used as a dumping ground for unopened post and miscellaneous files. Her fingers itched to set it right. She'd only been on secondment to the ECPU for less than a month and already her carefully ordered systems were falling into disrepair.

In the kitchen, alongside the jumbo caddy of Fairtrade tea bags and the dusty packet of Red Clover Infusions (which was supposed to help with Allyson's hot flushes, but smelled so unappetising that she never actually drank it), was a new brand of camomile tea. *Natasha's?* Cordy filled up the kettle and switched it on, wondering if it was worth checking.

'Hello, stranger. Guess you couldn't keep away . . .'

Cordy turned and grinned. Allyson was dressed in a floor-length batik-print robe – completely at odds with the functional surroundings of their North London office, but also completely perfect for her.

'Nice. Is that from your holiday last year?'

'Got it from Oxfam,' Allyson said, giving a little twirl. 'Not bad for a fiver.'

'Sugar or sweeteners?'

Allyson opened the cupboard and closed it again. 'Urgh, I think we might actually be out of both. Remind me to go to the Co-op on the way in tomorrow.'

'And the girl – Natasha, is it?'

'Yep. She drinks water. She might even be more of a health freak than you are.'

Cordy went to put the third mug back, then paused. 'Hot or cold?'

'Cold. From the tap. But I think she's probably all right for the minute. She usually has a big glass on the go. Anyway, how have you been?'

'Good. Can't complain.'

Apart from the fact that I can't seem to do anything right at the Unit. And the small matter of the psycho who seems to be stalking me.

'Jess is doing OK. And, you know, the Unit is keeping me busy.'

She turned away to hunt out a clean teaspoon. Allyson could be annoyingly perceptive at times, and she really didn't feel like getting into it with her. She was here to check up on J4C, not to unload more problems.

Angie looked at her carefully. 'So they're treating you well, those boys and girls in blue?'

Cordy tried not to picture the look Fiona had given her as she had left her office.

'Fine. But you know they're plain-clothes, right?'

Allyson laughed. 'You know what I mean. Missing us?'

'Of course. Seems busy,' Cordy said, 'the office.'

'When is it not?'

Cordy shot her a look. 'You'd tell me if you needed me to do a morning or two a week, wouldn't you? I'm sure I could work something out with ECPU.'

'To be honest, love,' Allyson said, passing her the milk, 'it's a relief not to have you on the payroll right now. I mean, don't take this the wrong way . . . you're still under contract and there'll always be a job for you here as long as you want it . . .'

'Jesus. Are the finances really that bad? I can take half-wages when I come back, if you need.'

Allyson blew on her tea. 'Might have to take you up on that. We didn't get that grant for the trauma-counselling programme and one of our major supporters is having a rough year with their investments. I was just about to send you an email about it. Anyway. Something will come up – it always does. Maybe the government funding will come through. Natasha just helped me put together a really solid proposal. I'll send that over too. Maybe you could have a quick read through it, if you've got a minute? See if we've left anything out.'

'Remind me. She's a student?'

'Graduated last summer. Edinburgh Uni. Her parents live in London, so she's fine with interning for a bit. I know it sounds awful,' Allyson said, lowering her voice, 'but I'm crossing my fingers that someone doesn't offer her a paid position in the next few months. With so much going on right now, it's good having her around.'

'I'll bet,' Cordy murmured, feeling oddly left out. 'But who's looking after the fundraising side of things?'

'The gala dinner's not for a few months. Hopefully you'll be back by then.'

'Oh definitely. We've got a suspect now at least . . .' Cordy stopped. 'But I'm not really supposed to talk about it.'

'Don't worry. I've got paedophiles coming out of my ears as it is.' Allyson smiled wryly. 'Sorry. Horrible image.'

'You've got new clients?'

'*So* many new ones. And ones who seemed to be sorted are now running up against new problems. Where to start?' Allyson put down her mug. 'Remember that family we were trying to set up with victim compensation? The Greenes?'

'The ones from Liverpool?'

'Yeah, well, the latest is that they've—'

'So sorry to interrupt.' Natasha put her head round the corner. 'But Allyson, I think you're going to want to take this one. It's that kid from yesterday who wouldn't leave a number.'

'Thanks, love.' Allyson gave Cordy a quick hug. 'If you've got time, stick around and we'll have a proper catch-up. But if you have to get going, give me a call tonight. And, if it's all right, I'll send that stuff over to you.'

Just then Cordy's own mobile went off.

'No rest for the wicked, eh?' Allyson said. 'Thanks for the tea, by the way.'

'Remember: sugar. From the Co-op.'

'What would I do without you?' she called, disappearing back into the office.

When Cordy fished out her phone she saw that the number was withheld. That often happened when someone called from one of the Unit's phones – something to do with the automated switchboard system – but she braced herself to hang up just in case.

'Hello?'

'Ah, Hunter, there you are. It's Tammy. For some reason I had the wrong number for you. Had to get this one from HR.'

'Right.'

'DeLuca said you'd nipped out. Are you coming back to the Unit today?'

Cordy glanced at the kitchen clock. Five thirty. *As long as I can still get to the clinic before seven* . . . 'I guess so.'

'Good. Because we've just had it confirmed that Mark's picture correlates with a partial image we've got from the house. Now there'll be no problem about getting an investigation warrant. We can just cite the screen-grab.'

'Oh, that's great news!' Cordy exclaimed, pathetically grateful that her impetuous visit to Mark's house had had a positive impact on the case at last.

'Yeah, because we were worried for a while that maybe he was just a bit-part player. But no. He's definitely one of the three main guys.' Tammy paused for breath. 'Anyway, it gets better . . .'

'Go on.'

One down, two to go.

'This afternoon I phoned around a couple of schools in the neighbourhood. Turns out Mark's stepdaughter, Laura, who was in Year Six, has been registered as home-schooled for the last few months. I managed to get hold of her old form teacher and she was saying that Laura was a smart girl, but that lately her behaviour hadn't been great.'

'What exactly did she say? The teacher.' Cordy pushed her tea away. It was getting cold.

'Wait a sec; I think I wrote it down.' There was a scrabbling sound, and then Tammy was back on the line, sounding jubilant. 'Thought so. Mood swings, basically. Bright and sunny one moment, tantrums the next. A falling out with some of the other girls – apparently she wet herself in gym class and there was a bit of teasing. Issues with homework and attendance. Teacher put it down to "family problems". Apparently there's a lot of that in that catchment area. Council estates, you know.'

Cordy grimaced. 'Jesus, a twelve-year-old suddenly becomes incontinent and no one thinks to look into it?'

'Apparently not.'

'So she didn't come back to school after Christmas?'

'No,' Tammy confirmed. 'And, reading between the lines, I reckon the teacher was more relieved than anything. Sounds like she's got enough on her plate. Told me that more than half the class were English as a Second Language, and then there's the ADD lot—'

Cordelia cut her off. 'Brothers and sisters? Mother? Grandparents?'

'No siblings. We're still working on the rest.'

'Right, I'll be there in twenty minutes.'

When Cordy looked into the office to say goodbye, both Natasha and Allyson were deep in telephone conversations. Not wanting to disturb them she slipped out and took the stairs out two at a time.

Laura. Lolita.

They were making progress. At last.

So who was Alice?

Chapter 33

spurs101:	thats it
clewis:	What?
spurs101:	im serious
	i cant hack this any more
clewis:	It's all right
	Look . . .
	just don't do anything stupid
spurs101:	whats stupid is sitting around here waiting for
	the shit to hit the fan
clewis:	It won't get to that.
	Calm down
	It's in hand
	Like I said, she won't be a problem for long
spurs101:	wait
	i don't want anyone getting hurt
	you know I never wanted that
	this is enough of a mess already
clewis:	I think it's a bit late to be worrying about that
	Don't you?

Chapter 34

The tarmac gleamed in the sun as Cordy edged into the right-hand lane to take the turning onto the quiet residential street. There were a couple of other ways to get to the Unit, and this wasn't necessarily the fastest, but it was definitely the most reliable. While the bigger roads got snarled with traffic, this one was always fairly clear, even during morning rush hour. And besides, Cordy was a creature of habit. Although she tried to curb some of her little rituals in public (forcing herself to speed up her hand-washing routine, for instance) she found the familiar contours of the route into work soothing and – she could admit this to herself – somehow necessary.

That morning the purr of the Suzuki helped her put her thoughts in order. After Tammy's phone call at the end of last week, Cordy had thrown herself in to building a psychological profile of Mark for the team to work with. For a man with Mark's background – council estate upbringing, absent father, history of petty theft and intimidation – money was power. It was easy to see why a scheme that made profits from sexual exploitation would appeal to him. As to when he had started targeting underage girls – that was harder to pin down.

What Cordy had found out was that Mark had married Laura's mother, Tina Parry, three and a half years ago, when she was thirty-one and he was still in his twenties. Neighbours complained of shouting and screaming, and Tina even got as far as having her husband charged with assault before dropping the charges at the last minute. Now Tina had reportedly moved on to a new partner, an electrician based in her home town of Birmingham who had children of his own from a former relationship. But, for some reason, Laura had got left behind with her stepfather. It certainly wasn't the first case of abandonment Cordy had seen in her professional life but . . .

Shit.

Cordy had been so deep in thought that she hadn't noticed the motorbike come up behind her. It was so close that its nose was almost nudging her back wheel. It was a Kawasaki Ninja, she noted wryly, or – to give the bike its nickname – the Ninja road bastard. Even from inside her helmet, the roar of its engine was deafening.

'Hang on a sec,' she muttered, irritably, as she moved over to let it pass. Usually she felt a sense of camaraderie with fellow bikers, but she was tempted to give this guy the finger. *Maybe he was in a rush to get somewhere, but still . . .*

'Watch it!' she yelled into her helmet, as the Ninja almost pranged her. If it hadn't swerved to the right just then it would have taken out her back lights.

'Look where you're going, you idiot.'

Glancing in the mirror she noticed the blacked-out helmet, the shiny-looking leather. No biking gang insignia.

Just some idiot poseur who should get back in the safety of his Ford Fiesta. What's he doing? There's plenty of—

Her whole body jarred forward as the Ninja bumped against the bike, clipping her petrol tank.

'What the—?'

Her knuckles whitened as she twisted round and saw the other bike slow down for a second, so that it was behind her again. She heard the accelerator roar back into life.

'Jesus!'

Cordy's first instinct was to hit the brakes and check for damage. *My beautiful bike. There must be some mistake.* But as the Kawasaki Ninja loomed closer, adrenaline kicked in and she wound back the throttle and kicked into a higher gear, desperately hoping that there was no one idling round the corner, knowing there wasn't time to get away.

The second impact, when it came, was announced by a screech of metal. The black-clad biker leaned into her, clearly hoping to slam her bike over. When she veered away he kicked out. There was a sickening crunch, Cordy's Suzuki was knocked sideways and it was all she could do to keep from spinning out of control. With a grimace she threw the handlebars in the opposite direction, counter-steering in a zigzag until she could regain her balance. By the time she pulled the clutch in and skidded to a halt, inches from a parked car, her hands were shaking. The other bike was gone. She hadn't even seen the registration plate. *Some detective she was.*

It took all her determination to get back on the bike. Riding to the Unit, at snail's pace, she jumped every time a motorbike appeared in her mirror. No Kawasaki Ninja. Pulling in, she realised that she was slick with sweat.

A quick check didn't reveal too much obvious damage – a dent in the body from the biker's kick, a nasty scratch in the paint – but she knew she'd have to call a garage and get it looked over properly. Cordy had to bite her lip as she traced the scratch with her fingers. It looked so painful.

She held it together long enough to smile hello to the surly receptionist, to change out of her leathers, splash her face with water and greet the team. Then she switched on her computer and saw the email. Work account this time.

Subject: Jessica

Guess it runs in the family, being a filthy slut. I can see the resemblance. Wish I could find one of the two of you together. But this will do me for starters . . .

'Bastard,' Cordy whispered. 'You fucking bastard.'

There was a link to a file-sharing site.

He knew her sister's name. He'd found a photo. Or a video.

Her eyes burned. Any second she was going to cry, right there at her desk. She squeezed them shut and tried hard to think of something else, something safe.

An empty beach. A sunset.

Less than a minute after she'd deleted it, another message popped up. Another unknown sender. Blank message line . . .

'How's it going?'

She jumped, and Anthony hurriedly took his hand off her shoulder.

'I'm sorry, you're busy . . .' Then he saw her face. 'Jesus, Cordy. What's wrong?'

Cordy could practically see Tammy's ears pricking up. *Gossip!* And if Bob started to wade in with his blundering brand of wisdom . . .

'Nothing,' she said quickly. 'I'm fine. But maybe we could go over Mark's profile. If you have a second.'

Anthony caught on fast. He straightened up, and in a much more casual voice he suggested they see if one of the media rooms were free.

'Good idea.'

Cordy couldn't look at him. Any hint of kindness would make her break down now, and that would mean they had won. Whoever *they* were. Only when she was sure that she had her feelings in check did she grab her file and follow Anthony to one of the little rooms off to the right of the Ops Room.

'Now what's all this about?' he asked gruffly, pulling out a chair for her before he sat down. 'Is the chief breathing down your neck again? I thought that was all sorted out. Or is it, you know, that stuff you told me about . . .'

Staring down at the table, Cordy told him about the

'accident' that morning, about the phone calls and emails that seemed to be getting nastier and more frequent by the day.

'And so there's . . . stuff. About me. Scanned-in photos. Maybe worse, I don't know. Video stuff that my uncle and his fucked-up friends shot, and that some creep's digitised.' She couldn't look him in the eye. 'But until today it was just me. Wild threats, that sort of thing. But now they want me to know that they know about my little sister . . .'

'And there's . . . stuff about her too?' Anthony asked gently. 'You might have mentioned a sister at some point, but you didn't tell me she was involved in the abuse.'

Cordy nodded, still avoiding his eye. 'She was. And I'm pretty sure there're images of her out there too.'

'So you think it's Mark and his lot?'

'There are other possibilities. Of course.' She shrugged helplessly. 'But it seems to be escalating, and I'm not really doing much work for J4C at the moment so I can't think who else would be so pissed off at me that they'd want to turn me into roadkill.'

'Jesus. You poor thing. Are you OK?'

When Cordy looked up she saw that his brown eyes were full of concern. She tried to smile.

'Ah, I'm fine. I'm a tough old bag, you know.'

'No you're not,' Anthony said firmly. 'They could have killed you.'

'You think I don't know that?'

He shook his head. 'I can't believe you've been keeping all this to yourself. Especially if it's related to the case.'

'We don't know that,' Cordy said sharply. 'And until we do, this is my business. OK?'

Anthony held his hands up. 'Fine. Whatever. But what are you going to do? You can't just keep on ignoring it. This is serious.'

Cordy let her head sink into her hands. 'I don't know. I just don't know. When it was just me – fine. I chose this line of work; I know the risks involved. I'm not stupid, or reckless. I can look after myself. But now they know about Jess . . . she's so vulnerable, you know?'

'Your sister?' Anthony asked. 'You don't really talk about her much. She in London as well?'

'Her situation's . . . complicated. I'll tell you another time. But she definitely didn't sign up for this. And if I'm putting her at risk by staying on the case . . .'

Anthony put an arm round her and gave her shoulders a quick squeeze. She knew he meant to comfort her, but she still shuffled away. 'Sorry, I'm an idiot. I keep forgetting,' he murmured, and moved away to give her more space.' I really can't believe this. It must be terrible for you. I mean, I've had threats and stuff in the past, but nothing like this. I can't believe they tried to make you crash. Did it look like Mark?'

Cordy closed her eyes. Her mind always seemed to work better when her adrenaline was pumping, and she could picture the other biker vividly. Not that it helped much. 'Could have been. I saw a flash of white skin. Right sort of build, but impossible to tell much more with the helmet and leathers.' She shrugged. 'And anyway, it could have been one of his cronies.'

Anthony nodded. 'Do you think they'll try again?'

'Jesus,' Cordy said, 'I don't even want to think about it. Like I said, my parents died when we were both pretty young, so I'm all Jess has got. If anything happened to me . . .'

'Don't say that!'

'You said it yourself. What's to stop them trying again?'

Anthony pulled his chair closer. 'Well, I hate to say this, but maybe you should think about taking a step back from the case.'

Cordy looked at him hard. 'What, let them scare me off?'

'Look, I know no one wants to get Mark and those guys more than you do.' His voice was solid and warm. She let the hard knot of anxiety in her unfurl, just a little. 'But what good is it going to do anyone if you wind up dead?'

'I hear what you're saying, but . . .'

At the sound of the door they fell silent.

'What's all this?' Bob asked, taking in the scene. 'DeLuca, do I need to get your wifey on the phone?'

'What do you want, Sampson?' Anthony asked, a hint of annoyance in his voice.

'Heard you guys were going through Mark's profile. Thought I'd put my penny's-worth in.'

'Well, we'd actually just finished so—'

Cordy cut in. 'It's OK, DeLuca.' She turned to Bob. 'Look, I might as well tell you. Someone tried to run me off the road this morning and I think it might have been Mark.'

'What? Are you OK?'

'Yeah. I'm fine. It was a black Kawasaki, a recent model by the look of it – I'd guess the new ZX 10R – in perfect condition. We call them Ninja road bastards. Lots of metal. Didn't get the plates, unfortunately . . .'

'So you crashed?' Bob asked, looking her over, as if for injuries. 'God . . .'

'No, but it was a close thing.'

'Well, I guess that's good.'

'Yes,' Anthony said. 'But still, it's worrying.'

Bob looked thoughtful. 'Mark doesn't have a motorbike registered, does he?'

'He could have borrowed it,' Cordy pointed out. 'Or, like I said to DeLuca, it could have been the ringleader. Maybe not the old guy – the biker had a pretty muscular build.'

'Right.'

Anthony weighed in. 'I was saying that she should be careful. There's no point putting herself at risk.'

'Really, I'm fine,' Cordy insisted. 'There's no way I'm going to let those bastards get me off their backs.'

Bob was shaking his head. 'Love, it sounds like you've had a nasty shock. But remember it could have just been some random tosser. I used to live near a local Hell's Angel chapter, and they don't get the name for nothing. Crazy bastards, the lot of them. Knife you as soon as look at you, some of them. Could have just been some bloke who gets his rocks off freaking out lady riders.'

Cordy's eyebrows shot up at the term 'lady riders', but she didn't rise to the bait. 'I know it sounds melodramatic, but it did seem . . .' – she searched for the right word – 'deliberate. You know, targeted.'

'All I'm saying, sweetheart, is that I've been in this business longer than I care to remember and no one's ever tried to ram me off the road.' He frowned. 'Look, love, don't take this the wrong way, but this case is horrible enough without imagining that every flare-up of road rage is an assassination attempt.'

'Sampson,' Anthony warned.

'So you think I'm paranoid?' Cordy's voice was icy. 'That I'm making this up to get attention?'

'Well, that's not actually what I said—'

'Forget it,' Cordy said, scooping up her file. 'And in the future' – she turned and fixed him with a cold gaze – 'keep your opinions to yourself.'

'You were the one who brought it up!'

'And I'm the one who's shutting it down.'

She slammed the door behind her.

The ceasefire, she thought ruefully, *is officially off.*

Chapter 35

Cordy toyed with her new phone, snapping it open and shut. Twice she scrolled down to the right number before pressing cancel.

This wasn't going to be easy.

She'd left the Unit early in order to prepare for her visit with Jess. Her plan was to have enough time to work out and shower before she headed over there, hopefully with most of the telltale tension released from her body. She'd left her bike in the garage, but she had the number of a car firm she knew she could trust.

But bit by bit she realised that she couldn't risk it. Whoever was driving the Ninja Kawasaki knew the route she took to work. If someone was still following her, she'd lead them straight to Jess. Even with the clinic's tight security, there'd be ways of getting at her. A letter from a 'school friend'. A phone call from an 'old teacher'. She could try warning the doctors, but if Jess noticed them treating her with kid gloves, she'd know something was up and it could trigger another bout of self-harm.

Jess wasn't stupid, and she wasn't a child. But right now, she needed Cordy's protection.

It was all too easy for Cordy to imagine her sister's fragile self-worth shattering at the first contact with these vicious perverts. Literally years of therapy would have all been for nothing. Jess would be starting from scratch all over again.

If that happened, she'd never forgive herself.

And what if they tried to hurt her? If they somehow wheedled their way inside the clinic?

Cordy couldn't even bear to think about that. It was too painful to hold in her mind.

In the end, she didn't have a choice. She couldn't see Jess until Mark and his cronies were in custody. She just couldn't take the risk.

But it was one thing to make that decision, and quite another to figure out how to explain to Jess that her only link with the outside world was about to be cut off.

The longer I leave it, the worse it'll be, Cordy thought, glancing again at the phone's display: 6.30. Jess would be expecting her any minute.

She dialled the number of the front desk.

'Afternoon. Please put me through to Jess Hunter in Room 704. It's her sister.'

'Ah, Cordelia. I'll put you through.'

'No,' Cordy said sharply. 'You've got to ask for the codeword. That's what we agreed for all Jess's callers.'

'But . . . well, fine.' She heard the receptionist sigh. 'What's the codeword?'

'Nemo.'

'Putting you through.'

The line only rang once before Jess answered.

'Cordy, that you?'

'Yep.'

'Running late?'

'Not exactly. That's why I'm calling.' Cordy put her hand to her forehead and wracked her brains for a good excuse. 'Thing is—'

'You're stuck at work,' Jess supplied. 'That's all right. Don't worry about it.'

'No, I'm not at work. I've, erm, got the flu. Pretty nasty,

actually. But,' she said quickly, 'nothing serious. I just need some rest.'

'Oh, go to bed then,' her sister said. 'I'll see you Thursday.'

'Will do. Thing is . . .' Cordy paused. *Why did I say the flu? Why not something like meningitis that'd buy me more time?* 'It's quite a bad flu. The doctor said a week at least. Maybe two.'

'But you're OK?'

'Yeah, fine,' Cordy assured her. 'I just don't want you to catch it. And you know what the doctors are like about spreading lurgies.'

Jess made a sound that wasn't quite a laugh.

'But I'll see you soon,' Cordy promised, hoping it was true.

'Right.' Jess's voice was dull.

'All right.' Cordy tried to think of something to say. The silence dragged on a few beats too long. In the end she blurted out: 'You know I'm sorry I can't come and see you?'

'It's fine,' Jess said, but her voice was heavy with disappointment. 'You're sick. I'll just . . . umm . . . anyway.'

'Love you, Jess.'

There was a pause. Cordy could imagine her sister playing with the half-heart necklace, tracing the smooth edges with her pale fingers. Eventually she muttered, 'You too. Get better.'

After her sister hung up, Cordy sat for a moment, wondering whether she should call her back. Even if she couldn't go to the clinic they could watch TV together over the phone, like they used to do when Jess's visiting hours were more carefully restricted. It would be good to hear her sister laugh.

The doctor said a week at least. Maybe two.

Cordy grimaced.

And what do I tell her after that? That I've got a stomachache? Hay fever? A mild case of leprosy?

Despite their recent progress, they were still nowhere near closing down the site and arresting the ringleaders. Two weeks was nothing on a case like this. Hell, they didn't have names for Mark's two cohorts yet. Or any concrete idea where the kids were being kept. It could go on like this for weeks. Months, maybe. And every single day Cordy would have to look over her shoulder, wondering where the next attack was coming from, wondering if Jess's safety had already been compromised.

The realisation sneaked up on her.

The only chance of resuming a normal life is to shut down the operation and lock up Mark and his cronies. Get to them before they get to me and mine. It's that simple.

Cordy leapt out of her chair and started up her computer.

Guiltily, she thought about how they'd all been so hung up on putting together background on Mark over the last week that the children had been sidelined. Cordy didn't even know if new clips were still coming in. But she had her notes from the old ones. And she had a security card to get into the Unit after hours.

'Come on, come on,' she muttered as Windows loaded up.

Seven o'clock. If she spent an hour here going over her notes, that'd give the stragglers time to go home. Then she could catch a Tube over to the Unit and stay as long as she wanted to, watching and rewatching the clips. Finding what she'd missed.

She skimmed back through her notes, adding the new information about Lolly. *About Laura*, Cordy corrected herself.

Laura. Kurt. Alice.

A detail nagged at the back of her mind, but when she tried to formulate it in words it slipped away, and all she was left with was the image of Alice's lost, haunted eyes burning into hers.

There was something she'd forgotten. Something she'd forgotten to do or check. And until she remembered, she wouldn't rest.

Chapter 36

'So do you have a flashing red light stashed away somewhere?' Cordy asked, with a grin.

'Funny, that's what all the kids ask when we go in to schools to talk about online safety.' Anthony raised an eyebrow. 'Why, do you wanna run some red lights? Live life dangerously?'

She coloured and looked hard at the road ahead. 'Just asking.'

'Whatever you say.' He sounded as if he might be laughing at her, but she didn't want to look over and check. 'Yes, I do have an emergency vehicle light, but no, I don't use it when I'm stuck in traffic jams. Although sometimes it is quite tempting.'

'I'll bet.'

For a few moments they drove on in silence.

It was Anthony who spoke first. 'Radio One or Radio Four?'

'Some sort of music. Please.' Cordy sank back into the soft leather of the sedan's front seat. 'Is it this comfy in the back?'

He laughed. 'I'm sure that's the last thing on the perps' minds when I sling 'em in there.'

A song that Cordy had never heard before played out, and she let herself get lost in the thrumming bass and bittersweet vocals.

Earlier that morning they'd got the call they'd all been waiting for. The surveillance team assigned to Mark had noted that he was repeatedly visiting a house on a quiet residential street in Beckton – Docklands area. At first they thought it might be his dealer, then – when they clocked him staying there overnight a couple of times – a new girlfriend? But they never caught sight of a woman, and when he was spotted bringing in bulging Sainsbury's bags and sloshing a bucketful of liquid down the drain, the detectives changed their minds. As far as they were concerned, this was *the* house.

Tammy had actually whooped aloud at the news, and Cordy had had to fight to go along with Anthony to recce the neighbourhood.

Now, making her way across London, her stomach was tight with expectation.

In ten minutes, we could be parked outside the house.

'So run it by me again,' Anthony said, taking one arm off the wheel to turn the radio down when the presenter started their spiel again. 'I was so buzzed about finding this place that I think I might have missed some of the details. Have to say, those CID guys did a great job.'

'Yeah, they're . . . great,' Cordy agreed, aware that her voice sounded a little flat. The truth was that she was trying very hard not to feel disappointed that it wasn't one of her leads that had taken them to the house. She'd been working night and day for the past few weeks. But, really, as long as they got the kids out and the perps banged up, who cared how they did it?

Only a really selfish, messed-up person would want to take the credit . . .

'So . . .' he prompted.

'Oh yeah, sorry.' Cordy scrabbled in her bag for the printout of the details. 'Right. So the house is detached. Twenty-seven Millhouse Lane. Deeds are registered to a Mr and Mrs Viner.'

'Finer?'

'Viner with a V. They're clean.'

'Look at you, getting in with the police lingo.'

Cordy ignored him. 'Give or take the odd speeding ticket. Anyway, they're in their sixties. He was in the army.'

'So he's the older guy, then?' Anthony asked as he pulled up for a red light. 'And where do we reckon she fits in? Enabler, or totally oblivious?'

Cordy shrugged. 'The other possibility is that it's rented out. I looked on Google Maps before we left and there're hospitals and the University of East London nearby. Plenty of people wanting short-term lets. And lots of that will be kept off the books. Cash in hand.'

'You're right. We should keep an open mind.' He peered forward to read the road sign. 'Can you check we're going the right way? I don't know this part of town that well. There's an *A–Z* in the glove compartment.'

'Next to the handcuffs?' Cordy quipped.

'Actually, they're right here.' Anthony patted his jacket pocket. 'Always prepared. Like a Boy Scout.'

He didn't smile. 'I'm telling you, it ain't pretty trying to restrain a suspect without them. Seen what animals are like when they're cornered? Well, it's like that sometimes. Jabbing and grabbing and biting like you wouldn't believe.'

'Right.'

When she didn't say anything else, he turned to reassure her. 'Look, don't worry. The boys on Mark will give us a call if he's heading over. We shouldn't have any direct contact at all today. If everything goes to plan, that is.'

They pulled up to Millhouse Lane. Cordy felt a sickening lurch in her gut as she noticed that many of the front lawns were littered with small bikes and plastic Wendy houses.

'You can see the appeal of the neighbourhood,' Anthony said grimly. 'Now, shall we start across the street?'

The lights were off in number 27, and there was no car parked outside. Still Cordy felt jittery, as if they were being watched.

'What if they're friends with the Viners and they tip them off?' she asked, quietly.

Anthony got out, paced around the car and held the door open for her. 'You'd be surprised how little community spirit there is these days. Even in these old working-class communities. And besides,' he said, closing and locking the door behind her, 'people tend to mind their own business, don't they?'

Cordy shrugged. She knew from experience that otherwise decent people were perfectly capable of overlooking the terrible things that were going on right under their noses.

If they don't believe it, it's like it's not really happening . . .

Anthony was already smoothing down his hair and ringing the bell. Despite her nerves, Cordy couldn't help but smile. Fiona had been right to insist on Anthony being among the fact-gathering team. He was just the sort of copper you'd most like to find on your doorstep – tall, handsome, and far too charming for his own good.

Mrs Sengupta from number 26 clearly agreed.

'Yes, I don't see why not,' she said, when Anthony put forward the possibility of the Senguptas having a couple of plain-clothes detectives doing surveillance in her attic. 'The only thing is that there's a load of junk all over the place. But I can always give it a clear-out this afternoon. It's about time I had a good sort through.'

'And you understand that we won't be able to reveal any information about the case?' Anthony checked.

'Yes, you said that.' Mrs Sengupta glanced between the two of them curiously.

'We can't afford to jeopardise the investigation,' Cordy put in. 'No one can know you have officers working from here. Not your friends, not your family – no one. It's vital that you're clear about that.' She had a sudden sick pang at the thought of word getting out, and the children disappearing, slipping through her fingers like ghosts.

Anthony softened Cordy's words with a smile. 'Of course, if you need to check with your husband . . .'

Mrs Sengupta ('Please, call me Bani . . .') laughed. 'Oh, he was always a big fan of *The Bill*. He'll love it.'

'That's great, Mrs Sengupta,' Cordy said briskly. 'But, like I said, I hope we can count on you both to be discreet. This is important. Really important.'

'Well of course . . .' She glanced up at the clock over the kitchen table. 'So, umm, I should have asked you this already. Do you have any idea how long the surveillance operation will last? It's just my daughter is visiting next week with our grandsons and the house will be quite crowded.'

Shit, Cordy thought, *she's regretting the offer already.*

'It's just—'

'Bani,' Anthony cut in. 'I don't suppose there's any chance of another cup of tea? I'm parched today and that last one really hit the spot.'

'Oh, of course.'

He rewarded her with a devastating smile. 'Thank you so much. You've really been so helpful.'

'Oh, I didn't bring the biscuits,' she said, jumping up and retrieving a packet of Jammy Dodgers from the cupboard. 'Here you go. And I'll just put the kettle on.'

'You,' he said, eyes twinkling, 'are an angel.'

Ten minutes later they were outside, clutching written permission from Mrs Sengupta sanctioning the use of their property for ECPU surveillance for the next week.

'You were brilliant in there,' Cordy admitted.

'And you,' Anthony said, mock-seriously, 'clearly never went to charm school.' He held up a hand to stop her protesting. 'Doesn't matter. We'll do a quick scout-around for side streets where we could base our Comms van for the raid, and then we should get back to the Unit so they can start getting a surveillance team together. Now we've got them in our sights there's no time to waste.'

'I feel like we should have a theme tune,' Cordy deadpanned.

'Let's get the perps banged up first,' he countered. 'And then you can go crime-fight in a unitard for all I care. And no, before you ask, I don't want to be cast as your trusty sidekick.'

'Pity,' she said. 'Think how much Mrs Sengupta would like seeing you in spandex.'

Chapter 37

Back at the ECPU, the heating was on the blink and Cordy shivered despite her thick jumper and extra pair of socks. She was worried that having lied about it for the last week, she now might actually be coming down with a cold. There was that telltale heat behind her eyes and she was getting through tissues like they were running out of fashion.

Karmic retribution, she thought morosely.

'Are we all here now?' Fiona sounded exasperated. She was staring pointedly at the empty chair around the desk. 'Where's Reynolds?'

'Making tea,' Bob said. 'She won't be a minute.'

Cordy shot him a look.

'What? She offered,' he protested.

'Well, let's get started and someone can always fill her in later,' Fiona said, standing up and pushing the door closed. 'Right, well, the big news is—'

'Sorry!' Tammy called. She was struggling to manoeuvre a tray of mugs into the room while holding the door open with her bum. 'Sampson, you lazy bastard, can you give me a hand?'

He jumped up and took the tray off her. 'Thanks, love. That's grand. What would I do without you?'

'Find another slave?' Tammy suggested, but she gave him a smile anyway.

Anthony cleared his throat. 'I think the chief would like to . . .'

'Thank you,' Fiona said heavily. 'Sit down you two, and listen. The phones are all diverted to voicemail, right?'

Tammy nodded.

'Good.' Fiona let out a deep breath. 'So. The surveillance team managed to get the infrared sensors working . . .'

'Don't know how you managed to wheedle one of those away from Customs and Excise,' Bob said, 'but I'm impressed. They always tell me to sod off whenever I put a request in.'

'And it looks like there are multiple bodies in the basement. Live ones, I mean.'

That shut everyone up.

Bob reached for his tea and then drew his hand back, as if thinking better of it.

'These people. Full-sized?' Cordy asked.

'Children, from what we can tell. Three of them. One adult upstairs.' Fiona gestured at the whiteboard, where they wrote up their notes about the case. 'It all fits.'

'So that'll be the ringleader then, we reckon? The guy from the Thai DVD?' Anthony asked. 'Any sign of Suspect number three – the older guy?'

Fiona checked her notes. 'He and Mark visit every couple of days. I've told surveillance that getting a clear shot of the grey-haired man and the "keeper" is a top priority. Anyway, the timing correlates with the last few broadcasts from the site. Which someone should watch, by the way. We need to check for any changes in the set-up. No point getting complacent now.'

'They need someone to keep an eye on the kids while they're filming,' Bob said quietly. 'Safety in numbers.'

'That makes sense,' Fiona agreed. 'Although I'd guess these children are now too traumatised to pose much of a threat escape-wise.'

'So, when do we go in?' Cordy blurted out. 'If he's there on his own, and he sleeps on a different floor of the house from the kids, it shouldn't be too difficult.' When no one answered she tried again. 'Should it?'

Fiona turned to face her head-on. 'I see what you're saying, but we've got to take this carefully. Really carefully. Remember that case in Florida last year?'

'It was cellar children again, wasn't it?' Cordy said, trying to think back. 'Sorry, I don't really remember the details. J4C only works on British cases. But I should know this.'

'It caused quite a uproar,' Fiona said, 'although I only got the full story from a friend who works for a government agency out there. Anyway, it was reported as a classic case of a rescue mission gone wrong. What the papers didn't report – because the Feds thought it best not to release the information – was that the whole place was rigged up with gas canisters. Soon as they broke in, fffffpt.' She shook her head. 'I think they got one kid out. Out of six. And some of the squad had to be hospitalised.'

'Guess they were worried about copycats,' Tammy said. 'That's why they kept it quiet.'

'Which makes sense.' Bob shrugged. 'But it's not like you can't get all this information on line, if you know where to look. There're so many unregulated how-to sites. Bomb-building, that kind of bollocks.' He stopped. 'Best not to think about it.'

'Jesus. So they gassed the kids. Actually gassed them? That *can't* really happen,' Cordy said, although even as the words left her mouth, she realised that it could. That it might again. 'That's—'

'Think about it,' Fiona said. 'If the children escape they'll tell the authorities about them. If they're rescued, they'll give evidence against them in court.'

'It's disgusting,' Anthony said, with sudden vehemence. 'It's not human. I hope to God that Florida has the death penalty.'

'That's not the issue,' Fiona said firmly. 'Or *our* issue anyway. We need to concentrate on retrieving those children quickly and safely.'

'Agreed,' Bob said. 'If we piss about too long they'll get wind of us and move the kids. Then we're right back to square one. Or worse.'

'These kids are much too valuable to just get rid of,' Cordy said, following his train of thought. 'Do you know how much Caucasian children like these change hands for?'

Bob shrugged. 'Yeah, but whether they kill 'em or sell 'em or move 'em out of the country, it'll still mean the same thing: those kids'll be lost to us.'

'That won't happen,' Fiona said sharply. 'The surveillance guys know what they're doing. Sampson and DeLuca, if you can put a proposal together – including what we need in terms of back-up and equipment – I'll go over it this afternoon and then take it to HQ first thing tomorrow morning. We need to have thought about this from every angle.'

'I'll watch the clips,' Cordy offered, 'and sketch out the layout.'

'Thanks. Any insight you can give us at this stage into the likely reactions of perps and victims would be very useful. And Reynolds, could you check the council offices? See if there're any plans of number twenty-seven.'

'I'm on it,' she said, downing her tea.

'We can't afford for anything to go wrong,' the detective chief superintendent reminded them. 'So check. Double-check. Triple-check. And then check some more. DeLuca, you'll liaise with the team on Mark.'

'Course.'

'Right.' Fiona looked at their expectant faces. 'What are you waiting for? Let's get going!'

Downing her cup of tea, Cordy headed for the media room. The temporary warmth it had given her was fading fast. More clips. More images to get stuck behind her eyes.

And maybe more messages.

She shook the thought out of her head and reached into her bag for a cleanish tissue.

Concentrate on the task in hand, Hunter.

Chapter 38

When we were in kindy there was a wall calendar and when it was your turn you had to go up and change the day of the week and the day of the month and the weather. One boy would always put that it was sunny even if it wasn't sunny but the teacher wouldn't tell him off because she liked saying it was sunny too. In December we forgot about the wall calendar because there was an advent calendar with chocolate in it, not like the one at home which was Mummy's when she was my age and is very special and you can't be rough with it and it doesn't have any chocolate in it.

You're supposed to write at the top of the page – day, comma, the something of something and then the year, even though the year hardly ever changed. That is what I should have done. I should have written it – not on my arm because there's not enough space but on the bunk or somewhere. Somewhere secret. Or I should have done like in Brownies when we add up points and put lines of five or is it lines of four and one slash through them? Then I would know how long it was. How long I've been down here.

They say I'll get used to it. That I'll learn to like it. But they don't know about my messages.

If you write a message in a bottle someone has to find it because that's the rule but how do you know if they found it and if it got to the right person? What if someone just put it in the recycling and didn't read the message?

It's been lots of days and maybe months too and my mummy and daddy still haven't rescued me yet. They are busy people with lives of their own, Mummy says, but they wouldn't wait so long I think. Not if they saw the messages.

I thought I was clever thinking up clues but if I was clever I'd have found a way out and I would know the day and he says if I'm smart I'll keep my mouth shut and smile and I'm not that smart.

Instead of clues I write my name on my arm. Not the stupid baby name they call me. My real name. I write it with my finger so often that it's funny that you can't see it there, that the skin isn't worn out.

They can't take my name away. They think they have but they can't.

Chapter 39

The door slammed so hard that the whole room reverberated.

'What did I say?' Bob asked, holding his hands up in defeat.

'You could have been a bit more tactful,' Anthony muttered.

'Oh, I don't know,' Cordy said dryly. 'What could be more tactful than suggesting she might be more of a hindrance than a help? I mean, granted, you didn't come right out and say that she'd probably fall to pieces and wreck the whole operation, but you did a pretty good job of getting the point across.'

'What, so you're best friends with Reynolds now?' Bob shot back.

'Well, I'd bet I'm further down her shit-list than you are right now.'

Bob sat down heavily. 'All I said was that she didn't have to do the raid if she didn't want to. I was just trying to make it easier for the lass. I wasn't expecting her to turn on the waterworks.'

'Should I go after her, do you think?' Anthony asked, looking uneasily at the door.

Cordy shook her head. 'Give her a few minutes to get herself together. And don't make a big deal of it when she comes back in.' She looked pointedly at Bob. 'We've got enough to worry about this afternoon. Isn't the chief supposed to be doing a briefing?'

'I wouldn't hold your breath,' Bob said gruffly. 'Word is that the infrared jobby is bust. Which is really all we need.'

'What, so we haven't got images of inside?' Anthony asked sharply. 'As of when?'

Bob shrugged. 'Doesn't look like it. Everything's going tits-up as usual.'

Cordy looked at her watch. Quarter past four. Just over twelve hours until they broke down the doors of number 27. *But if they were doing it blind . . .*

'Wait up,' Bob said. 'She's just emailed. Her office. Five minutes.'

'I'll go and get Tammy,' Cordy offered, picking up her bag.

'Tell her that, erm . . .' Bob floundered to a stop.

'I'll tell her how much you value her police work,' Cordy said. 'And that you're sorry that you upset her. But that you can't help being a blundering idiot.'

'And that you'll buy her a drink. A large one,' Anthony put in.

Bob groaned. 'You realise that means I'll have to go up and order some great big pink Cosmotini or some muck like that. I'll never live it down.'

'I'm sure you'll survive,' Cordy said crisply. 'See you in there.'

By the time that Cordy had persuaded Tammy that no, she shouldn't quit, and that yes, Sampson needed to think before he opened that big gob of his, the meeting was already in full swing.

'Right. Come in. I was wondering where you two were,' Fiona said, pushing a black and white surveillance photo towards them. 'Just got these through this afternoon. This is the guy we'll be looking out for. Suspect number one – the probable ringleader. He's the one we've seen entering and leaving the building most often. Always on his own. Stays overnight. No sign of the children.'

'Don't we have a better picture than this?' Cordy asked. The photo was clearly taken from the Senguptas' upstairs window with a telefocus lense. Although the resolution was good, a baseball cap covered most of the suspect's face. You could tell that he was white and clean-shaven, with a slim build, but his features were in shadow.

'This is the best we've got,' Fiona said. 'He never seems to take that bloody cap off, all right? Any more complaints?'

Cordy looked up, surprised. The detective chief superintendent was usually so calm and professional that it was a shock to hear her sound riled.

'And before you ask,' Fiona continued, 'yes, it's true that we've lost the infrared images. I've put in a request for a replacement scanner, but frankly it's not looking likely. The nearest one is being used to break a people-trafficking ring in Dover, and I don't see them handing it over in time. So . . .' She sucked in a deep breath. 'We'll have to work with what we've got.'

'But we won't know where the children are. Or their jailor, for that matter.'

'Unless of course they're in the same positions that they've been in every other night for the last few days,' the chief said dryly. 'Which is presumably where their beds are.'

Cordy swallowed hard. 'Yes, but if they're not? I'm just saying it's not ideal. From a child-safety perspective.'

'Well, from a child-safety perspective it's not ideal for a group of men to be keeping minors as sex slaves, but there you are.' Fiona smiled grimly. 'Now, as I was saying, Reynolds, you're going to be in charge of Comms?'

Cordy glanced over at Tammy. The young detective had managed to wipe off most of her smudged mascara, but her eyes still looked a bit pink.

'Yes. I'll be liaising between the team on the ground and HQ,' Tammy said, standing up a little straighter. 'In fact, when we're finished here I'll go check over the radios we'll be using. Would be good to have headsets too, in case things get nasty.'

'Which they won't,' Fiona said firmly. 'Not with the amount of back-up I've got in place. In fact, there's no reason that this shouldn't be a textbook operation. In and out in ten minutes.'

'Famous last words,' Bob muttered.

The team looked at each other.

Eleven hours to go.

When they'd gone through the plan for what felt like the millionth time, Fiona finally dismissed them.

'Get some sleep,' she said. 'I need everyone at the top of their game. I don't have to tell you that we really can't afford to make any mistakes tonight. Tone down the emotion.' She looked at Tammy, then at Cordy. 'And no going rogue either, people. You follow orders to the letter. Or I will personally see to it that your career in Child Protection ends here.'

Cordy fought the urge to spit out a retort.

We're on the same team, she told herself firmly. *Same team, different style.*

As they filed out, she caught Anthony's eye. 'Fancy a cuppa?'

'Across the road?'

Cordy nodded. 'I know we're supposed to go and get some rest, but there's no way that that's going to happen. Anyway' – she waited until Bob and Tammy had gone into the Ops Room – 'there's something I want to talk to you about.'

'Sure. Just give me a minute to finish off here.' Anthony held the door open for her. 'And then, *cara mia*, I'm all yours.'

Cordy rolled her eyes. 'No need to turn on the charm with me, DeLuca. Save it for the general public.'

'Or your wife,' Tammy retorted, without turning round, 'who left a message about an Ikea order, by the way. You might want to remind her that I'm not your secretary.'

'Five minutes,' Anthony mouthed, behind the young detective's back.

★   ★   ★

The café was full of well-dressed groups of mothers and students hunched over laptops. It was only Anthony's quick eye and slow smile that secured them the last table in the place – one so tiny that their knees almost touched under it. Cordy usually liked to rest her elbows on the table (despite all her grandmother's admonishments) but the restricted space forced her to be more ladylike. Anthony, as usual, looked perfectly at home, long legs folded neatly beneath his chair.

'So,' she said in hushed tones, spooning the froth off her cappuccino. 'Do you think Sampson was right?'

'About what?'

'About Reynolds staying with the van.'

Anthony frowned. 'Well, obviously he made a bit of a hash of it. But essentially – yes. I mean, the chief's managed to wangle a great back-up team. And there's only going to be one suspect. We don't *need* Reynolds there, and as none of us knows exactly what we're going to find . . .'

'In terms of, I don't know, trip-wires and things. Or in terms of the children?' Cordy asked. 'I mean, their condition.'

'Either. Both.'

She looked down at her cup. 'Does the same hold true for me?'

'Oh that's different. I mean, Reynolds is very young. And she's still inexperienced with these sorts of situations—'

Cordy stopped him. 'It's OK. I'm not about to storm out in tears. It's just that it got me thinking.'

He looked at her carefully. 'Is this about the threats? Are you still getting them?'

'It's not that I'm scared.'

He shook his head. 'You know I didn't mean that.'

She sighed. 'It's just . . . am I being selfish, is what I want to know? I want to be there when you guys crash through the door. I want to be there to help get the kids out and I want to see the look on those bastards' faces when they realise we've shut down their sick little business.'

Anthony pushed a stray lock of hair out of his eyes. 'If that's selfish, then I guess we're all selfish.'

'But I know exactly how dangerous cornered paedophiles are. And I'm all Jess has.'

'Your sister?'

'Yes.' Cordy ran the gold chain through her fingers until the half-heart locket was in her hand. 'My baby sister.'

Anthony looked up at her closely. 'I bet she's a beautiful girl. If she's anything like her big sister, that is.'

Despite herself, Cordy grinned. 'I told you, DeLuca, don't waste your charm on me.'

'Wouldn't dare.' He smiled back at her, and she couldn't help noticing how thick and dark his lashes were. *Wasted on a man*, her boss Allyson would say.

Anthony's voice ended her reverie. 'So you're wondering if you should take a step back now? Now that the investigative part of the operation's almost over?'

'I mean, of course I'll want to stick around to debrief the children and make sure they and their carers get the right support,' she said. 'But maybe it's ridiculous of me to want to be there for the actual rescue. I don't have the training, for one thing. I know I've signed the waiver forms, but Fiona will probably still make sure I'm posted round the corner where I can't get in the way.'

'Then stop worrying about it,' he said. 'At the end of the day no one's expecting you to do hand-to-hand combat with the resident paedophile. There'll be plenty of tough guys in bulletproof vests elbowing you out of the way to get a bit of the action.'

Cordy laughed. 'You're right. It's just that everyone seems so on edge, it's infectious. I guess I'm worrying about my role in order to avoid worrying about the outcome.'

'There you go, a bit of psychology with your coffee break. Although I usually prefer cake.'

'Sorry,' Cordy said, pushing the plate of biscotti towards him, 'I forgot we got this as well.'

'Halves?'

'Go on then.'

A bell jingled as the door opened to let in a new customer. They both turned sharply, as if to check it wasn't one of the team, and then swivelled back round, smiling.

'Seems like we're both a bit on edge today,' Anthony said. 'Unsurprisingly.'

'And I've been going on about myself as usual,' Cordy said, reaching for her half of the biscuit. 'What's going on with you? Outside of this crazy world of round-the-clock surveillance and dawn raids.'

'Well, we're doing a bit of redecorating,' he said, and then laughed at her expression.

'What?'

'You can always tell a single person. Their eyes glaze over at the first mention of home improvements.'

Cordy smiled. 'Sorry. Go on.'

Anthony shook his head. 'No, you're right. It's boring.'

'Compared with what's going down tonight, boring sounds pretty appealing. Go on. Talk to me about, erm, colour schemes.'

'You really don't know anything about DIY, do you?' He paused. 'Thing is, even I'm not into it. Actually, we've been talking about something quite, I don't know, ambitious.'

'Are we still talking power tools?' Cordy asked. 'Or the pitter-patter of little feet?' She steadfastly ignored the way her stomach contracted a little at the thought of Anthony starting a family.

'Neither, although . . .' He stopped himself. 'That's a whole other story. But we're actually thinking of going to Canada. Moving there, I mean.'

'Permanently?'

'That's the idea. But,' he said quickly, 'obviously keep this to yourself. The chief would have a hernia if she knew I was thinking of jumping ship. You know she's on at me to apply for promotion?'

'When are you thinking of heading off? I guess there're visas and stuff to work through.'

Anthony drained his cup. 'I mean, that's the thing. It's just an idea really. Angie's not that keen. And I can completely understand. It'd be a big move and she doesn't want to leave her friends and family. And she loves her job.'

'What about you?' Cordy asked. 'Would you be able to work for a similar unit over there?'

Anthony leaned back, away from her. 'To be honest, I wouldn't want to.'

'But you're so good . . .'

She stopped when she saw the pained expression on his face.

'I just can't do it any more,' he said, dully. 'It just seems to get worse and worse. And the more people we put away, the more sites we shut down, the more we find. It's like we said before – they're like cockroaches.' He repeated this quietly. 'Just like cockroaches.'

Awkwardly Cordy reached over and patted his arm. 'I'm sorry, I didn't mean to criticise.'

'I'm just so tired,' he said, looking up at her as if she could help.

'Of course you are,' she said, gently, 'and you've done great work. But it's not surprising you feel burned out. Who wouldn't, doing your job?'

'I feel like I'm letting everyone down,' he said quietly.

'Don't talk rubbish,' Cordy said. 'And anyway—'

'Can I get you anything else?' the young waitress asked, inclining her head towards Anthony.

'No thanks, sweetheart.'

'If you're sure . . .'

'Positive,' he said, ignoring her smile. 'Just the bill please.'

'Look, I'll get this,' Cordy said. 'You should get off home. Fiona's right, you need a proper rest before the raid.'

'If you're sure . . .' Anthony said.

'Yeah, get lost.'

'Well, see you at the Unit at three.'

'I'll be there, ready to kick some butt if I have to,' Cordy said. 'I mean, if the back-up guys need back-up.'

He didn't smile. 'Let's hope it doesn't come to that.'

Chapter 40

Even the big guys from the Rapid Armed Response squad were shuffling their feet and blowing on their hands to keep warm.

'The coldest hour is just before dawn,' one of them muttered.

'Shut it, Smithy,' another said. 'We don't need a fucking running commentary.'

The first guy looked over at Cordelia and Tammy. 'Sorry 'bout that language. Ginger's not used to being around ladies.'

'Now Smithy on the other hand . . .' He lowered his voice and the rest of the sentence got lost in muffled laughter.

Cordy ignored them both and turned to Anthony. 'How's it looking?'

'Nothing suspicious on the outside of the building, but we'll have to be careful when we get inside,' he said. 'I wouldn't be surprised if they've taken precautions. But these guys know the score.' He gestured over at a tall guy at the edge of the group. 'There's a bomb disposal expert going in with the first wave, just in case.'

She nodded, swallowing down a mouthful of bile. 'Right. And how we doing for time?'

He checked his watch, face tense. 'In a few minutes we'll get into position. After you hear us make an entrance, you'll wait at least a full five minutes before you go in. But keep an ear out for the radio. I'll let you know if we need you sooner or if you should hang back.'

'Got it.'

Now that they were at the site, Cordy was glad that she'd agreed to be part of the second wave. At first it had sounded like an excuse for keeping her out of the way, but now it really did seem like a good compromise. Her job would be to keep the children as calm as possible and reduce the level of panic. Even though they were trying to help the kids, there was no guarantee that they wouldn't meet with some fierce resistance. After all, why would they trust adults after what they'd been through over the past few months? Cordy remembered exactly what it felt like – the toxic mixture of anger and shame and confusion and misplaced guilt.

I can do this, she told herself. *In half an hour we'll have our man in custody and those children on their way to the hospital. Then the healing can start.*

All around her the half-dozen members of the back-up squad were double-checking their radios, their floor plans, their holsters. The detective chief superintendent was striding back and forth, keeping quiet and order.

'Two minutes, guys. Two minutes.'

Anthony caught her eye as he manoeuvred into position beside the RAR boys. 'See you inside.'

'One minute,' Fiona mouthed.

A cold sweat prickled at Cordy's neck. It hadn't seemed real up until now. So many forms to fill out and scenarios to work through and now they were really here, just down the street from where Alice, Laura and Kurt were locked away. *And if anything went wrong . . .*

Just then Bob shoved past. 'Coming through, coming through. Age before beauty.' Seeing Cordy's face he slowed down. 'You OK, love?'

'I'm fine,' she said woodenly.

'It'll all be over by the time we get in there,' Bob said, sounding a little disappointed. 'If I were a few years younger . . .'

He didn't get time to finish the sentence. At a signal from Fiona the first wave sprinted for number 27. The crash as they kicked open the front door caused lights to go on all down the street.

'Subtle,' Bob muttered, but like everyone else he was straining to see what was happening. After the last guy disappeared through the gaping hole where the front door had been there was an eerie quiet. No explosion. No shouting. No nothing.

Her heart thumping as though she was running a marathon, Cordy stared down at her watch.

One minute.

'They'll have him any second now,' Bob continued. 'Probably still asleep. Won't know what hit him.'

Cordy didn't answer.

One minute thirty. Two minutes.

'DeLuca's not even armed . . .'

Two minutes thirty. Three minutes.

'Why haven't they radioed in?' Cordy asked. 'What's going on?'

'Give 'em a chance,' Bob said, but he looked worried too. 'Are you ready to go?'

Cordy nodded, tightening her grip on the torch in her hand.

Three minutes thirty. Four minutes.

They all jumped when the radio crackled into life.

'. . . door . . . open. Over.'

Fiona held up her hand for silence. 'Can you repeat that please, over?'

This time everyone heard the message.

'Children gone. Suspect gone. Door to cellar left open. Over.'

'What? No!'

Without waiting to hear any more, Cordy turned on her heels and ran towards the house.

'Wait. No point going in now. The area hasn't been secured,' Bob called after her, but she ignored him. After waiting quietly for so long she needed to *do* something. Anything.

The children gone? Gone where?

Her heart sank even further as she stepped through the open doorway and into a darkened hall. The door to the cellar was right there, open for anyone to see. *Like an open wound*, Cordy thought, and then pushed the image away.

A man she recognised from before (Smithy?) came down the stairs and saw her standing there. 'Nothing,' he said, voice heavy with disgust. 'Empty. I mean, what the hell? Thought you guys had intel?'

'So did we.'

She followed him down to the cellar. No one had switched the lights on (*fingerprints*, Cordy thought, dully), but even by the light of her torch it was clear that the place had been cleaned out. But even worse than that . . .

Bleach. The whole place reeks of it.

Beneath the chemical smell was something tangy and cloying.

Faeces and urine, Cordy noted mechanically. *Like a zoo. Like they were animals.*

Looking around she saw that the small, high windows had been covered over with cardboard and the walls had been covered with thick padding, like a recording studio.

'Sound-proofing,' said Anthony grimly, stepping out from the shadows. 'Look, we need to get everyone out of here.'

'What happened? Where are they?' she asked, willing her voice to be steady.

'They're gone.' She was amazed he could be so professional, when the whole operation was falling apart around them. 'I'm going to pack this lot off and get forensics in here. We all need to get out.'

Although Cordy wanted more than anything to get back out into the fresh air, far far away from this makeshift prison, part of her mind was busy sectioning off the room, examining each part with a furious intensity.

'Wait. Those wall brackets,' she said. 'They must have used them for restraining the children. There might be something there. Hair, blood, body fluids. Or the bunk bed.' She stepped closer. 'Did you see that graffiti? Could pre-date the children – the whole thing looks ancient – but maybe not. The bed'll have been too big for them to move quickly but maybe—'

Anthony shook his head impatiently. He was already half-way up the stairs. 'Forensics will get all that, and we can work from the photos. We need to leave now. You might be contaminating the scene.'

'But if you just let me—'

'Now,' he shouted. 'Jesus, Cordy.'

Chastened, she followed him up the stairs. Watery morning light was beginning to creep in through the open door, shedding light on the rest of the house.

To her left she saw what looked like a living room, shrouded with white sheets. When a heavy-set member of the RAR backed into a sofa, thick clouds of dust flew into the air, making the whole team cough.

'Watch it, will you?' Anthony barked, before turning his attention back to his radio.

While he was busy clearing the house, Cordy darted down the hallway and stuck her head round doors, desperately looking for clues as to the children's whereabouts.

What she saw didn't give her much hope. It didn't look as if many of the rooms had been used in months, except a small, dark kitchen at the back of the house and a room on the ground floor, where a stripped-down bed took up most of the floor. Cordy felt the back of her neck prickle.

This isn't a home, it's a business premises.

Outside the quiet, tense atmosphere of earlier on had been replaced with frantic bustle and a lot of very vocal complaining.

'I hope we're still going to get overtime for this,' Ginger said. 'Complete waste of resources, if you ask me.'

'Keep it down,' his friend warned him, 'or the chief will make a necklace out of your bollocks.'

'Right, you lot,' Fiona said, snapping her phone shut and turning to the Rapid Response team. 'You can go home. I've talked to your unit and we'll do a debrief this afternoon.' She paused. 'Not the result we wanted, but thanks for your hard work.'

With only a minimum of grumbling, the back-up team handed back their equipment and got back in their van. Smithy gave Cordy a little wave as they drove off.

When their van had disappeared round the corner, Fiona turned to Tammy. 'How long until forensics are here?'

'It might be an hour or so,' Tammy warned. 'But we'll seal the building now, and I've already radioed for some uniforms to keep watch until they get here.'

'Thanks.' Fiona rubbed her eyes and looked around. 'Sampson, can you give her a hand getting the tape up?'

'I can. But is there any point?' Bob aimed a kick at an empty can of Red Bull that someone had left on the pavement. With a hollow ring it flew into the gutter. 'All I'm saying is that they clearly didn't leave in a hurry. If they were careful enough to scrub the floors they'll have been careful enough not to leave fingerprints.'

'Sampson . . .' Anthony warned, but Cordy shook her head.

'He's right. How the hell did they know we were coming?'

Fiona's phone rang, and she walked away as she answered it.

Bob looked at the rest of them. 'When I heard they'd scarpered I had a quick look round the back, just in case. Don't know what I thought I'd find – them all hiding out in the rose bushes or something. Obviously not. But that's how they got out, judging by the state of the garden. I guess we might be able to get some footprints. I can't believe it.' He laughed mirthlessly. 'This whole thing's a shit show. A total shit show.'

No one had anything to say to that.

Chapter 41

The sun was fully risen by the time they'd finished securing the site and were ready to head back to the Unit. While they were still standing around, waiting for a squad car from the local station to arrive, Mrs Sengupta came out with a couple of thermoses of sugary tea and coffee to find out how it all went. When she saw their faces, her body sagged a little beneath her colourful housecoat.

'So it didn't go according to plan? You didn't make any arrests?'

'I'm afraid that's restricted information,' Cordy said firmly.

'But all that surveillance . . .'

Cordy glanced at Anthony but he seemed so lost in thought that he'd barely registered Bani's presence.

'We're very sorry for any inconvenience caused, and very grateful for your help,' she said, a little stiffly.

The older woman shook her head. 'Oh, no trouble. No trouble at all.' With a last curious glance around, she retreated back inside.

All around them, the street's residents were getting ready for a day at work. Cars packed with gym kits and musical instruments headed out for the school run. Men and women in tracksuits took themselves or their dogs for a run.

To Cordy all these everyday sights and sounds took on a strange, nightmarish quality, as if the world were slightly out of sync – too bright, too loud, too ordinary.

It wasn't supposed to happen like this.

Tammy offered to stay behind with the detective chief superintendent to brief the uniformed officers and the forensics team, and no one put up much of an argument. In fact no one spoke much at all.

Slumped in the passenger seat of Anthony's car, the case ran through Cordy's mind like a broken record. In the end, as much to break the silence as anything, she started to run through the clues out loud.

'So obviously you've still got Mark who you can bring in and interrogate, right? And then there's the older man. We must have a decent shot of him by now. But I think we need to go right back to the start. To the children. Three children. We know Lolita/Laura's connection, but what about the other two? Since no missing children reports have come up as a match, the other options are parental/carer involvement, human trafficking – maybe from Eastern Europe? Or a child taken from a disaster zone. Or a foster or group home . . .'

She looked around but Anthony's eyes were fixed on the road. In the rearview mirror she could see that Bob's eyes were closed and that he was slumped against the back seat. Cordy knew that she should probably shut up, but she couldn't stop herself. It felt as if her head would burst unless she ordered her whirling thoughts into words.

'And then there're the messages that Alice has been sending.' She counted them off on her fingers. 'There's the Morse code. Maybe Alice is from a military family? And the song. Horses. The captain. I mean "down into the dark" – that's what she was saying – that fits, doesn't it? After all, they were in a cellar and there was no natural light. So maybe—'

'Shut up,' Bob snapped.

'Excuse me?' Cordy said coldly, craning round to look at him.

He slowly opened his eyes. 'I said, *shut up*. For fuck's sake. Do you really think we need to hear you wittering on?'

Cordy flinched. She had got used to a bit of banter with her colleague, but she'd never heard him sound so genuinely angry. 'Don't talk to me like that.'

Anthony looked as if he was about to say something but Bob wasn't finished. Not by a long shot.

'You know why they weren't there, don't you? Why those kids are still locked up somewhere? Being treated worse than . . . worse than animals?'

He didn't wait for an answer.

'You think you're so clever with your PhD and your stupid theories, going off like you can solve the case singlehandedly. Like I said before, Nancy Fucking Drew. Get a buzz from going after Mark yourself, did you? Well, I hope it was worth it. Because you scared them off. Until then they had no idea we were on to them. They were getting lazy. We were gathering evidence, building a case. And now the whole thing is fucked.' He slammed his fist against the car door. 'Well and truly fucked.'

Cordy felt as though the wind had been knocked out of her. 'Is that really what you think? That I—'

'If it wasn't for Hunter, we wouldn't even have Mark,' Anthony said firmly. 'And this morning wasn't her fault. Not in any way. Surveillance should have spotted something was up. I know they didn't have the scanner but still.'

'I'm just saying what everyone's thinking,' Bob muttered.

'No you're not,' Anthony insisted. 'You're pissed off. We all are. But pointing the finger at each other isn't going to help.'

A strained silence held for the rest of the ride back. With her eyes fixed straight out of the front window, Cordy oscillated back and forth between anger and self-doubt. *How dare Bob Sampson blame her for what happened at the raid! But*, a small voice said, *what if he's right?*

When they pulled up in front of the Unit, Bob got out so fast the car had barely stopped moving.

Can't bear to spend another second in here with me, Cordy thought, biting her lip.

Anthony moved much more slowly, methodically collecting his things from the glove box and the boot.

'I think we could all do with a cup of tea,' he said. 'I'll make it.'

'I'll give you a hand,' Cordy offered. The thought of going to the Ops Room alone and facing Bob's glowering face was not appealing.

As they waited for the lift, Cordy felt as though her limbs were made of lead. She couldn't ever remember feeling this tired, this wretchedly disappointed and confused.

If only the raid had been the night before. If only it had been earlier in the night. If only something hadn't spooked them.

Or someone, she thought grimly.

The kitchen was small and harshly lit, but still Cordy had an urge to close the door and lock out the outside world. *If only it was that easy.*

She reached to the back of the cupboard where she knew Tammy kept an emergency supply of biscuits. As her fingers closed round it, the colours of the room started to blur together.

Anthony looked up from filling the kettle. 'Hunter, you OK?'

To her horror, she realised that she was crying. And that she couldn't stop.

She dropped the biscuits on the side and leaned her face against the cupboard door.

Get a grip, Cordy. Get it together.

But it only got worse when Anthony came over and put an arm around her – instinctively, she twisted away, and then she started with the big, ugly, body-wracking sobs that turned her face red and made her nose stream.

'I'm sorry,' she choked, swiping furiously at her tears. 'I don't know . . . I need to . . .'

He backed away, obviously unsure what to do. 'Do you need a tissue? Shall I get . . . someone? Call someone?'

'No!' It came out more forcibly than she'd meant it to. 'I'll be OK in a minute.' Already the sobs were subsiding, but she couldn't seem to stop shivering. It was as though someone had turned all the heat in the world off.

Awkwardly, Anthony picked up both her hands and rubbed them between his. They felt surprisingly smooth and cool, and she didn't pull away. 'Don't listen to Sampson. He's talking out of his arse. These things happen all the time. You think you've got the perps pinned down but they get away at the last minute. It's part of the job.'

She squeezed her eyes shut. 'It's not just that . . .'

'I know. It must be doubly hard for you, knowing first-hand what those kids are going through.'

When she opened her eyes she saw that he was looking at her with such concern that she nearly started crying again.

An electric tone cut through the silence, breaking the connection between them.

Anthony dropped her hands. 'I'd better take that. Just in case.' He turned his back to her and held the phone to his ear. 'Hello?'

Not knowing what else to do, Cordy set out the cups and tea bags. Sugar for Bob. Sweetener for Fiona. She and Tammy shouldn't be too long now. While she kept her hands busy she tried not to hear the female voice on the other end of the phone.

Of course, his wife.

'Yeah, I shouldn't be back late tonight. I'll tell you about it then.'

A pause.

'No, I'm fine. Really. But thanks for checking in.'

Cordy opened the door. Anthony turned and gestured for her to wait a minute but she slipped out as if she hadn't seen him. She walked straight past the Ops Room and down the stairs that nobody used. For once she didn't bother to smile at the receptionist.

Mark had spotted her. Bob was right. She'd put the predators on the defensive, made them cautious. If they hadn't been so jumpy, maybe they wouldn't have moved the kids. And if it hadn't been for her meddling, maybe it would have been all over by now.

She needed to be at home, on her own, where she was safe. Where she couldn't screw anything else up.

Chapter 42

clewis: Thanks

You did the right thing

spurs101:   u reckon

clewis: Knew I could count on you

You were right – no one spotted us getting out the back way

We had plenty of time in the end

spurs101:   yeah

clewis: Like I said, we already had alternative arrangements in place.

Just as well you gave us the heads-up

After all, people could get hurt in that kind of situation

I told you that the boss-man is a bit of an amateur with explosives?

I reckon it's barbaric, myself

you there?

now don't be like that

really, are you there????

Chapter 43

'Go ahead.' Cordy moved aside to let Anthony pass. 'You know I'm no good at this.'

'You're the one with all the qualifications,' he said mildly, ringing the bell.

'I don't have a PhD in small talk.'

The door opened and an elderly woman peered out. She looked nervously back and forth between them.

'I'm not buying anything, and I ain't religious.'

Anthony hastily whipped out his ID and a mega-watt smile. 'I'm sorry to disturb you, but I was wondering if my colleague and I could come in for a quick chat.'

The woman lurched backwards. 'Oh God. My husband . . .'

'Oh no, it's nothing like that,' he assured her. 'Just after a little background on one of your neighbours. And a cup of tea would be lovely, of course. Mrs . . . ?'

'Mrs Willis. Daphne.' She gave him a wintry smile. 'You'd better come in then. Ignore the mess. I'll go and put the kettle on.'

Cordy tried not to grimace. If she had any more caffeine she'd be climbing the walls, but people always got so put out if you asked for water. They'd been going door to door all morning, and Anthony insisted on sitting down and having a cuppa with every single person, regardless of how well they knew the occupants of number 27. When Cordy had grumbled that it was a waste of time, Anthony had pointed out that it was the only way of getting decent information.

'It's not that people don't want to help,' he'd said. 'It's just that it's easier not to get involved. You have to form some sort of bond. Give them a reason to think a bit harder.'

Despite countless smiles and cups of tea they hadn't managed to find out much. Not yet.

While they took a seat on an overstuffed floral couch, Mrs Willis clattered about in the kitchen. The house had exactly the same layout as the one where the children had been kept, and Cordy found herself looking out for the door that led to the cellar.

'Soya milk OK? My husband is lactose intolerant.'

'Lovely.'

When Mrs Willis returned she seemed much less flustered. 'Now, what's all this about then?' she asked, placing the bone china cups in front of them. 'There's sugar in the bowl if you want it.'

Anthony looked at Cordy expectantly. She nodded slightly and turned to the older woman.

'Mrs Willis, we're investigating some suspected illegal activity at number twenty-seven.'

'Gosh, what kind? Nothing . . . violent?'

'I'm not at liberty to say,' Cordy said stiffly. She thought she saw Anthony's lips twitch. He'd teased her before about being so formal with the public. 'But we're trying to track down the people who were living in number twenty-seven, across the way. If you can tell us anything about the Viners – anything at all – that would be very useful.'

'Oh, well, they're a lovely couple. Or were, at least.'

Cordy and Anthony exchanged a glance.

'Were?' Cordy queried.

'Yes,' said Mrs Willis. 'She was a teacher and I think he did something for the local council. Meg and Gerry. But they moved to Spain a while back. I remember getting a postcard at one point, but I haven't heard from them in years.' She looked down at her hands. 'Such a shame. We used to know everyone on the street when we first moved here. Now no one even bothers to say good morning.'

'Do you remember if they had children? Grandchildren?'

'I don't think so. It was a while ago, of course, but I don't remember them ever talking about grandchildren. And people do, don't they?'

Cordy noticed her eyes stray to a framed family portrait on the wall.

'And do you happen to have the Viners' address in Spain?' Cordy asked. 'Or a phone number?'

Mrs Willis shook her head. 'I don't think so. Shame. Like I said, they were nice people. I'm sure they would never get mixed up in anything . . . off.' She smiled ruefully. 'You know, I would have liked to do something like that. Spain, I mean. Visit, at least. But my husband doesn't like to travel. The food doesn't agree with him, or so he says.'

'Well, thank you. You've been very helpful,' Anthony said, draining his cup and standing up. 'Here's my card. Don't hesitate to get in touch if you remember anything else. Or if that postcard turns up.'

Daphne took the card reverentially and slipped it into her handbag. 'Of course. Good luck with your investigations, officer. Officers, I mean. Sorry I couldn't be more help.'

After Mrs Willis's house, they continued down the street – knocking on doors, smiling, drinking tea. Most people didn't seem to have noticed the occupants of number 27 at all. A medical student from a shared house across the street said he had assumed they were squatters because the curtains were always closed.

'I just thought, good on them,' he said, running his hand across a couple of days' worth of stubble. 'It would be a shame for a nice house like that to go to waste, and there was never any trouble.'

The woman at number 25 remembered seeing a man with his daughter. They had been regular visitors for a while, but now the man was more often on his own.

'I only noticed because my son's about the same age,' she said.

'How old is that?' Cordy asked.

'Well, he's eleven. But it's harder to tell with girls, isn't it? They look so much more grown-up at that age.'

Anthony nodded. 'And the man. How would you describe him?'

The woman smiled apologetically. 'I wasn't really paying attention, you know? Quite attractive, I suppose. Youngish. Dark hair.'

'Black? White? Fat? Thin?' Cordy asked.

'White. Not fat, definitely. Bit flash-looking, in fact. You know, he always had a tan and stuff.'

'This the guy?' Cordy handed over a surveillance picture of Mark.

The woman screwed up her face. 'Could be him, definitely.'

'Definitely?'

She handed back the photo. 'Actually, I wouldn't say definitely. It's hard to tell, isn't it? I mean, I never even spoke to him. Just saw him around a few times.'

'Notice anyone else hanging around?' Anthony asked.

'Well, you know, I'm hardly here really,' the woman said. 'Today's my day off but I usually work in the centre of town, and then there're all the after-school activities to ferry the kids to. Seriously, I feel like an unpaid taxi service sometimes.'

'I'll bet,' said Anthony, handing over his card. 'But if you do remember anything. Or anyone . . .'

When they were back outside, Cordy turned to Anthony. 'Question.'

'Yep?'

'Why didn't we do all this before the raid? Maybe if we'd had more information . . .'

He stopped her. 'It's one thing knocking on doors to set up surveillance. That's a necessity. A calculated risk. But if we'd spent all day walking up and down the street like this, someone would have clocked us in no time. Anyway,' he said, looking down at his notebook, 'it's not like we've uncovered any startling new information. This is more just to make sure we're not cutting any corners. The chief is in enough shit already without us skipping anything.'

Cordy nodded glumly. At Anthony's prompting, Bob had apologised to Cordy that morning, but the atmosphere in the Unit was still tense, with Fiona spending half the time explaining to her superiors exactly what went wrong and the other half biting people's heads off. Worse still was the guilt that nagged away at Cordy at unexpected moments, like when she was standing under the shower, or waiting in the queue at the canteen. She tried to rationalise it away, but again and again it crept back. *This is your fault. This is all your fault.*

In some ways it would have been easier if Bob had still been openly blaming her. At least then she could get angry, could defend herself. The internal criticism was a hundred times harder to take.

'Fifteen down. Twenty-four to go,' said Anthony, striding over to the next gate.

'Wait.' Cordy pulled on his jacket.

From round the corner came the unmistakeable sound of hooves on tarmac. A minute later and a pair of mounted policemen came into view.

'Bloody typical,' Anthony muttered. 'This must be part of their beat. I can't believe all this was going on right under their noses.'

But Cordy was hardly listening. 'She must have heard the sound from the basement. The clip clop,' she said, with growing excitement.

'Who? Look, we should go and talk to them. They might have noticed people going in and out of number twenty-seven. Worth a try, anyway.'

Cordy trailed behind him, her head whirring.

The nursery rhyme from the very first clip.

This is the way the captain rides, clip clop, clip clop.

She'd been right about Alice's messages after all. What else had Alice been trying to tell them – to tell her?

I've got to get her out. The words came so strongly that for a second she thought she'd said them out loud.

Looking up she saw that Anthony had already waved the mounted policeman and policewoman to a stop, and was talking intently. With fresh determination she strode over to see what they knew.

Chapter 44

Bob stormed into the Ops Room and slammed his fist against the table.

'I knew it. The little scrote has skipped town. We should have gone straight over there after the raid. None of this fannying around.'

Cordy's heart sank. 'This is Mark we're talking about?'

He shook his head irritably. 'Who else?'

'Christ . . .'

'That slippery bastard,' Bob spat. 'We should have thrown the fucking book at him.'

When Cordy had got back to the Unit, Tammy told her that Bob and Fiona had gone round to Mark's place with the arrest warrant that had just come through. The hope had been that Mark might be persuaded to give up the others and the children's location in return for dropping some of the more serious charges. It was a mark of how worried they were getting about Alice and the others that there had been very little resistance to this manoeuvre. Now it looked more and more like they were running out of options. Not even the mounted police had been able to supply any fresh information about the occupants of number 27, although Anthony had gone back to the station with them to talk to other members of the patrol. The two they'd spoken to had never had cause to look at the place twice.

Evil hiding in plain sight, Cordy had thought grimly, on the ride back across London.

Now, instead of sitting down at his desk, Bob was pacing the room like a caged animal, bashing against tables and chairs as if he didn't see or feel them.

Cordy felt the frustration streaming off him. It was impossible to concentrate on anything else.

Finally she gave up and turned to look at him. 'So. What do we do now?' she asked.

'You,' Bob said, slamming a notepad down on her desk, 'can call the mother. Laura's mother. Lolita's mother. Whatever. Because, frankly, I don't trust myself to do it.'

'Right now?'

He nodded. 'If you would. Reynolds dug this out this morning, but we didn't want to call until we had Mark in custody, in case she tipped him off. Now there's nothing to lose.'

'You're sure it's OK for me to make the call?'

Bob shrugged. 'Well, you're supposed to be the expert in family trauma and shit like that. Go ahead and prove it ... We'll have her in for official questioning later. Right now we just need to find out where her scumbag ex has got to.'

Cordy took a deep breath and counted to ten before she reached for the phone.

In her work for Justice4Children she had talked with countless mothers of abused children – some of them humblingly brave, others shell-shocked, helpless and frozen with guilt. And then there were the enablers. And the predators. And the ones who just didn't give a damn.

For Cordy, those were the hardest.

As she dialled the number, she tried to get rid of any preconceived notions of the woman she was about to speak with. It was all too easy to assume the worst of adults in this situation, but the truth was that very often people didn't notice what was going on right under their noses. Or sometimes, Cordy admitted, didn't *want* to notice.

The phone rang for a long time before anyone answered.

'Hello?' The voice sounded surprisingly young.

'Afternoon. I'd like to speak to Mrs Jones. Tina Jones.'

'What's this about? Who is this?'

'Dr Cordelia Hunter. I'd like to talk to you about your husband, if I may.'

'If you're calling from the hospital you can tell him to try some other mug. I've told him before. He's not my problem any more. If he wants to get into stupid fights, then that's his concern.'

'I'm not that kind of doctor.' She took a deep breath. 'I'm calling from the Elite Child Protection Unit.'

'Never heard of it.'

'It's about your daughter. Laura.'

There was a pause, then: 'Go on.'

'I just wanted to check if you've heard from her lately? We're trying to track her and your husband down.'

'Ex-husband,' the woman corrected. 'As soon as the divorce comes through.'

'But Laura,' Cordy persisted, 'you haven't heard from her? Do you have a mobile number or anything we could reach her on? I don't want to alarm you, but—'

Tina cut her off. 'You from the social services, then? Don't listen to anything she says about me. That bastard has turned her against me. She used to be such a lovely little girl.' She sighed heavily. 'I know she looks like butter wouldn't melt, but she can be a nasty piece of work. Slapped me, last time I saw her. Her own mother. Well, there's only so much you can take. Honestly, I wash my hands of the pair of them.'

'So Mark has custody of her? Legal custody?'

'I've never seen a penny from him, did you know that?' She didn't wait for an answer. 'Tight bastard. So if he's after money, he can kiss my arse, if you'll excuse the expression.'

Cordy fought hard to keep her voice neutral. 'So when's the last time you saw Laura?'

There was a pause. 'I called her at Christmas and again on her birthday but the little cow didn't bother to pick up. Must be a good while since I've actually been in the same room as her. Bill – that's my new fiancé – keeps offering to have her over here, for a weekend or something. He's even offered to pay the train fare. Not that there's much space, mind. But she's made it clear she's not interested.'

'So you haven't seen her in the last six months?'

'Yeah, about that.' The woman suddenly went on the defensive. 'But that's not my choice. Not at all. She knows she's welcome here. Any time. She's my flesh and blood, despite everything. But she's made her choice. Apparently she's too good for us. Doesn't want to share a room with Bill's girl. Spoiled, that's what she is. I told her, when I was your age I never got new clothes or nothing like that, let alone clothes that make you look like some sort of footballer's wife! I never expected pocket money or anything like that. The way she talks, you'd think the world revolved around her. And of course she goes running to her stepdad when I try to put my foot down . . .'

There was a moment of silence after Tina ran out of steam. Cordy swallowed. Very gently, she explained that they were worried for Laura's safety. That there was a suspicion that she was being sexually exploited, and that her stepfather could be involved. So if her mother had any way of contacting either of them, she should let Cordy know at once.

She heard a sharp intake of breath, and then a low moan.

When the other woman managed to speak, it was obvious that she was struggling not to cry.

'I don't . . . No. No. He's wouldn't . . . I wouldn't have left her with him if I ever thought . . .'

'It's all right. I know it's a terrible shock, but we need to find Laura,' Cordy said. 'We need to make sure she's safe. That's all that's important right now. So if there are any school friends she might be in contact with, or any relatives of Mark's he might be staying with, you have to tell us.'

But Tina had clearly stopped listening. There was some mumbling and then, with a violence that made Cordy wince, she was shouting down the phone: 'The bastard. You better fucking get after him. Why are you wasting time blaming me for this? It's nothing to do with me. Don't you dare try and drag my name through the dirt. He's the one you should be going after. I'll wring his scraggy neck if he ever dares to show his face again. I always knew he was a dirty pervert but this . . . this . . .'

Behind Cordy, Bob muttered, 'Bit late to be playing the concerned mother now.'

Cordy shushed him and tried to calm Tina down. In the end she had to arrange to call back tomorrow, when it had had a chance to sink in. When she might be able to help them.

'Poor cow,' Bob said as Cordy hung up the phone and slumped down in her chair.

'Me or her?' Cordy asked, without looking up.

That got a dry laugh. 'Her,' Bob said. 'She hardly sounds like a candidate for mother of the year. But still, I wouldn't wish that call on my worst enemy.'

'It happens more than you would think, unfortunately,' Cordy replied. 'Mothers who abandon their children, that is. And not just in poor backgrounds either. But sometimes – particularly when a situation's got combative enough – walking away and disengaging just seems easier than staying. But it doesn't change the fact that she had a responsibility to her child. To leave her with a man with a history of violence . . . To not notice she'd been out of school for six months . . .' She squeezed her eyes shut, and let the flare of anger surge and fade again. 'Well, I guess it's no use laying the blame now. We just need to find Laura and get her away from Mark and the others. Then we can afford to worry about who's going to look after her in the future.'

She couldn't stop staring at the phone, dreading that it would ring and she would have to face that rage and hurt and guilt again. Despite all her training, all her professional experience, something inside her recoiled at the contact with such primal fear and anger.

At least my parents never knew.

The thought jumped into her head unbidden, but she pushed it away. There was too much work to do to linger on the past, too much at stake to get sidelined.

'You do realise she'll be ringing us on the hour every hour, from now on, demanding to know why her precious little girl isn't safe home in the bosom of her family?' Bob continued, going over and switching his computer on. 'That is, when she's not busy getting together a vigilante squad to go string up her ex.'

'Well, even more reason to find those children *now*,' Cordy said grimly. 'If we at least knew who the other two men were . . .' She froze a second, staring straight in front of her. Without another word she grabbed her bag and roughly pulled on her jacket.

'Where's the fire?' Bob called after her.

'I've got an idea,' Cordy said. 'I'll call when I get there.'

'God help us,' she heard him mutter, but she was already through the door, her mind back in that nightmarish basement.

Then, just as Cordy pushed the door to the stairwell open, Fiona called her name. When she spun round she saw the detective chief superintendent's face was even more serious than usual.

'Team briefing. Five minutes. Ops Room.'

The tone brooked no argument. Reluctantly, Cordy turned on her heel.

It'll wait, she tried to tell herself. *It'll still be there after the meeting.*

But in her heart was a childish fear that that wasn't true. That any delay would mean that the idea and the hope and the evidence would all melt away without trace, just like the children had.

Chapter 45

Ten minutes later, Cordy was recounting the contents of her telephone call with Tina to Fiona and Tammy. Bob stared morosely at the floor throughout.

'Reading between the lines, it sounds like Mark transferred his attentions from the mother to the daughter before Tina even moved out,' Cordy said. 'That is, if Tina wasn't a decoy in the first place.'

The detective chief superintendent nodded curtly. 'Sounds like the same old story. Question is, will she go on record? And if she does, will she be able to tell us anything useful?'

'Well, she sounded furious, which is more useful for our purposes than denial,' Cordy said, carefully. 'Like I said, there's been a gradual drop-off in contact, but at the very least she should be able to give us a list of Mark's friends and colleagues. It'll be a start.'

'Good,' Fiona said. 'When you next speak to her, try and get her to agree to a home visit. There might be old diaries, address books – that sort of thing – kicking around. Something concrete we can use as a lead. We'll send DeLuca along with you to take a statement, but I think it's best if you remain her primary point of contact.'

Cordy nodded. She wasn't exactly looking forward to the next call.

The chief had already turned to Bob. 'Any prints from Mark's house yet? Anything that might point us in the direction of his associates? It's imperative we get positive IDs on the other two suspects: the ringleader and the older man.'

'Not heard back yet,' he said. 'I'll keep you posted. But I'm not holding out much hope. I mean, from what we saw, it seemed like Mark'd ditched the incriminating stuff. Remember the gaps on the DVD shelf?' He sat up a little straighter. 'Mind you, I will tell forensics to check through the bins outside. If he's as stupid as he looks, they might find something.'

'Ooh, they'll love that,' Tammy said.

'If you're frightened to get your hands dirty,' Bob dead-panned, 'you don't go into forensics. You should hear those lads talk over a few pints. Some of the crime scenes they've been at ... well, let's just say that rifling through a pervert's garbage will be a bit of light relief.'

'Not our concern,' the chief said sharply. 'Reynolds. You were checking to see if we've picked up any webcasts since the raid.'

The young detective shook her head. 'Nada. Last one was late night, day before. It was the boy again – Kurt. Poor kid, he's so young ...'

'Right. Anything else. Any leads?'

Cordy hesitated. What she had wasn't really a lead so much as ...

'Yes?'

They all turned to look at her. Cordy bit her lip. Morale was bad enough without raising their hopes unnecessarily. *Or getting an earful about my airy-fairy methods*, she thought wryly.

'Did you have something to add, Dr Hunter?' Fiona persisted.

'Just that ... DeLuca is speaking to the mounted police patrol. They go right past the house. It's a long shot, but someone might have got visuals on the occupant or the third suspect.'

'Right,' the detective chief superintendent said wearily. 'If that's all, we should all get back to work. Dr Hunter – let me know how you get on with Mrs Jones.' She turned back to the others. 'Obviously I don't need to remind you all that timing is extremely critical, now more than ever. After that fiasco of a raid, I'm afraid our window of opportunity is getting narrower all the time. The longer we go without word of the children, the more likely it is that we'll be allocated to a new case. I know none of us likes it, but if we've still got nothing by the end of the week, we'll have to start seriously considering the possibility that the kids have been taken overseas.' She looked down at the table. 'Or worse.'

For a moment no one said anything.

Fiona's mobile went off. Her head snapped back up, business-like again.

'Child-minder. I'm going to take this. Keep me updated. I want to be on top of every new development, no matter how small.'

With the meeting over, Cordy took the opportunity to slip out of the room. Her heart was thudding in her chest and she had an unpleasant flashback to her own unofficial scout-out of Mark's home, earlier in the investigation.

This, she reminded herself, *is different. This time I'm not going to mess things up.*

When Cordy pulled up outside number 27, all looked quiet. If it hadn't been for the yellow crime-scene tape outside, you wouldn't look twice at the house. After locking up her bike, Cordy approached the place gingerly. For the first time she cursed the fact that her position with the Unit was so temporary, so poorly defined. *Specialist Consultant* – what did that even mean? If she were Anthony she could just stride up to the front door and flash her badge, instead of having to talk her way in. Of course she could have taken one of the team with her, but what she really needed was space and quiet to think.

As she got closer, she spotted a bored-looking officer standing guard at the entranceway. The door still swung off its hinges. Taking a deep breath, Cordy explained who she was and asked if it was possible to have another look round.

The officer shrugged.

'You guys are running the show. Forensics finished up here this morning. I'm just waiting for a locksmith and then I'm back to the station myself.'

'OK, I'll see you in a while,' Cordy assured him, as she pushed past through the entranceway and into the oppressive darkness of the hallway. Alone inside, she caught herself wishing she'd waited for Anthony to get back.

She shook herself. *Don't be an idiot. It's just a house. Bricks and mortar. That's all.*

But looking round, she felt the back of her neck prickle. There was something so desolate about the building, something that set her teeth on edge.

She'd been planning on heading straight down to the cellar, but instead found herself walking methodically through the ground-floor rooms, one by one, before taking the stairs up, not down. Although it seemed like few of the rooms had been used recently, there were still some scattered signs of domesticity, unnerving in their ordinariness. A supermarket-brand cereal box, up high on a shelf. A bar of soap in the downstairs toilet. A half-used loo roll on the shiny metal holder.

It was only when she'd mentally mapped out every room in the house, opened every cupboard, that Cordy finally went downstairs to the cellar.

Generally she liked to think of herself as a logical person. *Empathetic?* Yes. *Superstitious?* Definitely not. She was trained to look at the world as dispassionately as possible, and not let her emotions cloud her judgement. But, edging down the cellar steps, she couldn't shake the feeling that the terrible violence that had been committed down there had left a palpable taint, a residual darkness that lingered long after her fingers had found the light switch.

The room was even starker than she remembered. The space was about as big as her first London flat had been, but there the similarities ended. Between them, the perps and the forensics team had scrubbed any trace of human occupation away.

The ceiling was low, and the floor was unpainted concrete, cold and uneven to the touch. The mattresses that had featured in the webcast were gone, as were the fold-up chairs. The forensics teams must have removed the cardboard taped over the windows, because now there were new shadows in the corners of the room. But – Cordy's stomach twisted – the bunk bed was still there, pushed up against the far wall. It looked like one of Ikea's basic models – the same sort that would be found in thousands of children's bedrooms around the country. Here it looked vulnerable, out of place; its neat dimensions dwarfed by the empty space around it.

Cordy held her breath as she approached, hoping that her memory wasn't playing tricks on her. But no. There it was. Right where she first saw it.

Without waiting another second she slipped onto the bottom bunk.

This is where she lay. Where Alice lay.

With the mattresses gone, Cordy had to reach her arm to trace the jumble of lines carved into the wood on the underside of the bunk. The graffiti was all in one section, but so tightly packed and overlaid that it was like the bottom page of a notepad, or a broken Etch A Sketch. At first it was impossible to make anything out, to pick out any one word or picture. All she saw were the nail marks of someone desperate to escape, like an animal stuck in a trap.

It's not a message, it's a silent scream, Cordy thought despairingly. *No wonder forensics didn't flag it up.*

But she was determined to be patient. As the light from the windows slowly altered angles, she let her eyes focus and unfocus, let them follow each dent and line.

Gradually individual words and images separated themselves from the mass of scratches. Violent, ugly things. Words that children shouldn't know. But also hearts and stars and what looked like an angel or a fairy. A stick figure with a feathered cap, battling a pirate.

And then something else. Something that made her grab for her notebook.

A story. *Alice's story.*

She craned her neck and it disappeared, lost in the chaos around it. Panicked, Cordy pushed her head against the wall, closed her eyes, and counted to ten. With an effort of will she forced away the memories of her own past that threatened to overwhelm her, that tried to add their own dark marks to the jumble of scrawls. When she opened her eyes again, she let out the breath she had been holding, wanting to cry with relief. *There it was.* The world seemed to slow down as the puzzle untangled in her mind. Now that her eyes were hooked on the first words, she couldn't believe she hadn't seen it before, hadn't read what was right before her face.

Tail of Rebecca the Prinsess.

Rebecca.

Not all the words were legible and Cordy recognised the tortured cadences of victim-speak. For her, it was unmistakeable – the way a child retreated into the past, to baby language, as if the grown-up words adults had taught them would turn on them too and betray them.

But the story was there.

It took her a full half-hour to untangle a narrative of sorts from the mass of scrawlings, and even then she second-guessed herself, terrified that she was so desperate to find meaning that she was stringing nonsense together, twisting Alice's words for her own purpose. Hardly trusting her eyes, she took photo after photo on her digital camera.

But gradually, as word followed word, her confidence grew. *This was something. This was a message.*

Rebecca the Princess. A tropical island. An accident and blood and noise. A prince who was really a baddy in disguise. Who locked her in a dungeon.

Cordy's hand was shaking as she scribbled it all down – every letter, every misspelling. It felt like Alice was lying beside her, mouthing it for her. The thought was disturbing and comforting in equal measures.

When she'd finished writing and looking and taking pictures, Cordy just lay there a moment, letting it all sink in. She knew that the moment she left the house there'd be a flurry of activity – people to call, connections to make, information to gather – but for now, just for this minute, it was enough.

The message had got through.

And somewhere in her mind something clicked into place. It was as if Alice had handed her the end of a bit of a thread that would lead them both out of the labyrinth. Cordy hadn't got it all figured out yet, but for the first time since the investigation started she felt a fierce confidence that she would – that she could – rescue Alice and the others.

If only there was some way of letting her know …

But there was no time for idle wishes. Neither of them was living in the world of fairy tales.

Shaking herself out of her reverie, Cordy sat up, eased herself off the bunk and double-checked that she'd put her camera and notebook back in her bag. With only a brief glance backwards, she flicked the light off in the cellar, and the room returned to darkness once more.

Chapter 46

When we left I thought I'd won and they had seen everything. Not *them* but my mummy and daddy, who got the messages and kicked up a fuss, like they did that time in the restaurant when there was a black hair in the chicken salad. We got free ice cream, any flavour we wanted. Mum always says that I shouldn't make a fuss, but the restaurant was different and this is different too and I just want to go home. I need to go home right now.

Outside was night and they pushed and shoved with hands over our mouths, but maybe that was because they were angry that we had won and they had to let us free. But instead of free it was into the back of a smelly van and then here. Maybe it was a test. I used to like tests. Maybe the test was I should have bitten his hand. That's what they would have done in a book and run away but it was pushed hard and hard into my face and sounds didn't come out when I yelled for my parents. And they didn't come either.

Here is worse than there. I need to start from scratch because there are no messages here but they watch and watch all the time. So I'm still waiting to start.

They say we have to be extra extra extra quiet now but that is easy because there is nothing to say any more. I still spit out the special pills but maybe there's some in the food too because my eyes are heavy and they don't even close when the flash goes off any more. But I don't smile. They can't make me smile.

Lolly is lying next to me but scrunched on the edge of the mattress so her legs don't touch my legs because there's not enough beds now. She isn't crying and she isn't asleep.

I turn away from her to the wall. Blank wall.

There are no messages here and without the messages it isn't safe. Not safe at all.

Chapter 47

Fifth time lucky, Cordy thought grimly, as she picked up the phone to call yet another contact who she hoped might be able to shed some light on Alice's story.

She'd spent the last thirty-six hours methodically going through every possible interpretation of the narrative she'd untangled from the graffitied bunk bed. After trying out a hundred different possible theories, there was one simple conviction that she kept on coming back to: the accident on the tropical island – that was real. Alice had lived through that. All the marks of genuine trauma were there in the language and images she used, in the broken-down words, the stark, nightmarish cartoons. If Cordy could only connect the story to a real-world event, then she could start picking her way through the maze of theories and red herrings and false starts and work out who Alice was and how the hell she could track her down.

Cordy was used to examining her hypotheses and assumptions with a trained critical eye, but she just couldn't shake her hunch that she was right about this. Late last night she'd sat down with a list of natural disasters and terrorist attacks that could potentially fit Alice's descriptions and the probable time-frame of her ordeal. One by one she'd managed to eliminate them from her inquiries – thanks, in part, to help from the journalists and not-for-profit workers she'd met through her research and her work for Justice4Children. It was a slow, painstaking process, riddled with false hopes and deadening disappointments, but she refused to give up, worrying the problem like a dog with a stick.

Like a stupid bitch, she thought wryly, remembering one of the milder terms of abuse her anonymous email stalkers had hurled at her in an attempt to scare her off.

For a while, a recent series of bomb attacks in Thailand looked like they might hold the answer. After all, Cordy had reasoned, Bangkok was a hot spot for the illegal sex trade, and they had evidence that at least one of the suspects had travelled there in recent years. However, when she looked into it more closely, she realised that the explosions had all happened in built-up metropolitan areas – rather than on a 'tropical island' – and, moreover, there were no Caucasian children listed among the missing and the dead.

In the end there was only one place left on the list that had yet to be scribbled out.

As she picked up the phone to dial an old university friend, Cordy caught herself offering up a silent prayer to a God that she had long since stopped believing in, that this wouldn't turn out to be yet another dead end.

It was hard to hold an ordinary conversation when her heart was pounding in her chest, but Cordy just about managed to keep it together.

'Nikki, you're an angel!' she exclaimed down the phone. 'I really can't thank you enough.'

'Oh stop it. It's really not a problem. In fact, I'll send it right over to you.' Her friend paused. 'Obviously keep it to yourself. No one wants this ending up in the papers.'

'God no,' Cordy said. 'This is purely for the investigation.'

'Well, good luck with it. I . . . well, I hope it works out OK.'

'Thanks so much. I owe you one.'

At the other end of the line the woman laughed. 'Well, you definitely owe me a coffee. How long has it been since we met up?'

'Too long,' Cordy admitted. 'I'm sorry I missed the reunion drinks.'

'Well, we're having a dinner party on Friday. John's inviting a friend from Amnesty. Really nice guy, just split up with his long-term girlfriend. Smart. Good-looking. Tall ... even by your standards. Why don't you come along too?'

'Sounds great,' said Cordy, fiddling with her pen. 'Really. But, erm, you know, I'm probably going to be busy. Work and stuff. In fact, I don't mean to be rude but I should probably get going.'

'I think you'd like him,' Nikki insisted. 'How long has it been since you've had a proper date? And even if you don't hit it off, you know it'll be good food, better company. John's cooking, of course.'

Cordy laughed. 'Stop playing Cilla Black. Sorry, but I really have to go now.'

Her friend sighed. 'Well, just give me a bell sometime. When you have a chance to catch up properly.'

'Will do. And thanks again,' Cordy added, trying not to feel guilty. She'd fallen out of the habit of meeting up with her old university friends, and sometimes it felt as if she only ever called them when she needed something. *Like right now.*

'No problem. I'm emailing it over now. Just drop me a line if you can't open the attachment.'

A couple of clicks of the mouse and there it was: a working list of minors missing after the Haiti earthquake, compiled by the international aid organisation that Nikki worked for. These were separated into sections: children who had disappeared from hospitals and children who were missing, presumed dead, but whose bodies had never been identified. There were twenty names on the first list. Some only had approximate heights and ages; others were listed alongside detailed biographical information. Date of birth. Family photos. The contact numbers of relatives, should they ever reappear.

For once, this didn't feel like a dead end.

Cordy felt a wave of nausea as she read through the list.

Maybe some of these are international adoptions, she told herself. *It must have been so chaotic, and the situation so desperate, that no one was really bothering with paperwork.*

After all, there were legitimate adoptions over those first few days. A hundred to the Netherlands. Forty to France . . .

But Cordy had worked for J4C long enough to know that that sort of chaos encouraged exploitation as well as altruism.

After all, children were valuable commodities – and not just for agencies working on behalf of rich Western couples desperate for a family of their own.

An accident on a tropical island. A prince who was a baddy in disguise.

She shuddered and scanned through the names again. No Rebecca. No Alice. No Caucasian girl of the right age at all.

Doubts started to prick, but she was determined not to let them undermine her resolve.

An eight-year-old girl who is resolute and together enough to send secret messages under the noses of her captors was not born into an abusive situation, Cordy told herself for what felt like the thousandth time since she'd started working on the case. *So it's up to you to work out how she ended up in this one.*

The second list was longer, the names more anonymous. While the suspicion was that the children in the first section had been illegally removed from the country, the hundred or so in the second section were probably still buried under rubble, or jumbled with other bodies in the anonymous graves that had been hastily dug in what were once parks and gardens. They were on the list because they had relatives who hadn't given up hope of finding them alive. Or, at least, of finding their remains. Of knowing how and where to mourn their loss.

So many lost children.

Cordy ignored the tears that were pricking the back of her eyes, and ran her eyes down the list. She highlighted a couple of possibilities, but when she looked at them more closely she saw that these Beckys and Beccas had French-Haitian surnames like Templier and Pradieu. A quick call to Nikki confirmed her suspicions: there were only a handful of European or American holidaymakers on the list – that, and a few children of foreign workers – and none that matched Alice's description.

'And since ninety-five per cent of Haitians are black,' Nikki said, 'and a good portion of the remainder are mulatto, I'm afraid it doesn't look like your girl's on there. I'm sorry. I didn't mean to get your hopes up.'

After she'd hung up for the second time, Cordy just sat and looked at the screen.

After hours spent keeping herself tensely alert, Cordelia's shoulders finally slumped. It felt as though she'd come to the end of the line.

She picked up her pencil to cross out 'Haiti Earthquake' – the only remaining option on her list of disasters – but then she paused, the lead hovering above the page.

She's not on there. But that only means that no one's looking for her. What if her parents are dead?

What if whoever she used to be is dead?

Cordy laid the pencil down. Nikki had warned her that the list was far from complete. It had been almost impossible to put together accurate records after the infrastructure collapsed so completely.

Maybe it's too soon to cross this one off . . .

And maybe, she thought miserably, *I'm just wrong. Wrong about Haiti. Wrong about everything.*

On the screen in front of her, the names of the missing children swam before her eyes.

Snap out of it.

She shook her head irritably. So the lists hadn't confirmed her theory? Well, they hadn't proved it wrong either.

Every instinct in Cordy's body told her that she was on the right track. And, despite the disaster with the raid, and the team's doubts about her, she still trusted her instincts. Strip away the case studies and the theoretical knowledge and the modern technology and really, deep down, they were all she had.

Alice had had a normal, happy childhood. Cordy could read that in every message, every gesture of resistance. Which meant that the wild, fairytale story – the earthquake on the exotic island – was increasingly more plausible than the usual grey tales of neglectful foster parents, abusive institutions and broken families.

But it was one thing to have a theory of how Alice ended up in the house. It was quite another to find a way of tracking down her abusers and getting her out.

Cordy's stomach rumbled, interrupting her thoughts. She looked down at the digital clock in the corner of her screen. It was already twelve o'clock. Anthony had been holed up with Fiona most of the morning, strategising their next steps. Bob and Tammy were out talking to Mark's neighbours and tracking down his friends and family.

Cordy opened her desk drawer and took out a Nutri-Grain bar from the box she stashed there. A little guiltily, she pushed the button on her phone so that it would go straight to voicemail.

Now, if I can just get an hour uninterrupted, I can figure this out. I can make it up to them.

Doggedly she went back over the case, making a mental list of leads to follow up that afternoon, when she was due to call Laura's mother.

Did Mark ever take Laura sailing? Or out on a fishing trip? Or refer to anyone as 'the captain'?

Did he—?

Cordy stopped, eyes fixed on the screen-grab in front of her.

Wasn't that . . . ?

She clicked to enlarge the image and gave a sharp intake of breath.

It is. It definitely is.

At once she realised what had been nagging at her for weeks, the thing that kept on skirting the edge of her consciousness. Alice's scar. It *was* a symbol. And, as if a key had just turned in her brain, she now knew what it was.

How could I not have seen that? she thought, angry and excited all at once.

With her finger she traced the curved edge and the sharp pointed shapes at the edge. *Wings. Of course.*

She Googled the airline and there it was: the symbol of a UK-based, no-frills transatlantic carrier.

The key kept on turning.

This is the way the captain rides . . .

They were looking for a pilot, or at least someone who worked for the airline. Alice must have seen this symbol – either on the way to the UK or in the cellar itself. *A uniform, maybe?*

With trembling fingers she clicked through the FlyRite website.

The first thing she checked was the airline's routes.

Come on, come on, she muttered as pop-up ads for last-minute deals got between her and the information she needed.

When she was finally through to the right page, it was all she could do to stop herself from punching the air.

Against all odds, her hunch was right.

Although the airline didn't fly to Haiti itself, there were a couple of flights a week to the Dominican Republic. Cordy double-checked the flight map and sank back in her seat.

A thin dotted line separated the two Caribbean countries. A land border.

Gotcha.

Scrolling through the list of contacts, she found the number for General Enquiries. Without a moment's hesitation she picked up the phone. After a good twenty minutes of being shuffled around automated voice systems, she finally got put through to an actual human being.

'Good afternoon. FlyRite,' a woman mumbled. 'How may I direct your call?'

Cordy asked to be put through to the HR department, and, after a few minutes of Muzak, found herself talking to a bored-sounding young man. Remembering Anthony's teasing about her people skills, she cranked up the charm.

'You must be *really* busy. But it would be *so* helpful if you could just have a quick look at the crew records for me.'

There was an uncomfortable pause. 'Right. That's not really . . .'

'It's for the week beginning the tenth of January 2010,' Cordy persisted. 'It's flight FY 291 I'm interested in. UK to the Dominican Republic.'

The man sighed. 'Out of Heathrow?'

'That's the one.'

'I would have to dig them out,' he said, grudgingly. 'And there might be some data protection issues. I'd have to check. What's this about, anyway?'

'I'm calling from a specialist branch of the Metropolitan Police,' Cordy said, aware that she was carefully rationing the truth. He didn't have to know she was just a civilian adviser. 'I'm afraid the case is highly confidential. But your help would be very much appreciated. What did you say your name was again?'

'Tim.'

'Well, Tim.' She dropped the charm-school approach, and let a hint of steel show in her voice. 'I know you wouldn't want to get in the way of an official police investigation.'

He grunted, but a few minutes later he was back on the phone, and this time he sounded much more awake.

'That was about the time of that earthquake, wasn't it?' he asked. 'Everyone was in a right tizz. I remember there was a question mark over whether we'd be flying at all.'

'Oh I'll bet,' Cordy said, trying to sound casual.

If she was wrong about the flights, then maybe she was wrong about the FlyRite symbol. And if she was wrong about that ...

'But here we go. There was a flight out, as scheduled, on the Thursday into San Juan airport.'

'And the names of the pilot and co-pilot?' she asked, hurriedly.

The man paused. 'Well, I'm not sure I should really be giving out that sort of information. You know, what with security and everything.'

Cordy took a deep breath, and changed tactics. 'Oh, well, if you're not authorised to, I wouldn't want to get you in trouble with your boss. Maybe there's someone else I could speak to?'

'Well ...' He relented. 'I suppose if it'll help with your investigation ...'

'Oh it would,' Cordy said quickly.

'So. Looks like ... Cynthia Daley and Rajesh Kumar were flying that day.'

Her heart sank. Neither of those sounded like 'the captain', although she dutifully wrote down the names just in case. 'Right. Thanks.'

'Yeah, the way it works here is that the same crew sign up for a set route for a couple of months. Helps maximise efficiency,' he confided. 'Although, having said that ...'

'What?'

'We did have one swap. At FlyRite we pride ourselves on offering flexibility to our staff, wherever possible. It's part of our mission statement.'

Cordy fought to keep her voice calm. 'I don't suppose you have their name.'

'Who?'

'The person who swapped shifts,' she said through gritted teeth.

'Oh yeah. It's a bloke who usually does our East Asian routes. Err . . . SV. That's, yeah, Stephen Viner. With a ph. Do you need the other crew names too?'

'How old is Stephen?' Cordy blurted out.

There was a pause. 'Which branch did you say you were calling from, again?'

'Tim, you have been most helpful,' Cordy said firmly then, rather than waiting for a reply, she put down the phone, wrote down the name and circled it twice.

Stephen Viner.

I'm onto you.

Chapter 48

Cordy had always thought the expression 'my heart was in my mouth' a bit of a cliché – one of those pat phrases that football commentators said to ratchet up the tension. Now she couldn't think of any other way to explain it to herself. She felt as though she was going to choke, her throat was so tight and full. She'd always disliked public speaking, but what made it worse was that this was so important. She had to convince them she knew what she was talking about. That her wild theory might actually be true.

'So . . .' the detective chief superintendent prompted.

Cordy looked around. The team were looking up at her expectantly – all except Bob, who was still worrying away at the morning crossword. Anthony gave her a reassuring smile. She took a deep breath.

'I, erm, I know who we're looking for. And I know who Alice is.'

At this Bob put down his pen.

She glanced down hurriedly at her notes. 'Rebecca Smith. Eight years old, in January 2010. She was listed as killed in the Haiti earthquake, along with her parents and a younger brother. I got the information from the British Honorary Consulate in Port-au-Prince.'

'I don't quite follow,' Fiona said. 'The age is right, yes, but there are a lot of eight-year-old girls in the world. And it says she was killed?'

'*Listed* as killed,' Cordy corrected. 'But take a look at this.'

She passed round blown-up versions of the photos she had taken earlier that week. With a highlighter she'd painstakingly picked out the words of Alice's story so that they jumped out of the scrawling mass around them. To make things easier, she'd also written the words and phrases out in what seemed to be a logical order.

'Did you get these from forensics?' Fiona asked, gesturing at the photos. 'Because this is the first time I've seen them.'

'I took them myself,' Cordy said quietly. She waited for Bob to make some crack about *The Da Vinci Code*, but he too was staring at the pictures.

'And you got from this . . . to Haiti?' Anthony asked. It wasn't clear whether he was impressed or just plain sceptical.

'Via FlyRite.' Quickly, she explained about the scar and about the crew member who'd specifically requested to change flight shifts straight after the earthquake. 'So he was there in the aftermath, just across the border. Stephen Viner. Nephew of Meg and Gerald Viner who own number twenty-seven. I know it all seems circumstantial, but when you put everything together—'

Tammy shut her up by leaning over for a high-five. 'Jesus, Hunter, you're a dark horse. Why didn't you tell us any of this stuff?'

'Yes,' said the chief, more seriously. 'I told you I wanted to be kept in the loop about any signs of progress.'

'I've only just confirmed that it's the same Viner,' Cordy explained. 'I didn't want to come to you with half-baked ideas.'

Bob made a sound that could have been a snort, but Tammy was nodding furiously.

'You know what? We should get on the phone. This Stephen Viner might have form in other countries. Sounds like he travels a fair bit. He might even have had a practice run elsewhere.'

'Thailand,' Cordy suggested, surprised and grateful that the young detective was backing her up. She hadn't expected support from that quarter. 'He usually does the Southeast Asia flights.'

'Him and a load of other perverts,' Bob muttered. 'Those low-cost airlines have a lot to answer for in terms of sex tourism.'

'Well, if we're looking to gather evidence of Viner's career as a paedophile, Bangkok seems as good a place as any to start,' Cordy said. 'I mean, we've already seen those DVDs . . .'

She glanced over at Anthony, but he was still staring down at the photo of the graffiti, mesmerised.

'Let's not get our hopes up quite yet,' Fiona warned, but Tammy was already making notes on her iPhone.

'So I'll contact Interpol and see if I can talk to the Thai police.' She looked up, suddenly. 'You know, I heard about this happening after the tsunami. Children going missing. Turning up as domestic servants – slaves really – or sex workers. They're separated from their families. They're vulnerable.'

'You're right. Could have given him the idea,' Fiona said slowly. 'But even then . . . Sampson, DeLuca, what do you think?'

'I can't believe you spotted this,' Anthony said, looking up at last, and Cordy felt a warm glow suffuse through her body.

Bob was more prosaic. 'Yeah. Impressive. Still . . . bit far-fetched, isn't it?' He jabbed at the paper. 'I can't say I really get what this is on about. She thinks she's a princess, or what?'

Cordy struggled to keep her voice calm. 'No, it's a story. This is just what gave me the idea. Pointed me in the right direction.'

'And you think it'll hold up in court?'

'I think that if I'm right about Viner we can get enough dirt on him that we won't need to mention scars, songs or princess stories. You don't *start off* by keeping three children locked in a cellar and selling clips of them being abused to order. You don't need a PhD in psychology to work that out.'

Bob looked at her appraisingly for a beat or two. Then he shrugged. 'Right then. I guess it's worth a shot. I mean, what the hell else do we have to go on?'

'Reynolds, do you mind putting this up on the whiteboard?' the detective chief superintendent asked. Reynolds nodded, connected up her laptop and the screen behind them blazed into life.

'Dr Hunter, go on,' Fiona prompted. 'We have an eight-year-old – this Rebecca Smith is definitely the right girl?'

Cordy nodded. 'The passport picture in the system is old, but it certainly looks like Alice. Brown hair. Blue eyes.'

'So we have a white eight-year-old and a relative of the Viners potentially in Haiti at the same time. Say you're right – she wasn't dead, and he found her, somehow – how did he get her back to East London?'

Tammy scribbled furiously as Cordy cautiously aired her theory. That amid all the chaos it might have been possible for Stephen – or an accomplice – to win the girl's trust and claim she was his daughter.

'All he'd have to do would be to say her passport was destroyed. I mean, it happened to so many people. And all everyone wanted to do was get home.'

'And she'd play along?' Fiona asked.

Cordy shrugged. 'She's scared. She's drugged. She trusts him. All these seem like viable theories to me. Could have been a combination of all three. What matters is whether we think it's possible that he got her out of the country and into this one without documentation. If he had friends in various airlines and airports, that would have helped.'

Fiona was nodding, slowly.

'I'll have a word with Customs and Immigration – they should be up on the latest people-smuggling routes. In the meantime we can focus on tracking down Viner.'

'Wonder if his aunt and uncle knew what he was up to?' Tammy asked, typing 'Relatives?' and drawing a box around it.

'I wouldn't have thought so,' Cordy said. 'That's going to be a difficult phone call, when we get hold of them.'

The chief seemed distracted. She'd been staring down at the graffiti, but now snapped back to attention, as if her mind was made up.

'Sampson's right. We don't have a lot to go on since Mark's gone to ground, so this' – she leaned over and tapped the board – 'is what we focus our efforts on now. Who knows,' she said, giving Cordy a wintry smile, 'perhaps our specialist consultant will be the one to salvage this mess of an operation, after all.'

Chapter 49

spurs101:   where have you been???
            i've got something to tell u
            this is important all right
clewis: I'm not the one who's been acting weird, am I?
            You know I can still blow your cover, right?
            any time I want
            All it'd take would be a couple of emails
            Mud sticks
spurs101:   listen, will ya
            just thought ud want to know
            they haven't given up
clewis: What the fuck?
            Thought you said they had nothing
            we could have got our little friends out the fuck-
            ing country by now
spurs101:   its all right
            we can handle it
            just get everyone together and I'll explain it all
            in person
            wherever you want
            you there?????
clewis: yeah
            No offence . . .
            But how do I know I can trust you?
spurs101:   jesusfuckingchrist
            havent I proved it to you

```
              ???
              aren't I in as deep as you perverts ??
clewis:       All right
              Keep your pants on
              I'll have a word
```

Chapter 50

They all looked up expectantly as Bob came back into the room after his catch-up session with the detective chief superintendent. The clack of keyboards stopped, and a phone rang out, unanswered.

'Don't know what you ugly lot are looking so excited about,' he grumbled. He nodded towards the phone. 'Isn't someone going to get that?'

Tammy made a face and grabbed for it, muttering an interrogative 'ECPU?' down the line.

'So no progress?' Anthony asked.

Bob sat down at his desk. 'Ah, we're getting there. I mean, we'd be getting there faster if Interpol knew their arse from their elbow. And as for the bloody Thai police . . .' He grimaced. 'It's like I always say: too much sun addles the brain. Getting answers out of that lot is like trying to knit with jelly. Might as well not bother.' Seeing Cordy was about to protest he held up a hand. 'I'm not being racist. Plenty of useless people over here too. But I am dead serious about the sun. That's what I tell Jean when she's on about moving to the Costas. Seriously, couple of months there and I'd be struggling to do the crossword, I reckon.'

'That why you didn't finish yesterday's?' Tammy asked, holding the phone to her neck. 'Not cloudy enough for you?'

He laughed. 'Cheeky cow. I'd like to see you come up with an eleven-letter word for "solid".'

'Impermeable,' Cordy muttered to Anthony, who winked back at her.

'What was that?' Bob asked.

'Nothing important,' Cordy said. 'You're saying we can't get a warrant for surveillance until we find out if he's got form abroad?'

Bob shrugged. 'He's not on the Sex Offender Register over here, so we need something concrete.'

'But if we had someone watching him . . .'

He shook his head. 'I know; we'd probably get enough to bang him up for life. Mad, isn't it? Chicken and egg.'

'But I – *we* – know it's him.'

'Course, officially we don't. Innocent until proven guilty and all that.' Seeing her expression, Bob softened his tone. 'Look, welcome to our world. It's frustrating as hell. I know it's tempting to cut corners. Nasty case like this, sometimes all you want to do is go round and string them up yourself. I mean, it's not like they don't deserve it. And it'd save a hell of a lot of faffing around with bits of paper and court appeals. Not to mention the *Thai police*.' He twitched the mouse to bring his screen back to life. 'But what, we string 'em up? Then what? Decent folk banged up in jail and who's gonna go after the next lot?'

'I was talking about surveillance,' Cordy said stiffly. 'Not . . . I don't know—'

He cut her off. 'I know. But you gotta use the system. Because Viner and that lot will sure as hell be on the phone to their lawyers the minute they're in custody, trying to squirm their way out of it all.'

Cordy nodded slowly. 'I know you're right. I just feel like . . . he's getting away.'

'Not for long he ain't,' Bob said grimly. 'But look, I gotta get back to work.'

Anthony glanced up from his computer. 'Any luck with getting hold of Laura's mother again? We've still got the old guy to track down, remember?' He looked grey and tired, his tone sharper than usual.

'Nothing this morning, but I'll try again right now,' Cordy promised.

She dialled the numbers and heard the tone ring again and again. Nothing. She tried once more. Either Tina was out or she didn't want to speak to her. In the age of mobiles and voicemail there was something very desolate about the sound of a phone ringing out, unanswered.

With a pang she thought of all the phone messages that Jess had been leaving in the last few weeks. At first Cordy had been careful to return each call promptly, making her voice husky in a guilty attempt to keep up the pretence of illness. But as the days had gone by without visitors, her sister's messages had started coming at more erratic times. The middle of the night. During the day when Cordy was at work with her mobile switched off.

It was all too easy to picture Jess sitting on the other end of the phone, waiting and waiting and then hanging up when the disembodied voice explained how to leave a message or call-back number. Then, Cordy tortured herself, the rocking would start up. Or, worse still, the scratching that would tear into the skin of her arms and leave her fingernails bloody.

But even if Cordy answered her phone, what could she say?

That she still had a cold? That she was too busy to visit her sister? That she didn't want to lead dangerous paedophiles to her sister's home?

The thing Cordelia wanted most in the world was to protect her sister from harm and now she was the one hurting her.

She was getting fewer emails, and the calls seemed to have dried up altogether. Maybe it was time to risk a visit to the clinic? She dreaded the thought of using public transport, of having to rub up against so many strangers. But perhaps if she took the Tube into town then took a taxi out again, maybe she could feel more confident that she'd definitely get to Jess undetected . . .

Cordy turned to look at Anthony, but he was staring intently at his computer screen, shoulders hunched. She didn't feel that she could interrupt him to tell him about Laura's mother, much less to pick his brains about her personal problems.

If only it were all over and everything were back to normal. For everyone.

If only there was something I could do to speed things up a little . . .

Almost of their own accord, her fingers had opened her notebook on the FlyRite page. The HR extension was circled at the top right corner of the page.

With a little sweet-talking, Tim at FlyRite might tell me Viner's home address, she realised. *His 'legit' one, since he probably has somewhere apart from his aunt and uncle's place. I can't see him wanting to draw attention to number 27.*

That's all it would take. A quick phone call.

She stopped herself. It was that kind of thinking that got her into this mess in the first place. What was she going to do – go and confront Stephen and his cronies herself? Scare them off again? Risk the children's safety because she wanted her life back?

I'll pass Tim's contact number on to Anthony, she thought. *He can take it from there.*

'Right, people,' Bob said loudly, cutting through her thoughts. 'I, for one, am going to call it a day. What with the time differences, there's no way we're going to hear anything useful today, and I promised my wife I'd be home on time for once.'

'Fair enough,' Tammy said, swivelling round on her chair. 'I'm just going to finish up this report then I'll head off too. Anyone want a last cup of tea?'

'I'm all right, but I'll give you a hand,' Cordy offered.

'Boss?' Tammy called, but it took Anthony a few beats to answer.

'Coffee,' he said eventually. 'Thanks. Think I might be here a while.'

'It'll be that instant crap, if that's all right? I think we're out of the fresh stuff.'

'Whatever.'

Cordy glanced over at him. Usually Anthony would turn his nose up at the economy-brand instant coffee they kept for emergencies. Under the harsh strip lights, his handsome face looked a little drawn and his shoulders were up around his ears. 'What you working on?' she asked. 'Anything I can help with?'

'Maybe tomorrow. If I've made some progress.' He didn't sound very hopeful. 'Basically, there has to be a way of tracking down this third man – the older guy. Now we know Stephen Viner and Mark Jones we need to fill in the blanks. I reckon the third man must have been around the block. Maybe he's the one with the contacts?'

'Maybe,' Cordy said thoughtfully. In all the fuss over Mark and now Stephen, the shadowy third figure – glimpsed in so many of the most horrific of the clips – had rather slipped away from her. In her head she assessed the power dynamics amongst the suspects. Mark was the muscles of the group, the one who had complete emotional control over Lolita/ Laura – the oldest, and potentially the most volatile of the child victims. He himself was younger, and probably easily manipulated by the other men. She'd bet money that Viner – the captain – was in charge, and had been from day one. That would fit with her theory about Alice's abduction, and would also explain why he kept the children at his relatives' house. He'd be a classic Type A personality type – only comfortable when he was in complete control. The older man, who seemed so quick to lash out at the kids – what was his role? Could he be the group's strategist? The sinister brains behind the business venture?

'Two sugars then?' Tammy asked, interrupting her theorising.

'Yeah.' Anthony gave her a quick smile. 'Sorry, I know it's my turn. But I said I'd have something to show the chief tomorrow and so far I've got sod all.'

'Won't Angie be expecting you home for tea?' Tammy asked. 'You know it's coming up to six thirty, right?'

'I said she shouldn't wait for me,' he said, turning back to the screen. 'But that coffee would be great. Or whatever masquerades as coffee around here.'

In the kitchen, Tammy shot Cordy a significant look.

'Hmm? Was it just the one herbal tea and two coffees then?' Cordy checked. 'Or will the chief want something, do you reckon?'

'Did you hear all that?' Tammy asked. She turned to fill the kettle. 'Sounds to me like there's trouble in paradise.'

'All what?' Cordy was still thinking about what Anthony had said about Suspect number three. If Mark had brought along Laura, and Stephen had got Alice and provided them with a secure business premises, what did the grey-haired man bring to the deal? The little boy they called Kurt, maybe?

'The DeLucas.' Tammy stretched up to reach down some mugs. 'When they were first married he was always rushing home to see her. Shameless clock-watching. Now he hardly mentions her.'

'It's just the case. We're all a bit distracted.'

Tammy looked unconvinced. 'All our cases are like this. Well, not always quite this bad, but you know what I mean.' She lowered her voice, even though the corridor outside was empty. 'My theory is that she's been shagging around. I know that he looks like a player but that's just his style. When it comes down to it he's a bloody good guy. And she's a bit . . .

well, up herself, if I'm honest. Never a hair out of place. And she works with all those doctors.'

'I thought you liked her?'

'I don't *not* like her. I'm just worried about DeLuca, that's all.' When Cordy didn't respond, Tammy carried on in the same stage whisper. 'If Ang is messing around, she's mad. I'd feel so bad for him. Then again,' she grinned, 'it's not like he'd be on his own for long.'

'Sure that's not wishful thinking?' Cordy asked lightly. 'The marriage troubles, I mean?'

Tammy turned and gave her a hard look. '*I've* got a boyfriend, all right? Look, forget I said anything.'

'The kettle's boiled,' Cordy said, and busied herself with the herbal tea bags, milk and cheap instant coffee.

As she walked back down the corridor, mug in hand, she tried not to think too hard about what Tammy had said. As long as she'd known Anthony, she'd known he was taken. Out of reach. Safe. *But if he wasn't . . .*

She stopped herself. Life was complicated enough at the minute without taking Tammy's gossip at face value. She succeeded in rearranging her face into a bland smile by the time she pushed open the Ops Room door. Anthony, however, was still hunched over his screen, oblivious to anyone else.

Chapter 51

Now she wasn't visiting Jess three times a week, Cordy was finding herself spending more and more time on her home computer, answering J4C emails or obsessively going over the case notes and the psychological profile of Stephen Viner that she'd been tasked with putting together. Not only was she desperate to help move the case forward, but the hours she spent staring at the screen helped distract her from the unwelcome realisation that her personal life was a little on the empty side.

It wasn't that she didn't have friends, or that she never went on dates. She did – although, looking at her desk diary, she was embarrassed to see that the last one hadn't been for months.

God, I'm turning into an old maid, she thought, wryly. *Maybe I should give up and get a cat.*

The last guy she'd dated had been a handsome banker called Andrew. They'd met at a kickboxing gym in Soho and, after he'd helped her improve her roundhouse kicks, she'd slept with him for a few weeks until he started talking about 'where this was heading'. Not wanting to be tied down, she'd told him she was busy with work and deleted his number from her phone. And that was that. It was hardly a conventional romance, but it had suited her – clean, neat, and devoid of mess or dark corners, just like her beloved flat.

Maybe she shouldn't have deleted his number after all . . .

Cordy finished washing up her dinner plate, helped herself to a glass of cold tap water and an apple and returned to the computer.

When she clicked on the Refresh button she saw that she'd received three new emails. One was spam. One was a quick query from Allyson about the layout of the new J4C website. The third was more interesting. It was from helendavies@ theguardian.co.uk:

> Dear Dr Hunter,
>
> I'm planning a feature for the Family section of the paper and I would love to interview you about your work for Justice4Children. It would be an opinion piece about the upcoming debate on changes to the child protection legislation, to run in this weekend's issue. We would, of course, print the charity's details so that readers could make a donation to support your work.
>
> I'm afraid the deadline is a little tight on this, as you'd be filling the place of someone who had to pull out at the last minute. If you were able to meet me as soon as possible, I would be very grateful. I'm more than happy to come to your home for the interview, if that would be more convenient. Please send the details of a good time and place to meet to this address.
>
> Looking forward to hearing from you,
>
> Yours sincerely,
>
> Helen Davies, Features Ed

Cordy took a long draught of water and tried to decide how she should reply. J4C could definitely do with the profile boost, especially now that the buzz from her last article seemed to have faded away. A prominent feature would certainly help with Allyson's new fundraising initiative, and help her sell tickets for the charity auction that summer. Not to mention the fact that Cordy still felt guilty for not being in the office. Of course Allyson had agreed to release her right-hand woman for secondment to the ECPU. But, even though she always claimed she was doing fine, Cordy could see that her old boss was struggling without her.

On the other hand, there was no way that Cordy could afford that sort of media exposure while the ECPU case was at such a precarious stage.

If Mark opened the weekend papers and saw my mug staring back at him . . .

'Wait, isn't that the bitch who was sneaking round my place?'

The thought, horrible as it was, almost made her laugh.

But if it could run, say, a few weeks after that. When Mark and the others are safely behind bars. The debates aren't till next month, after all . . .

Since there was no contact number in the email, she picked up the phone and dialled the number for the *Guardian* switchboard.

'Helen Davies, please. Editorial.'

'Hang on a sec. Putting you through.'

First there was chirpy hold music, then a click.

A woman's voice. 'Hello . . .'

Cordy was about to respond, but the voice just talked over her, and after a beat she realised that it was a recorded message.

Damn. Shouldn't have called so late.

'. . . you have reached Helen Davies's phone at the *Guardian: Weekend*. Please do not leave a message. Please press 0 to return to the switchboard. I am currently taking a long-term sabbatical from the *Guardian* in order to work on an overseas project with VSO and will not be returning calls regarding current or future features, but if you want to reach me at hel—'

With shaking hands, Cordy hung up before Helen even finished giving out her email address.

What the hell? So who—?

Just then, the phone rang, making her jump out of her seat. It was turned up loudly enough that she could hear it in the shower or on the treadmill, and to her disordered mind its sharp tone sounded oddly malevolent.

Her hand hovered over the receiver for a beat before she picked it up.

'Hunter?'

Hearing Anthony's familiar voice she felt her shoulders drop a little. Up until then she hadn't realised that she'd been braced for another attack.

'You there?' he asked. 'Everything all right?'

'Oh fine, fine,' Cordy said. 'I mean, I just got this ...' She stopped herself. 'Not important. What were you calling about?'

'We're there.'

'What?' Cordy tried to drag her mind away from the email. Either Helen was back at the *Guardian* and had somehow forgotten to change her voicemail, or someone else was trying to ...

'Just heard from the detective chief superintendent. We've got enough evidence to get a search warrant for Stephen Viner's house. Turns out he doesn't live far from his aunt and uncle's place.'

'That's ... that's brilliant!'

'I know,' Anthony said, sounding much more like himself than he had done for the past few days. 'In the end what swung it was the money trail. Which I think we'd all pretty much given up hope of.'

'What, from the site?' she asked, sitting back on her heels.

'Yep. Took a while, but a guy from the fraud squad traced it all back to a bank account opened in Thailand a year ago. And get this: there are regular payments set up from there to accounts in the UK. Stephen Viner. Mark Jones. And another name, Arnold Ashton. At last, we know who the old guy is. Finally.'

'Halle-bloody-lujah.'

'I know!' She could hear his grin down the phone and wished, for a beat, that they'd both been at the Unit when the news came through. 'Anyway, no time to sit around congratulating ourselves. We're going in tonight.'

'Tonight?'

'Yeah. The chief's theory is that what went wrong last time was that Viner or one of the other men spotted the surveillance team.'

And Sampson's theory is that it was all my fault, Cordy added silently. Out loud she just said, 'Right. But don't we have to do a recce? Do we even know if the kids are at Viner's place?'

'That's the assumption we're working on.'

Cordy frowned. 'I mean, I know it fits with what we know of their operation. But under pressure power structures can alter in unpredictable ways. It's not inconceivable that they've switched it up and the old guy is playing warden now. We've always said his role in the group was pretty murky.'

Anthony, however, didn't seem to be in the mood to listen to objections. 'Don't worry, that's all been factored in,' he assured her quickly. 'So we're all coming back to the Unit. Reynolds has tracked down Viner's current address and the plan is to go straight in without giving them a chance to get the wind up. Wham bam, bang 'em up. Get the kids out. If they're not there, we go to this Arnold guy's place. Same night. I know it's not perfect, but it's better odds than we've had for a while.'

'Wow. Well, I guess that makes sense,' Cordy said, struggling to process all this new information. 'And I'm sure the chief will have planned for every eventuality.'

'Great. So see you there in an hour? That all right? The detective chief superintendent will run through how it'll work when she's got us all there.'

After she hung up the phone, Cordy turned back to the computer and deleted the email from 'Helen'.

Maybe there was a reasonable explanation. Or maybe it was a set-up.

Maybe someone just wanted my home address. Or wanted to lure me to a meeting and then ...

She shook her head fiercely.

Either way, she didn't have time to think about it now.

We're going in. Tonight.

At the thought, a surge of energy jolted through her body, making her skin tingle. She couldn't tell if it was fear or excitement or both, but whatever it was was better than anything she'd been feeling for a while.

She sprang to her feet. If she hurried she could shower and change and still get to the Unit within the hour.

For a second the thought drew her up short. What was the proper attire for a night-time bust on a paedophile ring? Something familiar and domestic to help the children to trust her? Head-to-toe black, like a cat burglar?

The idea made her smile, and with a pang she wondered what Jess would have made of her sartorial dilemma. On her better days, Jess would pore over fashion magazines, pointing out to Cordy looks she liked and loathed.

But it had been a while since Cordy had been there for a good day.

When it's all over, she promised herself, *I'll be there for her again, just like before.*

Just as long as nothing goes wrong.

Chapter 52

spurs101:	theres been a change of plan
	gotta meet this evening
clewis:	Tonight?
spurs101:	yeah
	same place and time
clewis:	Ah, but we never go out without leaving a
	baby-sitter
	☺
spurs101:	look theres no time for mucking about
	this is serious
clewis:	Maybe you should plan on coming round and
	playing with the kids afterwards?
	Have a little hands-on fun
	I'm pretty sure that'll be all right with the others
	Only if you want to though
spurs101:	mate
	if you don't watch your back the only hands-on
	fun any of us will be having will be with our big
	butch cell-mates
	so you'd better be there
	all of you
clewis:	Fine
	I'll see what I can do
	Don't forget your balls are on the line too.
spurs101:	ud never never let me forget that

Chapter 53

'Sorry I'm late,' Bob said, letting the door to the Ops Room slam behind him. 'You wouldn't have thought the traffic would be too bad this time of the evening, but I got stuck behind a couple of bloody buses in that section where they're taking out the—'

'It's fine. Take a seat,' the detective chief superintendent said firmly. 'Now where was I?'

'Back-up,' Tammy reminded her.

'Yes. Or rather, lack thereof.' Fiona's frown deepened a notch. 'I'm afraid we're going to have to do without the RAR team this time. I knew it was unlikely given the late notice, but I thought it was still worth making the call, in case there was a team on standby. Apparently not.'

'But we're still going ahead tonight?' Bob checked. 'I didn't come all the way over here for nothing?'

'We've just been talking about that,' she said. 'So if you have any thoughts—'

'Speak now or forever hold your peace?'

Fiona gave him a quick smile. 'That's about the size of it.'

Bob looked around. 'Just us, right? Well, it's not ideal . . .'

Cordy followed his gaze. Tammy was still in her crumpled work clothes, but with her usual court shoes swapped for a pair of designer trainers. Anthony was in jeans. Fiona looked incongruous in an immaculate twin set and trouser suit. Cordy herself had opted for gym clothes. She wanted to be ready if running, or even fighting, was involved. Not that it would come to that.

'Of course we've told the local station,' Fiona continued. 'So there'll be a squad car or two on alert. We'll have uniform who can be on the scene in minutes if need be.'

Anthony cleared his throat. 'I think it's now or never,' he said. 'We just can't afford to let them slip away again.'

Although his words didn't seem to be aimed at anyone in particular, Cordy felt them like a stab in the gut.

Trying to put aside her worries about the children's safety, she blurted out her piece. 'There is no doubt in my mind that if they get wind of this second raid they'll take the children out of the country without a second thought. Since Stephen Viner is still showing up for his job, we can be pretty confident that that hasn't happened yet. Despite the risks involved, this does seem like our best chance of breaking the ring.'

Bob nodded. He turned to Tammy. 'DC Reynolds? What do you think?'

Tammy's eyes widened in surprise, but she soon regained her composure. 'I agree. We should go in tonight.'

'Good,' Fiona said briskly. 'That is, in fact, the decision I came to.' Ignoring Bob's grin, she started handing out sheets of paper.

'What's this from?' he asked, looking at the top sheet. 'Google Maps?'

The chief nodded. 'No time to pull up official street ordinance, so we work with what we've got. This is the layout of the road. I've circled the target's residence, and marked on where I think we should park the van. We'll go back to that in a second. Turn over and you'll see a rough outline of the timings.'

'Midnight raid,' Bob said, sucking on his teeth. 'Atmospheric.'

Anthony's head shot up. 'I thought we said eleven, didn't we?' he asked, turning to Fiona. 'When did that change?'

'What, are you worried about your beauty sleep?' Bob asked. 'Because I think it's all right to stay up past your bedtime this once.'

'Shut up, Sampson,' Anthony snapped. 'Now is not the time.'

Fiona glared at them both. 'The specific timing isn't the most important thing right now. Could slip back. Then again, if we're ready earlier there's no point hanging around.'

'So no need to synchronise watches, then?' Cordy said, and there was a flutter of nervous laughter that cleared the air.

'What's important,' Fiona continued, 'is how we minimise the risk for the victims. That means getting the kids out *before* confronting the suspects, if at all possible. Which I think we can do.' She looked around at them. 'That is, if we plan and run this thing seamlessly. With the minimum of screwing up.'

'From their earlier MO, we're only expecting Stephen Viner to be there, right?' Cordy checked. 'With the children, I mean.'

'Well, let's keep our fingers crossed that they haven't tightened up their security after last time,' Bob muttered. 'If all three of them are there and we haven't got proper back-up, things might get messy.'

A chill ran down Cordy's spine. She had never thought of herself as anything other than fearless – after all, many of her favourite pastimes came with a risk of serious injury. But the prospect of venturing into a nest of paedophiles suddenly hit her full force. Her body tensed and her senses sharpened, as if she was squaring up to an opponent in the ring.

This was really happening to her. To them all. Tonight.

If the others noticed a change in Cordy, they didn't say anything. When she managed to get a grip on her adrenaline and tune back into the conversation, the chief was talking about what they'd do if they broke in and the children weren't there.

'. . . but my bet is that Viner could be scared into turning his mates in. Course he's going to lead us to the kids if the alternative is taking the full whack himself. He'll want to see the others share the blame. Misery craves company, after all.'

Anthony let out a mirthless laugh from the corner, but when Cordy looked over he wouldn't meet her eye. Instead she looked down at her watch. Half nine.

In two and half hours they'd be breaking down the door, not knowing what they'd find inside.

A cold shiver ran down her spine.

Chapter 54

The sudden wail of a distant car alarm made them all jump. The owners must have been out of earshot because it kept going off, each iteration shredding Cordy's nerves a little more.

Through it all, the road ahead of them remained stubbornly clear.

'What the hell is keeping him?' Fiona snarled.

Bob pressed a button on his watch and peered into its illuminated face. 'Almost eleven.'

'How many times did we go through this? Jesus.' The detective chief superintendent rubbed a hand across her eyes, then turned to Tammy. 'I thought you said he was heading straight here from the Unit? If I'd known he would go AWOL I'd have insisted we all squash in the Comms van. For Christ's sake, he's the one who wanted it all moved forward.'

Tammy looked up from her mobile. 'I'm sorry. I've left a message, but he's not picking up.'

'Well, leave another one, then! This is a joke.'

'Chief, it's not Tam's fault,' Bob put in. 'Probably just took a wrong turn. I'm sure he'll turn up any second.'

If Fiona heard him she didn't make any sort of acknowledgement. Instead she stomped off muttering something about checking on the radios.

Tammy and Bob exchanged elaborate shrugs.

Cordy knew that she should step in and try to defuse the situation. She'd had the training, knew the techniques.

Problem was, right that minute it was all she could do to keep a hold of herself. Her blood was thrumming through her veins, and every sense seemed strangely heightened. Against her will, her eyes flicked across the road again. Parked opposite them, round the corner from Stephen Viner's house, was a motorbike, gleaming in the streetlights. It looked just like the Kawasaki Ninja that had tried to run her off the road.

Probably just a coincidence, she told herself firmly.

And even if it's not, tonight will put an end to all that. After tonight, everything will be back to normal.

Despite the mental shakedown, it was hard for her to wrench her eyes off the bike. Cordy bit her lip. Remembering Bob's reaction she was loath to point out the vehicle to the rest of the team. Besides, they had enough to worry about for one night. Plenty of time to investigate further and call forensics in when the perps were safely banged up.

Still, when the detective chief superintendent muttered for the hundredth time, 'Where the hell is DeLuca?' Cordy was hard pressed not to join in. Out of all of the team, he was the only one who'd understand. He'd know what to say to get her mind off the hulking motorbike and back to the children they were about to rescue.

If he ever shows up, that is.

She tried to draft a mental list of all the possible logical reasons for his tardiness.

He's been called away by a family emergency. She shook her head. *No way. He'd call and let us know.*

He's lost in East London and his phone has died.

He's had an accident . . .

Her stomach, already tight with nerves, convulsed, and for a second she thought she might throw up.

Calm down, you idiot, she told herself. *He'll be fine. We'll be fine. The kids will be fine.*

Eventually.

Strange things were happening to Cordy's sense of time, so that when Bob cleared his throat it could have been five minutes or two hours since the last person had spoken. A glance at her phone told her it was fifteen minutes.

'Look. Let's just go in, shall we?' he said. 'It's eleven thirty. The longer we fanny about out here, the more likely they are to get wind of us. The lights are off. With any luck Viner will be asleep and we'll be in and out in ten minutes – DeLuca or no DeLuca.'

Cordy turned to Fiona, pretty sure that she'd make a speech about sticking to the plan and following protocol, but instead she just nodded grimly.

'So should I still stay with the van?' Tammy asked.

'Yep,' the chief said, straightening up and suddenly sounding much more like herself. 'The local station are on call for back-up, if needs be, so just keep your eyes and ears open and we'll radio in if there are any issues. Hunter and Sampson go in with me. Everyone miked up?'

Cordelia and Bob looked at each other and nodded.

'Two minutes. Then we'll go in. And don't forget the breaching pack.'

'I'm on it,' Bob assured her, picking up a squat black battering ram and moving it from hand to hand, as if testing its weight. 'Can't believe DeLuca's missing all the Action Man stuff. It's his favourite part of the job.'

Now that the waiting was almost over, a strange calm descended on Cordelia. She felt her breathing regulate and her senses sharpen, as her hypervigilance kicked in. It was like time was slowing down, and the whole world was coming into perfect focus. She remembered the feeling from the most horrific time in her life, remembered how it helped her see clearly when all the world was going mad around her. She hoped to hell it'd do the same this time.

This is it: the chance we've been waiting for.

She looked around and every back yard, every rubbish bin, every chained-up bike seemed picked out in sharp detail. The moon was hidden behind a cloud, but there was so much light pollution that the sky glowed a dull purple.

It's never truly dark in a city, she reminded herself, gratefully.

The detective chief superintendent took a last look along the street and nodded to the team. 'All right then. Three. Two. One. Let's go.'

The next thing Cordy knew she was running down the street towards the house that backed on to Stephen's and hurtling over the small wall that sectioned off its front garden. Adrenaline coursing through her veins, she had no problem negotiating the much larger fence at the back of the house. Pausing a second to catch her breath, she glanced up – Stephen Viner, the one they called the captain, lived in this house. It all looked so ordinary – a plain, redbrick terrace, in a scruffy little garden littered with cheap plastic furniture and a rusty barbecue. For an instant Cordy felt a stab of uncertainty. What if they'd somehow got the wrong place, and were about to scare the living daylights out of some poor civilian family?

Maybe we should ...

But when she looked up, Bob was already at the back door. There was a crash and a few muttered curses and then they were inside, throwing their torch lights through doorways and taking the stairs two at a time.

'Hunter, sounds like the kids're up here!' the chief called. She'd entered right behind Bob, leaving Cordy to bring up the rear, as planned. 'First door on the left. You get them out. We'll find Viner.'

At the top of the stairs, Cordy swivelled left and tried the handle of the nearest door. Locked. Muffled sobs from behind it confirmed that Fiona was right – they'd found the kids.

Firstly she scanned the door for wires, holes, or anything that might indicate a booby-trap.

Nothing.

'Stand back! Away from the door,' she shouted. The battering ram was still downstairs, but a sharp, well-placed kick was
all it took to break it down.

Inside, the darkness seemed to have a deeper, danker quality than in the rest of the house. Instead of lighting it up,
Cordy turned the torch on herself, so that the children would
be able to see her clearly. She gave them a beat to take her in
– take in the fact that she was an adult, a woman, a stranger.
Although time was desperately important, she also knew that
the last thing she wanted was for the children to panic and
hurt themselves or each other.

'It's all right,' she said, forcing her voice to be calm and
gentle, despite knowing that Viner could appear any minute and
block their escape. 'I'm here. It's OK. We're going to go outside
together. No one will hurt you. Just come with me. It's OK.'

She tried to ignore the bangs and bumps coming from the
rest of the house. Bob and Fiona would have to shift for themselves. Her focus was here. The children.

As her eyes grew accustomed to the light, she began to make
out their shapes in the darkness. Mark's stepdaughter, Laura.
Kurt. And, huddled against the far side of the room, the girl
they called Alice: Rebecca Smith. The tiny box room was hot
and reeked of urine and something metallic and medicinal.
The children were all pressed into the shadows, faces averted,
as if they wanted to melt into the walls. The two girls shared
a child-sized mattress and the little boy – Kurt – was crying
quietly on a chair in the corner. Something scuttled across the
floorboards and the crying got louder.

'You all right?' Bob said, coming up behind her and peering past her. 'Fucking hell,' he murmured. The sight of the
children seemed to take all the breath out of his lungs, but he
quickly shook himself and recovered his voice. 'Let's get them
out of here. Viner's gone. Done a bolt, maybe, or—'

'He's out.' A small voice came from the corner of the room.

'What?' Bob asked, squinting into the darkness. 'Can't we get a light on these kids?'

'Keep the beam on the floor,' Cordy hissed as he aimed his torch straight at them. The younger kids put their hands over their faces but the older girl – Laura – didn't flinch.

'I said he's out. Gone down the pub. I'm in charge.' She put her hands on her thin hips. 'They'll be back any minute, you know. You'd better go or else.'

Bob made a move as if to speak, but Cordy shushed him.

'That's OK. Laura, is it?'

The girl chewed her lip. 'Lolita. Or Lolly. No one calls me Laura any more. I'm not a baby.'

Gently, Cordy edged towards her, stopping when she was a little over an arm's width away. She had to fight the urge to scoop up the three slight children and forcibly carry them to safety. But she knew how desperate these kids would be – how fragile and raw – and she didn't want to do anything to freak them out further.

'Do you want to come downstairs?' she asked, moving aside so there was a clear route to the door. She saw the girl hesitate. 'It's OK, you know. You're all right now. You're safe. You won't get into trouble.'

But Lolly crossed her arms across her chest and stood her ground. 'No. I'm in charge. My Mark will beat you shitless if he finds you here.' She looked around, squinting. 'There's a button I'm supposed to press—'

'What button?' asked Bob sharply.

'Button for when the nasty people come and try and take us away.'

Bob and Cordy exchanged a horrified glance. It was Cordy who recovered first.

'Let's go to the window, Lolly. We're not nasty people, so you don't need the button. We just want to talk. Maybe your friends can come over too?'

'They're not my friends,' the little girl said, but she'd turned away from the tangle of wires in the corner of the room and was sizing Cordy up. 'Do you have any chocolate?'

'Maybe,' Cordy said, glancing anxiously at the other children. Neither of them looked as if they would touch the home-made device (in fact they'd hardly moved a muscle since she entered the room), but it was increasingly clear that she needed to get them all out of there, right now. 'But maybe if you're in charge you can ask the others to get up too?'

'Fine. Up, you lazy fucking sods!' called Lolly, sounding more like a middle-aged builder than a pre-teen girl.

Obediently they creaked to their feet, heads still hanging towards the floor. Kurt was furiously scratching something behind his knee. Alice/Rebecca's eyes were fixed on the floor.

Bob was just radioing through an update to Fiona when they all heard Tammy's panicked voice over the radio.

'They're coming back. Repeat, suspects are approaching the house. Four suspects. Over.'

'Four?' Bob queried, snatching up the intercom. 'Not three?'

'Confirmed. Four suspects,' Tammy replied. 'Squad car standing by. Get the kids out of there. You have less than five minutes. Over.'

'All right,' Cordy said, turning to face the children. She bent down and tried to look them each in the eye in turn, making sure none of the tension of the situation was leaching into her voice. 'Now it's time to go outside. Let's see how fast you can go. Prizes for the quickest and carefulest.'

'No, we're not allowed,' Lolly said firmly. 'I have to stay here. We all have to stay and you have to go.' She took a step back from Cordy.

Just then they all heard the creak of the gate.

From the corner Kurt let out a keening wail.

'I told you—' Lolly began, but Bob interrupted her.

'Quiet. All of you. Now,' he hissed.

Instantly they obeyed.

Used to taking orders, Cordy thought, sickened and saddened to her core. She glanced over at the other, smaller girl, who was writing something with her finger in the layer of dust, crumbs and tissues that covered the filthy floor.

And if anything goes wrong . . .

But before she'd even had time to formulate the thought, she heard the key turn in the lock. And then something that made her gut flip over in confusion.

Chapter 55

Cordy could tell from the way Bob's eyes bulged that he'd heard it too. Holding a finger up to her lips, she crept to the door and strained to listen.

The voices from downstairs were loud and furred with alcohol. Cordy thought she recognised Mark's nasal tones.

'Thanks for getting that last round, mate. Owe you one.'

But it was the next voice that was shockingly familiar.

'Well, we can't all be tight bastards.'

'DeLuca?' mouthed Bob. 'What the—?'

Cordy held up a hand to stop him and asked in a hurried whisper: 'Was there an undercover element to the operation I wasn't told about?'

'What? You think we wouldn't have told you?'

'Never mind. No time for that now.' Cordy's mind was whirring. 'Look, did we close the back door after us? I don't think I did.'

'Wait up.' Bob paused for a beat before nodding. 'Yeah, I pulled it to when I went back downstairs to look for Viner. Just in case someone saw it hanging open and called the cops.'

'Good. That'll buy us a little more time to get the children—' She broke off as she heard Anthony starting up again. This time the voice was less clear, as if the men had moved out of the hallway and into one of the downstairs rooms, and no matter how hard she listened, all that Cordy could make out were scattered words. Quickly, she made a decision. 'Wait here. I'll check it out, and find where the chief has got to. If she's sticking to the plan, Tammy won't call for back-up until the children are safely outside. The last thing we want to do is provoke a hostage situation.'

Bob gestured his head towards the children, who were watching them with wide, preternaturally serious eyes. 'I'll stay here with this lot. But don't be long. We need to get out.'

On the way out of the door, Cordy caught a flash of movement. She froze in place, willing whoever it was to leave without seeing her. If the motorbike outside belonged to Viner, and he and his mates really had tried to run her off the road, there was no saying what they might do if they caught her on their territory. She assumed a fighting stance, ready to take on whoever was on the other side of the door. But then the movement came again and she almost laughed with relief. Fiona.

'Chief,' she hissed.

Cordy saw the detective chief superintendent jerk her head backwards, and then spin round, one hand going for her baton.

'Jesus, Hunter, it's you!' she mouthed back. 'You scared the crap out of me.'

'Bob's in the box room with the kids,' Cordy said, without missing a beat. 'I'm going down a little to find out what's going on.'

'Careful,' Fiona warned, but Cordy was already creeping over to the stairs and crouching down so that she was partially hidden by the banisters.

Finally, she could hear what was going on.

'. . . and I was like, mate, you must be kidding me. I wouldn't trust my own mother with that amount of money and I hardly know you.'

Mark again?

There was laughter and then an audible beat before Anthony could be heard.

'So, you gonna give us a look at these films of yours or what? Don't tell me you got me back here on false pretences.'

A voice Cordy didn't recognise – *Stephen Viner – the captain? Or the old guy, Arnold?* – said, 'Maybe another time. Laptop's upstairs.'

Anthony again. 'Ah, bring it down. I mean, if it's a hassle—'

The man didn't let him finish. 'Look, it's getting late. Another time, maybe. Did you want a beer for the road?'

'Cheers. But back in the Fox and Hound you did say—'

Another voice cut in. 'Cap'n, I told you he's all right. Let him have a quick squiz. What's the harm?'

There was a pause. Cordy felt as if electric cables connected her to Anthony downstairs. She seemed to feel every twitch of nerves and surge of adrenaline as they both waited to hear Viner's reaction.

Whatever Anthony's playing at, she thought, crossing her fingers, *I hope it's bloody working.*

Eventually Cordy heard Viner clear his throat. 'Well, I guess it's not a problem. I mean, if Arnold says you're OK, then you're OK, I guess.'

'Cheers. That's very decent of you.'

But Viner wasn't finished. 'In fact, I can do one better. Why don't you come and meet the stars of the show?'

'Well, sounds good, but, to be honest . . .'

Unable to wait for the rest of Anthony's answer, Cordy crept back up the stairs and into the box room.

Inside, Fiona was holding a whispered exchange over the radio with Tammy outside, keeping one eye on the children. Bob had managed to break the lock on the window and was testing whether or not the roof of next-door's extension would take his weight.

'They're coming up,' Cordy blurted out, without preamble. 'We get the kids out *now*.'

'What the hell is DeLuca up to?' Fiona asked, gently marshalling Lolly and Kurt towards the window.

'No idea, but we don't have much time,' she whispered. 'Sampson, that escape route OK, do you think?'

'If it'll hold a fatso like me . . .' He didn't bother to finish the sentence. 'Right. I'll go down now so I can lift them the last bit. See you outside in a few minutes.'

'But we're not *supposed* to,' Lolly protested once more, before allowing Fiona to lead her out of the window. 'You've got to have rules. Someone's got to be in charge.'

Kurt said nothing, but stubbornly refused to put down the battered backpack he clutched to his chest. With the men likely to appear any second, Fiona gently lifted him – backpack and all – down onto the roof three foot below, and into Bob's arms.

'You got the last one OK?' the chief called.

'Give me a sec.'

The one they called Alice was sitting on the edge of her mattress, staring at the words she'd drawn on the dirty floor. Now Lolly had got up, Cordy could see that the bedding was covered with lurid stains and she quickly shifted her eyes away.

The little girl didn't even look up as the others disappeared out of the window. Cordy hunched down in front of her, so that their faces were at the same level.

'Alice . . .' she said gently, first trying the name the child would have become accustomed to. There was no response.

When dealing with a traumatised child, Cordy generally tried not to touch them without their permission, but this was an emergency. Obviously Anthony would do his best to keep the men downstairs, but there was no way of knowing how much time he'd be able to buy. So Cordy reached across and gently touched the child's arm to get her attention. There was no response. Looking at her was like looking at a statue, rather than a living, breathing child.

'Look, I know it's scary but we've got to go.'

Nothing.

'I'm Cordelia, remember? I was here before too.'

Nothing.

'They're coming back, so we need to go.'

Cordy thought she spotted the smallest possible narrowing of the eyes at that. She shot a glance at the door. Was she imagining it, or was that a creak on the stairs?

'Look, Rebecca . . .'

At the name the girl's head snapped up, and for the first time she looked Cordy bang in the eyes. The intensity of her stare almost made Cordy falter.

'Rebecca,' she tried again. 'Come with me. Please.'

For a moment it looked as though that was all the response Cordy was going to get. She did a split-second assessment. In another thirty seconds she'd have to forcibly carry the traumatised girl to the window, or else barricade the two of them inside the room and hope for the best.

What, and wait for those predators to come and find us?

No, Cordy thought. *I've got to get her out of here.*

Just as she was taking a step forward, there was a jerky movement. Without a word the girl stood up and walked over to the window. Stiffly, as if she hadn't used her limbs in a long time, she lowered her skinny body onto the roof next door, where Fiona and the others were waiting to help her down.

So she was watching, after all, Cordy thought.

But there was no time to think about that. As soon as Fiona had made sure the last child was safely on the ground, she called up to Cordy.

'Right, you next. Make sure that Reynolds gets those kids off to hospital, then get in the van and wait for us to finish this off.'

Cordy shook her head fiercely. 'Leave? No way.'

'It wasn't a suggestion.'

'Look, I want to help arrest these monsters. Back-up isn't even here yet, and DeLuca's put himself on the line.'

'You know, if they don't kill him, I will,' Fiona snapped. 'Look, you're not a police officer. You don't have powers of arrest. And you need to get out of here.'

Cordy paused, horribly torn. She desperately wanted to stay with the victims, and make sure that they got the best care possible. On the other hand, the children were safe now, and there wasn't much she could do until a medical team had looked them over and they'd been given a chance to rest and recover somewhat.

And meanwhile her friend was trapped in a nest of vicious predators, who could turn on him at any second. It was three against one. She had to help even up those odds.

'Sorry,' Cordy said, her hands curling into tight fists, 'but I can't do that. Tammy knows the procedure. Child services should be on their way. They'll get the kids to the hospital. I'm staying right here.'

Through the open window, Fiona gave her a hard stare, but there was no time to argue, not when the suspects could appear any minute.

'Fine,' she said at last, pushing the broadcast button on her radio. 'Sampson, Reynolds, you copy this?'

'Confirmed.'

'The squad car's on its way, right?' the chief asked.

Tammy's voice came over the intercom. 'Two minutes. I made the call as soon as I saw the kids were out.'

'Copy that. Tell them to come in all sirens blazing. Will be good to have them in case things turn nasty. Meanwhile I'll get down off here, nip round and secure the back door, while Sampson goes round the front. We'll close this thing down.'

While the detective chief superintendent clambered down into the back garden, Cordy closed the window and slipped out into the corridor. It had not escaped her that she hadn't been included in the chief's plan, and now, beneath the thump of adrenaline was a flush of embarrassment. Should she really be here? Fiona was right. She was an amateur. A civilian. Was now really the time to be playing cops and robbers?

Cordy shook herself. She needed all her alertness, all her hyper-vigilance. Because, right this second, she and Anthony were the only team members left in the house.

Her vague plan had been to listen to see if she could pinpoint exactly where the men were in the house, but at the sound of a downstairs door being opened she panicked and slipped into the nearest room.

As she looked around, her heart fell. The artsy photographs of little boys and girls, the travel knick-knacks, the steward's uniform hanging on the back of the wardrobe – it all added up.

Stephen's room.

Another noise on the stairs made her pull the door to, leaving only the smallest crack to look through.

Suddenly she felt a wave of claustrophobia wash over her.

Three suspected paedophiles were sitting downstairs and instead of taking her chance to get out she was here: in Stephen's room, with the door still ajar.

Trapped in a predator's lair.

Chapter 56

There in Stephen Viner's room, the years fell away, and Cordy experienced the horribly familiar sensation of retreating inside her body. She was no longer a strong, educated woman – a biker, a kickboxer, a specialist consultant for the Elite Child Protection Unit. An adult. Instead she was a network of nerves, muscles and vulnerable flesh. It felt as though someone had torn her skin off and left her entirely exposed. Cordy could almost smell her uncle there with her – the sharp tang of sweat mixed with the sickly sweet smell of cheap gin.

He's not here, she told herself again and again. *He's not here and it's not the same.*

Her heart was pounding as if it wanted to escape her ribcage, and for a few seconds it was all she could do to wrestle her breathing under control and put her thoughts back into some semblance of order.

The children are safe outside in the van, she told herself. *The worst is over.*

So why did she feel such a palpable threat still looming over her and the rest of the team? Why did she catch herself moving into a fighting position, every nerve in her body taut as a violin string? Even as she assessed the situation, she felt an old, primal part of her gearing up to counter a vicious attack.

Cordy shook her head to clear it.

Anthony. That was the focus now.

Inching back towards the slightly ajar door, she put her ear against the crack, and heard the continued rumble of conversation coming up from downstairs. Anthony's voice was the easiest for her to pick out, and she was amazed to hear him sound so natural and confident. Something about his tone helped scare away the last few demons, and as moment followed moment, Cordy felt herself returning to normal, her adult self reassembling its protective armour and logical thought processes. What mattered now was the raid, not the skeletons in her closet.

'. . . Yeah, who did that guy think he was back there in the pub? Rambo, or what? Must have been all of five foot nothing. Well, I reckon he won't be back in that place any time soon.'

There were a few snorts of laughter at this and the sound of clinking bottles.

Anthony has the situation completely under control, she thought, with a tug of admiration. *He lured all three of the guys here together and gave us enough time to get the children out. Now, when Fiona and Bob come in with the arrest warrants, he'll be on hand to help subdue the suspects. A threat from the direction they least expected it.*

She remembered the lecture he gave her after she scoped out Mark's house.

So much for playing by the rules.

She stifled a smaller voice that wanted to know why he hadn't let her in on the scheme. For once she'd dropped her defences and let Anthony see what lay beneath her professional demeanour (the 'Ice Maiden mask', as her boss Allyson liked to call it). She'd told him about the threats, about her family, about her background. But he'd kept all this to himself.

But this isn't about you, Cordy reminded herself, as she felt the memories threaten to gain ground again. *It's about justice for those children. And if Anthony's figured out a way to prevent any of those rats fleeing the law, then no one has any right to complain. He'll get a big enough dressing-down from Fiona as it is, without me sticking my oar in.*

But a turn in the conversation downstairs pushed all these thoughts aside.

'Look, I should go and check on the kids.'

'Want me to come too, Captain?' Anthony asked.

The man laughed. 'You don't have to call me that, you know. But yeah, why not? Come on up.'

This time the creaks on the stairs were distinct and unmistakeable.

When Anthony spoke again ('Nice place you've got here'), Cordy almost jumped out of her skin. A strange echo effect made it sound as if he was right there in the room with her. Looking around she spotted a battered-looking laptop on the desk under the window. Wrapping her hand in her jumper sleeve to avoid adding new fingerprints, she nudged the mouse. The screen sprang to life. Because of the strange camera angle – more like CCTV than anything else – it took her a few seconds to recognise what she was looking at: the box room, now empty. Viner must have rigged up a remote webcam, because his and Anthony's voices were now being picked up by the microphone and bounced back into the room where Cordy was hiding. The effect was unnerving, but it certainly made listening in a whole lot easier.

'So Arnold was saying that you look after the security side of things?' Anthony said.

'You know, I did my research and that and it seems like the mistake people make is to integrate it into the building. Then you're stuck there, obviously. No plan B.'

'So we're talking cameras?' Cordy could tell that he was working hard to keep his tone casual. 'Portable cameras? Like CCTV?'

'Yeah that. But, I mean, that's a given. What with digital technology there's no need for bulky shit no more, and you

don't have to be in the same building to check everything's
OK. No. Arnold's more on about the *other* side of things. You
know, cleaning up our tracks if the shit hits the fan. I know
every fool thinks he can rig up some explosives, but that
system needs to be portable too.'

'Right.'

'I know the old boy doesn't like it. But, like I told him, you've
got to think in terms of worst-case scenario. It's worth shelling
out a bit more for that peace of mind.'

Cordy went cold with fear and horror. Anyone would think
he was talking about installing fire alarms, rather than a home-
made explosive device, designed to dispose of his child victims
in the event of a raid.

'Gotcha.'

'And, like I said,' Cordy heard Viner say, 'mine might not
look pretty, but it'll do the job all right. Won't be much DNA
or shit left if that thing goes off.'

As the voices got nearer and clearer, Cordy's heart-rate
accelerated once more. She glanced down at her watch. At this
rate, Bob and Fiona would come crashing in at any second,
just as Anthony was getting the ringleader to confess to his
crimes in front of the camera. She had to warn them, so she
made a snap decision.

'Hunter to Comms van, over,' she hissed into the intercom.

After a few seconds of static crackle she heard the reply.

'Comms van to Hunter. All set in there? Over.'

'Tam, you've got to hold them back for a few minutes,'
Cordy said, dropping all attempts at following protocol. 'No
time to explain. Just trust me. It'll be worth it. Over.'

While she was talking to Tammy, she never took her eyes
off the laptop screen. The shadows in the room altered as
someone opened the door. Two bodies glowed out of the
grainy image. Viner was shorter than Cordy had pictured
him, a good head and shoulders below Anthony. The

camera angle showed up a round bald spot on the centre of his head. She watched, eyes frozen to the moving image, as Viner started pacing back and forth, kicking the mattresses around.

Oh shit.

Now the voices were crystal clear. She clicked the symbol on the side of the screen to start recording.

'All right. Very funny. Where are they then?' She saw Anthony looking around, confused.

'An Oscar-worthy performance,' she muttered, trying hard not to be too impressed.

'Fine. I get it. Some sort of joke. Well, just wait a sec.' She saw Viner walk towards the door and disappear out of frame. She didn't need the help of the webcam microphones to hear him hollering down the stairs: 'Mark. Arnold. Get up here, you bunch of losers.'

More stair sounds and soon the small room was packed with male bodies.

For the first time, Cordy got a good look at the elusive third member of the team, the most vicious of the three: Arnold Ashton. She shivered. With his cardigan and neat grey beard he looked like the sort of grandfather who would have a ready supply of boiled sweets.

What did you expect, Cordy? she asked herself. *That he'd have devil horns and 'pervert' tattooed across his chest? Come on, you've been in the child protection game too long for that.*

Cordy could tell from their body language that Mark and Arnold were on the defensive. It was clear from the arms crossed against their chests and their dropped heads that Viner was very much in charge. By comparison, Anthony looked watchful and alert, ready to pounce.

But Viner was the one she was worried about. He was turning his head to face them each in turn, and his voice was starting to reveal more than a hint of steel.

'Come on, guys. You got me. Where are they? This ain't funny no more.'

'Loll,' Mark called, peering behind the door and into the cabinet under the sink. 'Lolly. Come out now, you little bitch. Game's over.'

'They're not in here,' Arnold said quietly. Cordy watched him move over to the door and finger the splintered wood near the doorknob. 'Was the door open when you got up here?'

'I don't . . .' There was a sudden bang as Viner kicked the door. 'Fuck, it wasn't locked, was it?'

'In which case—' Arnold started.

'All right, what the fuck is going on?' To her horror, Cordy saw Viner turn slowly to Anthony. 'It's you. It's you, isn't it? I knew something wasn't right about you.'

Because of where the camera was pointing, it was impossible to gauge Anthony's reaction to Viner's sudden attack. All she knew was that he held his ground and kept his mouth shut.

Viner took a step closer, jabbing his finger into Anthony's chest. 'You interfering bastard. What the fuck is this all about? Arnold said I could trust you. Said you were on side. Well, fuck this.'

Cordy saw Arnold put a hand on the captain's arm. 'Stephen, calm down. He didn't even know where we've been keeping them. There'll be a logical explanation. Kids could have broken the door down, somehow. I always said you should have put in a bar or something. You keep the front and back doors double-locked, don't you? Yeah? So they can't have gone very far. Mark, do ya wanna go check the other rooms?'

Cordy thanked God that in their panic they didn't think to check the window, and see that the lock had been broken.

But the thanks died on her lips when she saw the impression on the captain's face.

'I'm not going to fucking calm down,' Viner shouted, shaking Arnold off. 'He's a rat. He's screwed us all over.' He lunged for Anthony but with unexpected speed the detective grabbed his arm and twisted it behind his back.

Mark, who had been heading out through the door, stopped on the threshold.

Fuck. It's three against one.

They'll tear him to pieces right on the webcam.

I've got to get help. I've got to go and back him up.

Cordy dashed out of the room and into the corridor. Arnold yelped in surprise as she crashed into him, but her whole focus was on getting to Anthony. For a second her eyes locked with his through the open doorway. She saw something in his face that took her breath away. A desperation and despair that was animal in its intensity, and then a sudden flame of determination.

'Get out of here,' he mouthed.

Cordy shook her head. For a beat everyone seemed frozen in place, and then all at once Mark was lumbering towards her. 'You! You fuckin' bitch. Come here.'

Cordy took a few steps backwards, back into Viner's bedroom, bracing herself for a fight, when she heard something that stopped them both in their tracks.

It was Anthony's voice – as cool, calm and collected as it was when he talked about what he'd been up to over the weekend or whether they should expect rain that afternoon. But it was what he said that froze her in place.

'Well . . . guess that's it, then. All right, Captain. Let's see how good your security system really is.'

From the webcam, it almost seemed like slow motion, as Anthony dropped Viner's arm and lunged for the corner of the room where Lolly had pointed out the 'safety button'. He must have already scoped out where the switch was amidst the tangle of wires, because only seconds later there was a gut-wrenching explosion.

A scream cut through the noise and light and chaos and after a few seconds Cordy recognised it as her own.

Chapter 57

It's just like I'm back there back in the holiday place hotel and everything is going wrong and it wasn't supposed to be like this and where are they where is anyone I know? Here there is no one good to see but there are so many people and the nee-naws loud and loud and gone and loud again. There was a bang and now everything is ruined.

A lady comes and ladies are better Mummy says if you are lost but best is not to get lost in the first place and she is not the same lady from inside. The lady stranger is saying we will be OK but what does she know and the OK after the last time never happened. She comes down next to me and I am ready in case she tries to touch me but she doesn't because I cry when she gets too close.

And I am not OK and I want my mummy and my daddy and my brother and my school and my room and I say that or maybe I don't because no one seems to hear. The woman has blonde hair and all the shutting my fucking yap must have made my words funny because I say again and she just gives me a blanket. It smells like our old new car and I want to put it over my face and smell it and make everything else go away.

Lolly is here too but she's not listening. She's looking at the house and the fire and the holes and the rubbish and she is howling like a dog howls at the moon in cartoons. She won't take a blanket and she won't stop.

Chapter 58

In the seconds it took Cordy to realise what the hell was going on, fingers of acrid black smoke had already started to curl into the hallway, turning the air near the ceiling a deadly shade of grey.

Fire.

I've got to get out of here.

The impact of the explosion had slammed her body against the wall. It would have been worse – much worse – if she hadn't already been back in Viner's room. Reaching up she felt the wood of a doorframe and pushed the door closed, securing herself inside the room – Viner's room – away from Mark and the others. Even amidst the chaos her mind was working clearly. She couldn't afford to be caught now when her guard was down, and the air would be clearer the further she got from the box room.

Or what used to be the box room.

She refused to let herself think about that right now.

The jolt to her body made her wince, but there was no time to check for damage just yet. She looked around, noting the toxic fingers of smoke that were creeping round the doorframe.

The laptop.

I've got to get out of here, but I can't go without that laptop.

Her first thought was to leave by the same route as the children – out through the window, across the roof of next-door's extension – but the idea of leaving Anthony behind was enough to make her grab the laptop, put her sleeve to her face and pull the door back open.

Cordy hesitated on the threshold, disorientated. Now the corridor was eerily silent and the darkness was compounded by the clouds of smoke and dust that filled the air. Cradling the laptop against her body, she looked around for the door to the box room. It should have been just to her right, but everything looked strange and different, and the ringing in her ears made it hard to concentrate.

Just as she was getting her bearings, a body slammed into her, shoving her hard against the wall.

'What the—? Wait!'

But whoever it was had already flung her aside and was racing down the stairs.

Outside she could hear sirens wailing.

A fire engine. Hopefully a squad car or two.

They'll get him, she thought grimly. *Whoever it is.*

The corridor seemed much longer than she remembered. Maybe that was just because it was so hard to move through, now that the carpet was littered with debris and the top layer was choked with smoke. Only the smooth, warm feel of the laptop in her arms reminded Cordy that she hadn't fallen into a nightmare. That this was real.

She must have somehow missed the door to the box room, because her fingers found the door to the bathroom at the end of the corridor. Cursing herself, she turned round.

There is no time for mistakes.

It was just then that she stumbled over something on the ground. At first she thought it was just a pile of clothes or bedding, but there was something about the way it gave against her shin that made her look more closely.

Jesus.

A body.

For a moment all she could think about were the waxy corpses from old horror films. The ghostly pale. The red lips. The technicolour blood. Any moment now someone would shout 'Cut!' and the actor would spring back to life and wipe his make-up off.

The sound of a window shattering brought her back to reality.

There's no director here, calling the shots. So get a move on.

She bent closer to the body, and even before she'd wiped the soot from his mouth she knew.

Anthony.

Anthony's dead.

Everything in her body urged her to shake him back to life, to insist that he stop mucking around and get out of there before they both got killed. But before she got a chance, her first-aid training kicked in and she was on her hands and knees, checking his vital signs, laptop blindly placed behind her. Although his pulse was weak she felt a faint breath on her cheek and almost collapsed in relief.

The elation didn't last long.

Looking up she took in, for the first time, the hole that the explosion had blown into the outer wall of the house. The cold air gusting in must have been fanning the flames, because the children's mattress was turning into a ball of fire. Crouching just outside the room, the heat was so intense that Cordy had to close her eyes for a second. By the time she opened them, she had made a decision. It wasn't safe to stay there and wait to be rescued. If the building's structure had been damaged, the whole thing could come down at any second. The smoke and carbon monoxide in the air was making Cordy's head spin, and she struggled to set aside the random thoughts that were flooding into her brain, like the time she'd argued with her sister over a book they'd both read where the men were all strong and heroic and the women all beautiful and in dire need of being rescued.

Well, Cordy thought grimly, *if anyone's going to be doing any rescuing round here, it's me.*

There was a splutter and Anthony started moving his head.

She reached down and grabbed his hand. 'DeLuca. We're getting out now. It'll all be OK.' She looked at him intensely, noticing that his shirt and trousers were drenched in blood. 'Don't try to get up.'

He seemed to be trying to say something. She leaned closer.

'Go. Leave me here,' he croaked. 'It's all over for me.' She stared at him for a beat. It sounded as if he meant it.

Something dark and twisted was starting to untangle in Cordy's mind, but her sharply honed survivor's instinct told her that she couldn't afford to focus on it right now. When she spoke, her voice was brisk and businesslike. 'Shush now. I'm sorry, but this is going to hurt.'

She reached for the laptop, tucked it down her tracksuit top and zipped it up. It slipped about a bit when she moved, but it was the best she could do. She'd need both arms for Anthony.

Hooking one hand beneath each armpit, she started to drag him along the corridor towards the stairs, blocking out his cries of pain whenever she tripped or banged his body against the wall.

It's ten metres. Five metres. Two metres, she told herself, arms screaming under his dead weight. *And then downhill from there.*

Out loud she kept up a constant patter of encouragement. 'You're doing great. Well done. Nearly there.' And after a particularly piercing shout of pain, 'You'll thank me for this eventually.'

When they got to the stairs, she found that the easiest thing to do was to crawl down and drag Anthony after her. With each bump of the body, Cordy gritted her teeth and tried not to think about the irreparable damage she might be doing to his back, legs and head.

Anthony had stopped trying to talk now, and the quiet whimpers were worse than anything that had come before.

Those bastards, Cordy thought, letting the anger bring strength to her protesting muscles. *I'll make sure they pay for this.*

It seemed like hours – but could only have been minutes – before she was at the bottom of the stairs, in the hall, out onto the steps. The cool night air was so clean it hurt her lungs. She heard a scream of a fire engine's siren in the distance.

'Watch out, love,' a paramedic ordered, gently pushing her aside to get to Anthony. He put his face to the man's chest, then grabbed his wrists, checking for a pulse. 'Give us a hand,' he shouted at his female colleague. 'This one needs resus. Now. And someone stem the flow on that wound!'

The medic began pushing down on Anthony's chest and Cordy had to turn away, choked with shame.

I know how to do that. Why didn't I stop and do that?

'Get an oxygen mask on him. Quickly now.'

A female voice this time. 'He's not responding. Do you want the ECG?'

'Got it. Right. You ready? Clear! And . . . clear!'

There was a series of dull thuds as Anthony's body jerked up and back down on the stretcher. As the paramedic cut his trousers off, Cordy realised to her horror that the blood she'd seen earlier was now pouring freely from the mangled remains of his pelvis.

Someone – could have been anyone – wrapped a silver foil blanket around Cordy's shoulders, but all she could do was stare at the floor and listen to the sound of Anthony dying. The slackening rhythm of the heart massage. The frustrated 'Come on's of the paramedics. The terrible silence that meant they'd given up on him. That it was too late.

When the medics tried to examine her she batted them away, furious to find tears coursing down her cheeks.

She'd dragged a corpse to safety.
It was all her fault.

The laptop lay at the floor by her feet, gleaming in the moonlight like an accusation.

Chapter 59

It's like a doll's house. A doll's house that someone has taken a sledgehammer to, Cordy thought, looking up at the ruined building. Large sections of the side wall had been blown away, exposing the interior of the house to the neighbours' curious gazes. The garden was strewn with bits of brick and plaster and items so out of place – a television remote, a cheap plastic razor, a novelty toilet-roll holder – that it resembled a modern art installation.

Cordy closed her eyes for a beat or two, blocking it all out.

The only way to get through the night was to switch onto automatic pilot. Close down her feelings. Do her job. In the morning . . . Well, she'd deal with that when the time came. *If* it came. At the minute it felt as if the night would just go on forever – one long, unrelenting nightmare.

Another siren swelled in volume as a second fire engine approached the house, causing yet more lights to flick on up and down the street. Looking up, Cordy saw that the fire was already under control. Jets of water had damped down the flames, revealing the full extent of the smoke damage.

There goes our evidence, she thought grimly.

Although she'd insisted to the medics that she was fine, Cordy found it harder to stand than she'd expected. Her limbs, usually so strong and sure, felt weak and unreliable. Gritting her teeth, she tossed aside the thin metal blanket and hobbled over towards the Comms van, where Tammy would be able to give her an update on the children.

At least that *went according to plan.*

On her way she passed a group of police and medics crowded around something on the floor. Craning over their shoulders she saw that it was another body. Her heart convulsed. Who next? Bob? Fiona? She'd assumed they'd been out of blast range, but she felt that she'd assumed wrong about a lot of things lately. Steeling herself, she took a closer look.

The relief knocked the breath out of her.

Not one of ours. One of theirs.

The captain. Viner. He must have been flung from the building by the blast.

This time, looking at the soot-blackened corpse, she felt nothing. It was as though Anthony's death had drained the last drop of empathy from her. Coolly, she ran her eyes over the body. From the twisted angles of Viner's spine it was clear that they'd never get a chance to take him to court. Her snap assessment was confirmed when she saw the crime-scene photographer step back and the medic move in with a body bag.

'I know I'm not supposed to say this, but good riddance.'

Cordy turned to see Fiona standing behind her. The older woman looked her over.

'You OK, Hunter?'

Cordy nodded, not trusting herself to speak.

'Wait. Turn around,' the detective chief superintendent said sharply. When Cordy did, the chief was looking at her with a strange expression in her eyes.

'What is it?' she mumbled. 'Is there something on me? Is it blood?'

'No. It's . . . Whose laptop is that?' Fiona asked. 'Is it Viner's? Jesus, I can't believe you managed to hold on to that.'

Cordy looked down, confused. Hadn't she left it by the ambulance? But no, there it was, nestled under her arm.

'Yes. But I didn't get . . . I couldn't . . .'

She must have looked as if she were about to faint, because Fiona called over a couple of uniformed officers and asked them to show her to the Comms van.

When Cordy looked back she saw that the detective chief superintendent was already busy directing the photographers, surveyors and the forensics team. From watching her calm, authoritative gestures, you'd never have thought that she'd just lost a friend and a colleague. Cordy was pretty certain that she was one of the only people picking up the woman's emotional 'tells' – the slight quiver in her voice when she raised it, the hand clamped down by her side as if she didn't trust herself not to do something terrible with it. But to the rest of the world she looked like a woman in control – of herself, and the situation.

That's how I should be, Cordy upbraided herself. She shook off the young man in uniform who was guiding her by her elbow.

'You all right, Miss?' he asked, glancing over at her. 'Want to sit down? You've had a nasty shock.'

'It's Dr, actually,' she said. 'And I'm pretty sure I can take it from here.'

Tammy smiled gratefully when she saw that it was Cordy knocking on the van, which was parked safely around the corner from the crime scene.

'Thank God you're here. I've had my med check and debrief. Have you?' Cordy nodded. 'There was supposed to be a social services team here to take the little ones for medical treatment and psych evaluation but' – she looked nervously at the children, who were, to Cordy's dismay, still sitting in the rear seats – 'things didn't go quite to plan.'

'They should have gone straight to the hospital,' Cordy hissed, taking care to keep her voice low. 'We went over this, for God's sake.'

'I know but—'

Cordy cut across her. 'Oh, never mind. There're more important things to worry about right now. Is everyone OK?'

'You mean apart from . . .' Tammy couldn't finish the sentence, her bottom lip wobbling.

'Apart from what happened to DeLuca.'

'Yes.' The young detective looked up at her, and Cordy could see that she was trying very hard not to cry. *Jesus Christ, the last thing those kids need to see are bawling child protectors.* 'Yes,' she said more firmly, then continued more quietly, 'Sampson managed to catch Mark as he came out through the front door, but the third guy – Arnold Ashton – got away. In fact Sampson should be back any moment. Then I can take the kids to the hospital myself.'

'And you guys,' Cordy asked, turning to look at the children. 'Are you OK?'

Laura shrugged, thumb jammed in her mouth. She had wrapped a red blanket round and round herself so that only her pale face could be seen above it. When Cordy tried to catch her eye she turned and looked out through the window.

'We told her Mark was fine,' Tammy said in an undertone. 'Had to. She was screaming blue murder. Anyway, after that she calmed down. Now I can't get two words out of her. That one either. I thought she was going to at one point but nah, nothing.'

She gestured her head towards Rebecca, who was squeezed next to Lolly, rocking like an animal in a zoo.

Cordy inched a little closer. 'Rebecca. Are you OK?'

But it was as if she wasn't even there. The flash of recognition – of connection – that she'd felt up in the box room had gone, and for some reason that felt like the worst of all the terrible things that had happened that night.

Worse than Anthony? a little voice piped up. *Worse than that?*

Hurriedly she turned to Kurt, whose skinny arms were crossed against his chest.

'Kurt? Is there anything you need?'

He muttered something.

'Sorry, what was that?' She leaned closer to hear better.

'I said, you can fucking leave me alone you silly bitch whore.'

Despite her experience with abused children and their victim-speak, Cordy was still shocked to hear the words come out of such a tiny, angelic-looking boy. She backed away, and he shoved his hands down the front of his trousers and glared at her, his thin arm pumping mechanically up and down.

The girls didn't even seem to notice.

Classic oversexualised behaviour, Cordy noted. *We have to separate these kids ASAP.*

But while it was impossible not to feel horrified at the damage that had been inflicted on the children, already the professional part of Cordy's brain was ticking over, working out the best combinations of therapies that would help them work through what they'd endured at the paedophiles' hands. The terrible abuse that they'd then have to revisit for the trial.

Her plans were interrupted by a sharp bang on the van.

'Open up. Incoming.'

When Tammy slid the door open, she saw Bob standing there. About ten metres behind him she clocked Mark, cuffed, standing with a couple of uniformed officers. Fragments of pathetic excuses drifted over on the cold night air. Cordy glanced quickly at Laura, but if she'd noticed too, she didn't make any sign.

'Cordy.' Bob Sampson stopped, staring. 'Jeez. You look like shit.'

To her shock she laughed: a ragged, strange sound. When she touched her face, her hands came away black.

'Sorry, Sampson – didn't get a chance to fix my make-up.'

For a second they looked at each other. There was no need to say anything. Cordy knew they were both thinking the same thing.

DeLuca should be here too.

Cordy steeled herself against the tears that she could feel building up behind her eyes.

But Bob was never one for emotional moments.

'Reynolds, the chief said you can head back to the Unit now. Child Services are now on hand to take the kids to hospital. And Hunter, come and help me with this, will you?' he asked. Without waiting for a response he headed back over to Mark and the officers.

Cordy glanced over at Tammy.

'Oh, I'll be fine,' the young detective said. She lowered her voice. 'Are you sure you don't want to go to the hospital too? Smoke inhalation can be really serious, you know. No one would think any less of you.'

Cordy shook her head. 'Thanks. But I can get it checked out in the morning.'

'You coming or what?' Bob called and, grateful to have something to do, Cordy slipped out of the van and slammed the door closed.

As she walked over towards the four men, she took a good hard look at Mark. Surrounded by policemen, he looked smaller than Cordy remembered, but despite the fact that his arms were being pinioned behind his back, he still maintained at least a glimmer of his old arrogant swagger.

'You!' he said as Cordy approached. 'I knew you, the moment I saw you back there, you fucking bitch.' In an undertone he added, 'And I know where you live.'

Cordy ignored him, and turned to face Bob.

'Has he told you where Arnold Ashton lives yet?'

Bob shook his head, looking for all the world like a disappointed head teacher. 'I'm afraid he hasn't.'

'I told you, I don't know nuffin,' Mark said, swivelling his head this way and that as if looking for someone to back him up. 'Those guys are fuck-all to do with me. Never seen them before in my life. I swear. I ain't done nothing wrong. There's no fucking way I'm going down for this.'

'Oh, are you not?' Cordy asked. 'Because from where I'm standing, it looks like you're wanting to take the full rap for this. Cos that's what'll happen if your mate gets away.' She turned to Bob. 'How long do you reckon he'll get, all told? I mean, if we pin the whole thing on him: planning, kidnap, child molestation, money laundering, killing a police officer.'

'Who the fuck said anything about killing anyone?' Mark asked, clearly struggling to keep his cool. 'Don't give me any of that good cop/bad cop shit. Where's my lawyer?' He looked around, as if expecting a lawyer to materialise any minute. 'I want my fucking lawyer. This is going to make me suicidal. And I need medical attention! I'm injured!' he continued, gesturing to a small cut on his forehead. 'You can't deny me that. I have rights!'

But Bob was ignoring him, busy counting on his fingers. 'I reckon he should get out by the time he's – what? – sixty. That said, it's not a . . .' He stopped, seemingly to choose his words more carefully. ' . . . a *pleasant* experience, being in jail for sex crimes. Especially against children.'

'You do hear some horrifying stories,' Cordy agreed.

Mark jerked round to face her full on. 'That's bollocks. I didn't do nuffink.'

That's when Bob drew up to his full height and let him have it. 'You know what, you're fucking scum. But you know what else? There's even lower scum than you. Do you think that old bastard Arnold Ashton would hesitate one second before turning you in, if he thought it might give him an easier ride? No way.'

'After all, he just left you here, didn't he?' Cordy put in.

'Nah, mate.' Mark caught himself. 'Anyway, I told you, I don't know a fucking thing.'

'Yes,' Bob said emphatically. 'He fucked off and left you to take this shit all on your ownsome. We've got an officer down too. D'ya know that? Do you know what happens to cop killers? I don't even want to tell you what happens to cop killers.'

'That's a load of shit,' Mark said, but his shoulders were starting to sag. 'I didn't kill no one.'

Bob saw him weaken and moved in. 'Well, your mate Viner's dead.' At this news Mark's head snapped up but, before he got a chance to ask any questions, the detective ploughed straight on. 'And Ashton's buggered off. So, as things stand, you're the only one up for it. So bear that in mind, you little fuck.' He let that sink in for a second. 'Look, just tell us his address. We'll find it out anyway, but this will be quicker. This will show you're willing to cooperate. And he never has to know. Then we'll get a paramedic to check you over.'

'This is all bollocks.'

'It's up to you,' Bob said, shrugging. 'I mean, this is just my job, mate. I'm not the one looking at life at Her Majesty's pleasure.'

Mark mumbled something.

'What?'

'Mannerton Gardens. Two something. Two A?'

Bob cracked a smile. 'Right, that wasn't so hard, was it? Come on. You can ride along with us.'

'But you said—'

An 'accidental' jerk on the arms silenced Mark, and after Bob had thanked the local cops, the three of them headed over to Sampson's patrol car.

Cordy walked a little in front, unnerved by the feeling of Mark's eyes on her back. Bob had radioed the chief to tell her what was happening and she was also going to set off with a squad car and meet them at Ashton's.

The drive there was tense. Mark kept up a running monologue about how unfair it all was, and how all cops were twisted.

'We've been set up. I never did shit. Ask my stepdaughter. She'll tell you I had nuffin to do with it.'

'Shut it,' Bob said, and rammed his fist on the toughened plastic screen that separated them. 'Or I'll shut it for you.'

By the time they got to Mannerton Gardens, a squad car was already sitting outside and Fiona was holding onto a bowed-looking Ashton.

'How the fuck did you beat us here?' Bob asked.

'Good thing we did,' the detective chief superintendent said. 'This *suspect* was trying to burn his stash. Photos. DVDs. Luckily we got to him before he'd destroyed his home computer.' She nodded over to where it sat, wires trailing, in the middle of the lawn.

'You won't get anything off that,' Ashton spat. 'I can guarantee it.'

Bob came up close to him and looked him up and down. 'Oh, I guarantee we will. We've got a young man on our tech team who does this sort of thing in his sleep.'

'You're bluffing.'

'Just wait and see.'

'I've got this covered,' the chief said, stepping forward. 'Forensics are on their way. So if you want to get these two *gentlemen* back to the station . . .'

'Done,' Bob said, roughly grabbing hold of Ashton's shoulder and pulling him round to the other side of the car. 'In you go. Watch your head now.'

For a tense moment Cordy thought he was going to smash the old man's head against the bodywork, but at the last moment he reached up a hand and guided him safely inside.

Without another word, she got back into the front seat, feeling utterly drained.

She glanced at the clock. It was impossible to believe that only a couple of hours had passed since they had been sitting round the corner from Viner's house, planning the raid.

Meanwhile, Mark was still busy alternately whining, demanding medical attention and protesting his innocence in the back. Cordy tried to tune him out, like an irritating song on the radio, but when no one interrupted him, his self-assertions just grew louder and more forceful. By the time they were halfway across London, he had really worked himself into a lather.

'All I'm saying is, even if we did what you said we did, who are we hurting, really? I mean, it's capitalism isn't it, supply and demand. Isn't that right, Arnold? That's what you always say.'

Slowly the older man turned and stared hard at his fellow prisoner. Quietly, precisely, he said: 'Just shut your fucking face.'

'Thank you,' Bob said from the front. 'At least we agree on something.'

The rest of the ride passed in silence.

Chapter 60

The harsh, halogen lights of the ECPU foyer made Cordy's head throb. On Fiona's insistence she'd gone home for a few hours after they'd given their statements, and had had their official individual and team debriefs, and full medical check-ups, but despite her exhaustion she'd found herself lying in bed, staring at the ceiling, unable to sleep. At one point she had reached for a sleeping pill, but the thought of waking up and having to remember last night's events all over again stayed her hand. Now it was 10 a.m., she was back at work, and the building was buzzing with life. The normally surly receptionist greeted her with a smile. Cordy tried to return it, but her face didn't seem to process the instruction. By the time she'd forced her lips to twitch upwards, the girl at the desk had turned to take a call.

On the way into work Cordy had stopped off at the Unit's safe house in Bermondsey. The house mother had told her that the children were back from the hospital, but they were still asleep. She promised to ring Cordy when they were up and about. Unit policy was that child victims were to have a few days' rest and recovery time before any official statements were taken, but Cordy was keen to establish a rapport as soon as possible. Their abusers had been the only care figures in the children's lives for months now, and it was vital that they were made to understand that some adults could be trusted.

And, Cordy admitted to herself, she wanted to talk to Rebecca, the one her captors had called Alice. Wanted to get to know this little girl who reminded her so strongly of her former self. The girl whose messages seemed aimed straight at her.

Not to mention that focusing on the children seemed like the best way to tear her mind away from the image of Anthony lying there amidst the rubble. Then covered in a blanket. Taken off to the morgue.

How the hell had that happened?

As she waited for the lift, Cordy went over the implications of last night for what felt like the thousandth time. But instead of theories, all she ended up with was a series of unanswered questions that cycled endlessly through her head, shock still marring her normally clear analytical skills.

He wanted to take justice into his hands.

I, more than anyone, can understand that.

But why would he put himself in so much danger? Why try to kill the men, when the team were waiting outside to arrest them? Why risk his own life to punish them? Did he think Stephen was bluffing about the explosive device?

And then there was that look he gave me . . .

With a ding the lift was there, and Cordy squeezed in amongst the assorted police officers and administrative staff.

'Fifth floor please.'

As they went up, the questions gathered pace.

How did he make contact with the men? Why didn't he tell us? Why didn't he tell me?

It was opening the door to the Ops Room that broke the obsessive thought cycle.

There it was. Anthony's desk – looking for all the world as though he'd left it a moment ago to nip to the toilet or make a round of tea.

Hastily, Cordy shut the door again, and went to track down the rest of the team.

She found Bob and Fiona in Fiona's office.

'Thought you were supposed to be resting,' Bob said brusquely when she knocked on the door.

'Good morning to you too,' Cordy said. 'What's happening?'

Bob pulled a face. 'Arnold Ashton's refusing to talk without his lawyer present, so we left him to stew for a bit. Which means we're in for another fun session with that mouthy scrote Mark.'

'You can observe if you like,' Fiona said, pushing herself up off the desk. 'Might be useful to have your thoughts.'

'Will do. But have neither of you had a chance to sleep?' Cordy asked, taking in their drawn faces.

Fiona shrugged. 'Had a quick lie-down on the sofa. I'll be fine. When a police officer gets murdered. Well, it's our job as his friends and colleagues to get him justice. That said, I sent Reynolds home a few hours ago – she was in pieces. Sampson's insisting he's good to push on through.'

'Plenty of time to sleep when you're dead,' Bob quipped, and then turned ashen. 'Bollocks. I didn't mean—'

'Let's go,' the chief said crisply. She turned to Cordy, 'Let's see what Mr Jones has to say for himself.'

It was an uncanny feeling to sit behind the one-way glass, seeing Mark and her colleagues and knowing that they couldn't see her. Mark – perhaps thanks to his long rap-sheet, or perhaps just because he'd seen a lot of cop shows – kept looking around, sometimes staring right at Cordy as if he knew she was there. Whenever that happened she caught herself inching away from the glass.

But right now the suspect was too busy protesting his innocence to worry about hidden cameras or the like.

'How many times do I have to say this?' he whined. 'I know nothing about it. Nothing.'

Fiona sighed. 'Once more, how did you get involved with Stephen Viner and Arnold Ashton?'

'Never met those blokes in my life before. Met 'em down the pub, in fact.' He was grinning, as if pleased with this particular bit of invention.

'But your stepdaughter was locked in Viner's house,' the detective chief superintendent pointed out. 'And we have extensive footage that shows a connection going back almost a year, as well as bank transactions that prove your involvement with both Viner and Ashton.'

'Yeah, and?' He crossed his arms in front of his chest.

'And do we have to go through this all again?' Bob asked wearily. 'Come on. You know how it works. You're gonna get nailed for this. And you're gonna go down. The only question is whether you're prepared to be a sucker and take the rap for your friends, or whether you play it smart.'

'You'd love that, wouldn't you?'

'No,' Bob said simply. 'What I'd love is for you to get the maximum sentence.' He turned to Fiona. 'Look, boss, I told you this was a bad idea. We've got a strong case already. And Ashton'll tell us everything we need to know. Not to mention the children themselves.'

'Lolly'll back me up, you'll see,' Mark said, but his sneer was starting to falter.

'Perhaps. But there're two other victims in custody,' Fiona said coolly.

'Look, this is clearly a waste of time.' Bob scraped back his chair and stood up. 'Let's get Ashton in here instead. He doesn't seem like the sort to take one for the team.'

'Wait,' Mark said. 'Just . . . Hold on a sec.'

'Yeah?'

There was a pause while the suspect fiddled with the piece of paper in front of him, setting out his legal rights. 'Thing is . . . none of this was my idea.'

'Well, I figured that you weren't exactly the brains behind the operation,' Bob said.

Mark ignored the dig. 'I mean I was getting along fine. I got laid off but I had a nice little sideline in—' He stopped abruptly.

Fiona leaned forwards. 'Look, we're not interested in minor misdemeanours here. We just want to hear about the Internet scheme.'

'I think getting reported to the social is the least of your worries,' Bob added.

Mark shot him a poisonous look. 'Fine. So I used to sort some of my friends out. I mean, just weed and stuff. And, err, you know, special-interest stuff. Home-made videos and photos and shit.'

Cordy felt her stomach churn.

Fiona didn't even look up from her notes. 'Did any of these videos feature your stepdaughter, Laura?'

Mark shrugged. 'She liked the attention. She'll tell you herself.'

'Go on.'

'So anyway,' Mark said, clearly warming to his theme. 'I was dead subtle about it. Used to just do it down my local, and people would come to me, you know? Word of mouth, I guess. Not a load of money, but pretty decent. Anyway, you get to know the type, right. So one day this old geezer – Arnold, that is – comes up to me and I think he just wants to buy a DVD or some shit like that but turns out he got one from a friend and was after meeting Loll himself.'

'Had this happened before?' Bob asked.

'Not like someone I didn't know. But he seemed all right and he was offering a couple of hundred quid if I took Loll round to his mate's house. So it was all his idea, really.'

'Did he give you the money then and there?'

'Nah,' Mark snorted. 'He's too tight a bastard for all that. Half up front and half afterwards, that was the deal.'

'Then what happened?' Bob asked.

'Not much to tell, really. So the first time was all right and I met the other guy Viner – the Captain, he liked to be called – and it became sort of a regular thing. Loll didn't mind. She's a good girl. And after a bit there were other kids there and stuff.'

Fiona looked up sharply. 'How many kids?'

'Just that Alice one to start with. Moody little bitch. There'd be others that'd come and go – be there for a weekend or something. Then the boy showed up. Not that I'm into that,' Mark said, quickly. 'I'm not queer or nothing. But, you know, live and let live.'

'And you never asked where they came from?' she asked.

'None of my business.' He smirked. 'In my world, it's best not to ask too many questions.'

'And the Internet scheme,' Bob prompted. 'When did that happen?'

'Ah, that was definitely the Captain's thing. All his idea. Called me up one day and said he'd seen this site in the States doing, like, pay-per-view, and did I want to try it out and I said, look, mate, sounds like a hassle, but if you want to do it, go ahead. And fair dues, once it was up and running it was a nice little earner.'

Fiona nodded blankly. 'Is that when Laura started sleeping at Viner's house?'

Mark shrugged. 'Yeah, probably. I mean, her mum just left her with me. No money or nuffin, you know what I mean? To be fair, I stuck it out for a bit but after a while it just seemed easier to leave her with the others. Bit of company for her, you know? And, to be honest, it got her out of my hair.'

'And you took turns to stay overnight with the kids.'

'Only when Viner was on stopover somewhere. Still.' Mark sucked his teeth. 'Bit of a pain in the arse. Arnold was always on at him about getting transferred to short haul. Hah. Like he'd go for that.'

'And this happened how frequently?'

'Dunno. Sometimes. Sometimes they just used the remote webcam. Look. I was just helping out, that's all,' Mark said, then lapsed into stubborn silence.

Fiona's phone went off.

'One minute.' With an apologetic look at Bob she stepped out into the corridor.

Now that he was alone with Mark, Bob's face hardened.

'Detective Chief Superintendent Andrews is called away from the room, ten thirty-five.' He reached back and flicked off a switch. After a brief hesitation he turned to Mark. 'Right, you scumbag.'

'Scumbag? I like that. As soon as the fucking tape's off . . .'

'There is one more thing I want to ask you about. While we're all cosy like.' He looked down at his notebook. 'Where were you on the morning of March the fifth, around nine a.m.?'

'Well, I ain't exactly got my diary to hand . . .'

Cordy felt a cold shiver running down her spine. She, at least, knew where this was headed.

'Well,' Bob said firmly. 'Try and think back. We're investigating a suspected automotive attack that took place on Lemington Road. Now, does that ring any bells?'

'Automotive attack?'

'You tried to ram my colleague off the road on your motorbike,' Bob explained, nodding towards the two-way glass. 'That clearer for you?'

'Look, mate,' Mark said, sitting back. 'I just do what I'm told.'

'So you admit that you were responsible?'

'Nah. All I'm saying is that it wasn't my call. And anyway, that bitch had it coming. Did you know she came sniffing round my place, no warrant, no nothing?' He put his hands behind his head and leaned back further. 'Half a mind to do her for trespass or some shit like that.'

Behind the glass, Cordy's heart was racing.

Why was I so fucking stupid? If he gets off on a technicality ...

'Yeah. Great idea,' Bob said sharply. 'Then we can hit you with a counter-charge of attempted murder.'

That shut him up, and helped slow Cordy's pulse down a little.

'Sorry, folks,' Fiona said, coming back in. 'Now where were we?'

For a few minutes Mark sulked, looking down at his hands and answering questions with single-word answers. It looked to Cordy as if Bob and Fiona were about to wrap it up, when the detective chief superintendent tried one final question.

'So why did you move the kids from Twenty-seven Millhouse Lane, then? Whose decision was that?'

For the first time since the talk of the 'accident', Mark looked up and smiled a weaselly smile. 'You'll have to talk to Arnold about that. Bent copper, by the sounds of it. Same psycho that tried to blow us all up.'

'Anthony DeLuca?' Bob asked sharply. 'The man from yesterday?'

Mark just shrugged. 'Like I said. Talk to Arnold Ashton. I don't know nothing about it.'

'All right,' Fiona said, standing up. 'I think we'll stop it there. You've been very . . . helpful.'

'Any chance of a burger? Cheeseburger would be good. Maybe a Coke or something. I can't concentrate when I'm hungry.'

'We'll see what we can do about getting you some food,' Fiona assured him.

Cordy saw Bob's hand clench into a fist on the table and, looking down, saw that her own were twisted painfully together.

'I mean even just some chips or something. I know my rights, you know.'

'Like I said,' Fiona said grimly, 'we'll see what we can do.'

Chapter 61

Under the harsh neon of the corridor lights they avoided each other's eyes.

Bob muttered something that sounded like 'a fucking cheeseburger' but when Cordy shot him a look he was already squinting at his phone, checking for messages.

Fiona was looking down at her notes, frowning, and Cordy had a strong impulse just to slip away, to leave them to sort out the mess themselves.

Not my problem, she tried to tell herself. *I'm a temporary consultant. That's all. Not even a proper part of the team.*

But the creeping numbness she felt told its own story.

'What did I miss?' Tammy asked, rounding the corner and joining the rest of the team outside the interview room. 'Who'd you have in there? And did either of 'em roll over yet?'

'Weren't you supposed to be going home and resting?' Bob asked.

'Well, I did. For a bit.'

Cordy looked at the purple half-moons under the young detective's eyes and knew she was lying.

Fiona dragged herself away from her notes long enough to catch Tammy up on the interview. When she got to her final question she hesitated.

'Did he say anything about DeLuca?' Tammy pressed. 'About how he infiltrated the gang?'

'No,' the chief said slowly. 'But he implied that Detective Inspector DeLuca was . . . I don't know.'

'Bent,' Bob supplied.

'Fine. Bent,' she said. 'According to Mark at least. We haven't spoken to Arnold Ashton yet.'

But Tammy was already shaking her head. 'Well of course that's what he'd want them to think. Double bluff. He wasn't stupid.'

'I was thinking along the same lines,' the detective chief superintendent admitted. 'Yes, it was stupid and dangerous – utterly reckless, really – to go undercover without the proper intelligence and resources, and I'd have been the first to call for disciplinary action. But we all knew DeLuca. He was an honourable man and a dedicated child protector – one of the best I've ever worked with – and he died in the line of duty.'

'Mark's generally full of bullshit,' Bob put in.

'Bullshit,' Tammy repeated softly. 'That's all it is.'

'I mean,' Fiona said, 'there was no way DeLuca could have known that Viner would detonate the device. We figured they'd have a defence system, but—'

Here Cordy had to cut her off. 'But it wasn't Viner who pressed the button. It was DeLuca. I saw it with my own eyes.'

There was a beat's silence.

Fiona shook her head decisively. 'But that doesn't make any sense . . .'

'Just look at the camera feed from the laptop if you don't believe me.' Cordy hated herself for what she was about to say, but she knew she couldn't keep quiet. 'And if Mark's just talking bullshit, how did the suspects know about the first raid?' She paused, knowing her words were explosive and wanting to choose them carefully. 'Look, I don't like it any more than you do, but I think we need to start seriously considering the possibility that DeLuca was in this deeper than we first thought.'

Before anyone else realised what was happening, Tammy had taken a step forward and jerked her hand back to slap

Cordy across the face. Instinctively Cordy blocked her, grabbing Tammy's arm and twisting it behind her back. For a second she was tempted to push upwards – no one got away with hitting Cordy any more, in or out of the ring – but when she felt the girl's body go limp she just let go and pushed her away in disgust.

'Reynolds!' Fiona yelled, barrelling forwards. 'What the hell? Do that again and I'll personally make sure this is your last day in the force.'

But Tammy wasn't listening. She was staring at Cordy, her face seemingly drained of blood. When her voice came it was strangled with rage.

'In deeper?' She cradled her arm against her body. 'What the fuck are you on about? What, you think DeLuca was involved with those perverts? You hardly knew him! You swan in here and think you know better than everyone else—'

'Calm down, love,' Bob said, putting an arm on her back. 'We're all gutted about Anthony.'

But Tammy shook him off. She was still staring at Cordy, who felt as though she was frozen to the spot, unable to say a word in her own defence.

'I can't believe this. If it wasn't for you he'd still be alive,' Tammy spat. 'You were the one who jeopardised the whole operation. He was cleaning up your fucking mess.'

'If it wasn't for Hunter,' Fiona snapped, 'Sampson and I would be dead too. She was the one who told us to wait a few minutes, remember? Back when we were all set to come crashing in and arrest those guys, right before the explosion. If she hadn't, we might all be on the slab. Is that what you'd prefer? And what makes you think that it could possibly be acceptable to physically assault a member of the team?'

'She's not one of us.' Tammy shook her head, eyes dull. 'She's nothing. And she's not going to bad-mouth DeLuca any more.' Her voice cracked a little. 'It's not fair. He's not here to defend himself.'

Fiona looked as if she had quite a bit more to say, but Bob stepped in between the women.

'Come on, love,' he said, forcibly taking his young colleague by the shoulders. 'Let's go and get you a cup of tea.'

'Good idea,' Fiona said. Her voice was calmer now, but there was a telltale tightness in her lips. 'Are you OK, Dr Hunter?'

'Fine,' Cordy managed. She turned to Tammy. 'Let's talk about it later, all right? We're all upset.'

Tammy shrugged, not meeting her eye. Bob patted her shoulder, looking awkward in his new role of peacekeeper.

The detective chief superintendent smoothed out her crumpled suit and gave them a stern look. 'Right. It's been a hard night for everyone. Maybe I was wrong to try and start getting statements from the perps straight away.' She looked at her watch. 'So. Here's what's going to happen. I don't want to see any of you before three p.m., at the very earliest. Go home. Go to sleep. And come back when you're ready to do your jobs. And that means,' she said, eyeballing Tammy, 'no more fisticuffs. Got it?'

'Sorry, Chief,' Tammy said at last, before Bob steered her away. She looked up at Cordy as if thinking about extending the apology, but reddened and turned away.

Great, she hates me, Cordy thought. *Which is all I need.*

When the others left, Cordy found herself still standing in the corridor, unable to work up the effort to move. Her body ached from slamming into the wall the night before. On her arm she could see an angry bruise already starting to bloom. She traced its outline, then pressed a little harder against the tender flesh, momentarily distracted by the familiar swell of pain.

She can't bear to think that Anthony might be anything other than the hero in this situation.

The sick thing is, I hope she's right. Because if she isn't . . .

Again she saw the determination on his face as he pressed the button. But her exhausted brain refused to finish the thought. She would look at the laptop footage the next day.

Chapter 62

When Cordy walked into the Ops Room the next morning, Tammy studiously failed to look up from her call.

Lovely. The silent treatment.

They'd successfully avoided each other all yesterday afternoon, and Cordy had hoped that the young detective would have got over herself in the interim. After all, Tammy had to realise that she wasn't the only person affected by Anthony's death, that the rest of the team was suffering too.

Apparently no such luck.

'Morning.' Bob gestured across at Tammy's bowed head. 'She's trying to track down Kurt's mother. Sad story. Homeless, from what we can gather. Teen runaway, maybe. Or a crackhead on the game. Anyway, sooner we find her the better. Are you in with the shrink this morning?'

Cordy nodded. 'It's Laura's debrief. In fact, I'm just picking up some files and then heading over.'

'Rather you than me,' Bob muttered, and turned back to his screen. 'That stuff's enough to give you nightmares.'

When she was leaving the room, files tucked under her arm, Cordy couldn't help but glance at the place where Anthony should have been sitting. Although his death was far too raw for people to start using the desk as a dumping ground, already it had acquired a patina of disuse. The pint glass that Anthony kept constantly to hand ('never knowingly dehydrated,' as Bob had quipped) was empty, and Cordy's fingers itched to tidy up the bulging in-tray.

He's gone. He's actually gone.

The thought struck her with all the intensity of a fresh realisation, despite the fact that it had already hit her over and over again in the past thirty-six hours.

But the children, she reminded herself, *are here.*

And one of them's waiting for you right now. So pull yourself together and get your arse over there.

'I like your necklace,' Laura said, as soon as Cordy walked in. 'Can I see it?'

Automatically her hand flew to her chest, covering it but, looking again at Laura's face, she found herself gently lifting the chain over her head. 'Sure. If you're careful.'

When Cordy handed over the locket, the little girl clamped her fingers over it, as if she'd never give it back. Her pretty face hardened as she shot Cordy a look that was part cunning, part outright defiance. But when it became clear that no one would tell her off, she unclenched her fingers and had a proper look at it.

'It's pretty,' she said. 'A pretty one.'

'It's half a heart,' Cordy said, reaching over to press down the clasp for her. 'My sister has the other part.'

'Right.' She closed it again quickly, with barely a glance.

The child psychologist, a pale woman with thin, greying hair and a bright silk scarf, took that as her cue.

'So Laura . . .'

'Lolly,' the girl corrected, dropping the necklace on the desk. Cordy tried not to wince. Her grandmother had given her and her sister the matching necklaces soon after the crash that had left them orphans. It meant more to her than anything she owned, including her beloved motorbike.

'Lolly. I'm Karen.' The psychologist made no motion to touch the girl, but gave her an encouraging smile. 'And this is Cordelia.'

'Cordy is fine. We've met already.'

From Lolly's blank face it was unclear how much she remembered of the night of the raid.

Or how much she's allowing herself to remember, Cordy thought, hearing again her screams as the house burned.

Karen nodded, and turned back to the girl. 'First things first: this is a safe space. You can talk about anything you like. I won't be writing anything down. This is just for you, OK?'

The girl shrugged.

'Nothing you say will get you in trouble with your stepfather, or Arnold Ashton, or the Captain, as he made you call him sometimes,' the psychologist said.

'What do you want me to do?' Lolly asked, staring at the half-heart pendant again.

'Just talk to me. About anything you like.'

'About the dirty stuff?' The way she said it made Cordy's heart contract – it was so matter-of-fact, as if she was talking about a subject she didn't like at school.

The psychologist's expression remained bland and benign. 'If you like.'

'I'm not supposed to.'

Cordy leaned forward. 'It's OK to now. I promise. The men are talking to the police already. We just want to hear your side of things.'

Lolly carried on looking down at the table and the silence dragged on.

Karen and Cordy looked at each other, both clearly reluctant to push her.

Eventually, in a dull, flat tone, Lolly started talking. It sounded as if she was retelling the story of some book or film she only partly remembered, or had perhaps heard about second-hand. But even with the distance that this implied, the story was hard to hear. Rather than talk about how Mark's abuse had begun, she cut straight to the point where the

Captain and Arnold had become involved, as if that was when the 'dirty stuff' began, in her mind.

'He smelled bad – the old one – but you've got to be a good girl. Sometimes it was him and sometimes it was the Captain and sometimes it was . . .' She shook her head before she carried on. 'And sometimes it was your turn and sometimes not. Sometimes they brought other kids.'

'Kids you knew?' Cordy asked, gently.

'Seen 'em around,' Lolly said. 'Some of 'em. He didn't care about them. About any of them.'

'Go on. You're doing really well.'

'I'd been going there for a bit. Weekends, mostly. The Captain's place. Then that girl Alice was there and then it was more and more.'

'And would Mark go with you?' Cordy asked.

At the mention of his name, Lolly's head snapped up and she focused her full attention on Cordy. It was unnerving, like watching someone brought back to life by a shock of electricity.

'Mark? You know Mark? He's not hurt, is he?' Up until this point the words had been halting, but now they came spilling out of her mouth, sometimes tangled together. 'They said he wasn't hurt but sometimes people lie. Can we go home now? He said it wouldn't be for long and then we could go home and it would be like before. Please can I go home? Is Mark coming?' She craned her neck around as if expecting him to appear any moment.

The psychologist glanced at Cordy and she nodded.

Karen cleared her throat. 'Now, Lolly, I know this is hard to hear but Mark has done some bad things. The police are making sure that he doesn't do more bad things.'

'He's not arrested?' She looked back and forth between them. 'He is, isn't he? He's locked up. You've locked him up. This is a joke.'

'Lolly,' Cordy put in gently, 'I know you're worried about Mark. But he's in a safe place. Now we're just trying to get him the help he needs.'

Karen nodded. 'You don't need to worry about Mark for a bit. We're here to help you.'

Lolly slammed her little fist down on the table. 'You . . . you pigs should take your fucking pig noses out of other people's business.'

'Is that what Mark says?' the psychologist asked.

'Why are you keeping him away from me?' The girl's voice was getting louder and more hysterical. 'What did I do? I didn't do anything? Why are you doing this to me?'

Karen waited until she paused for breath before replying, in the same low, calm voice. 'Are you OK, Lolly? Do you want to take a break?'

But the girl had turned to Cordy, and her eyes were pleading. 'Where am I going to go if he's locked up? He's my daddy now. He loves me. He said he does. He said everyone would try to turn me against him. He's right, isn't he?'

Cordy took a deep breath before replying. 'Lolly, it's going to be all right. We don't have all the answers yet, but we're here for you. And, like I said, we're going to make sure that Mark gets help too. Remember that.' She glanced across at Karen. 'Why don't you guys go and get a Coke from the canteen and we can talk some more in a bit?'

'That's a good idea,' Karen said brightly. 'We can chat again after a break, when everyone's feeling nice and calm.'

'Lolly?'

'Whatever.'

'Great. Maybe, in fact,' Cordy said, looking round at the stark interior of the interview room, 'we can head out to the park and talk there. Feed the ducks.'

At this Lolly rolled her eyes. 'I'm not a baby, you know.'

'Well, you don't have to, but I'm definitely going to be feeding them,' Cordy said. 'I've been saving my crusts for weeks. No wonder my hair's so straight.'

'Not funny,' Lolly pronounced, but Cordy thought she caught the ghost of a smile on her lips.

'I'll check with the detective chief superintendent,' Cordy said when she clocked Karen's sceptical expression. 'But I'm sure it'll be OK.'

'Well, I could certainly do with some fresh air,' the therapist said, bending down to pick up her voluminous black handbag.

'See you guys in, say, twenty minutes,' Cordy said, waving a goodbye. 'Can I take this back?' she asked, gesturing at the necklace. 'Or do you want to look after it for me? Until this afternoon.'

The girl nodded, eyes down, fingers running through the gold chain.

'I'll keep an eye on it,' the psychologist mouthed. 'Looks valuable.'

'Only to me.'

Outside Fiona was waiting, pacing back and forth in the corridor.

'Sorry, I was about to come to your office,' Cordy said. 'We're just taking a quick break. Laura's debrief.'

Fiona barely waited for the end of the sentence before launching right in. 'So I've just got off the phone to Tina, Laura's mother.'

'You managed to get hold of her again then? I called and called yesterday afternoon, but never even managed to leave a message.'

The detective chief superintendent nodded. 'Social services managed to track down a mobile number for us.'

'Well, that's a relief . . .'

The door to the interview room opened and Lolly and Karen came out.

Fiona gave the pair of them a smile and then sharply hustled Cordy down the corridor and into her office. Instead of sitting in her chair, she just leaned heavily against her desk. She didn't offer Cordy a chair either.

'So, I'm afraid it's not looking good,' the chief said, as soon as she saw the door was closed. 'Apparently Tina Jones, the mother, says she can't *handle* her daughter right now. That's a direct quote.'

Cordy winced. 'Foster home, then?'

'They're trying to sort something out. Poor kid. She saying much?'

'More than I expected,' Cordy said. 'And I think if we get her in a more friendly environment this afternoon, she might open up even more.'

'Good,' Fiona said, 'because so far she's our best hope as a witness. Kurt's so young and word from the safe house is that Alice, I mean Rebecca, is still refusing to speak.'

'I should go and talk to her.'

'One at a time,' the detective chief superintendent said. 'Focus on Laura for today, please.' With a sigh she stood up and walked around her desk. 'Well, that's all really. Report back when you've finished, will you?'

Cordy saw that she was being dismissed, but there was a question that had been nagging away at her ever since the raid, making sleep impossible and turning the waking world into a blur.

Now that she had the detective chief superintendent alone she couldn't *not* ask it.

She paused on the threshold. 'So, DI DeLuca. I can't seem to stop thinking about what the hell was really going on back there. I know we're working from the assumption that DeLuca was somehow undercover, but we both know that that doesn't make a hell of a lot of sense.' She took a deep breath. 'And I have a couple of theories that do. In confidence, what do you think really happened?'

'I think that I'd rather not talk about this,' Fiona said wearily, 'just as I'm about to phone his wife and persuade her to give us access to his personal computer.' She let that sink in for a beat or two. 'And I don't need to tell you, that's not going to be a fun phone call.'

Cordy swallowed heavily. 'I'm sorry, it's just . . .'

'And quite aside from that, I've got Mr Ashton holed up with his lawyer night and day plotting God-knows-what.' She turned away from Cordy, towards her computer screen. 'And I'll be damned if I'm going to let the defence pick holes in the case because my best child defender decided to turn vigilante. So if there's nothing else?'

'Sorry, I'll leave you to it. And good luck. With the phone call, I mean.'

It wasn't clear whether she heard or not, but just before Cordy left the office she heard the detective chief superintendent pick up her heavy desk phone and start tapping in numbers.

Chapter 63

She was riding over to the safe house when she got the call. Feeling the vibration in her jacket pocket, she checked behind her and, after waiting for a bus to go past, pulled over to the side of the road.

Still straddling the bike, she flipped her phone open. 'Hello.'

'Cordy . . .' The line was bad, but it was a male voice. A deep one. Stupidly, her heart skipped a beat.

'Hello?'

Of course it couldn't be, but it sounded a bit like . . .

'Sorry, it's me. Sampson. Have you got a sec?'

'Well, I'm on my way somewhere. Can it wait?' she asked curtly, furious at herself for being so deluded.

What, you're expecting a phone call from beyond the grave, now?

'Just calling to say that I've called a team meeting for this afternoon.' There was a pause. 'I really think you should be there.'

'At the Unit? What time?'

'Soon as you can get back here.'

Cordy cursed under her breath. It was three days since the raid, and she still hadn't had an opportunity to talk to Rebecca. Now that the doctors had certified that the girl's health was stable, Cordelia was supposed to be spending the afternoon with her. It felt as though the whole case had been building towards the moment when she'd finally get to know the girl behind the messages, and now the moment was being delayed. *Again.*

'Cordy, you still there?'

'Yep.' A passing cyclist shot her a filthy look, and she glared back.

Jesus, I'm not even in your way.

'So you're heading back now?' Bob persisted.

'Yeah. Looks like I am.' Cordy flicked her ignition back on. 'This'd better be worth it,' she muttered, but not until Bob had already hung up.

Back at the Unit she found the others already sitting round the table in the middle of the Ops Room.

'Sorry, shall I get tea or anything?' she asked, hovering for a moment.

'No,' Fiona said simply. 'Just sit down.' She turned to Bob. 'Well then? What's this about?'

Cordy looked up, half expecting him to crack some inappropriate joke like he would have done in the old days, but his expression was grim. 'Right. So while the tech boys have been going through Viner's laptop, I've been taking a look at Arnold Ashton's.' He tapped it vaguely, and Cordy did a double take. It looked almost exactly like her home laptop – she'd assumed it was Bob's, or another member of the team's. 'Mick restored the hard drive for us last night, so that's what I've been doing all morning.'

'And?' Fiona asked.

'And luckily for us he's a methodical sort of guy. There was a lot to sort through, and I haven't finished yet. Bank statements, that sort of thing. Emails all filed away.' He paused, looking deeply uncomfortable. 'And look. There's really no easy way to say this.'

'So spit it out.' The chief crossed her arms in front of her chest. 'Come on, Sampson, we don't have all day.'

'All right. Listen then. This is a conversation between, whatever he calls himself: "clewis".'

'Like C. S. Lewis? Or I suppose Lewis Carroll? *Alice in Wonderland*?' Cordy asked.

He shrugged. 'Yeah, probably something like that. And another guy – "spurs101". Sorry, I should have got copies made. There's just so much of the stuff. But I'll read out the important bits.' He cleared his throat. 'So anyway, this was from February the twenty-eighth, about ten o'clock in the evening. "Clewis" asks if the other guy has the information he promised, and spurs101 just writes out this number – 0734987098 – and then an email address.' He turned over the scrap of paper in front of him. 'Wait, I wrote that down too.'

'Batoutofhell7 at gmail?' Cordy said dully. Hearing the familiar digits had turned her blood to ice, and now she could feel her body growing numb and the world around her slowing as the missing pieces slotted into place and she finally forced herself to look at the bleak, ugly picture that was emerging.

She saw his face. The look on his handsome face.

Anthony. I trusted you. I knew you were in this deeper than anyone wanted to admit, but to hang me out to fucking dry.

'That's the one.'

This can't be real. He wouldn't have done this. He couldn't have.

'I'm sorry, I'm not following,' Fiona said. 'Should I be?'

Bob glanced across at Cordy. 'Those are, umm, Dr Hunter's personal contact details. I know we should have come with this to you earlier, Chief, but after her first contact with Mark, Hunter's been getting harassed by these losers. Emails. Phone calls. That's what it was, wasn't it?' He looked over at Cordy. She just nodded.

Mentally she was replaying every single conversation she'd ever had with Anthony. Every single jagged little fact she'd entrusted him with. She'd handed him the weapons to tear her apart.

'And you didn't think it was worth telling me this before?' the detective chief superintendent asked. 'Jesus, I thought I was supposed to be the one in charge? I can't believe you kept me in the dark like that.'

'Hang on,' Bob said. 'There's more. This one came a few weeks later, right before the initial raid. It's spurs101 again.' He cleared his throat and looked down at a print-out in front of him. He'd highlighted a couple of lines, seemingly midway through the chat. 'All right. It's all set for tonight. You need to get the fuck out of there and have it all cleared up by ten at the latest. Don't worry about the guys across the road.' And then clewis thanks him and says—'

Tammy interrupted him. 'This is bollocks. It's obviously some sort of elaborate set-up.' She looked around, eyes pleading with them to agree. 'I mean we were talking about this guy Ashton being the brains behind the operation, weren't we?'

No one answered.

Tammy took their silence as tacit agreement. 'So clearly this is his contingency plan. Maybe he was planning on blackmailing Anthony?'

Bob looked as though he was trying to come up with something to say. Fiona, to his right, had put her glasses on and was flipping through the print-outs of the online chats.

Cordy let out a deep breath. She felt the shock beginning to wear off, but with the thaw came a terrible ache in her heart that made it difficult to put words together. 'Look,' she said quietly, 'I've seen this before.'

'What?' Tammy said, but Bob shushed her.

'I studied it in fact,' she said, trying to remember some official terms she could hide behind – then, on second thoughts, rejecting them. The team deserved better than jargon. 'There have been several cases of cops with unlimited access to obscene images of children finding themselves having … confusing feelings. Viewing those images day in, day out is mentally corrosive because of the indecent, toxic material. It wears you down, like an acid.' She couldn't look at the others as she said this. It felt as if she was accusing each of them personally, taking their bravery and dedication and turning it

against them. 'And,' she went on, 'especially when the work-
load is heavy and resources are limited, things like routine
debriefs and proper emotional support services can fall by the
wayside.' At that Fiona gave a little snort, but Cordy ploughed
straight on. She'd gone too far now to stop and worry about
tact. She felt the pressure of the unsaid words as a physical force, pushing to get out. 'The mentally toxic material is
forbidden, and it's not uncommon for that to give it an . . .
erotic charge. The child protectors realise what is going on,
are frightened and disgusted with themselves.

'They're becoming the very thing they've vowed to fight.
But when the boundaries get blurred, there's no one they can
talk to about it. No one who understands, except maybe—'

'Except child rapists?' Tammy said, and Cordy winced. 'Is
that what you mean? Because if you are accusing DeLuca of
some sort of . . . conspiracy, you need more than wild accusa-
tions. Fuck it, the man has a reputation. A wife . . .'

'Enough hysterics,' Fiona said sharply. 'There's an easy way
to sort this out.' She nodded to a laptop bag in the corner of
the room. 'I haven't been looking forward to doing this, but I
think it's time we checked DeLuca's personal computer. I got
a squad car to pick it up this morning.'

'What did you say to Angie?' Bob asked, going over, lifting
the laptop out and onto the table, booting it up.

'Told her we thought he might have saved some case notes
on it. Stuff that'd help with the prosecution.' She didn't meet
his eye. 'Thought there was no point worrying her at this stage
in the game.'

There was a heavy silence as Windows started up and, after
consulting the log-in details that Angie had copied out of his
personal organiser, Fiona signed in.

'Do you want me to do this?' Bob asked.

'I'm fine finding my way round a computer,' Fiona snapped.
'Although exactly what I'm looking for . . .' She scrolled

through folder after folder of holiday shots and pictures of the office Christmas party. Cordy had to look away when one shot filled the screen: Anthony's handsome face, grinning like a loon, telltale spots of pink on his cheeks and a plastic cup in his hand.

'It wouldn't be on the shared drive,' Bob pointed out. 'Look for anything marked Personal or Private or Work.'

'Or password protected?' Fiona asked, sitting back.

Bob swore under his breath. 'That'd be a good bet.'

Fiona tapped out a couple of possible passwords then looked up, frowning. 'Guess we'd better get Mick in. Presumably he can crack something like this in two seconds.'

'Try some Spurs players,' Cordy suggested, but they made their way through the entire squad with no success. In fact, it wasn't until they typed in the head coach – after some furious Googling from Tammy – that they finally gained access to the file.

A couple of clicks later and the screen was filled with obscene images of girls – young girls – stripped naked and posed with each other or childish props. A battered Raggedy Ann doll. An oversized lollipop. Some were tarted up in make-up and cheap, lacy underwear, but most looked exactly like what they were – children.

'Are they—?' Tammy said, turning away.

Fiona slammed down the screen and nodded. 'Definitely underage. You don't get images like that on mainstream porn sites.' She shook her head. 'Jesus. I don't believe it. I mean, I don't want to believe it. But it's there. On his bloody home computer. He was hardly even bothering to hide it.'

'So there was no undercover mission,' Tammy said. Her voice was muffled and when she turned back to the group, Cordy saw the tears running down her face. 'That was . . . that was all . . .'

'There was no undercover mission that I knew of,' Fiona confirmed, shaking her head sadly.

'No,' Cordy said. 'No undercover mission. Nothing like that. Or, at least, maybe only at the end. Right at the end.' The hurt and betrayal knocked the wind out of her lungs and she found she couldn't say anything else, not even to stop the young detective crying.

How could I not have seen what was going on right under my nose? she thought, closing her eyes against a wave of nausea. *How could I have been so stupid? I saw him with them, saw him push the button, and even then it didn't click. So much for my training. So much for my fucking instincts.*

'We'll have to go through this all very carefully,' Fiona was saying. 'Build up a proper picture of what happened when. There'll be reports. An official investigation . . .'

Bob was staring at Anthony's empty desk, as if daring him to come back and face the music. 'This morning I still thought . . . I don't know. That there might have been some sort of explanation. Something to get him off the hook. Anything. Maybe this spurs101 was someone else entirely? I wanted to believe that so much I even had myself convinced . . .' He pushed his fingers into his eye sockets, as if wanting to blot out the room and the people in it. 'But not now. Not now I know he was going home and probably jerking off to this filth. Christ, I introduced him to my grandkids . . .'

'Sampson,' Fiona said, a warning note in her voice. 'This isn't helping.'

But he continued, his voice dangerously low and quiet. 'Now I want to kill him. I want to tear him limb from limb. I want to see him suffer.'

'No need,' Cordy said sharply. 'He already did the job for you. And he took one of them with him.'

'So what, we forgive and forget now?' Bob asked. 'Because he had a crisis of conscience at the end? Well, I don't give a shit. He could have blown the whole nest of them to smithereens and that wouldn't have changed the fact that he was one of them.' Fiona held up a hand but he didn't stop. 'For fuck's sake, he was working against us the whole time. He was their man on the inside.'

'Don't say that,' Tammy said. 'You don't know that for sure.'

'DC Reynolds is right. We still don't know exactly what happened,' Fiona reminded him. 'And we can go back and forth forever arguing about what DI DeLuca did and didn't do, did and did not intend. How much was pretence and how much was real. But right now we have more pressing matters. We're all in shock, but it doesn't change anything. Our priority is still to build a watertight case against Mark Jones and Arnold Ashton.'

Cordy nodded slowly. 'I agree. Two men are dead. Out of our hands. But we can make sure the other two never have the opportunity to hurt children ever again.'

After that no one spoke, but the humming of Anthony's laptop grew so loud in Cordy's ears that she had to leave the room.

Chapter 64

Thank God for waterproof mascara, Cordy thought, staring at her reflection in the mirror. She'd locked herself in the small Ladies loo eight minutes ago in order to have a good cry, and now she'd give herself two more minutes to stop blubbing and get herself looking vaguely sane and normal. Seeing how red her face was, she splashed it again with cold water, washing away the last vestiges of snot and tears.

The ten-minute cry was a survival technique she'd perfected long ago – although thankfully she'd had much less frequent recourse to it in recent years.

Still works though, she thought, registering, like a neutral observer, how the tension had left her shoulders now that her breathing was returning to normal. How the fog in her head was lifting.

She checked the time on her mobile.

Another minute and I'll be good to go.

In the end it took a surprising amount of willpower to push the lock back and step out into the corridor again. But she did it, with thirty seconds to spare.

You will not think about Anthony, she told herself sternly, *for the next ninety minutes at least. Then you get another ten minutes of feeling it. If you need to.*

'Coping by numbers' was what her boss Allyson had dubbed it, the one time Cordy had tried to explain the system to her.

'Know what, babe? If it works for you, it works for you,'

Allyson had said. 'We've all got our own weird little coping devices. And at least yours is pretty benign.'

Unlike Jess's, Cordy added silently, thinking of the ugly criss-cross of scars that covered her little sister's thin, pale arms.

The thought of Jess stiffened Cordy's resolve. She'd see her again tonight, for the first time in weeks. She knew her little sister would be feeling worried and probably a bit abandoned, but she would do whatever it took to make everything OK again between them. Besides, as far as Jess knew, Cordy had just been fighting a nasty bout of the flu. She never needed to find out who the real fight had been against.

'Visitor for you in reception,' Bob called, as soon as she was back in the Ops Room.

'Early,' Cordy observed. 'I guess that's a good sign.'

'Kurt's mum, is it? I saw that you'd booked out the interview room.'

Cordy nodded. 'Social services are coming in half an hour, but I thought we'd have a chat first.'

'Well, let me know how it goes. Poor woman'll have a hell of a lot of hoops to jump through before she gets that kid back,' Bob said, turning away from Arnold Ashton's computer to look at her head-on. 'You still all right to do it? This afternoon was a bit . . . you know. Reynolds has gone for the day. She was neither use nor ornament in that state.'

'Can't say I blame her. But I'm fine.'

'Tougher than you look, aren't you?' Bob observed.

Maybe, Cordy thought. *Maybe not.*

Kurt's mother turned out to be a small, pretty girl with a nervous habit of fiddling with her long chestnut hair. She couldn't have been more than twenty or twenty-one, but she was dressed in an ill-fitting trouser suit that looked as if it had seen better days, and a cheap imitation Chanel quilted handbag.

Charity shop respectability, Cordy thought, remembering her own hit-and-miss attempts at looking like a responsible adult after she left the group home. *Nothing like striking out on your own to mess with your fashion sense.*

Before they were even in the lift, the girl, Cheryl, was breathlessly apologising to her son, to Cordy, and to the world in general.

'It sounds stupid but I just didn't know.' Her eyes were wide and she kept her arms hugged across her torso, like a defensive barrier. 'I was going through such a bad time, trying to find somewhere to live. Some work. I'd just split up from my boyfriend and he didn't want to know about either of us.' She gulped audibly, ran a quick hand over her eyes and launched straight into it again. 'You know, lots of the hostels don't let you have kids with you, and I mean we did have this little flat but there was a problem with the neighbours and that meant we were way down on the list and my parents made it clear that they had washed their hands of me. They've never even met him, you know? Thomas, I mean. That's his real name. On his birth certificate.' She fished it out of her bag and showed Cordy. It was protected by a cheap plastic sheath, but still the corners were looking a little dog-eared.

Cordy nodded and let her get it all out.

'And even when I was working all the money went on childcare and people think you're scrounging if you're on benefits but I'd like to see them try and pay for food and clothes and pay the bills on what we were getting every month.'

'Sounds tough,' Cordy said gently, holding the door open for her and guiding her into the interview room. 'Is that when the grey-haired man approached you?'

Cheryl nodded. 'Am I going to make a statement? Because I can. I've written down everything I can remember.' Again her hand went into her bag and came out with a sheaf of lined, loose-leaf paper, written over in biro. 'I've been going over and over it in my head. You know I've been looking for him everywhere for months? Retracing my steps. Talking to people in hostels, on the street. At first I thought I just needed to get a job and a place to live, and then they'd send him back to me. But I did, and they didn't. It's been such a . . . I don't know. A nightmare. I can't even tell you. Sorry, I'm rambling, aren't I?'

'You're doing fine,' Cordy assured her. 'I'll get a colleague in to take a statement later this afternoon, if that's OK. And there'll also be some people from social services here to talk to you about Kur . . . Thomas.'

At the sound of her son's name Cheryl's lip quivered. 'How is he? Can I see him? Did they—?' She clearly couldn't bring herself to finish the question.

'You can see him later today. He's safe now. But he's been through a really hard time, and it'll be a while before he's ready to trust adults again. Even you,' she said gently.

Cheryl let out a mirthless laugh. 'I don't blame him. He should hate me for what I did to him. I knew we should have stayed together. I knew it. But this guy said he was from a charity, that he could give Thomas a good home. That I could visit whenever I liked. Get him back when I was in a position to support him properly. And I am now.' She delved in her bag again and came out with what looked like a pile of pay slips. 'Here.' She thrust them into Cordy's hand. 'Anyway, everyone said it was too good to be true. And then the number he gave me didn't work and I should have gone to the police then. Should have gone. But I wanted to believe that everything was OK, that he was happy.' She stared down at her thin hands. Cordy noticed that the polish was chipped and that they were ragged around the edges, as if she'd been biting them. 'So stupid. So bloody stupid.' She looked up, eyes suddenly fierce. 'He's a good boy. What the hell did he do to deserve all that? He don't deserve a mother like me.'

'You know what?' Cordy said gently. 'Of the three children, Thomas is the lucky one. You know why? Because he's the one with a parent around who really loves him.'

Cheryl shook her head. 'I'm a terrible mother. He's better off without me.'

'I just don't think that's true. But you should know that they're not just going to hand him over. You're both going to have to be patient while they make their assessments. It's going to be a while.'

'Assessments?' Cheryl sounded terrified.

Cordy's phone buzzed and she quickly checked the message. Social services were downstairs too.

'Don't worry about that right now. I'll be back in a minute,' she promised, standing up and handing back the pay slips. At the door, she turned to look at Cheryl. 'Let me just say this. This wasn't your fault. You didn't know that this is what would happen. I don't know much about your current situation but please remember this was the paedophile's fault. Maybe you didn't make all the right decisions, but it wasn't your crime, it was theirs. And I do know that you've got a chance to help Thomas recover. Which means that both of you are luckier than you'll ever realise.'

It wasn't until she was outside the room that Cordy realised that she was close to tears herself.

Not for another sixty-seven minutes, she told herself firmly.

As it turned out, those sixty-seven minutes came and went and Cordy was too wrapped up in her work to notice. Shortly after Fiona came into the interview room to start taking Cheryl's statement, Cordy got a call from the safe house. Rebecca had been asking after her. Her heart leapt at the news. Leaving Cheryl in her case-worker's capable hands, Cordy bolted down the stairs and out to her bike.

Finally, she thought, revving the engine, *a chance to find out who the little message-leaver really is*.

The Unit's safe house was down a quiet suburban street in Southeast London. It looked just like any other semi on the street, complete with neat front garden and swings in the back one. *The last place anyone would think of looking for these kids*, Cordy thought, with a surge of gratitude.

The house mother met Cordy out on the driveway. She looked like the sort of person who would be entirely unfazed by whatever life threw at her.

Which is just as well in her job, Cordy thought, with a mixture of admiration and envy. So often her own interactions with child victims were short and semi-formal, designed to achieve some aim – preparing them for giving evidence in court, dealing with a specific behavioural problem. There was something very appealing at the idea of just being on hand to help with the healing process, hard as that might be.

'Susan,' the woman said, extending her hand. 'Nice to meet you at last.'

'Likewise.'

'Come in. Rebecca's in the kitchen. They tell me you've seen a copy of the doctor's report?'

Cordy nodded. 'Clear signs of extended abuse. Sexual, physical, emotional.'

Susan waited while Cordy locked up her bike, and then beckoned her inside. 'She's on a course of antibiotics to clear up the STD, and she's a little underweight, but apart from that she's OK. But she's still hardly speaking. But one thing she did say was about a nice lady, which we think is you.' She smiled, a little wryly. 'Don't be offended if it's not. But I knew you wanted to speak to her, so I thought it was worth a try.'

'Thank you,' Cordy said. 'I'll see what I can do.'

Rebecca was sitting exactly in the middle of the far side of the kitchen table. It sat eight, and the vast expanse of wood either side of her made the girl look even smaller and more fragile. In front of her was an A4 piece of white paper, which she was covering in minute pencil drawings, too dense to decode.

'Rebecca, look who it is.' The girl didn't look up, and Susan made an apologetic face. 'Well, I'll leave you guys to it. There's juice in the fridge and biscuits in the tin over there. Help yourselves, and give me a call if there're any problems.'

'Can I sit down?' Cordy asked. There was a movement that might have been a shrug, so Cordy slid into a seat diagonally across from Rebecca. 'What are you drawing?'

The girl said nothing; just put her arm up to shield the paper, as if she were taking a test.

'That's OK. It can be private.' Cordy reached into her backpack and got out a battered copy of a children's hardback. She'd had to make a detour to the local library to get it, but she hoped it'd be worth it. 'Do you mind if I read to you? I know you're not a baby, but I like reading aloud. And this is one of my favourites.'

Still Rebecca didn't look up. The determined way she gripped the pencil, gouging it into the paper, made Cordy think of the carvings on the bunk bed – the words and pictures that had led her to Rebecca, and might even show her the way to lead Rebecca back to herself.

If I read this right, she reminded herself, crossing her fingers.

Flicking past the dedication and the title page, she found the first page, took a deep breath and began. '*All children except one grow up.*'

There was a dull thud as Rebecca set down her pencil. For the first time Cordy felt the girl's eyes upon her. She pretended not to notice, and carried on to the next line.

'*They soon know that they will grow up, and the way Wendy knew was this.*'

'Can . . . can I see?' The voice had a roughened, jagged edge, more like an old woman's than a young girl's.

When Cordy looked up, she saw that Rebecca was reaching her hands over towards the book, fingers straining to touch it.

'Here you go,' Cordy said, passing it over. 'You like *Peter Pan* too?'

'Mummy used to . . .' There was silence as the sentence petered out. And then suddenly something cracked and the girl was sobbing so hard that Susan dashed back into the room.

'Everything all right?' she asked, looking hard at Cordy.

'We're OK,' Cordy said. 'We'll be OK.'

'Sorry,' the girl choked, 'I'll stop.'

'You don't have to. Let it out,' Cordy said, desperate to put an arm around the girl's heaving shoulders; knowing that any kind of physical intimacy could be unwelcome.

Susan bent over and whispered in Cordy's ear, 'You know, that's the first time she's cried? That she's shown any kind of emotional response?'

Cordy was about to say something about trauma and the healing process, but Rebecca silenced her by suddenly sniffing back her tears and looking directly at Cordy.

'They're dead, aren't they – my mummy and daddy? The Captain and the Old One lied, but they didn't lie about that.'

It wasn't a question.

Cordy nodded, confirming that they did die in the earthquake; that she, Rebecca, had survived, and the crying started up again.

Looking down at the skinny little girl, wracked with sobs, Cordy made a decision.

I can't leave her to get through this on her own.

And I won't.

Chapter 65

'So you're sure you're not going to come?' Cordy asked once more, cupping her mobile to her ear.

'I just can't, love. Not now I know what he did. I just can't stand there and pretend . . . not that, you know. I mean it's good that you're going and everything. I just don't—'

Cordy cut him off. 'Calm down, Sampson, don't get your knickers in a twist.'

He let out a snort. 'Touché. But Hunter, you'll give my best to Angie, won't you? Poor kid. She must be a mess.'

'That I will.'

Cordy looked over to where Anthony's widow was standing by the church entrance, smiling wanly at all the well-wishers. Even with her face etched with grief and her slim figure hidden behind a severe black dress, she was clearly beautiful, and Cordy had a sudden pang at the thought of how happy Anthony could have been, how differently the story of his life might have played out.

If only he'd talked to someone, rather than letting himself sink deeper and deeper into the muck he was supposed to be clearing up.

But what could he have said? 'I know it's wrong, but I'm finding myself aroused by abusive images of minors'?

Where was the safe space for a conversation like that?

On the other end of the line she heard Bob sigh. 'Anyway. What's the latest on Rebecca?'

'Way to change the subject.'

'Sorry. But they don't really tell us much. Last I heard she'd told you her best friend's name?'

Cordy smiled at the memory of that little breakthrough. 'Yes, Jemma Swanton. And it didn't take long to find her family. Surprisingly unusual surname. They put us in touch with Rebecca's aunt. You know, little Jemma still wore a friendship bracelet that Rebecca had made her – she hadn't taken it off, because she said she still missed her friend.'

Bob coughed at the other end of the line. Cordy wasn't sure, but she thought he might be trying to hide his emotional response to the story. She could barely believe it herself when she thought back. They hadn't reintroduced the girls yet – it was far too soon for Rebecca, and Jemma needed to be clear that she mustn't ask her friend what had happened since the earthquake in Haiti – but they were hoping the girls would get to meet at some point in the future. Not least because Cordy would never forget seeing, for the first time, that faint glimmer of something that looked like hope in Rebecca's eyes when she'd passed on the message that Jemma Swanton missed her.

Most importantly, the Swantons had known the Smith family, and knew that there was an aunt who lived in Hampstead, in North London. Caro Smith was unmarried, a GP, and quite a few years older than Rebecca's father would have been – but she had been extremely close to the family, and had rushed over to meet Cordy and the social services teams, kicking off the process of formally adopting her niece as quickly as she could, in spite of admitting she might be out of her depth with a lot of what Rebecca had gone through.

Cordy continued, 'She's asked me to stay involved in Rebecca's life. As a sort of extra "foster aunt". And I think I should. They say I'm the only one she opens up to. The only one she trusts. She's getting there with Caro – and they're spending some time alone together now – but I can't ignore that she needs me, that perhaps they both do.' There was no way Cordy could explain to Bob the pang she felt when she saw Rebecca retreat back into herself at the end of their sessions, like a snail retreating into its shell. This was a little girl who'd lost everything, but who was a fighter, a survivor. And who needed Cordy like no one – apart from Jess – had needed her before. The turning point had come when Cordy had brought up the messages, and Rebecca had just stared at her, not saying a thing, not breaking eye contact. That time when Cordy left, the little girl had started sobbing – a sound that wrenched Cordy's heart and made her even more determined to help Rebecca learn she wasn't just a victim, she was a survivor – this little girl who reminded her so much of another little girl (just as hurt, just as determined) who'd had to struggle on alone half a lifetime ago.

She thought about trying to find a way of saying this to Bob, but at that moment the people who had been milling around outside were now starting to make their way into the vestry. Cordy watched the hardcore smokers finishing up their cigarettes, passing around chewing gum, standing up and dusting off their dark clothes.

'Look,' she said down the phone. 'I need to go in a minute. We can talk about this when I'm back this afternoon, but basically Rebecca . . . well. She needs me.'

Bob was silent for a minute. 'You know we're not supposed to get emotionally involved with cases, right?'

'I think it's a little late for that.'

Down the line, she heard him laugh. 'Well, I still think you're over-involved, but I guess I'm going to have to trust your judgement on this one. After all, seems like you've got pretty good instincts. You know, for a woman.'

Good instincts, yeah. Except for that Anthony-shaped blind spot.

'Well, that's very observant of you. For a man.'

'Fair dues.' His voice grew serious again as he took his leave. 'All right, kid, I should let you go. Chin up. And give Angie my best.'

'I'll tell her you're thinking of her.'

She was about to hang up, when he added, in a quiet voice: 'She won't understand why I'm not there.'

'Trust me; she's got more to worry about than the whereabouts of DCI Bob Sampson.'

'You're not going to—'

'No. Fiona and I talked about it, and I convinced her that telling Angie wouldn't help at this stage.' She looked over at Angie, who was now standing alone on the porch, staring off into the graveyard. Although she was safely out of earshot, Cordy still found herself lowering her voice. 'Of course it'll almost certainly come out in the trial. And she must know something's up – your absence notwithstanding, this isn't exactly the ceremony you'd expect for an officer who'd gone down in the line of duty. But until then, why should we ruin her memories of him? I mean, that's all she's got left, isn't it?'

After she rang off, Cordy braced herself to go and introduce herself to Angie. Up until now she'd been able to make excuses for hanging back, but now there were no weeping relatives, no grim-faced friends between her and Anthony's widow.

'Mrs DeLuca?' she asked, approaching slowly. 'I'm Cordelia Hunter, a colleague of your late husband's.'

Angie shook her head as if to clear it, and dragged her eyes to Cordy's face.

When she spoke her voice was surprisingly level, with only the faintest, telltale tremor. 'Cordelia. Nice to meet you, finally. You're the PhD, right? Anthony was a big fan of yours. If I'd known how pretty you were, I'd probably have been quite jealous.'

A sharp stab of pain entered Cordy's heart, as she found herself remembering Anthony's ready smile, the way he'd roll his eyes when Bob went off on one of his rants. For a second she felt as though she was the one who had betrayed him, rather than the other way round.

'Well,' she managed, 'he was obviously devoted to you. I wish we could have met under happier circumstances.'

Just then a black-robed vicar appeared and stepped in between them.

'I'm sorry, ladies, but the ceremony is about to start. If you'll just come this way . . .'

Angie smiled at him apologetically. 'If you don't mind giving me a minute to pull myself together, I'll be in shortly.'

The vicar looked a little disgruntled – *probably got a wedding or a christening straight after this*, Cordy figured – but answered mildly enough. 'Of course. Take your time. See you inside.'

Cordy made to follow him, but Angie touched her arm to stay her. 'Sorry. I'm sure I'll see you at the wake as well. But there was one thing I wanted to ask . . . now, when there's no one else around.'

'Yes?' Cordy asked breathlessly, feeling a little sick.

Am I going to have to lie to this poor woman's face? Or tell her that her husband was aroused by explicit images of underage girls? That he was conspiring with the paedophiles he was supposed to be putting away? Allowing them to continue raping children for profit?

'It's just . . .' Angie took a deep breath. She was obviously struggling to find the right words, and in the end they all came out in a rush. 'You were there, weren't you?'

'At the raid? Yes I was.'

'So. Was it—? I mean, I know it wasn't worth it, because he's dead. And that's . . . nothing could be worth that. But are those men going to be sentenced at least?' Looking down, Cordy saw Angie was twisting her wedding ring round and round her finger, as if she couldn't stop. 'What I'm saying is, he didn't die for nothing, did he? Please tell me he didn't.'

Cordy took a deep breath. 'Well, the children are safe now. And yes, we have enough evidence to put the two men who survived away for a long time. And if it wasn't for Anthony . . .' To Cordy's horror, her voice cracked on his name. 'And if it wasn't for Anthony, then one or more of them could have escaped justice. Could have been free to find new victims. So no, he didn't die for nothing.'

'Really, ladies, I hate to rush you at this difficult time,' the vicar said, popping his plump face around the church door. 'But I think we'd better get started.'

'Sure,' Angie said, quickly wiping her eyes. 'Sorry for the delay. And thank you,' she said more quietly, gripping Cordy's arm so hard it left finger marks. 'I needed to hear that.'

And maybe so did I, Cordy realised, watching the other woman straighten her shoulders and brace herself for the coming ordeal.

Nothing will ever undo the harm he did. Nothing can ever make up for the way he helped those perverts continue their reign of terror over those children. For the way he betrayed us all.

But in the end he could have tipped them off again. Could have left himself. Instead he led them into a trap and he had at least tried to warn me before he hit the button, not to mention the fact that he took one of them with him. She pushed her hair back out of her face and followed Angie inside, slipping into a half-empty pew at the back of the church.

He couldn't live with what he had become. It's sad he took the coward's way out, but I can't even begin to imagine facing that kind of inner demon. Before she could think about it any more, the organ sounded and the assembled congregation shuffled to its feet.

The ceremony was sad and beautiful but Cordy didn't have any more tears left to cry – not even when Anthony's mother (a short, plump woman, with her son's soulful brown eyes) described how open and friendly he was as a boy. How he could never bear to keep a secret from her. How she had looked forward so much to the day when he would bring her a dark-haired son of his own – a day that would now never come.

'*Suffer the little children to come unto me and forbid them not, for of such is the kingdom of God . . .*'

Cordy winced as the vicar read out the familiar prayer, and was grateful that everyone around her had their heads solemnly bowed. Looking up, she caught Fiona's eye. The older woman's expression was so deeply bereft that Cordy had to look away.

Thankfully, the service was almost over. Just the burial to go.

She had put her phone on silent, but when she checked it after the final hymn she saw she had a text message from Susan, the house mother at the Unit's safe house.

Rebecca, Caro & I are still at the coffee shop. I said we didn't have to stay but R said youd be sad. C U soon x

She'd met Rebecca, her Aunt Caro, and Susan earlier that morning, back when she hadn't been sure whether to go to the funeral at all. It'd been drizzling outside and they'd all been sipping hot chocolate, looking out at the glum weather.

'It's horrid out there,' Cordy had said, grimacing.

Rebecca had just shrugged. She was still far too quiet for Cordy's liking, but every day there were fresh signs that the clouds were parting, and that the scars – both mental and physical – would one day heal over. The other two were also battling through.

'How are Thomas and Laura doing?' Cordy had asked the house mother, quietly, when Caro and Rebecca had gone up to the counter to choose a cake. She had to bite her tongue to stop herself saying 'Kurt and Lolly'.

'Not bad,' Susan had said. 'Thomas has been moved to a more' – she'd glanced at Rebecca and lowered her voice – 'a safer place. He's got a lot of issues to deal with, poor love. He doesn't remember much about before he was there. And Laura's been moved to a really nice interim foster home.'

'I'm so pleased. If it's OK, I'd love to get the details so I can drop by and see her soon.'

'That'd be good.' Susan had flashed her a warm smile.

Cordy had looked at her watch. 'I ought to go,' she'd said. 'Although maybe I should give it a miss,' She wavered. But then, to her surprise, she'd realised the little girl had returned to the table and was standing right beside her.

'You should say goodbye,' she'd said, in the tiniest voice. 'Saying goodbye is important. If you can.'

Susan and Cordy had exchanged a look, before she'd put on her coat, told the two women and the vulnerable little girl she would see them later, and stepped out into the drizzly rain, walking resolutely towards the church.

Saying goodbye is important.

A light drizzle had started up during the ceremony. Cordy stepped out of the church and moved with the congregation to the freshly cut grave, listening to the vicar's familiar words.

'*We commit his body to the ground; earth to earth, ashes to ashes, dust to dust . . .*'

Not far away, Fiona and Tammy stood together, a little apart from the huddles of family and friends. Tammy looked as if she'd been crying.

'*. . . and the corruptible bodies of those who sleep in him shall be changed, and made like unto his own glorious body . . .*'

Angie had pushed away the solicitous arms that had been offered to her, and was standing on her own, a clod of earth grasped tightly in her hand.

At the vicar's signal she threw it onto the wooden coffin that lay in the grave, and others followed suit, covering the gleaming wood with dirt.

When Cordy threw her own handful, she tried to imagine that her rage and hurt would be buried too, along with Anthony's body.

Because you've got to live to fight another day, she told herself. *And that means letting go.*

Cordy was still staring at the grave.

Live to fight another day.

EPILOGUE

'Come in, come in,' Cordy cried, as she opened the door to Caro and Rebecca.

As she opened the door, she was overwhelmed with emotions. Her first thought was that this was actually the first time she'd had guests in years. Secondly, she noticed how well Rebecca looked. The little girl had put on a bit of weight since they'd last seen each other – and it suited her. But more than that, she was smiling. Actually smiling.

'You look well, Rebecca,' she said, coming down to the little girl's level and looking her in the eye. 'Auntie Caro's been feeding you well, hey?'

The little girl gave a tiny mischievous laugh, and looked at Caro for approval. 'We made chocolate brownies, Cordy! We made them for you!' She reached behind her back and pulled out a Tupperware container. 'Can we have one now?'

Cordy grinned. 'In a minute. Go and wash your hands first.' She pointed towards the only internal door in her loft apartment. 'It's through there. I'll come with you if you like?'

'Don't be silly, Cordy. It's just hand-washing!' answered Rebecca, running off in the direction of the bathroom.

Caro leaned over and hugged Cordy hello. 'She's been *soooo* excited about seeing you, you wouldn't believe. And she's been way better since the trial. Fewer tantrums, eating the food I make for her, even the nightmares aren't coming so often. Especially in the last week or two, it's like a different girl. I mean, could you have imagined her giggling like she just did, or going into a room on her own, when she first came to me? She's like . . . well, she's a bit more like the little girl she was before . . . before it happened.'

It had been over six months since the ECPU had freed Rebecca, Laura and Thomas. The court case had been and gone, with Rebecca giving video evidence, which helped incriminate both Arnold Ashton and Mark Jones, who had both been sentenced to ten years in prison each, for kidnap, child molestation, money laundering and rape. Rebecca, at least, seemed reassured that they wouldn't be out for a long time.

Rebecca came bouncing back out of the toilet, and proceeded to start exploring Cordy's flat. She stopped dead at the photo in the frame by Cordy's bed, however.

'Who's that?' she asked, reaching gently towards it, as if scared that touching it might get her in trouble.

'That's . . . that was, is, my sister, Jess. A few years ago.'

'Did she go in an earthquake too?'

Cordy's heart contracted. 'Not exactly, darling.'

'Poor Jess. Perhaps she needs an Auntie Caro?' Rebecca mused quietly, moving to the photo to study it more closely. Cordy turned around to see tears in Caro's eyes. 'I don't like photographs of me,' she continued.

'Me neither,' Cordy smiled. 'But I do like brownies! And sitting in the sunshine!' She opened the door to her little roof terrace, with its view across Blackheath.

'Swanky,' Caro said, looking out. 'This view's pretty. Do you have parties up here?'

'What are you talking about?' Cordy said, gesturing to the table, which she'd laid out this morning. 'This *is* a party right here. We've got carrots. We've got hummus. Apple slices. I made some sugar-free lemonade . . . And, um, now I think I'm forgetting something . . .'

'The brownies, Cordy!' replied Rebecca delightedly.

'Ah, yes, these brownies. Let's try one, then.' She prised open the Tupperware container, to find four large chocolate brownies, decorated prettily with pink writing icing – stars, hearts and some letters too.

'Look at what they spell!' instructed Rebecca.

Cordy smiled – the little girl was evidently still finding ways to message. But her pleasure turned to concern as she looked at the letters written on the brownies: E, V, L . . . However, in that instant, Rebecca snatched the box back from her. 'Oops, they got in the wrong order on the way over,' she said grinning as she rearranged them. 'There!' she said, handing the box back to Cordy and grinning again announced, 'I think you're going L-O-V-E them, Cordy!'

After they'd left, as she sat with her MacBook on her lap, on the roof terrace and watching the sun set, the smile Cordy had been wearing all afternoon faded a little. In the months since the trial, she had grown accustomed to deleting even seemingly innocent emails from unknown sources. Although Mark and Arnold were safely in prison, members of the Online Sex Offenders' Community continued to harass her – although the phone calls had stopped. *For now, at least.*

There was one particularly hostile opponent who seemed intent on getting through to her. She'd shown his emails to the team at ECPU. A name had come up.

A name from the past.

Someone who'd never been brought to justice.

Cordy quickly scanned through her emails, but for once there was nothing suspicious. She let her shoulders drop, forced herself to breathe more deeply.

Let's not worry about that today. One battle at a time.

She printed out a copy of an email that Laura had sent to her. In it she complained about all the extra homework she had to do to catch her up with the rest of her year group, and how she wasn't allowed to watch much TV but, reading between the lines, it seemed that her new foster home was working out fine.

Laura signed off: 'Come and visit me!! I'm bored to DEATH in the countryside.'

Boring is good, Cordy thought. *Boring is exactly what she needs.*

She was just about to sign off when an electronic ping told her a new message had arrived. When she clicked it open she saw that it was from Detective Chief Superintendent Fiona Andrews, written in her typically brusque style.

Dear Dr Hunter,

I hope that this finds you well. Now, I'll cut to the chase. We'd like you back on the team. I know you've returned to your job at Justice4Children, but given the outcome of the last case, I hope you might realise that – while your work there is valuable, what you can do for our team could be above and beyond that. We couldn't have managed without you last time – something perhaps we didn't admit freely enough at the time. In fact, however much I disapproved of your methods at the time, I must admit that, had it not been for the DeLuca situation, you might have led us to the children even sooner.

So, I am delighted to be in the position to offer you a permanent place on the Elite Child Protection Unit team. We have secured funding for a one-year contract, with the hope of extending it further. It can start as soon as you're able to organise a replacement at J4C. Please do give it your fullest consideration (not least because Bob Sampson has taken to asking me daily when you're returning!).

Kind regards,

Fiona.

Cordy was overwhelmed. In that instant she felt six feet tall. *So they want me back*, she thought. *They must be gluttons for punishment. But there are a hell of a lot of predators out there and I've got plenty of fight left in me . . .*

Still, she would make Fiona wait for another day, she decided, as she clicked the email closed. Today she wanted to hold on to her happy afternoon with Caro and Rebecca. But, as she brushed the brownie crumbs off the table, and took one last long look at the beautiful sunset, she knew there was really no choice. If she could save just one child, help turn one more victim into a survivor, then she knew it'd be a job well done.

Interview with Shy Keenan

You are the author of two bestselling non-fiction books, including the memoir Broken. What made you decide to move into writing fiction?

There was so much I wanted to say, that I felt unable to say, until I moved into writing fiction. And then . . . well, it was like being set free, really. But at the same time as being liberating – it was also very scary. Especially having spent so much of my early life being told I was a liar, then my adulthood proving I wasn't . . . and now I get to make stuff up for a living – that was daunting! Inventing Cordy Hunter was an amazing experience though: she has the ability to find strength in the things that test her the most, and I love that.

How did you conceive of the character of Cordelia Hunter? And will we be seeing her again?

She's definitely not me – not least because she takes risks I never would! But in her, there is obviously a person I sometimes wish I could be, and a strength, self-empowerment, and sense of purpose I admire enormously. But more than that, I also wanted to show that even the worst possible circumstances can make someone strong. That however hard a person's childhood is, it doesn't have to defeat or define them. So perhaps she is also the personification of the fighting spirit inside me – the part that fights hard to never let the bad stuff win.

Why did you make her sister, Jessica, so very damaged, when Cordy herself seems so confident?

In some ways Jess and Cordy are two sides of the same coin: the broken side, and the surviving side. I wanted to demonstrate this through their characters, and specifically look at how two different people who have essentially gone through the same childhood experiences can end up taking two very different journeys in life: one to an admirable survival and one to abject misery. Thankfully, I'm very pleased to say that in my own life – as well as through my advocacy work – I know many more Cordelias than I know Jessicas.

In the novel, Rebecca/Alice is abducted from Haiti in the aftermath of the earthquake. Is this sort of thing really a frequent occurrence?

Frighteningly so. Paedophiles prey on the innocent and the vulnerable, and nowhere are children more vulnerable than in the aftermath of a natural disaster. It's horrific but paedophiles have been known to swarm these disasters areas – where children can be 'easily disappeared'. Thankfully, particularly since the tsunami of 2004 and Hurricane Katrina in 2005, the international police forces have become hyper-vigilant towards such activity, and now move extremely fast in order to protect children and the vulnerable as best they can in these natural disaster zones.

You experienced violent abuse in your own childhood. Did writing the novel bring up any tough memories?

Yes it did. But it gave me an opportunity to look at those situations with new eyes. Not as a frightened helpless child trapped in some very twisted grown-ups' world, but as a grown-up looking in. And in a strange way, looking back from a safe place gave me real peace and closure, as it enabled me to truly understand some of what was going on for me when I was a child, which was simply that they were perverts and child abusers, and I was just an unlucky vulnerable child.

A key element of the story is Rebecca/Alice's messaging – which helps lead Cordy to the children. Is this something you have experience of?

Messaging is a very typical response to traumatic abuse in childhood, and I myself would leave messages as a child. Messaging is like a very mild form of hypergraphia (obsessive writing) which is often found in battered children who've suffered frequent head trauma. But the more I talk about it, the more I find people like me. And that makes me feel less alone. I didn't want the little girl to be alone though, which is why I gave her Cordy. Because I personally hated how lonely I felt, and wanted Rebecca to have some hope of being safe again.

How much of the novel is based on real life?

All of it and none of it! The situations and individuals are completely made up. But I certainly drew experience from my own life and the thousands of people I've met in the course of it. One thing I am very pleased to say is fictional is my depiction of the police and child services, who are thankfully much better in real life than in my novel. It's been both my personal and professional experience to have worked alongside some of the most incredible child protectors, who are faster, quicker, better than the ones you'll find in *The Stolen Ones*. In particular, I'm extremely glad that I've never encountered anyone who worked for the police who went bad – thank God! – but I must say it was interesting exploring what might happen if one did.

Aside from writing novels, what other projects are you involved in at the moment?

We are setting up the Phoenix Foundation charity to help develop groundbreaking advocacy, support and recovery services for victims of paedophile crimes. There's lots still to do and we're not there yet; in the meantime if you personally need support, or know someone who does, here are some good contacts:

National Society for the Prevention of Cruelty to Children (NSPCC): http://www.nspcc.org.uk/

Childline: 0800 1111
Help for adults concerned about a child: 0808 800 5000

National Association for People Abused in Childhood (NAPAC): http://www.napac.org.uk/
Tel: 0800 085 3330

The Samaritans: http://www.samaritans.org/
Tel: 08457 90 90 90

Child Exploitation and Online Protection Centre (CEOP): http://www.ceop.police.uk/

And if you think a child is at immediate risk, please call 999 and report it.